GREENWICH MEAN TIME

Reed Bunzel

coffeetownpress

Kenmore, WA

coffeetownpress

A Coffee Town Press book published by Epicenter Press

Epicenter Press
6524 NE 181st St.
Suite 2
Kenmore, WA 98028

For more information go to:
www.Camelpress.com
www.Coffeetownpress.com
www.Epicenterpress.com

Author's website: www.reedbunzel.com

Greenwich Mean Time
2023 © Reed Bunzel

ISBN: 9781684920358 (trade paper)
ISBN: 9781684920365 (ebook)

Printed in the United States of America

For Kimberley Cameron: Friend, adviser, and agent supreme.
Merci beaucoup.

The twin-engine Beechcraft took off from Haifa, Israel at twelve past nine local time.

Eighteen minutes later, as it passed through the ten-thousand-foot threshold, the pilot deactivated the dual Mode S transponders and ADS-B tracker, then pushed his way through the curtain that separated the cockpit from the main cabin. He stood there, hunched over because of the aircraft's low ceiling, and studied the five passengers aboard this private flight: three men, two women, ages from thirty-two to forty-nine. All were facing forward, as if expecting him to make an important announcement, or perhaps begin serving them cocktails.

Instead, he produced an Israeli-made BUL Cherokee handgun, polymer frame with rosewood grip, 9x19 mm parabellum caliber. He aimed it at the man seated in the front seat, left side of the aisle, seatbelt unfastened. No reaction from him or his four compadres, all of whom by now had inexplicably drifted into a mental zone of disconnected reverie, a detached sense of being in which here was there and now was then. Real was fleeting, truth was elusive.

And life was death.

It was over in seconds. Ten quick shots, two in each forehead. Then the pilot returned to the cockpit and squirmed into his seat behind the controls. He pulled back on the throttle and put the plane into a steep dive, calculating forty, maybe fifty seconds until it would hit the water. By now the tower in Haifa would have lost the Beechcraft on radar, and others would be working frantically to track it—contact him on the radio, speak with other towers along the coast, and do everything that could be done to locate it.

He maintained speed, his military training coming back to him. He kept one eye on the sea, one eye on the altimeter. Twenty seconds to impact, then fifteen. At the last possible moment, he pulled the nose up and leveled the aircraft off until it was flying just fifty feet above the surface. To all the investigators and experts and media pundits who would dig into the plane's disappearances for weeks afterwards, it would appear to have simply vanished from the sky.

The pilot then made a gradual but full right turn—one hundred sixty degrees—using his own pocket compass to determine direction. At this point he didn't really have a fixed destination; all he wanted was to be well over land again before slowly climbing up to cruising altitude. Conserving fuel was critical to the success of his strategy; the higher the better.

Eventually the coast of Lebanon appeared in the distance. As he crossed over the seaside town of Jiyeh he began his ascent, hoping to appear as just another aircraft gaining altitude as it approached from the Mediterranean. There was a slight risk of encountering the country's underwhelming air force, but he figured that by the time they realized he was in their airspace and scrambled their Embraer fighters, the plane would already be out of it.

At five thousand feet he shrugged the parachute onto his back. Not the one his employers had provided—they had surely incapacitated it— but the one he'd personally packed last night. He'd already activated the autopilot, set to take the plane up to thirty-thousand feet and then fly due east until the tanks ran dry.

At six thousand feet he opened the rear door. Not an easy task, due to pressure and velocity, but it finally swung outward and was quickly grabbed by the force of the wind. It ripped off and went tumbling end over end, plummeting toward the arid terrain below.

Ten seconds later the pilot stepped out, hoping his calculations were correct and that he would come to earth in friendly territory, and not fall into the hands of the Syrian Arab Republic...

Chapter 1

<u>**Wednesday, June 16**</u>
Karakoram Mountains, Pakistan
6:58 am Greenwich Mean Time, 12:58 pm Local

As brothers they were bound by blood, and as brothers they were sworn to kill.

Alashir was the elder of the two, his name given in honor of a legendary 17th-century Baltistani king who vanquished an entire people and commandeered a vast mountain territory in Northern Pakistan. His younger sibling was called Shahazim, in memory of a proud rebel who had killed sixteen Kashmir separatists during the war of 1947, before being felled by a bullet to the head. Both were tribal heroes whose glory and infamy had grown through the decades, totemic lore that inspired the mountain folk to fill the high valleys with resounding songs of conquest and death. Their discordant wails and melodious chants served as grand yet tragic reminders of victory and darkness for all those who dwelled in the deep shadows of the Karakoram Range, where eternity came swiftly and unexpectedly from all corners.

The two men had been watching the small band of hikers since the first hint of daylight slid over the ridge to the east. Alashir had spotted them first, although he'd actually smelled the thin trickle of smoke that spiraled up from their smoldering fire at first light. The trio of *ajanib* had spent the night in a makeshift camp beside the river three thousand feet below in the narrow valley; from there it was a trek of five hours up the precipitous trail that had been carved out of the side of the rock wall. If one was swift.

Alashir and Shahazi were swift, but these three trespassers clearly were not. How easy it would be to slash the throats of the two men who walked in the lead, then take the head of the lazy straggler as a prize. They had collected many such trophies in Syria and Iraq during their days with the Salafi jihadists but, now that the ideological climate had changed, they had returned to the land of their birth and were waiting for the political tide to turn. Afghanistan was next.

"*Kaffir ko mout*," Alashir proclaimed as he handed the binoculars to his brother. Death to the infidels.

"*Khilafat zindah raho*," Shahazi replied with disdain as he spat on the rocky trail. Long live the caliphate.

Monica Cross pressed tightly against a shard of granite that jutted from the edge of the cliff. To her left the craggy wall seemed to rise forever into the deep blue umbra; on the right it seemed to drop forever to the dark valley floor below. She dared not look.

The trail was hardly more than a yard or two wide. Every tentative step along the crumbling moraine taunted her with the threat of death, and reminded her just how uncertain life truly was. The mountain peaks seemed to stretch forever into the heavens, up where the gods must live. Earlier that morning, when she had stood at the bottom of this valley and glanced upward toward the lightening sky, she thought they might never make it to the top.

Monica was already drained from this morning's hike. After a tasteless breakfast of trail mix and reconstituted citrus drink, she and her companions had set out on foot again for another long trek. Smug and imperious, the two men quickly outpaced her with speed and indifference borne of cultural misogyny. *Good*, she'd thought: *the less contact I have with either of them, the better.*

She was mostly thinking—*fuming*—about Branson Dahl, the travel writer who had a reputation as a conceited and arrogant womanizer. Monica had met him just once before this trip, two weeks ago when they were introduced at the offices of *Earth Illustrated* magazine in New York. Within ten minutes he had shamelessly revealed himself as an intolerable narcissist with only two apparent interests: himself and anything in a skirt. *#MeToo* to the max. He'd made it quite clear he was delighted they would be spending a week together in search of the perfect photographs to illustrate his cover story on the majestic beauty of the mighty Baltoro Glacier.

When she had arrived at the Islamabad Serena Hotel four days ago, she had found a handwritten message from him inviting her to dinner. Intrigued by the prospect of tasting some of the local cuisine, she was dismayed to find the schmuck had ordered braised Turkish lamb cutlets to be served in his room, along with a bottle of Dom Perignon and eleven roses. Even more appalling was how the king-sized bed had been turned down and a single rose—the last of the dozen—was set on what she presumed was to be her pillow.

"I trimmed my beard for later," he'd explained in a soft, confident voice as he popped the cork on the champagne. He was the sort of man many women would find attractive: tall and tan, rugged features, crystal blue eyes—coarse, blond hair, square chin and firm jaw—a Robert Redford type. That night he was wearing a hotel bathrobe loosely—*very loosely*—cinched around his waist. "The sensation on the skin is to die for."

That was the end of the evening, at least as far as Monica was concerned. After her hasty retreat to her own room she called down and ordered herself a plate of *batata harra*—spicy fried potatoes—and a pot of black tea. Then she read an Alafair Burke novel until she was too tired to keep her eyes open.

Now, three full days later, Dahl remained ruffled by Monica's rejection, and was doing his best to let it show. "You're going to have to bust some serious ass if you expect to keep up," he'd taunted her three hours ago as he and Ahmed set off on the trail. "See you at the top."

By late morning she had covered just three miles of this stark, barren terrain. Her thighs ached and her feet burned. She longed for a shower. She imagined one now as she set one foot in front of the other: hot water flowing from chrome faucets, lathering real shampoo into her hair, drying off with a soft microfiber towel. Other amenities came to mind: food cooked in a real oven, chilled chardonnay in a glass, clean underwear. It all seemed incredibly distant now, and as she trudged up the track her mind raged with the agonizing events of the last six months.

Top of the list was Phillip. He had been her husband, her lover, and her best friend. He'd just turned thirty-six when the car he was driving skidded on a patch of black ice on the New York State Thruway, three days after Christmas. Now he was dead.

Monica tried to suppress the dull throb of pain she feared would linger long after his touch faded from her memory. Her chest tightened and her eyes grew moist, a common symptom that she hardly even noticed anymore. Her world had been cleaved in two by his death, and the waves of numbness continued to wash over her as regularly as the ebb and flow of the tides. She felt like a beach that had been laid bare after a torrential storm, exposed for all to see. And now, as she picked her way up the steep mountain trail in one of the most remote locations on the planet, one hundred and seventy days after his death, she remained awash in the familiar sense of total desolation and loneliness.

His memorial service had almost filled the Unitarian Church on Lexington Avenue, and was defined by fond memories, generous tears, and heartfelt laughter. Monica had held herself together just long enough to make it home to their condo on the Upper West Side, where the silence and emptiness caused the dam to overflow as soon as she closed the door behind her. Her sister Kathleen had dropped by later, but insisted she couldn't stay the night. Around midnight she found herself alone with amorphic shadows in the corners of her mind and eventually, after all the tears had drained away, she had slipped down the hall and crawled into her own bed. It was twice as large as it had seemed just a week before, and there she had burrowed under the duvet her husband had hated, until she'd dry-sobbed herself to sleep.

She hadn't wanted to go on this photoshoot, not in the beginning. It would be her first field assignment out of the country since the accident, and she thought it might be too much, too soon. A lingering vulnerability made her feel on edge, and her usual self-confidence seemed on the verge of cracking. But Kathleen had convinced her she needed to break out of her cocoon, while her editor, Arnie Kelso, had patiently eased her anxieties about traveling to a distant land. Reluctantly she had said "yes," and over the ensuing days her misgivings turned to anticipation. She'd boarded the plane at JFK with a renewed sense of adventure, convinced it was the start of a new chapter in her life.

Now she lowered her weary body onto a rock and massaged her right leg. The muscle was really tightening and she could feel the stiffness working its way up to her knee. She wiggled her toes inside her stiff hiking boots and shrugged her backpack off her shoulders. She looked up, saw the glow from the sun etched on the distant peaks towering above this mountain pass, casting off a deep, gilded glow that gave this range its name: Spine of Gold.

That's when she heard it: a short squeal ahead of her on the trail, followed by an empty silence. And it was in that silence that she felt the sudden grip of unspeakable fear.

Ahmed was the first to die.

Alashir lunged from behind a crag of rock and drove his eight-inch blade through the guide's ribs and into his heart. Instinctively the guide's hands went up to his chest, clutching at life as it gushed from the wound. His mouth opened wide, gasping for one last breath as mortality greeted him forever.

To his credit, Branson Dahl managed to utter the most pitiful of screams before Shahazi's knife slashed him across the throat, the curved edge slicing deep into the vertebral venous plexus just above his C-2. Somehow, he was still alive when his assailant nudged him over the precipice, waiting until somewhere below a dull thud echoed up the granite wall.

The two brothers embraced each other, comrades in arms who had killed many men in their call for jihad. Then they turned and, without uttering a word, quietly made their way down the trail to confront the straggler who clearly was the weakest of the three.

They covered the distance with such stealth that Monica barely caught a flicker of motion. Alashir came into view first, knife clenched in his fist. Tall and muscular, his frame carried power and a lot of bulk. His skin was dark and leathery, and what she could see of his face was haggard and cruel. She restrained her instinct to run; on this trail she wouldn't get far.

Then Shahazi came into view behind him, and her fear turned to raw terror.

He, too, carried a knife in his hand, and a sneer on his lips. He raised the blade above his head and charged at her with a ferocious snarl. Acting on sheer instinct, Monica pressed her body against the rock wall and kicked out with both feet, dodging the blade and hitting him squarely in the stomach, hard and unexpected. He uttered a loud grunt and toppled backwards, his hands flailing outward as he released his grip on the knife. He managed to grasp a rock at the edge of the trail, but it came loose and he disappeared over the side in a torrent of screams that faded into the depths below.

Alashir froze as his brother tipped out into nothing. Then his eyes filled with fury and he lunged for her, wrapping his arm around her neck and yanking her off her feet.

In an instant Monica was pinned on her back against the rocky trail, staring into the hardened eyes of her attacker, which were dark and penetrating, projecting a thirst for blood and revenge. A menacing grin crept across his face as he raised his knife, the midday sun glistening off the jagged blade as he held it over her. The grip on her throat tightened, and a wave of panic engulfed her as she felt an overwhelming certainty that she was about to die.

Then the eyes blinked in shock, the darkness in them turning to a look of disgust as he realized he was wasting his time on a mere woman. What was this whore doing here on this trail, in this treacherous corner of the world? Monica sensed the hesitation in his eyes and, without thinking, wrapped her fingers around a stone lying on the ragged path. Gripping it tightly, she brought it down against the side of his skull and heard something crack. Blood gushed from his left ear, but she wasted no time as she shot the heel of her fist into his nose.

Alashir howled in pain and anger as his head jerked backward. Monica flexed her hips and thrust him off her, narrowly escaping the razor-sharp blade as it slashed down and glanced off a chunk of granite. She scurried out of his reach and saw that his nasty grin was back, a deep scowl etched in his eyes as he snarled something under his breath.

Monica couldn't comprehend what he was saying, nor did she wait for him to finish. She lashed out with her foot and kicked him in the teeth, the sudden impact causing him to lose his grip on the knife. It went skittering across the narrow trail, and she retrieved it just as he clawed his way to his feet. She held it in front of her with two hands and made an awkward slashing motion, trying to look as menacing as she could while not revealing the terror that was gripping the deepest recesses of her mind.

The man growled something else, then lunged at her again. They both hit the ground hard, the impact causing her to let go of the knife as he grabbed her hair. He jerked her head with such force that she thought her neck might break, which clearly was his intention, if he didn't strangle her first.

But Monica had not done all that yoga and tai-chi over the last few months for nothing. Following Phillip's death her doctor had suggested she refocus her mental and spiritual energies, leading her to sign up for night classes at a studio on Amsterdam Avenue. She'd almost given up after the first week, but had convinced herself to give it a month. Then another month, and another. Not as useful in a fight as Tae Kwon Do or Aikido, but over time she learned about the spiritual energy of the *ching*, *ch'i*, and *shen*, and how yin and yang reflected perceived opposites in the phenomenal world: light and dark, cold and hot, soft and hard. Good and bad, life or death.

Now, as she lay pinned on the mountain trail, the only mobile part of her body was her left leg. She raised it up around his shoulder and gave it a quick jerk, then twisted her body sideways, rolling to the very edge of the trail. She felt the earth disappear beneath her, and again she was seized by panic. With one hand she clung to a crag of granite; with the other she clawed at the hands that now were trying to choke the life out of her. The grip on her throat was tight, but she was able to slip her fingers around one wrist. She dug her nails in and felt his hold loosen, but she knew it would tighten again if she let go.

Monica summoned all her strength and arched her body, trying to thrust him off her. She managed to wriggle to her right, to the very edge of the trail, when she felt something hard under her back. At first, she thought it was another rock, but then she realized it was the knife. If only she could get a hand on it, she might be able to jab it into his mouth.

Problem was, Monica would have to either let go of his wrist or the rock that was keeping her from tumbling over the edge of the cliff. She took a gamble and released her grip on the granite shard and grabbed wildly for the knife. She snaked a finger around the carved bone handle and pulled it close to her chest. Then, wrapping her fingers around it tightly, she jabbed the tip against the nearest point of flesh that was not her own, and pushed.

It happened to be his left ear, the one she had already hit with the rock. The blade pierced his tympanic membrane, penetrated the vestibule and the cochlea, then slipped into the opening through which the nerve endings were connected to the brain. The *external acoustic meatus*.

At that point Monica felt his choke hold let go.

At the same time, she felt the weight of her own legs pull her to the edge. Her attacker's now-limp body lay draped over her arm, his dead weight all that kept her from slipping away. She dropped the knife and grabbed at the ground as her arm began to slide out from under his lifeless form. Her fingers tried to find purchase, but there was nothing to hold on to, nothing to keep her from going over the side. She felt gravity grip her mercilessly, and then she was gone.

The drop seemed like an eternity but actually lasted no more than a second. She landed some twenty feet below the trail on a rocky outcropping, twisting two ribs on impact. An instant later she began to tumble down the steep hillside, bumping and bouncing over boulders that had been deposited there by melting ice eons ago, and supplemented when the trail had been carved out of the cliff.

When she finally hit bottom, she bounced off yet another rock, and a rivulet of blood opened in her scalp. Her left ankle had become twisted on the way down, and several of her fingers seemed to be dislocated from the force of impact. She lay there on her back a moment, looking up at the pale blue sky above, wincing at the agony of her ribs pressing against her lungs.

Monica inhaled several more ragged breaths, then glanced up at where she imagined the trail must be—a hundred yards, maybe two hundred above her? It seemed impossible that she had tumbled this far and survived. A sharp spasm gripped her chest, and she tried shifting her body again, a motion that instantly was followed by another slice of pain.

It was somewhere in between these bouts of torment that she noticed the shards of glass and scraps of metal scattered about. At first, they didn't strike her as odd or out of place, because the drop and her injuries had momentarily disoriented her. But as she came to terms with the steady throbbing that racked her body, the reality of where she was began to sink in. She was stranded on the side of a mountain in the middle of northern Pakistan, her body awash with pain, not a living soul within miles. She had just killed two men who seemed to have come from out of nowhere and attacked her, and she had no doubt that her traveling companions — Branson Dahl and Ahmed Javid—were dead, as well.

And, scattered around her, were the remains of what seemed to be a long-ago plane crash. Twisted pieces of fuselage, fragments of broken windows, and shredded luggage were strewn across the mountain ridge. To Monica's right lay the contorted cabin of an airplane, the cockpit crushed by the impact, wings and engines sheared clean off. And, protruding through the open doorway, the remains of a man who—by the look of things—had been dead for a very long time.

She was too tired to scream and, besides, it just wasn't in her. She felt a little lightheaded and realized she was hyperventilating, confused and on the verge of shock. No one knew where she was, and the trail sure as hell wasn't a major thoroughfare to anywhere. It was a good path for horses and goats and, obviously, jihadist rebels dressed in smelly camo, if that's who those bastards were.

She glanced around, thinking the body of her first attacker had to be down here somewhere, hopefully farther down the hillside, and preferably dead. She tried to straighten her legs, but the throbbing in her ankle was almost unbearable—same thing with her ribs—same thing with everything, it seemed. She blinked back the burning pain and checked her body for signs of blood. There was a little, mostly from scrapes and gashes on her arms and legs, and her scalp; but nothing major, no serious artery leakage. Good news: she wasn't going to bleed out.

The flipside was, she was dead if she didn't do something soon.

But what? She was a good forty miles from the closest village, a tiny outpost that sold produce and spices and, oddly enough, bootleg copies of American CDs. The nearest hikers were probably days behind her, and moving at a snail's pace. She'd abandoned her backpack and cameras up on the trail, where one of her assailants now lay dead. Maybe some traveler would stumble across them, wonder what had gone down here and peer over the edge. Maybe they would spot her at the bottom of this rocky cliff, along with the wreckage of a private aircraft.

Damn. What had she stumbled upon?

The sun was directly overhead now, just past noon in northern Pakistan, about fifty miles east of the Afghan border and west of China, with the disputed territories in between. Over the past few months a half-dozen militants had been killed in the area during a spate of infighting, something the consular officer at the U.S. embassy had repeatedly pointed out the day before yesterday when he'd tried to dissuade them from making this trip. Not safe for a woman to travel, a lesson that had been confirmed just a few minutes ago. Not safe for anyone, actually.

"Rebels are crossing through that region every day," he had warned her. "They will kill you as soon as look at you."

Monica took a moment to flex her feet. The pain in her ankle was excruciating, but she could move it. She slowly pushed herself up and tried to put weight on it…not much at first; just enough to see if it got any worse. She took a step forward, and when it didn't collapse, she did it again. Each one of them was agonizing, but she couldn't just remain where she was.

Plus, she was morbidly intrigued by the wreckage and the remnants of the dead body in the doorway. Her years as a photographer flying in and out of wildfires and floods and earthquakes had steeled her against the sight of death and destruction and, while she was facing her own mortality, she was curious about this mangled plane that somehow had ended up on the side of this mountain.

And whoever else might be inside.

She made it halfway to the doorway near the rear of the aircraft when her ankle seized up in a fit of pain. She was wearing her good pair of hiking boots, and she could feel her ankle swelling against the leather uppers. She wiggled her toes, then made a circular motion with her foot to test the flexibility of her ankle. Not good, she thought, possibly broken after all, *dammit*.

It took her a few more minutes, but she eventually made it to the open hatch. The corpse she had seen from a distance turned out to be no more than a skull with a mandible, a withered torso, and one intact arm. The other arm had either been torn off in the crash or carried off by a hungry carnivore; maybe both.

The body carried the tattered fragments of a men's dress shirt; faded blue, with a collar that one time had been white. Much of his flesh had been chewed away over the passing years by mountain-dwelling mammals, and both of his eyes had been removed, probably at the pleasure of the same creatures of prey.

It didn't require a forensic investigator to determine cause of death, given the pair of holes in his forehead, centered just an inch apart.

Whatever had brought the plane down, this man—body, corpse, cadaver, whatever he was—had been shot prior to impact. Twice, in fact. Execution style.

What the hell happened here? Monica wondered. *Who was this guy? Where had this plane come from, and what was it doing here in the middle of nowhere?*

A flicker of motion to her left caused her to freeze as a shadow slid out of the periphery of her vision. Someone—*something*—was here with her, just a few yards away. Had her first assailant survived his plunge into the maw of death just as she had, and now was coming to finish her off? Or had she just seen the ghost of one of passengers who had died in the crash? She dared not move, dared not say a word.

Then she heard a bleating sound, and she ventured a slow, careful look to her left. Monica had read Branson Dahl's article, which explained that wild sheep inhabited the high mountains to the east, while ibex and markhors lived along the steep, craggy cliffs. She released a shallow breath of relief when she saw a mountain goat munching on a tuft of grass at the nose of the wrecked plane, chewing with a calm indifference to her presence. She closed her eyes and tipped her head back with a relaxed sigh, her heart now pumping on overdrive as it poured adrenaline through her veins.

Under different circumstance she might have laughed, but the horror that engulfed her wouldn't allow it.

When she opened her eyes again nothing had changed. The goat remained where it was, casually grazing on his lunch. It took a step closer, took another bite. Step, bite. Step, bite.

The cadaver in the doorway, however, wasn't going anywhere.

Taking care not to disturb his repose, Monica edged her way into the gloomy fuselage. She found herself in the back of the plane, where there was yet another body belted into one of the rear seats. Remnants of a floral print dress and lace collar told her this passenger had been a woman and, like the man in the open hatch, she also had received two bullets just above the bridge of her nose.

Monica felt her mouth go dry and pressed back a wave of nausea. She tried not to think who the dead woman might have been—how she had come to be on this plane—and instead turned her attention to the forward part of the cabin. All but one of the windows had fractured upon impact, and a thick film of dust was everywhere. She waited a moment for her eyes to adjust to the subdued light, then glanced around the crumpled fuselage.

There were eight seats, four on either side of a narrow aisle that had been made even narrower by the force of impact. They had been crafted from what appeared to be plush leather that had shredded upon impact, tufts of padding scattered about. Hungry carnivores had definitely been in here, devouring everything that was carbon-based and grabbing the rest to line their nests. Some of the seats had twisted around to face sideways, and Monica found more bodies buckled into three of them.

That made five in all.

She carefully edged her way toward the front of the plane, pausing briefly to inspect each victim as she went. Each one shared the same telltale mark of two holes in the forehead, same placement and spacing as the man in the doorway and the woman she'd found sprawled across the rear seats. Each of them had been murdered while they were strapped into their seats. Except for the one in the doorway, who might have been moving about the cabin when he'd been killed, then maybe dragged to the door by a predator.

In any event, all of them appeared to have been killed prior to the crash.

Monica attempted to stand, but the crushed ceiling prevented her from straightening fully upright. Remaining in her hunched position, she turned her attention to the cockpit, wondering if the same fate had befallen the captain of this ill-fated flight.

There was no forward door on this plane, just a flimsy curtain that could be pulled closed to separate the pilot and first officer from the rest of the passengers. It was hanging from its runner in shreds, the ragged marks of sharp claws telling her all she needed to know. She gingerly pushed it aside and found that the nose of the aircraft had been flattened upon impact, the windscreen exploded into thousands of glass jewels. The instrument panel had been pancaked inward against the twin side-by-side seats, apparently with such force that it would have brought instant death to anyone who might have been sitting there.

But both seats were empty; no pilot, no copilot. Which might offer an explanation of who shot the five passengers of this plane. Or, maybe, who the corpse in the doorway was.

It was then that she noticed a metallic emblem affixed to the bulkhead wall to her left, a simple line of stylish lettering that read:

King Air 350 XER

Monica was no expert on airplanes, but she knew from her travels that a King Air was a turboprop rather than a jet. Which meant that, as nicely appointed as it may have been in the past, this was no high-end private aircraft leased by rock stars and celebrities. They traveled in Lears and Citations, enjoying their champagne wishes and caviar dreams. This plane probably had been on a charter flight and had lost its way, coming down in the mountains of northern Pakistan.

With each of its passengers shot in the head. *Double taps.*

Acting purely out of professional curiosity, she pulled out her cell phone. The screen had cracked during her tumble down the cliffside, but the camera function seemed to work. The small lens was nowhere near the quality of the professional gear she'd left up on the trail, but it was good enough in a pinch. She snapped a photo of the empty cockpit, then turned back to the main cabin and took another, and then another, and another.

By the time she finished, she'd captured several dozen images of the plane and its deceased occupants. Once again, she wondered how long ago this had happened, what had brought the aircraft down. There were no signs of fire, which was odd unless the plane had run out of fuel. Yes; that fit the storyline that was beginning to form in her head. Someone—the pilot, maybe—had murdered all the passengers, then had bailed out. That would explain why the cabin door was missing. She knew it was near impossible to unlock a hatch at cruising altitude, but what if it had been opened before the cabin had pressurized? Could the aircraft have continued on a pre-set course until the tanks were empty, then come to earth here in the remote mountains of northern Pakistan?

The big question was *why*? Why had the pilot killed them all, then jumped? The twisted wreckage was not just the aftermath of a tragic crash; it was the scene of five premeditated murders. Who were all these people, and why did they all have to die?

As Monica slipped her phone back inside a pocket of her hiking vest, she noticed a black briefcase that appeared to have been dented from being tossed about the cabin. At first glance she thought it was one of those expensive metallic carry-ons sold at pricey specialty stores. Upon closer examination, however, she realized it was made from—*what was that material called*? Carbon fiber; that was it. A label affixed between the latches read:

EQUINOX

It seemed to be an equipment case, and its two combination locks were sprung, probably from the force of the crash. Inside were two layers of gray egg-crate padding, on both the top and bottom. Matching compartments for a four-by-six rectangular object had been cut into both halves of the foam, but whatever had been wedged in there now was gone. The protective packing had partially granularized from the elements, and she saw marks where tiny teeth had chewed some of it away. That's when she found the adhesive label that read, "EMF shielding guaranteed to block up to 99% RF radiation."

Monica had seen those very words on the vinyl bag in which Branson Dahl had kept his laptop computer. This was back in New York, before the ill-fated night at the hotel in Islamabad and, when she had inquired about it, he'd said—like the smug little shit he was—"you've never heard of a Faraday bag?"

Determined not to let his egotism mess with her nerves, she'd Googled the term later. Learned that a Faraday bag was designed to block electromagnetic fields, preventing the penetration of wireless signals or radiation and thus protecting whatever was inside from digital theft. For the average traveler, this meant data on passports and credit cards was safe from hackers and identity thieves. This carbon fiber case, however, was a different matter, and it appeared someone had gone to great lengths to protect whatever had been inside.

Which easily begged any number of questions: Why had all these people been killed, and where was the pilot? What information was on the object that had been housed in this case? What was it doing on this plane, and who brought it on board? And, probably most important of all, where was it now?

Chapter 2

Tuesday, June 23
NEW YORK
11:48 am GMT, 6:48 Local

"Goddamit, Petrie. That damned hard drive has to be there somewhere. How can it not be in that bloody airplane?"

"I'm just telling you what I've been told, sir," Diana Petrie replied in a calm and restrained voice that had come to be known as her trademark. It was more than that, in fact; it was the cornerstone of her very being and the driving force that had allowed her to break the glass ceiling of power when other women were simply figuring out how to wash it. "You need to settle down and let me do the heavy lifting on this."

"Settle down? You're telling me to settle down?" Thousands of miles away The Chairman had removed his Berluti shoes and was slowly tapping his hand-carved ebony cane across the oversized Persian rug in his wood-paneled drawing room. He stopped in his tracks and deliberately turned to look back at her. Or, rather, at the wall-mounted videoconference unit that was transmitting this private discussion, through an array of signal scramblers and encryption devices, from his island outpost off the coast of Scotland to the heart of midtown Manhattan. The twenty-first floor of the Graybar Building, to be precise, located on Lexington Avenue adjacent to Grand Central Terminal. "We're not talking about the complete boxed set of the remastered Beatles on that hard drive," he fumed. "That's Goddamn *Equinox*—"

"I know what it is, sir," Petrie replied, her measured tone like an even keel plowing through rough waters. She was in her late fifties, close-cropped hair the color of a subway rat and eyes just as probing. She had never considered herself particularly attractive and, as with most of her astute observations, this one was dead-on. Intelligent and imperious, she had long ago stopped worrying about her appearance, her lack of friends, or the growing ranks of people who might consider her an adversary. She felt comfortable in her own skin, despite its almost translucent hue and—unlike her ego—a tendency to bruise easily. "Wherever it might be, we will find it."

"Wherever it might be?" The Chairman repeated, his words crackling like the embers of a fire on a cold winter's night. "Are we certain that Goddamned photographer didn't bring it down the mountain with her?"

"As certain as we can be. She and her belongings have been thoroughly searched."

The old man had momentarily wandered out of range of the camera, and Petrie could swear she heard him pound his fist on something hard, followed by some muffled cussing. "Do you even have a goddammed clue where that thing *might be*?" he fumed.

"Not at this very moment, no," she replied, refusing to give rise to his legendary temper or acknowledge his vulgarities. "But we will find it."

She was seated in an uncomfortable executive chair, positioned behind a scarred oak desk in a room totally devoid of any trappings or embellishments that could even remotely betray its true business function. That function being to serve as the bricks-and-mortar headquarters of the fictitious J.H. Black Headwear, LLC, a dummy corporation owned by a holding firm set up through an offshore shell company that was a subsidiary of the Greenwich Global Group. It was a clandestine entity that operated entirely within the deepest confines of the dark web, and had never manufactured or sold a single hat in its seventy-plus-year history. Nor were there any plans to do so anytime soon.

Petrie's encrypted laptop sat on the desk in front of her, and the fifteen-inch HD screen revealed The Chairman's every move in his book-lined library that screamed of British pretense—as long as he didn't stray too far left or right out of camera range.

"Does this lack of information even bother you in the slightest?" he pressed her.

One of the first lessons she learned when she was named to the G3 executive board almost three decades ago was not to engage in The Chairman's infamous rhetoric. With that in mind she said, "Sir, we have the finest intelligence resources working on our behalf. Wherever it is, we'll find it."

"The bloody thing was supposed to be at the bottom of the goddamned Mediterranean," he continued to fume. "What the hell happened to that plan?"

"Payne Stewart," she said, folding her hands squarely in her lap.

Thaddeus Stone, the ninety-eight-year-old Chairman whose haggard face Petrie was studying on the screen, at one time had been publicly recognized as the founding partner of Colfax Stone, Plc, a London-based securities company that had earned him many millions of pounds over his decades-long tenure. He had been forced to step aside from that position thirteen years ago when he reached the mandatory retirement milestone of eighty-five, an edict that would have caused most men of his stature to harbor ill will and resentment. But Stone had viewed his newfound freedom as a gift and a godsend, allowing him time to busy himself fulltime in his covert role as the leader—and last surviving architect—of the Greenwich Global Group, a clandestine and extrajudicial venture founded in the months immediately after the end of World War II. It took its name from the prime meridian that passes through the Royal Observatory in Greenwich, England, and which serves as a sort of "ground zero" for all time zones around the world. The final draft of the pact developed by the organization's original founders was signed at that particular location in late January 1946, thus giving it its name.

Despite his age, he would retain his current position—as prescribed by the firm's original charter—until death or dementia made his leadership either impossible or impractical. Parallel events that, by all accounts, were fast approaching.

"What the fuck does a dead golfer have to do with anything?" he fumed at the camera, its steady red light beaming at him like the laser sight of a sniper's rifle.

"Payne Stewart was on a routine flight from Orlando to Houston in 1999 when something happened to his plane," Petrie explained patiently, like a schoolteacher explaining the Law of Quadratic Reciprocity. "It lost cabin pressure, and everyone on board blacked out. Air Force pilots tracked the aircraft, but there was nothing they could do. Eventually it ran out of fuel and plunged into a field in South Dakota, over a thousand miles off course. A tragic accident."

"We had nothing to do with that," he said, his automatic defense mechanism kicking in.

"Of course not," Petrie replied. "I only mention it to illustrate how accidents happen."

"This is different, and you know it," The Chairman said. "It was a total fuck-up from the start, and now we find out everyone on board that plane was shot. Twice, just to make sure."

"Not everyone was shot, sir," she reminded him. "Pakistani authorities counted five bodies in the wreckage, and U.S. investigators confirm that. There was no sign of the pilot."

The Chairman rubbed the crown of his head, which these days consisted more of scabs than follicles. His eyes were dark and cloudy, his ruddy skin scarred from where the doctors had periodically scraped off masses of basal cells. At one time his clothes had come from a tailor on Savile Row, but this morning he appeared to be wearing gray flannel trousers whose crease had long ago fallen out, and a stained cardigan sweater that sagged on his gaunt frame. Except for the pricey shoes he'd kicked off his feet, he dressed more like a beggar in central London.

"You're saying the bloody wanker shot them all?"

"It appears so, but at this point no one is officially confirming or denying a thing. That would put a negative spin on an already inexplicable situation."

"It's already been all over the news," he reminded her. "It's not easy to dispute ballistic evidence."

"All because one hysterical woman spent four days at the bottom of a cliff and was so delirious she couldn't remember what she saw," Petrie ventured.

"Rubbish…we can't keep the true cause of death under wraps forever."

Petrie hated to admit it, but he was right. There was no getting around the double-taps in the foreheads of all five victims. Whether or not this truth was being covered up by the Americans or the Pakistanis, maybe even the Brits or Israelis, it still endured. As Aldous Huxley had once prophetically proclaimed, "Facts do not cease to exist because they are ignored."

"And that's where we start," she told him.

"What the hell does that mean?"

"It means we pursue this incident in a logical and straightforward process."

The Chairman shot her a dark look through the camera lens in his drawing room. "As I recall, that bloody plane was supposed to blow up over the Mediterranean," he said.

"We knew at the time that our plans had gone awry," Petrie reminded him. "Its whereabouts remained a mystery to the world, until fifty-two hours ago."

"There are almost two hundred million square miles of land on this planet," he said. "Almost one hundred twenty-five billion acres. For a plane that was supposed to disintegrate over the ocean, how do you suppose it ended up where it did?"

"It ran out of fuel, like I said," she replied. "Our independent search of the wreckage confirms the tanks were empty."

The Chairman continued to glare at her, through the lens. He sensed she was avoiding the reality of the matter, and he was not accustomed to being treated in such a fashion. "Then what the fuck went wrong?" he seethed.

"The only way all this could have happened—with the fuel tanks empty—was if the entire assignment was hijacked."

"By the pilot." The Chairman scowled as he digested what she was saying. "That fucking snake, Phythian." Correctly pronouncing the name *FITH-yun*.

"As you said, everyone else confirmed to have been on board that aircraft was shot and killed," she said, by way of confirmation. "Phythian was at the controls, and our source on the scene says he does not appear to be among the dead. Process of elimination."

The Chairman rolled his clouded, glaucomic eyes. For the past six years he'd assumed—as had the entire global intelligence community—that Rōnin Phythian had been wiped off the face of the earth when the plane he was flying went down. *Farewell and good riddance, Achilles' brach*, as Thersites had said to Shakespeare's Patroclus. Now this unwelcome and uninvited development erased all that.

"So Phythian was running his own game," he said, his words coming out as a statement rather than a question.

"We suspected it at the time, when not a shred of the aircraft was found," Petrie reminded the old man. "Seems he covered his tracks well."

The Chairman nodded and stared at the floor, as if a solution to this immediate problem might be lurking there amongst the carpet mites and cigar ashes. Eventually he looked up and said, "Our partners paid damned good money for that bloody thing to go down. Along with all everyone on board."

"Don't forget the hard drive," she reminded him, bringing the discussion back around to the source of his original tirade.

"Equinox."

"Yes, Equinox. The contents of which the five passengers on board the King Air were conspiring to reveal to the world. That's why this videoconference is top priority."

"Then enough of this bullshit," The Chairman said with an exasperated sigh. "It's time we got the others on the line and filled them in on this bloody clusterfuck."

"They're all standing by, and I've already briefed them on the details." Petrie tapped a few pre-programmed function keys on her laptop, then said, "Adam...Simone...Eitan. Are you all there?"

Almost instantly the screen divided into four quadrants. The image in the upper left quadrant was The Chairman, who abhorred these virtual meetings unless necessity dictated, which this morning it did. To the right of him on the upper row was Adam Kent, late-forties, squarish nose and angular cheekbones, dimpled chin, dark hair. Eyes that Petrie knew were brown but, because of the camera quality on his mobile device, just looked like black dots. Or maybe it was a set of vanity contact lenses. One never knew with Kent who, as the newest recruit to the G3 executive board and head of logistics, also seemed the most squirrelly.

Directly below him was a woman with an angular jaw, thin lips, wiry blonde and silver hair pinned up in a tight bun. Her name was Simone Marchand, and her cheeks showed the blowsy signs of rosacea, but Petrie knew from her personnel file that the reddish hue actually betrayed her fondness for expensive vodka. To her left and below The Chairman was Eitan Hazan, a bald man sporting a dark tan and a bent nose that appeared to have been flattened either by a fist or the butt of a gun. He never spoke about it, but Petrie—given her unfettered access to the G3's personnel files—knew the injury had occurred during Operation Entebbe more than forty years ago, when he was a young recruit trying to prove himself to the Mossad.

Missing from the video array was a Frenchman named Martin Beaudin, whom Petrie and The Chairman discreetly had not included in this encrypted videoconference. The keeper of all G3 secrets, his true identity and whereabouts were closely held in strict confidence, and not even the other board members knew of his existence—or his function. The Group's original post-war charter stipulated that an internal, innominate auditor be appointed to "guard and protect" its business matters with exacting care, a responsibility Beaudin undertook with the same conviction and dedication that his own father had applied to the role before him.

Known as The Locksmith—*Le Serrurier*—he was Petrie's point-person from the moment word of the discovery of the wreckage had come down from the mountain. He had contacts inside every intelligence agency and team investigating the crash, and whatever they knew, he knew.

"I am your eyes and ears in this, madam," he'd told her. "Trust me."

Trust him, she did.

As Petrie had told The Chairman, all those present had been briefed on the nature of this call, and none of them seemed pleased with the circumstances that made it necessary. All confirmed their presence with the word "here," as if their faces on the screen didn't provide sufficient evidence. Followed by the requisite, "good morning, sir," addressed to the shriveled Chairman, to whom the word *smile* was a non-starter.

"All of us have other things to do, and I thank you for giving up your time to participate in this video chat," Petrie began as she leaned back in her chair. "As I mentioned in the briefing I sent you earlier, we're faced with a highly serious and sobering issue."

"Communications are secure?" asked the man named Kent, who was seated on a bench in the Ellipse, just south of the White House. As the most recent addition to the executive board, he still questioned the protocols the other directors took for granted.

"Completely," she assured him. "Simone…good to see you. How's Trixie?"

"Nursing twelve stitches," Simone Marchand replied, not a single muscle in her face giving the slightest flicker of movement. "She had a tumor removed yesterday. The vet says she'll recover completely, but she has to wear a cone of silence for a few days. *Mon Dieu*."

"I'm really sorry," Petrie replied. "My poor Diesel was confined to one of those when I got him neutered. It drove him crazy."

"Excuse me, but we're facing a crisis of global proportions here," The Chairman snapped from Square Number One.

"And I have a meeting at the Knesset in thirty-two minutes," Eitan Hazan in Israel added, glancing at his watch. "Chairman of the Foreign

Affairs and Defense Committee." As if that made his time more valuable than anyone else on the screen, which he was arrogant enough to believe it was.

"Let's get on with this, then," Petrie agreed. These things always made her feel like a border collie trying to herd a clowder of cats. "I assume everyone has read the files and viewed the videos?"

Three brusque nods and verbal "affirmatives"—not including The Chairman—confirmed that they had.

"Okay. Just to keep us all on the same page, King Air 350 number 00-JKA—registered to a private charter firm in Belgium—went missing six years and two months ago on a flight from Haifa, Israel, to the island of Malta. The aircraft disappeared from radar eighteen minutes into its flight, over the Mediterranean Sea. Search and rescue vessels were immediately dispatched to the area near where the last transponder signal was detected, but no sign of the plane was ever found. No wreckage, no human remains. Highly mysterious, but not without precedent. After two weeks the search was called off. Eventually it was presumed that the plane plunged into the water at such a steep angle that it ended up on the bottom. An unlikely scenario, but we had the recent disappearance of Malaysia Air flight 370 working in our favor. The possibility of an explosion was discounted, since no wreckage was spotted. The entire incident remained a riddle, right up until the discovery of the turboprop in northeastern Pakistan."

"We're certain it's the same plane?" Simone Marchand asked. She was seated on a retaining wall in *Jardin d'Erivan* in her beloved Paris, just four blocks from her apartment. A tourist boat was drifting up the Seine behind her, about to disappear under the *Pont de Invalides*. Unlike the laptop Petrie was using on her desk in the Graybar building, she was patched into the call through her iPad via Bluetooth. Also scrambled and encrypted.

"The registration numbers on the fuselage match those of the missing King Air," Petrie confirmed. "And the company that owned the missing aircraft confirmed it's theirs."

"How did it end up where it did?" Eitan Hazan asked from Menakhem Stern Square in Jerusalem. In addition to his board position, he was in charge of overall strategy for the G3. "Best guess."

"I'm not prone to guessing, but logic suggests the pilot engineered a sophisticated hoax and diverted the plane's course back over land, overriding his assignment."

"After killing all the passengers on board the plane," the woman named Simone said.

"Two shots each," Adam Kent affirmed from Washington. "Pop-pop."

"The details are in dispute," Petrie said. "If those people were, indeed, shot, all we know is it happened before the aircraft came back down to earth."

"What kind of plane is a King Air?" Kent wanted to know.

"It's a twin turboprop built by Beechcraft. This one was a 350 XER, which stands for extra-extended range. Fitted with larger tanks that allow it to fly close to three thousand miles without refueling."

"Far enough to make it all the way to northern Pakistan?" he pressed.

"The outer edge of its range. The theory is the plane went into a gentle glide when the tanks ran dry, adding additional miles to its flight. That's why there was no explosion or evidence of fire at the scene, no bodies burned beyond recognition. Their identities are in the files you received, but I'll go over them briefly just to refresh all our memories."

She touched her keyboard again. Gone was the matrix of faces that looked like an aging *Brady Bunch*, replaced with color photographs of the five men and women who'd had the misfortune of being on the King Air 350 XER that fateful day over six years ago. Those who were participating in this videoconference from their remote locations would be seeing the same imagery on their own digital devices. Secured and encrypted, as always.

She highlighted the first photo, in the upper left of the screen, and said, "This is Pascal Bergeron, thirty-eight at time of death. Born in Lyons, France. Educated at *École des Ponts Paris Tech*. Headed R&D at a global IT firm until he founded his own digital security company known as *Securatique*. Annual sales of over two billion Euros the year before he died."

"Bribed his way out of a sexual assault charge in Poland, if I'm not mistaken," Adam Kent said from his perch in Washington.

"Three of them, to be exact," Petrie confirmed. "All eventually were dropped posthumously. Next is Avigail Eichorn, age thirty-one. Israeli-born, kibbutz background. Hebrew University degree in physics, mandatory military service. Suspected Mossad connections, possibly through her father, but never confirmed. Uber-patriot to her nation and her people."

Eitan Hazan nodded with an impassioned frown, trying his best to disguise a sudden flare of guilt. He'd managed to keep his connection to the Eichorn woman a secret for over six years, something he doubted even Petrie knew of. Not even during the G3's investigation of the plane's disappearance, nor the subsequent flaying he'd received for his role in the mission's total failure.

"She was rumored to have had a relationship with Bergeron," he observed, purely as a diversionary tactic.

"Intimate?" Simone Marchand wanted to know, simply because she was into such things.

"We suspect so, but we're not sure of the nature," Petrie replied as she watched Hazan try not to squirm on the screen. "It didn't seem relevant at the time, and still isn't."

She then ran through the other three passengers on the plane. A Vietnamese national living in Brussels named Binh Phan, forty-six years old and former programmer for a major global search engine based in Stockholm. Also an accomplished hacker suspected of numerous purloined files uploaded to Wikileaks and other online sites that claimed to support political truth and transparency. Number four on her list was Bruno Richter, forty-one at the time of his death. He'd served as an investigator for the Federal Criminal Police Office in Germany for almost two decades, but a year prior to the crash he'd quit to join Bergeron's security business, which specialized in investigating cybercrimes and cryptocurrency scams.

"Last on our list is Katya Leiffson," Petrie announced. "Thirty-four years of age, born in Reykjavík. Graduated from the University of Iceland top of her class, completed two years of post-grad work at Cambridge. Economics background, but she transitioned to business journalism a year before her death. She was building quite a reputation investigating money laundering and financial fraud, and was one of the early forces looking into the Panama Papers a few years back."

A momentary pause followed Petrie's recap, both in the austere office of the *faux* hat company on the twenty-first floor of the office building in Manhattan, as well as the secure locations in Washington, Paris, and Jerusalem. And Gray Rock, off the western coast of Scotland in a windswept sound known as the Firth of Clyde. She gave them all time to absorb the information, and waited for one of them to throw out the next question.

"You haven't mentioned Phythian," Simone Marchand said, adding a touch of French flare to the pronunciation: *FEETH-yun*. "Wasn't he the pilot of the plane?"

"He was, and we all breathed a collective sigh of relief upon the initial reports of his death," Petrie replied. "The hard truth is, the discovery of the plane in the mountains suggests there's good reason to believe he bailed out of it and very likely survived the jump."

"Excuse me," Adam Kent said from Washington. "This was all before my time here. I read the brief you sent earlier, and I remember the incident from when it was in the news. What's a bit murky to me is this person you call Phythian."

A prolonged silence followed as everyone on the line waited for someone else to speak first, as if they all might contract a deadly virus just by coming in close contact with the name.

"Rōnin Phythian was the most efficient contractor ever to work for the G3," Petrie finally explained. "As the dossier I sent—and you read—lays out very clearly."

"Yes, it does, up to a point," Kent replied. "Maybe I'm particularly dense, but what's so damned special about this guy?"

"Just about everything, if you get right down to it. Fifty-two years old when he went missing, which would make him fifty-eight today. Born in Cranston, Rhode Island. Father was a janitor in the local church the family attended, and his mother pressed garments in a dry-cleaning shop in their Fiskeville neighborhood. Tested significantly above average on both the Stanford Binet and the ASVAB. Father's name was Owen Phythian, deceased, third-generation American. Mother's name was Maria Doyle, Irish heritage on her father's side, also deceased."

"Sounds pretty special to me."

Petrie ignored Kent's annoying sarcasm and continued. "Rōnin Phythian graduated from the University of Rhode Island, ROTC—" she pronounced it *rot-see* "—then served twelve years as a Marine, where he was trained to fly Prowlers and Super Hercules. Also learned how to shoot, among many valuable qualifications for his subsequent line of work. Master sniper, small arms fire, hand-to-hand combat, experienced with explosives. Both making and defusing them. He was exceptionally effective while in our employ, but not for those particular abilities."

"I assume his departure from the Marines voluntary?" he interrupted.

"It was, for reasons that are immaterial to this discussion." Phythian's general discharge from military service was an omission of choice, as was her decision to skirt—at least for the time being—the true nature of

Phythian's deadly skillset. "Like I said, everything you need to know about the man is in his profile." *Which you clearly haven't spent any time studying, numb nuts*, her tone implied.

Like a dog gnawing on a rawhide bone, however, Kent was not about to let go. "And this Phythian was at the controls the day that plane went down?" he pressed.

"He was," she confirmed. "His background with the Hercules gave him the experience to fly turboprops, such as the King Air. Not the reason we initially recruited him, but useful in a pinch. Again, it's all in the file."

"Enough of the bloody backstory," The Chairman said. "Tell us what the fuck we're doing to distance ourselves from this debacle. And then remedy it."

"Our hands are clean," Petrie assured him, following their pre-arranged dialogue to the letter. "We covered our tracks thoroughly six years ago regarding this incident, as we always do with any mission. Our involvement is totally untraceable, no evidentiary connection to the G3 of any kind."

"Except for Phythian," Marchand pointed out. "He's the loose end in all of this."

"Whatever happened in that plane six years ago was strictly off-the-books improv," Petrie said. "He was told that his assignment was to disable the plane, set it on a crash course, and bail."

"Why lease a clunky old turboprop instead of a jet?" Kent asked, out of the blue.

"That plane was anything but clunky, and definitely not old," she replied, her patience growing thin almost to a molecular level. "But since you asked, the answer is easy: If you jump out of a jet, the wing will kill you instantly. The door of a King Air, however, is in the rear, making a clean jump possible. Phythian knew this. The story we'd given him was we had a recon team standing by to rescue him even before the aircraft went into the sea."

"All of which was total horseshit," Kent ventured. "Could he have known that?"

"This is Phythian we're talking about," Petrie reminded her, and everyone else on the call. "That's why we took what we thought were extra-guarded measures, to make sure he wouldn't get wind of our end game."

Those extra-guarded measures had been Eitan Hazan's responsibility, and the full weight of the mission's failure had landed on him when it fell apart. Now, six years later, he continued to feel a stinging guilt about the entire matter. Especially since it was the focal point of this conversation, and his smudged fingerprints were all over it. There was nothing he could do but stare straight ahead at the camera lens on his tablet, knowing what everyone on this call must be thinking. Everyone but Adam Kent, who had not been affiliated with the G3 at the time, and wasn't aware of Eitan's involvement.

"He must have turned off the transponders just before he nose-dived to simulate a crash," Kent mused aloud. "Then, just before he hit the water he leveled off. When the time was right he switched the controls to altitude pre-set, put the plane in climb mode, then opened the door and jumped before the cabin had a chance to pressurize."

"As I said, Phythian was a highly experienced pilot and well-equipped to improvise when the need arose," Petrie concurred. "He would have known what he was doing."

"If he managed to survive this game of his when he bailed, where on earth do you think he might be?" Marchand asked as a thin cloud swept in front of the sun, casting a shadow across her ruddy face.

Her question was enough to revive the interest of The Chairman, who appeared to have almost drifted into a midday nap. "Yes…where the bollocks is the bloody bugger?" he asked through a crackle of phlegm.

"As of last count, there are one hundred ninety-five individual countries on this planet, spread across six continents," Petrie replied, extrapolating from his own observation a few minutes earlier. "That includes the Holy See and the state of Palestine. If Phythian didn't die after stepping out of that plane—a strong possibility that none of our thoughts and prayers can change—your guess is as good as mine which one of them he might be calling home."

Chapter 3

12:02 pm GMT, 3:02 pm Local

Rōnin Phythian was not dead; far from it. And, as Diana Petrie had surmised, no one's thoughts or prayers were going to alter that truth anytime soon.

At that very moment he was stretched out on a slight knoll in Tarangire National Park, the harsh afternoon sun baking the low ridges of gneiss and pre-Cambrian rocks for which this region of Africa was known. He'd found a patch of dry hardscrabble hours ago and had positioned himself behind two igneous boulders on a craggy mound that an ancient seismic convulsion had thrust upwards from the valley floor. The rocks were elongated and egg-shaped, coming together a foot from the ground, and they provided a perfect V-shaped platform.

He was propped up on his elbows, about a hundred yards above a dry wash that just a month ago had been flushed by seasonal floods. The rains had been more plentiful than normal this year, which was a boon for the thousands of animals that lived in this vast section of the Serengeti. The first clouds had rolled over the massive Masai Steppe in November, the initial drizzle sweeping across the parched land in shimmery gray veils, and later in thick sheets that fed the first rivulets and streams. Then the wet season had begun in earnest, and the valley filled with runoff that flowed northward to the Tarangire River. Mammals and reptiles and birds migrated to the lush ecosystem, cohabiting the land with a wary *esprit de corps* as they fed and drank at the natural watering troughs.

Now the land was drying rapidly, most of the moisture either having evaporated or leeched into the ground. The earth here consisted of stony soils, sediments and clays, and volcanic ash deposits that yielded the rich loam found throughout the region. Many of the larger animals already traveled northward where more plentiful sources of water might be found, but some would remain here until the very last drop of moisture was gone.

Phythian's right eye was pressed against the lens of a high-powered scope, and he was watching one of those animals right now. It was a large elephant with long, curved tusks that had been worn to crude buds at the end. *Loxodonta Africana.* She was large, standing close to ten feet at her shoulders, and was using her trunk to probe the dry scrub in search of grasses and roots. Another half dozen elephants, all of them smaller, casually grazed nearby. As evidenced by her size and almost regal demeanor, this one clearly was the older matriarch, and she exuded the stature of a protective leader who would gladly fight off all attackers.

He knew African elephants lived in social units consisting of mothers and their young, as well as sisters and their female cousins. Males left the herd when they matured around fourteen years of age, wandering off to join an *ad hoc* band of other bulls, departing from the bachelor pack only when it was time to find a mate. Once that reproductive task was completed, he would leave the female to begin gestation of a new calf, a period that lasted twenty-two months.

The rifle scope was powerful, and its array of hand-ground lenses magnified several scars on the grand creature's weathered gray hide—mostly old wounds, but a few newer ones, as well. These suggested she'd already suffered through a number of territorial battles and, by all appearances, had emerged victorious from all of them.

Phythian locked his crosshairs on the side of elephant's face. The animal was a good five hundred yards distant, but the scope he was using was a Schmidt & Bender 5-25x56 PMII telescopic sight—known for its exemplary magnification and parallax adjustment from 10 meters out to infinity. That meant that, at this distance, the elephant's head more than filled the lens, and Phythian could even see the caramel hue of the animal's huge, wondering eyes.

The scope itself was affixed to a McMillan Tac-50 long-range anti-personnel rifle. The TAC-50 was a manually operated, rotary bolt-action gun almost exclusively used by snipers who sought long-range accuracy and terminal results. Just a few years back one of these weapons—in the hands of a Canadian shooter—had taken down an ISIS target at two-point-two miles. That worked out to three thousand, seven hundred seventy-two yards; eleven thousand, three hundred sixteen feet. Just over seven times the distance currently between Phythian and the elephant.

Phythian kept his gaze on the animal for about ten seconds, watched as it calmly grazed the dry wash, totally unaware that a deadly rifle scope was zeroed in on its every move. Two scopes, in fact, although Phythian was about to reduce that number to zero.

Very slowly he moved the crosshairs of his Schmidt & Bender 5-25x56 PMII off the elephant's head and pivoted them to the right. The fifteen-degree movement took a good ten seconds, the lack of speed being critical in not alerting the mammal to his presence. Phythian was well-positioned not to let the afternoon sun reflect off the powerful lens or the rifle itself, but he was taking no chances. Even the slightest change in light patterns might betray his location.

It took him another twenty seconds but Phythian finally located his actual target. This one was a human being, a man dressed in high-end safari camo and wearing matching headgear to help him blend in with the surrounding flora. Just like Phythian, he was hiding behind a pile of rocks but, unlike Phythian, his goal today was to take down the graceful giant that he'd fixed in his own scope. Phythian knew from tracking this man that he was shooting a .700 Nitro Express 17.8×89mmR big game rifle fabricated by Holland & Holland of London, this one purchased in a private sale for one hundred thousand U.S. dollars. The .700 cartridges themselves went for one hundred bucks apiece. The weapon was fitted with a Zeiss Conquest 5-25×50 Black Rapid Z 1000 scope which, at just over a thousand dollars, was a bargain. It typically was used for long-range hunting, especially predators and big game.

The hunter and his mercenary Tanzanian guide named Chandu were here in the heart of Tarangire National Park, where neither had any business being. The same thing could be said about Phythian and his sniper rifle, but he was there for an altogether different purpose, one that he believed could only affect the natural balance of the park in a positive way.

The man with the high-priced gun was Russian. Phythian had picked up that valuable detail from the structure of his thought processes as well as the language he'd used on a satellite phone call. That had been the night before last, when he and his guide had settled in for the night at a remote hunting camp that officially did not exist inside the park. Despite the constant threat of poachers, a few park rangers could be persuaded to look the other way if the proper incentive was introduced. Hence the camp site with all the creature comforts expected by a man who was paying ten thousand dollars a day to bag an elephant: king-size bed, eucalyptus fiber sheets, *en suite* bath, and a fully stocked wet bar. Women were available for an extra charge, but they had to be arranged in advance. Singularly determined in his purpose, the Russian had not done that.

Phythian had been following the hunter and his local guide for three days, ever since he'd picked up their trail on the road from the small airport in Arusha. The Russian stood out immediately after stepping down from the private Falcon 50, the elongated metal gun case giving away his true intent here at the edge of the Serengeti. Phythian had shadowed the pair at a distance for the past sixty-eight hours, studying their habits and determining their route the same way a professional bounty hunter would follow a suspect through the toughest terrain. Patiently stalking his prey, assessing the Russian's every movement and behavior. Waiting for the precise moment he would attempt his kill shot.

Which, Phythian knew, was imminent on this searing African afternoon. The temperature was well over one hundred, and even in the shade of the acacias and baobab trees it was hovering in the upper nineties. The air was quiet and still, except for filmy waves of mirage where the last remnants of the wet season were being reclaimed by the sun. Wispy tendrils of smoke and dried animal dung dispatched a thin but fecund aroma.

The Russian had lined up his scope on the elephant, from about four hundred yards out. He could have gotten much, much closer, but he was into it for the thrill of the shooting as well as the ultimate trophy. He came from a long line of hunters who collected mementoes of their killings, particularly his oligarch father, who was too busy controlling the price of Asian oil to have ever bagged an elephant.

At thirty-two years old, young Vasily Sokolov was about to make a point to his old man.

He studied the elephant as his finger gently settled on the trigger. He was waiting for the graceful animal to turn her head, just slightly, which would make it easier to place the bullet directly into the skull through the right ear hole—a one hundred-dollar .700 nitro cartridge, something nature had never anticipated during hundreds of thousands of years of skeletal evolution.

The elephant lifted her head slightly and turned just right, while the Russian applied steady pressure on his finger.

A single shot exploded across the dusty savannah. Birds rushed into the air at the sudden disruption of solitude, and the elephant jerked her head anxiously. She recognized that sound, knew what it had meant to other elephants. She'd seen them fall, seen what the humans did to them once they arrived on the scene with their saws and their knives.

But that was not the case this tranquil afternoon in Tarangire National Park. No elephants would be killed today, at least not in this part of the world. Humans definitely, including the one now lying lifeless behind his pile of rocks. A look of shock in his empty eyes, blood pouring from a gaping hole in his chest. He still had the long gun in his hand, and the highly paid Tanzanian guide was frantically checking his pulse and screaming hysterically. But the now-dead body of the eager poacher who just a couple seconds ago had been the son of a billionaire Russian petroleum exporter was downwind of where the elephant and her herd were grazing, which meant the animals knew none of this.

They returned to their foraging, and a few seconds later the memory of the shot and the bustle of startled birds had faded on the warm Serengeti breeze.

Phythian remained motionless for a long time as he absorbed the full serenity of the moment. The beauty of nature was all around him, from one horizon to the other: earth and sky, flora and fauna. It was all so incredibly vast and immensely satisfying: immediate and permanent. Like life and death, and all that fell between the two.

Five minutes later—or maybe it was fifty—he took a much-needed drink of water from the canteen he'd buried deep in the dirt, which was cooler than the shade. He hadn't been able to quench his thirst while waiting for the shot, and now he helped himself liberally. Careful to leave enough for later, he slipped it into a pocket of his rucksack, then carefully packed up his rifle and prepared for the long journey home.

Chapter 4

"Phythian was known to have at least four passports, as well as sizable bank accounts in a half dozen countries," Diana Petrie summarized from her spartan office in Manhattan. "It wouldn't be difficult for him to go to ground anywhere on the planet."

"There's almost a billion surveillance cameras around the world," Eitan Hazan replied. Time was ticking down until he had to leave for his meeting at the Knesset, and he couldn't wait to escape the scrutinizing eyes of this videoconference. "If he made it out of that plane alive, he's operating totally under the radar."

"As I said, his IQ is well above average," Petrie agreed. "Plus, he has a distinct advantage when it comes to human behavior and thought."

"That's why he was such a valuable asset." This came from Simone Marchand, who wore the hat of G3 finance director in addition to that of executive board member. Somewhere close by a Parisian police siren wailed, then faded in the distance. "Other than the financial hit, none of us was heartbroken that Phythian was gone. In fact, we considered it a blessing in disguise."

"And now it seems you've been dancing on an empty grave," Kent said. *You*, not *we*. And certainly not *I*. "How many assignments was he responsible for?"

"Ninety-eight, over a ten-year period," Petrie said. "Plus, he had a one hundred percent completion rate. No one had ever achieved a perfect score before Phythian came along."

"The deadliest man alive," Marchand added, a hardened look in her eyes. "And for all we know, he still is. Alive. And probably just as deadly."

"Will you all stop your fucking hand-wringing!" The Chairman boomed, or at least his version of a boom, considering his compromised lung and vocal capacity. "None of this is getting us any closer to fixing this cock-up."

A long silence followed, and Petrie took a moment to regain her composure, as well as her temper. For about the tenth time in as many minutes she wondered, not just hypothetically, when this *bloody privileged arsehole* might succumb to his host of diseases and put them all out of their collective misery.

"As has already been stated, we don't have one shred of evidence suggesting where Phythian might be," she said. "Not surprising, given his unbelievable skillset. And the fact that every assignment we ever gave him was completed without issue. Whoever the target, no matter the reason, Phythian got the job done."

"Except his last one," Adam Kent observed. "I'd call that an issue."

Petrie didn't respond, not right away. The prick had signed a lethally binding NDA when The Chairman had personally brought him into the fold, but he'd not been read in on all operations prior to his arrival. Including this one, until now.

"As we've discussed, Phythian believed his job was to nose-dive that plane into the sea, killing everyone on board," she finally explained. "We were convinced that he didn't know the layered nuances of the mission."

In an a-ha moment of clarity, Kent said, "He was both the contractor and the ultimate target."

"Phythian's assignment was to get the plane to altitude and then manipulate the airflow systems to cause everyone to drift into unconsciousness," she replied. "Once he was sure they were out for good he would bail, using a chute that had been stashed in a forward compartment. He was told that a rescue boat would be standing nearby to whisk him to safety before a search and rescue team arrived on-site. Since the wreckage would be scattered over a large area, one missing body—his—wouldn't be questioned."

"But that's not what happened," Kent pushed.

Petrie inhaled a long, deep breath, then slowly let it out. Hazan stole another glance at his watch, hoping this wouldn't take much longer. They all were hoping the same thing.

"A block of C4 disguised to look like cheese was planted in the galley," she said, looking directly into the camera lens. "It was put there by an outside party, the detonator set to go off at cruising altitude. No traceable connection to the G3 or, even more important, Phythian. Every precaution was taken to make sure he wouldn't learn of this subplot, given his acumen for sniffing such things out. The fewer human touch points between him and us, the better."

"Let me guess: terrorists would be blamed."

"We had a whole scenario in place, with two groups set to take credit," Petrie confirmed. "Clearly we miscalculated. We now know the transponders in the wrecked cockpit had been deactivated not long after take-off, which tells us Phythian likely got wind of the plan before he even left Haifa. Probably flew just a few feet above the sea and changed course mid-flight, coming back over land somewhere over Lebanon or Turkey. He would have set the system on autopilot at some point to make it fly a steady route until it used up whatever fuel was left in its tanks."

"And when he got to an unpopulated area he bailed." Simone Marchand finished for her. "After disposing of the C4."

Adam Kent fixed the camera with impatient eyes and said, "Look: For the past eighteen minutes you've nibbled around the edges, hinting at how threatening and formidable this Phythian was. *Is.* I know I'm sort of the new kid on the block with this sort of thing, but don't you think it's time to come right out and explain why it was necessary to kill him?"

Kent reminded Petrie of the annoying suck-ups in her college classes who sat in the front row and peppered the professors with questions, when they clearly could have read the books listed in the syllabus and not wasted everyone's time. She nodded, trying not to reveal her growing impatience, then said, "As you know, all our contractors are skilled in a broad spectrum of lethal techniques. Heart attacks, strokes, accidents, overdoses, muggings. Whatever the job calls for, staged to make certain the forensics can never point back to us. Phythian's expertise lay in a totally different M.O., a particular skill that defied all belief."

It was called begging the question, and she waited patiently for Kent to ask her to go on. He went for it, saying, "What the hell are you talking about?"

"Not to oversell it, but Phythian possessed capabilities that defied every molecule of brainpower of anyone who ever came in contact with him," Petrie continued. "In one sense he was your everyday Joe, with a very modest apple-pie-and-baseball upbringing. Working class family, blue collar parents, public schools, church on Sundays. He played stickball in the street, pick-up basketball on weekends. Cut school when he was older. Things typical kids do."

"So, what the fuck sort of name is Rōnin? I mean, what is that? Gaelic? Norse? Celtic?" Kent pronounced it with a soft "c," like the Boston basketball team.

"Actually, it's Japanese," Petrie explained. "A rōnin was a samurai without a lord or master, back during the country's feudal period. Although there are many variations on that interpretation. His mother supposedly got it from the film *Harakiri*, which she saw while she was pregnant with him."

"Can you please get to the bloody *significance of it all*?" The Chairman pressed her.

Eitan Hazan glanced at his watch, emphasizing the point.

Petrie allowed herself a moment to stem her frustration and regain her concentration, then continued. "Phythian's father had a gambling problem," she said. "Horses, mostly. Trotters, as they call them in New England. Over the years he got into the Providence mob for over thirty grand, with no way to pay it back, much less the weekly vig. The blue-collar dream gone awry. Anyway, two days after Phythian's thirteenth birthday, a local enforcer snatched him off the street. He and an associate took him to an old flooded quarry, and threatened to kill him if he didn't help them pull a jewelry store heist that would pay his old man's debt in full. Phythian refused, and they threw him over the edge. He fell thirty feet to the water and landed on his head, bursting an eardrum. Subsequent scans showed other forms of physical trauma had been inflicted to the right side of his cerebrum."

"Is this going somewhere?" Kent asked, feigning a yawn.

If he'd been in the same room with her, she would have hurled her chair at him. Instead, she said, "Where it's going is that he was rescued by a couple of teenagers who were skinny-dipping at the quarry that afternoon. They called the police, and when Phythian woke up in the hospital the next day, he heard his parents talking about him. Praying for him to pull through."

Kent stared at her, through the camera lens in his tablet, waiting for the *Goddamned point* he knew had to be coming.

"Except his parents weren't saying a word," Petrie continued. "Not out loud, at least. They were just standing there, silently beseeching God above to save their son. The father quietly admitting his gambling sins and promising to lay off the bottle, the mother promising she would never, ever lust after her son's phys ed teacher again. Anything and everything they could do to bargain with the Lord Almighty to let their boy live. And Phythian heard it all."

When she finished her tale no one uttered a word, since they'd all been subjected to it before. Except Kent, who said, "You're saying the sonofabitch woke up a mind-reader."

"The best we can speculate is that, because of his traumatic brain injury, he acquired a hyper-attenuated competence in extrasensory consciousness," she clarified. "A proficiency that one day, with a lot of assistance and investment from Uncle Sam, would lead him to become the most dangerous killing machine the world has ever known."

"What a fucking load of horseshit. Sounds more like some comic book hero with superhuman powers. Maybe you should call him Psycho Man."

Petrie ignored Kent's cynicism; she'd dealt with far more dubious reactions to Phythian's skills ever since her first encounter with him at The Farm more than twenty years ago. "Believe it or don't, he was good at what he did. Too good, and he became a very real threat. The plane crash was supposed to eliminate that threat, but now it appears he's out there. And very likely alive."

"Well, the fact that we haven't heard from him in all this time tells us he's well off the grid," Hazan observed. "Either that or he is, in fact, dead."

No one spoke because no one had anything constructive to add. Eventually Petrie said, "My assessment is, he's content with letting bygones be bygones. I knew the man better than anyone—Christ, I recruited him— and I can assure you, he doesn't have a vindictive bone in his body."

Simone Marchand's eyes were wide open, revealing a deep sense of anxiety, if not palpable fear. "With all due respect, Diana, the man's a professional assassin, and we tried to kill him."

So is everyone on this call, by extension, Petrie wanted to point out, but didn't. "The fact that it's been more than six years since the crash tells me that, whatever dark corner of the world he's living in, he likes it there. No need to come out of hiding now."

"The discovery of the plane changes everything," Eitan Hazan said, shaking his head. "For the past six years Phythian has known what we— the G3—tried to do to him."

"And now he knows that *we know* he may have survived," Marchand added. "He could either continue to make himself scarce, or come after us and seek revenge."

"Which means we need to find him," Kent concurred. "Now, as in yesterday."

Anxiety is a thin stream of fear trickling through the mind, Petrie thought, her mind going back to a book she'd once read but couldn't put a finger on. Or maybe it was a play she'd seen.

"Waste of time," she countered. "If Phythian really got out of that plane alive, we're woefully ill-equipped to track him down. And even if we did, he'd know we were coming."

"Then what do you suggest we do?"

"We wait," she said, calm and resolute. "If our friend is hellbent on getting revenge he'll come for us, when time and circumstance suits him. And he knows that, when he does, we will meet him measure for measure."

"Meanwhile, we deal with the photographer," The Chairman ordered, his voice resolute and immutable. "Whatever she knows or doesn't know, it's too much of a risk. Terminate her."

Chapter 5

The first three times Monica tried calling her sister, the phone rang straight to voicemail. On the fourth try she finally managed to get through, but only after a series of squeaks, pops, and hisses. The switchboard at Abdulaziz Medical Center in Islamabad was a hand-operated rig that had not been improved upon since its installation decades before, and its antiquity showed.

Patrick Butler was out of town on business, but his wife Kathleen—Monica's sister—was home, upstairs in bed. It was late in New York—close to two in the morning—but she was awake, savoring the afterglow of her just-completed phone sex with Lance Hendrix, the young dealer she'd recently employed at the gallery she managed in Greenwich Village.

She picked up the phone on the second ring and said, "Oh my God, that was the most unbelievable experience I think I've ever had." She started to say "goodnight" again when she heard a noise that sounded distant, something definitely not Lance Hendrix.

"Kath?"

"Monica—is that you?"

"Kath...thank God you're off the phone." Monica released a sigh of relief that seemed to have clogged her lungs all day. For the last week, come to think of it. "I've been trying to get through to you for hours."

"I'm sorry...business," her sister lied. "Major transaction at the gallery, haggling with the Japanese. Ten-hour time difference. Or maybe it's nine." She felt a twinge of guilt as she recalled the things Lance had told her he would do to her if she ever let him get close enough to demonstrate what sort of lover he really was. "Where are you calling from, anyway?"

"Pakistan," Monica replied. Her cracked ribs felt as if they were stabbing her whenever she spoke, causing her to keep her words to a minimum.

"You're still there?" Kathleen asked. "I thought this was just going to be a quick trip. Snap a couple photos, come on home."

Like most people, Monica's sister had no real grasp of what a professional photographer did. Just point and shoot, download the images. "That was the plan," she said. "But…well, something unexpected came up."

"It had better not be that prick…what's his name—?"

"Branson Dahl?"

"If he touched you, I'll kill him," Kathleen snarled. She'd never met the bastard, but after Monica told her about their meeting at the magazine's office, she took an instant dislike to the creep. "One slow piece at a time."

"You're too late," Monica said with resignation. "There was an accident."

"What do you mean, an accident?"

"I'll explain everything when I get home," Monica said. "Hopefully they'll release me tomorrow."

"Release you? Monica—are you in jail?"

She had to laugh at that, then said, "Jail? No…nothing like that. I'm in the hospital, in fact. I just called to let you know everything's all right."

"Why wouldn't it be? Look, Monica…you never could keep anything from me. What the hell's going on?"

Monica wasted no time filling her in, which was why she'd called in the first place. She had to tell someone, and it was too late in New York to call Arnie Kelso, her publisher at *Earth Illustrated*. He'd convinced her to take this assignment in the first place, and she knew he'd be worried sick about her, blaming himself for everything that had happened. Unable to do a damned thing to help her, which would only make him feel more frustrated and helpless. Maybe later tonight, when the time zones added up and he would just be arriving in the office.

She began by telling her sister about the beautiful but arduous trek along the narrow trail through the Karakoram Mountains ("they sound absolutely lovely"), then described the absolute sense of beauty and solitude ("that must have been truly marvelous to experience"). She recounted the attack by the two jihadists or terrorists or whatever they were ("oh, my God") and how she had fought them both off ("un-fucking believable"). She finished with her fall from the trail and the discovery of the twisted airplane wreckage.

"That was you?" Kathleen blurted out when Monica finally finished her story. "They didn't say who…oh my God, I had no idea."

"Good news travels fast," Monica said. "The embassy here is trying to keep me out of it."

"Lester Holt said everybody on board the plane was killed. I'll be damned…my little baby sister, in the news."

Not exactly in the news yet, Monica thought as she rearranged the pillow behind her head, again wincing from the stab of pain. Her doctor had told her that reporters from a dozen news organizations were demanding to speak with her, but the consular officer from the embassy was keeping them at bay. She'd been brought into the hospital the night before last, after being carted out of the mountains on a litter fashioned from a blanket and two stripped saplings. Some hikers crossing the mountains had found her backpack and had called out to whomever owned it. Monica had heard them and yelled "please help me," over and over. Unable to rappel down the mountainside, one of the hikers went off in search of help. He returned fourteen hours later with two farmers and a coil of rope, and together they were able to hoist her up the steep slope.

The initial pain in her ribs and ankle had been displaced by a numbness that she guessed was the onset of physical shock. It had enabled her to withstand the jolting trip over the rugged mountain track back to the village of Gilgit. There, a local doctor of some sort pronounced her fit enough to be loaded into the back of an old lorry, which transported her down the Karakoram Highway to a better-equipped and more sophisticated hospital in Islamabad. Abdulaziz Medical Center, to be precise. Somewhere along the way she had passed out and hadn't awakened until she was being wheeled through the door of the small emergency room.

"Look, Kath…I have to go," she told her sister. "Phone service here is sketchy. I just called to let you know I'm okay, and I'll be home soon."

"Well, you tell the doctors there to take good care of you," Kathleen Butler told her. "And if you'd like to have your older sister come over to be with you, just say the word—"

"Don't even think of it," Monica told her. "Soon as they give me my walking papers, I'm on the next flight out."

"You'll give me a call when you get out of there?"

"Count on it," Monica assured her, and then hung up.

She slipped the phone back onto the table next to her bed and stared at the cracks in the ceiling. Her cell phone had been misplaced during her rescue and she felt naked without it. She glanced around at the starkness that surrounded her, wishing she could get the hell out of here, yet comforted that she was alive. She was in a room shared by two other patients, both of them Pakistani women who probably had no knowledge of English, nor any comprehension of the story Monica had just told her sister.

Her body ached every time she moved. Stranger still, her eyes filled with moisture when she thought about Branson Dahl and Ahmed Javid. She couldn't shake the gnawing feeling that she could have done something to save them, but most of all she felt guilty for not dying. And that's what ached the most, an ache she remembered from that frigid night Phillip had been killed on the New York Thruway and her life had cracked wide open. For months afterwards, Monica had wished herself dead as well, unable to conceive how her life could continue without him by her side. How could she live without the man who had given her everything and had expected little in return, and had shared her very body and soul? The man who had smiled at her and talked to her and listened to what she had to say, and who respected her feelings and her dreams and her passions.

The past seven days had been a blur, evolving not in a single stretch of time, but rather in brief outtakes flashing in between periods of near-death and the paralysis of fear. Monica had spent two nights huddled in the wreckage of the crashed plane halfway down that rocky cliff, clinging to every thread of reality she could summon. She only began to lose perspective when she was lying safely in the back of the lorry, the steady jouncing over the rough surface reminding her of her own mother's arms gently rocking her while she slept.

The woman in the bed next to hers was mumbling, carrying on in her sleep about something that seemed to be quite upsetting. The other woman was awake, unleashing a torrent of words Monica did not understand but which sounded like a sort of local curse. Monica was caught in the crossfire and decided she had to get away. She raised herself to a sitting position and slowly swung her legs over the edge of the bed, gingerly touching her feet to the linoleum floor. The padded hospital socks provided a layer of insulation and she attempted to stand, but her chest stung with a sharp burn and her ankle throbbed as she placed her full weight on it.

The hallway outside her room was empty except for the government suit who was sitting in a chair outside her door. He was leafing through an old copy of the *New Yorker*, chuckling at the cartoons, and glanced up when he heard the door open. His name was Brian Walker, and he was the same consular officer who had lectured her and Branson Dahl last week about the hazards of traveling near the disputed territories.

"Mrs. Cross...you finished your phone call." He was on his feet in a flash, and slipped his hand under her elbow to assist. "I'm sure the doctor doesn't want you walking around, not in your condition. Please, let me help you back into your bed."

"I don't want to go to bed," she told him firmly. "My back is beginning to ache and my ass is falling asleep. What do you say we go for a walk?"

Brian Walker really didn't know how to respond. Babysitting an injured American who had ignored his earlier warnings did not constitute an important matter of state. He had cautioned her and the writer named Dahl about wandering off the marked trails, and had warned them that rebels and terrorists had been sighted hiding out along the remote pathways. But they were like many other Americans abroad, possessed of the imperious notion that nothing bad could happen to them because they were from the United States. Still, because of the tragic end to Monica Cross' ill-fated trip, he was trying—as best he knew how—to be civil and polite.

Walker was tall and rugged in a collegiate sort of way, dressed in a lightweight suit and blue shirt, and a boring yellow tie that he'd loosened at the collar. His hair was short, his face clean-shaven, and his shoes freshly polished and shined. As a bureaucrat on the rise, he was single-minded and ambitious and, in his early thirties, young for his rank but not for this posting.

He glanced up and down the hallway but saw no sign of Dr. Mugheri, Monica's physician of record. "All right...five minutes. Then I'm taking you back to bed." He liked the way that sounded, and under his suit he felt his skin flush.

"Such a deal," Monica said. "All right, Mr. Walker...let's go see the sights."

The hospital had been built in the middle of the last century, and looked every inch the part. Chipped masonry walls, peeling plaster, industrial grade linoleum worn down from untold feet over the decades. Suspicious stains oozed from tiles in the drop ceiling, and lighting came from bare tubes that hummed and buzzed.

"Any word from the doc how much longer you're in for?" Walker asked as he gently cupped her elbow in his palm.

"No more than a day, I hope," Monica shrugged. She winced as even the slightest pressure made the pain in her ribs almost unbearable. "I'm told they need the bed."

Walker glanced sideways at her and shook his head, just a touch disappointed. "I think you need a long vacation," he said.

"I don't want a vacation," she rebuffed him. "I just want to go home."

"Believe me, that I can understand," he said. "Of course, before you leave, a lot of people would like to talk to you before about your experience up in the mountains."

"You mean the reporters downstairs?" she sighed, trying hard not to cause herself any more pain than she had to.

"How do you know about them?"

"Dr. Mugheri told me."

Walker's top priority was to keep Monica Cross away from the hungry pack of media hounds that had been gathering from the moment she'd arrived. While he gave the impression that he was with the State Department, he actually was on the FBI's payroll, and his duty was to obfuscate as much as possible while sounding sincere. The circumstances surrounding the plane's disappearance six years ago had been suspicious, but now that it had been found—with five murdered passengers inside—a lot of very powerful people suddenly were very nervous. His boss at the Hoover building in Washington had made it clear that *his* boss wanted the entire affair to go away soon, the quieter the better.

"Please forgive me for bringing it up, but I'm sorry you had to see all that," he said, trying to sound genuinely sympathetic. "It must have been a shock, first losing your colleague and guide, then stumbling across the wreckage of the accident—"

"Oh, it was no accident," Monica informed him, lowering her voice a notch.

"Of course, it was," Brian Walker corrected her. "That plane flew into the side of the mountain and everyone in it died on impact."

"No," Monica shook her head. "That's not at all what happened."

"They've conducted autopsies on all the victims, and the reports are quite clear," Walker insisted. "'Severe multiples injuries,' I think they called it."

Until this moment, Monica and Brian had been moving slowly down the hall, but now she stopped and stared at him. "They didn't die as a result of the crash, Mr. Walker." She felt odd calling this young man who was younger than she "mister." "They were shot."

He gently gripped her elbow, turned her until she was facing him. "I believe you were under quite a strain at the time, Mrs. Cross—"

"It's the truth," Monica insisted. "The pictures prove it."

"What pictures?"

"The ones I took with my phone."

"So, where's your phone?" Walker humored her.

"Your people claim it's missing," she replied.

But Walker just shook his head and smiled. "We have no record of any cell phone, and you were rather incoherent when you were brought down from the mountain," he reminded her. "No one has seen these pictures you keep mentioning."

"That's bullshit," Monica said. "You people are just doing what you do best."

"And what is that?"

"Covering it up."

"No one's doing anything of the sort," he insisted. He tried to get her moving again, but she wasn't buying it.

"I know what I saw," she said. "I was there."

"Yet there's no evidence to back up what you're saying."

"Sure there is," Monica replied. "I took dozens of photographs—the bodies, the bullet holes, everything. That's all the evidence I need."

"And we'd love to see them," the arrogant prick of a consulate official who really worked with the FBI said with his annoying smile.

She didn't respond, letting her silence say it all.

"If it's any solace, we do have the cameras from your backpack," he told her. "You left them on the trail."

"That was before I found the airplane," Monica reminded him.

"They look like they were very expensive," Walker said. "I'm sure you'd like to have them back."

In return for what? she wondered. "They belong to me."

"I'll make sure they're returned to you before you leave," Walker assured her. "Come... let's walk a bit."

They walked. He helped her along the hallway, strolling slowly as she tested the strength of her twisted ankle and attempted to erase the trauma of the past seven days. She realized she looked a mess: snarled, dirty-blonde hair framed her bruised face, and the hospital gown was not her best look. But Brian Walker looked past all that, focusing instead on her amber eyes that burned with an intensity he'd rarely seen since he'd arrived here.

When they reached the end of the corridor she stopped, and turned to face him. "Tell me, Mr. Walker—"

"Please, ma'am. My name is Brian."

She forced a smile and said, "All right, Brian. Tell me...why are you here?"

"I was assigned to make sure you're comfortable until you're well enough to leave."

"That's very kind, and I want to apologize for my lack of manners earlier. But what I mean is, why are you here in Islamabad? Most of what I've seen of this place has been from a hospital window, but it seems to me this isn't a particularly choice posting."

"There's no question, this country may be one of those dustbins of the world," Walker said. "Not long before you got here an American businessman was killed when his Jeep ran over a road mine outside Mohra, and a week ago two missionaries got hit by snipers. A team of Brits was ambushed down in Karachi the other night, and now there's the case of you and your colleague, which has drawn considerable attention around the globe. Not quite as romantic as Paris, but you can't judge a diplomatic posting based solely on its wine and cheese."

She peered out a window that was reinforced with wire-mesh that overlooked the skyline of Islamabad, such as it was. When she had arrived here eleven days ago, she had expected to find old mosques and buildings crumbling from the ages, and had been surprised at all the steel and glass going up.

"How much longer do you have here?" she asked him.

"Three more months and counting," Walker replied.

"And after that?"

"I'm slated to be transferred to Ankara," he said.

"Well, there you go. That's in Turkey, which is right next to Greece."

"Plenty of ouzo and feta," he agreed, without much enthusiasm. "And I assume you're heading straight home when the doctor says you can go?"

"New York," she said as another thrum of pain seized her ankle, causing her to grimace. "I wonder what time it is there."

Walker glanced at his watch, something that looked like a cross between a diver's chronograph and a gaudy timepiece that was found at an airport kiosk. "Just past two in the morning," he told her.

"You have that thing set on Eastern time?" Monica asked.

"Three time zones, in fact. Here in Pakistan, back home in DC, and Greenwich Mean Time in London."

"That has to do with the prime meridian at the Royal Observatory, or something like that. Right?"

"It's where all time around the globe is measured from, more or less," he said. "And if you intend to get out of here on time tomorrow, I should probably help you back to your room."

"A splendid idea," Monica replied. She clutched his elbow as they slowly shuffled back down the hallway, and thanked him for the tour when they arrived at her door.

"Always at your service," Walker replied with a slight bow of his head. Then he seemed to remember something that had been jostled loose from his brain and said, "The other night, when you were brought in here, you mentioned something about a briefcase—"

She let go of his elbow and tried not to wince as each step caused another spasm to wash through her. "I did?"

"You don't remember?"

"I'm afraid I don't recall much of what I saw up there in the mountains," she told him. Not true, not by a long shot. She remembered just about everything from the time she encountered the rebels on the narrow trail to the agony of being hoisted up the cliff from the crash site several days later. "I hope I didn't blurt out anything too embarrassing—"

"Don't worry. No one else knew what you were talking about, either. Except you mentioned something about a black case with foam padding inside."

"I must have been hallucinating," she said with a shrug. "Or high on pain meds."

"That's what the doctors thought. But now that you're up and about... well, do you have any idea what you might have been talking about?"

Monica's intuition kicked into gear, telling her that Walker was fishing for information while trying to appear blasé. Despite his affable, off-hand manner, she sensed a subtle urgency to his questions, even though they were disguised as everyday chatter. She hated to lie, but yes, she remembered the briefcase with a label on the side that read *Equinox*. She had snapped several photos of it, inside and out, before the total blackness of that first night had fallen upon her, when she was certain she would either freeze from the biting cold or, even worse, die a slow death on the side of this desolate peak and her remains would never be found.

"I'm sorry," she said, shaking her head.

"Well, if you remember anything—*anything at all*—please let me know," Walker told her.

He started to assist her back inside her room, but they were cut off by a nurse who was not pleased that he'd been touring the hallways with one of her patients. She reprimanded him fiercely, barking at him in a language Monica did not understand. Walker responded politely and with great deference, and Monica was astounded that he could speak the language with some efficiency. The nurse rattled on at him in a furious tirade to which he could do nothing but listen, and finally he acquiesced to hospital protocol.

"It appears you were not to get out of bed without the permission of our friendly nurse, here," he finally translated for Monica. "You were not to be on your feet, and I was not to take you for a walk. You are to get back in bed, and I am to take my leave from this hospital."

Monica looked from him to the nurse, then glanced in at the bed she had just crawled out of only ten minutes before. The woman who had been sleeping nearest the window—the one who incessantly chanted in her sleep—now was curled up in it, under a mound of blankets. Monica glanced back at Walker and said, "Since you seem to be proficient in the local tongue, could you please ask her why that person is in my bed?"

He relayed her question—crudely, it seemed—and the nurse snapped an answer. When she had finished, he told Monica, "Florence Nightingale, here, says the patient in your bed was getting chilled near the window, and the doctor was concerned that she might get pneumonia unless she was moved."

"But it's okay if I get pneumonia?" she asked.

"Doctor's orders," Walker replied. "But look on the bright side...it's only for one more night. She says you're out of here in the ayem."

"The what?"

"AM. The morning. It seems the parole board came through. Your doctor is going to take a look at you during morning rounds and, if you check out, you're free to go home."

Chapter 6

Eitan Hazan's story yesterday about a time-sensitive meeting at the Knesset was a ruse. There was no meeting, at least not in Jerusalem, and definitely not one that had forced him to bail from the G3 videoconference a few minutes early. He'd offered his sincerest apologies to everyone on the encrypted call, then had jumped into the backseat of a modified Audi A8 that had pulled to the curb fifty yards down the street from where he'd been sitting.

The car whisked him to Ben Gurion Airport, thirty-five miles outside the city, whereupon he caught a non-stop commercial flight to Berlin. Six hours after leaving Jerusalem he'd checked into the five-star Das Stue, using his personal credit card to cover the room charges because this visit was off the G3 books. His first order of business upon arriving in the German capital had been Dr. Frieda Lange, a lovely professor of animal anesthesiology at the Koret School of Veterinary Medicine back home in Rehovot. She also was connected—in ways he was never able to understand, and she had never explained—to the Finance Development unit of the World Bank in Brussels. Some things were best left unsaid, and she made it well worth his while not to ask too many questions.

This morning he was up early. Dr. Lange had slipped out of bed a little after two, allowing him a total of five hours' sleep. He would have preferred more, but the room service coffee was strong and did its job. As did the two Dexedrines he'd swallowed with a gulp of grapefruit juice, a variation on a theme that had been driving him since his first mission in Uganda many decades ago. Back when he was a young man, subsisting on a rush of youthful exuberance and a naïve quest for adrenaline.

Now he was seated in an anteroom on the third floor of the Israeli Diplomatic Mission, constructed of Jerusalem limestone and glass, and located in the *Schmargendorf* district at *Auguste-Viktoria-Straße*. He was four minutes early but, on this particular morning, time did not matter—not only because he didn't have to catch his flight back to Jerusalem until tomorrow, but also because the gentleman with whom he was meeting had a reputation for never being on time.

He busied himself by gazing through the floor-to-ceiling window in the reception area, then retreated to a post-modern Bauhaus-style sofa that looked like a Mies van der Rohe knockoff. He briefly scanned the front section of that day's *Jerusalem Post*, which arrived by diplomatic pouch every morning precisely at eight-fifty. The headlines weren't too far from normal: an attack on a tanker in the Persian Gulf, thought to be the work of the Iranians, an escalation of Hezbollah attacks on Israel's West Bank settlements, the surge of anti-Jewish nationalism in Austria and Germany.

Which, if anyone were to ask, was the official reason listed for Eitan Hazan's visit to Berlin in the first place. Formally recorded in the embassy's public calendar, just in case some meddling whistleblower requested it someday. Confidentially, however, he was here for an entirely different purpose.

At sixteen past the hour a polite yet mousy young woman with buzzed black hair and a small opal nose stud, sitting behind a desk also designed in the Bauhaus style, informed him in Hebrew that the Foreign Minister had arrived. The man was prepared to see Eitan Hazan, if he would kindly go through that door, there, and proceed to the office at the end of the hall.

"No need to knock," she assured him. "He's expecting you."

Hazan wouldn't have knocked even if the Foreign Minister's assistant hadn't told him not to bother. His name was Lior Eichorn and they were family, Eitan being his older cousin by two years, which meant that typical business formalities were totally unnecessary.

Despite their connection through blood and mitochondrial DNA—their respective mothers had been sisters—eons had passed since the two men had set eyes on each other. They'd spoken on the phone dozens of times, but the last occasion they had been in the same room at the same time had been the memorial service for Lior's daughter, Avigail Eichorn. She had been one of the five passengers who had been presumed dead in the disappearance of the Belgian charter plane six years ago, and Eitan had attended the *Levaya*, which had been held even though no remains had been recovered at the time.

Eichorn had not been Foreign Minister back then, and he preferred to think that his daughter's untimely death had nothing to do with his subsequent climb up the rungs of power. A former member of the Knesset—hence the slim validity to Eitan Hazan's excuse yesterday—he'd held a top position within his party and, following the narrow election of the current Prime Minister, had been awarded the post of Minister of Energy and Water Resources. Two years ago, he'd been offered his current role in the cabinet, and it was rumored that he had his eye on the top prize—if the quixotic political winds continued to blow from just the right direction.

"*Shalom*, Lior," Hazan greeted him as he approached his cousin's desk. The carpet was as soft as a forest floor, and the ambient light streaming through the tinted windows reminded him of a redwood grove he had once visited in California. "*Nekhmad lir-ot otkha shuv.*"

"*Shalom*," the Foreign Minister echoed, coming around his desk and enveloping Hazan with arms that resembled tree roots. "So good to see you, especially on such short notice."

"Yes, I apologize for that," Hazan said. "You're looking quite well, considering your hectic schedule."

"Someone needs to personally look in on our outposts from time to time," Eichorn said with a throaty rumble. "Please, please…have a seat."

Hazan preferred to remain standing. He had acquired a leg cramp from a particularly impossible contortion involving Dr. Lange's thighs last night, and his right quadricep ached. He'd massaged it afterwards and even paced around his room for a good fifteen minutes, trying to work out the knot. Yet it remained.

He followed his cousin's lead and lowered himself into a stylized chair with soft black leather that looked like a mongrel love child of Eames and Ikea. Eichorn settled into an identical chair across a glass table that held a hand-carved onyx *Aryeh Yehudah*, the iconic lion with its roots firmly planted in the Book of Genesis, and which traditionally symbolized the Israelite tribe of Judah.

"Your message said you have news of Avigail," Eichorn said, getting right to it. The two cousins were family but had never been particularly close, and each knew the other's respective time was invaluable. Small talk on idle topics was not their way, and neither of them had any interest in sharing observations about war, finance, or politics. While both men were personally affected by the global ramifications of all three, there was only one purpose for this meeting.

"Not the news you wanted, but yes," Hazan replied. "I came as soon as I got definitive confirmation."

"You're referring to the plane that was found in Pakistan?"

Hazan offered a grim frown. "I'm afraid so. The same plane your daughter was on. I can't tell you how sorry I am, Lior—"

Hazan made a motion to get up from his chair to comfort his cousin, but Eichorn raised his palm, indicating for him to remain seated. They'd already exchanged one round of man hugs, and that was enough.

"I heard a rumor that all the victims were shot," the Foreign Minister countered, a fierce darkness in his eyes. "What do you know about that?"

"I heard it, too. Seems that's all it was: rumors."

"Then tell me how she died," he said, remaining in his chair.

Eitan Hazan knew the words his cousin wanted to hear, as well as those he needed to know. Some of them being mutually exclusive. "We have evidence that suggests it was oxygen deprivation," he explained, going with the G3's official line in order to distance himself from any complicity in the tragedy. "The plane ascended higher than it should have, and everyone on board passed away."

Lior closed his eyes and went to an inner place where he had hoped he would never have to return, a darkness that had been waiting to finally engulf him ever since the King Air turboprop had disappeared from radar six years ago. When he finally regained his composure, he regarded his cousin with a thoughtful gaze. "A moment ago you said 'we have evidence,'" he noted. "Whom, might I ask, is we?"

"As with you, there sometimes are things of which I cannot speak," Hazan replied.

Eichorn slowly shook his head and took a deep breath of air that, until now, Hazan hadn't realized smelled of women's perfume. He wondered what his cousin had been up to before he'd arrived. Or was the proper question, *with whom*?

"You trust your private intel over the official line?" Eichorn asked him.

"Don't you trust yours?"

The Foreign Minister nodded: good point. Despite the global reach of the Americans, British, Russians, Chinese—even the Vatican—he viewed his country's *Mossad* as the premiere source of global intelligence. Certainly, the Israeli intelligence agency didn't get everything right, and the tentacles of its activities were as deeply entwined with the nation's politics as the CIA or MI6 were with theirs, respectively. But at least the politics were Israeli, which made it more palpable—and actionable. None of the bullshit that its western allies always seemed to be spreading with one hand, while dangling the carrot of foreign aid with the other.

"Does your private intel explain how the fuck that plane ended up where it did, thousands of miles beyond where everyone thought it had gone down?"

"Facts are scattered, literally, all over the side of that mountain," Hazan replied. "Investigators from six countries are up there, poring through everything. Meanwhile, we're developing some theories."

"I don't want fucking theories!" Lior Eichorn fumed. "This is my daughter we're talking about. I want the truth."

A movie image of Jack Nicholson flashed in Hazan's brain, something about not being able to handle the truth. Which certainly would have been the case here, were the truth not so malleable and if Hazan wasn't so professionally involved in it. It was something his cousin must never learn, under any circumstance.

"And what would you do with it?" he asked. "The truth."

It was a largely rhetorical question, but Eichorn actually considered it for a moment. Then he said, "Eye for an eye, tooth for a tooth."

Hazan understood his cousin's raw anger and impatience, but his own nature was to balance it against the canonical wisdom from Ecclesiastes: *There is a time for everything, and a season for every activity under the heavens.*

"Don't even start thinking like that," he cautioned his cousin.

"I started thinking like this six years ago when my Avigail was taken from me," Eichorn seethed. "Somewhere in this world there exists a person who deserves reprisal of the most cruel and ferocious kind."

And an eye for an eye leaves everyone blind, Hazan thought—ironic, since his direct planning of the fated mission meant he deserved to be the first to forfeit his vision. "I understand how you feel, where your mind is going right now," he said. "But revenge won't bring Avi back, and it won't turn back time to a better day."

"Then what would you advise me to do, *cousin*? Recite the *Kaddish* one more time and act as if nothing ever happened? Ignore the empty place at the table, forget the laughter and the promise and the joy of life reflected in my daughter's eyes? I want to know who did this, and cause that person— man or woman, I don't care—to rue the day he was born. And you can help me with that."

Hazan suspected Lior knew of his connection to the G3 and, thus, knew he was complicit in the deaths of hundreds of top-profile targets around the world. Israeli intelligence surely would have told him about the *faux* hat company that maintained offices in Manhattan, but which otherwise had no physical location. It had no country, no payroll, no bank of record. All contracts were handled by the executive board and its chairman, all wet work was executed by independent contractors, and all financial transactions were handled through cybercurrency exchange. In fact, Eichorn's own government had employed the G3 on multiple occasions, always with positive results and extreme satisfaction. Even though the Israelis usually preferred to work alone, there was always a time when outside assistance—and plausible deniability—proved beneficial.

Confidentially, *Mossad*'s own intel had showed that none of the usual terror suspects had brought the Beechcraft King Air down: not Al-Shabaab, not Boko Haram, not ISIS. There was no evidence of a bomb, no call after the fact to take credit. The Americans denied any involvement in the incident, same as the Brits and the Russkies. That left only one other *bona fide* player in the world with the reach and resources to make it happen.

The one Eitan Hazan worked for.

Eichorn said nothing for a moment as he rose from his chair and walked over to his desk. He sat down in a leather chair that seemed to swallow him whole, then clasped his hands together on the bare surface in front of him. "You know who was responsible for this, don't you?" he demanded. "You and that damned dark web outfit you're connected to."

"I have no idea what you're talking about—"

"Don't insult my intelligence or try my patience, Eitan," Eichorn seethed, spittle forming on his pudgy lips. "I asked you a simple question, and I want an equally simple answer."

"Restraint and composure are a marvelous antidote to animus and revenge," Hazan told him, not moving a muscle.

"Spare me the platitudes." Lior Eichorn glared at him, then reached into a drawer and pulled out what Hazan recognized as a Jericho 941 pistol. It was a semi-automatic, double-action weapon developed for Israeli military use, and it made sense that the Foreign Minister would keep one in his office. He pointed it at his older cousin and said, "Give me the name. Now."

Hazan had faced the business end of a gun too many times to count, and he hardly flinched at the sight of this one, unexpected as it was. "You're not going to shoot me," he said with a detached and measured certitude.

"The name," Eichorn repeated, holding the weapon steady.

Hazan knew the Jericho 941 was always ready to fire in double-action mode when de-cocked, also knew his cousin's shooting history while serving with the Israeli army. Damned good aim, in practice and in the field. No need to test him here.

"Put it down and I'll tell you."

"With all due respect to blood and marriage, you first."

Hazan saw this wasn't going to end well if he didn't comply. Even though he'd been sworn to secrecy on the G3's version of the Ten Commandments, he had no intention of laying down his life to protect the identity of the rat bastard who'd paid to have Avigail and everyone else on that plane killed. And while he didn't really think his cousin would actually pull the trigger, why risk it? It was a complicated matter, with many government agencies ponying up a portion of the highly inflated tab to make sure the aircraft went down and that their collective secrets, contained on the hard drive known as Equinox, would disappear forever. Additionally, one especially callous American had laid a lot of money on the table six years ago to make sure a particularly squalid transgression from his college days remained buried forever.

Hazan could continue to pivot and deny and obfuscate, but lying would only exacerbate the issue if the truth every surfaced. As a former U.S. president had observed, "The search for a scapegoat is the easiest of all hunting expeditions."

"My gift to you, cousin," he finally said. He approached the Foreign Minister's desk, palms raised outwards, then bent down and whispered a name in his ear. "Do with it what you will, but do it wisely."

"*Toda*," the Foreign Minister replied, exhibiting neither shock nor surprise at the name he'd just been given.

"*Shalom*, Lior."

Chapter 7

Carter Logan burrowed his head deep into his pillow and tried to kill the throbbing in his brain.

The traffic noise outside his Kalorama apartment in Northwest Washington was notably deafening this morning, the horns and sirens burning in his skull like a soldering iron. The constant pulsing felt like a pneumatic hammer pounding nails into his occipital neuralgia, each jolt aligning with the steady rush of blood through his veins and causing his cranium to feel as if it were splitting in two. A wave of nausea washed through him, and he correctly placed the blame for this pain on the gin he'd consumed the evening before. The gin and the vodka, and then the red wine. Followed by the shots of Scotch that had chased him into the vast abyss that ended in an amnesic blackout.

That's how it had been last night, a true bender that began when the online notice had popped up in his email Inbox. He'd almost forgotten that he'd set up the search parameters that would feed him an update whenever her name appeared in the news. But there it had been:

Google Alert—Katya Leiffson

Six years. That's how long it had been since he'd typed her name into the search window, just three days after her plane disappeared over the eastern Mediterranean. In those early days she'd been all over the news, and the daily reports he'd received sometimes contained twenty, even thirty news stories about her. Not one of them had been conclusive, everything at that point highly speculative. Such as, "family and friends are holding out hope that Katya Leiffson will be found alive" or "a candlelight vigil will be held tonight for Katya Leiffson in her home outside Reykjavík." Over the days and weeks that followed, the alerts became more ominous, as in "Katya Leiffson's family are now coping with the idea that her body may never be found."

Well, it *had* been found, a week ago in a mountainous ravine near a glacier in northern Pakistan. Positive identification had been slow, given the condition of her remains after six years of exposure to the elements and the peculiar circumstances of the plane's disappearance in the first place. The four news stories delivered by Google last night all reported the same details: essentially that, after all this time, the mystery of her whereabouts had been solved.

In those first few months six years ago, Logan had denied the truth, holding out hope that this had all been a mistake. She hadn't actually boarded the chartered plane traveling from Haifa to Malta, and one day she would call him from an airport somewhere in the world and all this would turn out to be a poorly scripted TV drama. Grief was woefully adept at playing strange tricks on the mind, and he'd continued to hang on to a thin thread of false reality.

The Google alert last night had unraveled everything. Logan's eighteen months with Katya tumbled through his mind as he'd stared at the words on his laptop:

Crash Victim Identified as Katya Leiffson

Now it was official. She was deceased, the suspected cause of death listed as altitude asphyxia, pending autopsy. The words on the screen had induced him to crack the seal of the gin bottle, and the thought of a pathologist cutting into whatever remained of her body with a rotary saw had caused him to swig a large gulp even before he splashed a double dose into his glass.

They'd met in London, almost eight years ago. Hard to believe it was that far in the past. He'd been sent there by the *Washington Post* to report on the rocky relationship between the U.K. and the European Union, while Katya was pursuing a story about offshore banking and global money laundering. Their paths had crossed in, of all places, the Royal Observatory at Greenwich, where they'd each taken a few hours away from their respective assignments to view the legendary clocks and the historic time ball, and straddle the prime meridian line. They'd ended up grabbing a pint at a pub near the footbridge at the Cutty Sark replica, which later evolved into dinner at an Indian restaurant in east London's Brick Lane. That turned into hours of conversation, made easier by the fact that Katya spoke fluent English, as well as Icelandic and German.

Over the next eighteen months they arranged to be together whenever they could manage, and Skype served them well when their travels kept them apart. Sometimes for months at a time. He'd proposed to her on her second trip to Washington, presenting her with a ring he'd selected after thoroughly researching carat, cut, clarity, and color. She'd said "yes" immediately, but had not wanted to set a date, not just yet. There were things to do, places to go. Plus, she'd just started a new job at *Der Spiegel* in Hamburg and was working on a story that was very hush-hush. If she told him about it, she'd have to kill him. That sort of thing.

The story had taken her to Israel, a brief journey whose final leg would return her to DC after a quick stop in Malta. She'd be gone just a few days, no more than a week.

"Sorry, babe, but this one is big," she'd apologized via Skype the night before she left Haifa. God, how he'd loved her accent. "You'll understand when you read it."

"No worries," he'd said. "Do what you need to do, and I'll see you when you get back."

Then, all of a sudden, she was gone from his life.

Logan managed to stumble into the bathroom, where he chased four Advil with a huge gulp of water. He ran a brush across his teeth, splashed water on his face, decided he could shave later. After he got something in his stomach and maybe went for a run along the Rock Creek Trail.

Scratch that thought: his feet pounding on the pavement surely would cause his pulsing skull to burst at its fragile seams.

One of the positives that come from being downsized out of a job was that your hours became your own. Eleven months ago, he'd found himself without a salary, health benefits, or three weeks of paid vacation each year. The internet had been rearranging the deck chairs of the news media for years, and one day he was told that his desk was being given to a young reporter who was coming up from Richmond. At least that's how he'd explained it to himself, although he knew his growing love affair with the bottle played a major role in his redundancy.

Eight weeks of severance pay had helped numb the pain, and he'd managed to find a gig with a syndication company that licensed his twice-weekly articles to forty-six newspapers around the country. The pay was about half of what he'd been making at the *Post*, and he was just barely able to cover his rent and light bill. But if he went to the free museums on the weekends and bought bottom-shelf booze he just managed to get by. Plus, there was talk of a podcast that never seemed to get off the ground.

Logan brewed himself a pot of white label coffee from the Safeway in Georgetown and settled down at his desk. His laptop was open and, after moving the touchpad, the monitor came to life. After the screensaver disappeared, he found himself staring at the same Google alerts that had caused last night's bender in the first place.

Yes, Katya Leiffson was definitely gone. The wreckage of her plane had been found, her remains identified. There would be no changing the facts, no turning back time, no rewriting history. He wondered if the pear-cut diamond he'd given to her that night at *L'Auberge Chez Francois* in Great Falls had been on her finger when she'd been found.

He wiped away one final tear that had not fallen last night, inhaled a deep breath, and went to work. Thinking as his fingers flew across the keyboard, *I'm going to find out whatever the fuck brought that plane down, even if it's the last thing I ever do.*

He had no idea at just then how prescient those words might turn out to be.

Chapter 8

"Sleep well, Monica Cross," Dr. Mugheri said as he hovered over his patient, looking down at her closed eyes. In days past he would have departed the hospital hours ago and left the overnight supervision to the nurses, but he'd taken a particular interest in Monica since she'd been thrust into his care. Therefore, tonight he remained long after the other doctors had gone home to check in on her one last time.

And Monica did sleep like a baby. A drugged baby, because he'd given her a strong sedative to ease her pain and help her sleep. One-point-five milligrams of Clonazepam, administered all at once rather than spread out over the day in three equal measures. She drifted off quickly after he left her in the darkened room, and soon the effect of the drug vanquished the anxiety that had been building in her.

She'd sunk into a sleep deeper than anything she'd experienced in weeks, almost slipping into an abstract trance. Billows of bright colors washed through her eyes like the undulations of a lava lamp, and once or twice she heard the rhythmic beat of drums in the distance. She didn't know it at the time, but she was experiencing a harmless side effect of the sedative that was flowing through her veins. The waves and flashes were fueled by the effect of the drug on her optic nerves, and the pounding she heard was the rush of blood pulsing through her head.

Only once during the night did the colors take shape and the drum beats form real sounds. The room had been darker than she thought possible, and with the darkness came a comforting stillness. Stillness except for the gentle creak of a door opening on old hinges and the shuffle of soft-soled shoes on the hard linoleum floor.

Monica flicked her eyes open and blinked rapidly in the dark. She just barely made out the other beds, the thin line of light coming in from the corridor. She lay there, waiting for her vision to adjust, and was certain she saw a form hovering in the shadows. She sensed more than watched it glide across the room to the bed where the once-babbling woman now was sleeping, also like a baby. Was someone really in the room, Monica wondered, or was it just the lingering effect of the drugs?

Real or not, she could feel a presence. Just as she could feel a shiver rattle through her body on a cold New York morning, when an icy chill froze the glass in the window and the city almost seemed to come to a stop. Except in this case, she sensed not the frigid grip of winter, but the presence of pure evil.

The ghostly specter—whatever or whoever it was—muttered something she could not decipher. She heard a faint moan as the sleeping woman moved gently in the darkness, perhaps rolling over to find more comfort. After that Monica drifted off to sleep again, and none of what she thought she'd heard or seen came back to her when she finally awoke the following morning to a quiet room.

Chapter 9

Supreme Court Justice Colin Wheeler knew he was in deep shit. He also knew it was shit of his own making, no question about it: guilty as charged, no hung jury, no appeal, no SCOTUS decision forthcoming.

His problems began the moment the blond vixen knocked on his door at the Franklin Pierce Hotel in Southwest Washington. A discreet phone call placed to an even more discreet number, which operated with the utmost discretion, had delivered her to his room right on time, as lovely as promised. Five feet, nine inches of lithe, supple elegance, hair seemingly spun from gold, eyes poured from the clear waters of the Caribbean. Body courtesy of Victoria's Secret, form-fitted into a shimmery white dress cut well above the knee, enticing neckline that laid waste to any need for imagination.

Eager to let the evening's activities commence, he'd promptly invited her inside his suite, then quickly closed the door behind her and threw the security latch.

"Good evening, Justice," she'd said in a beguiling yet playful purr. There seemed to be a bit of an accent buried in there, possibly one of the Carolinas, or maybe it was just some corn-fed flyover state. He was too distracted to tell the difference, or to give it more than a passing thought. "Or do I call you Mr. Wheeler?"

"My first name is Colin," he told her. "Let's dispense with formalities and convene in my chambers." A sweep of his hand indicated the door to the bedroom.

"Then you must call me Linda." Not her real name, of course. Not even close.

"Would you care for a cocktail, maybe a martini or a gin fizz?"

She winked at him and said, "Are you giving me a bar exam?"

It took him a second to get the lawyer joke, then said, "The thought never occurred to me. In fact, I think we should get right down to oral arguments."

"After which I'm sure you'll hand me a stiff sentence," she countered as she leaned up to kiss him. Cinching the deal, which he'd been told would cost him the usual two grand for the hour. Plus, there would be a generous gratuity at the end.

She gently took him by his manhood through his trousers and led him across the soft carpet into the bedroom. It was large and spacious, the same suite he always got whenever he called the confidential toll-free number and arranged for a little extracurricular roguery, which worked out to once every other month. A man with business interests in Vegas and Atlantic City had handed him the embossed card with the ten digits on it not long after Wheeler first took the bench.

"One call gets all," he'd explained on the downlow. "Use it or lose it." And the new Justice had used it, a different girl each time, never an objection raised and no questions asked.

The bedroom walls were a muted cream, mint trim and accents, a massive king-sized bed with a firm mattress and far too many pillows. It was the bed Wheeler was eyeing now as he began to unfasten his top collar button.

"What do you say we dispense with all briefs," he suggested as he drew her toward him.

"As long as you can sustain an objection for hours, we'll be in good shape," she replied with a giggle.

"Believe me, everything we do will be in strict adherence to the penal code," he cracked, going for one last joke. "All I ask is…fuck, *what the hell was that*?"

The Supreme Court justice instinctively slapped a hand to his skin, just below his left ear, where some kind of insect seemed to have nipped at his flesh. More likely stung it, sharp and deep, sending its long proboscis deep into the tissue. But there weren't any bugs up here on the tenth floor, definitely not any that could be that fierce and venomous.

Venomous because he felt the paralyzing effects of the drug within seconds, roughly at the same time he saw the large needle the woman who called herself Linda was pulling out of his neck. The unexpected injection contained a strong dose of succinylcholine chloride, a short-acting depolarizing neuromuscular blockade designed to disrupt the cholinergic receptors of the parasympathetic and sympathetic nervous systems. In other words—those that mattered most to Supreme Court Justice Colin Wheeler—the anesthetic properties kicked in almost instantly, causing a sort of rapid onset muscle relaxation that allowed doctors a brief window in which to perform short procedures that lasted no more than seven or eight minutes.

Problem was, the slinky blond with the supple body and centerfold curves was not a doctor. Nor was Wheeler in need of an emergency tracheotomy. He was, however, naked: stark naked, not even wearing his navy-blue Fruit-Of-The-Loom briefs. Second, he was strapped into a leather chair positioned in front of the built-in desk out in the suite's living room, his ankles and wrists bound to it with some sort of soft fabric that seemed like a silk scarf.

A similar length of fabric was fastened across his mouth, loose enough to allow him to breathe but not to emit anything more than a muffled grunt. Same material as the noose that had been secured around his throat and strung up through the sprinkler pipe directly above him. What alarmed him most was how tightly it was stretched, forcing him to sit up straight and keep his chin upright, or risk blacking out from the lack of oxygen.

How long had he been unconscious? Long enough for someone to have done this to him, someone who now was typing on a laptop computer that had been set on the desk. *His* laptop, he realized, the one he kept on his desk in his library inside his home on Dexter Street, near Glover Archibald Park. The two-story brick colonial he shared with his wife Cynthia, who was out of town visiting her sister in Ohio.

"Hang in there, Sweetums," Linda cooed as she typed something on the keyboard and then fingered the touchpad. She wore nitrile gloves on both hands, he noticed. This was not a good sign. "We'll be done in five, no more than ten minutes."

"How...who...*what the fuck do you think you're doing?*" he demanded, his voice raspy from a side-effect of the medication, deeply muffled because of the scarf that bound his mouth.

"What I'm doing is playing with your computer," she said, her voice even and cold. "See that thumb drive there?"

A memory stick was protruding from a slot in the side of the laptop, a flashing red light indicating it was hard at work doing something.

"You get the fuck out of here—" he told her, chewing his words through the scarf.

"Or you'll do what, Mr. Wheeler? Call the cops? Beat me with your limp dick? Fat chance. But to address your question—what the fuck I'm doing—I'm downloading photographs onto your hard drive. Along with some videos. And what do you think those pictures and videos might be, you're probably wondering? Well, since you can't really ask, on account of your ligatures and the gag, I'm going to tell you. Even though I don't have to, since it's not part of the job description. Just a courtesy, one judge to another."

"You're not a judge," he snarled through the scarf.

"We all are, to some extent," she said. "Although the Bible warns us not to be. Anyway, as I was saying, tomorrow morning the kind folk of Washington will wake up to the news that Supreme Court justice Colin Wheeler died in a suite at a hotel in Southeast DC, apparently killed by autoerotic asphyxiation. The police and medical examiner will reach this mutual conclusion based on the evidence, namely the scarf tied off to the overhead pipe, up there, and the visual imagery on the computer. Which, unfortunately, is going to be embarrassing to your wife and grown kids, since it contains nude photographs of children, specifically young boys engaging in sex acts too lurid for me to mention in any detail. Suffice to say, not only will you be dead, but your illustrious judicial career will have gone down in flames. Reputation shot, character assassinated, every court decision questioned. And your community standing turned to rubble. Not that any of it really matters, because you'll be dead."

Colin Wheeler could scarcely believe what this harpy was telling him. It was crazy talk, total lunacy. No way would she get away with it. Closed circuit surveillance was found on just about every block in the city, and her arrival at the hotel had to have been picked up by dozens of cameras. Then again, she seemed confident and fearless as she went about downloading those disgusting images onto his laptop, and he suspected she'd been careful with her every move. Just as he thought he'd been, which was why he'd selected this hotel in the first place.

"You're out of your fucking mind," he snarled through one hundred percent pure silk.

"Ironic, don't you think, that judge and executioner have come together at last, in such an auspicious way?"

"My security detail will be looking for me," he said, grasping at straws.

"I don't think so, Mr. SCOTUS. Or should I say Scrotum?" She fell silent for a minute as she plugged a different device into another slot, then tapped a few more keys. "You see, when I did my preliminary research, I was astounded to learn that, unlike cabinet secretaries and key members of Congress, Supreme Court justices don't have any mandatory security. I mean, sure, you have coverage on request from the U.S. Marshals Service, and most of your colleagues accept protection at least some of the time. But you—well, you're all loosey-goosey, keeping them on standby for when you need them. Which you don't seem to do very often, for reasons that got us to where we are tonight."

"Fuck you," he managed to say.

"Yes, that was your seminal objective tonight. Alas, the streets of Washington—like those that lead to hell—are paved with reckless intentions." Her fingers began flying across the keys again, and this time she worked for several minutes before she stopped.

"No one will believe this," he mumbled. "Not in a million years."

"Oh, but they will," Linda told him, almost purring in his ear. "The evidence will be overwhelming, hundreds of pictures on your hard drive."

"You put them all there just now. Someone will figure it out."

"Not likely. There's a nifty program I found online that allows me to permanently change the attributes of any file on your computer. That means not even the top forensic analysts can know when each file was actually downloaded onto your computer, which will make it look as if you've been collecting them for years. Kinda cool, don't you think?"

Her bright and cheery manner was causing his contempt to boil over, and he tried to scream. Not loudly, and not for very long, because Linda tugged on the scarf that extended up over the sprinkler pipe and served as the noose around his neck. He choked until he almost turned blue, whereupon she released her grip.

"That's how the asphyxiation part of this works," she explained. "Unfortunately for you, you're going to miss out on the erotic aspect."

It began to sink in that Supreme Court Justice Colin Wheeler actually might die here, in this hotel room, in a most grotesque and abysmal manner. He squirmed and thrashed as he thought about death, humiliation, disgrace, and shame. But his efforts were no use. The woman named Linda seemed determined, and she'd said she'd done this sort of thing before, dozens of times. Did that mean she was a contract killer? For Chrissakes, who wanted him dead? How much was this skeezoid being paid? Well, two could play at that game; after all, the slush fund that covered this room had millions of dollars in it.

"How much are you getting for this?" he gasped through the scarf. "I can pay you more."

"Please, don't grovel," she told him. "You have no idea how that annoys me."

"A million. *Two million.*" He tugged and pulled at the bindings again, but his efforts only seemed to make them tighter. Then, out of the blue, he said, "Ligature marks."

"That fabric doesn't chafe or leave a trace." More typing for another few seconds, and then she said, "Okay, I think we're good to go."

"Go where?" he asked, his spirit momentarily brightening.

"Figure of speech, I'm afraid," she told him.

"You can't do this. You'll never get away with it—"

"Just to make it easier on you, here's what you're going to feel," she said, ignoring him. "First, you're going to experience a lot of pressure to your throat, like you did when I pulled on the noose just a minute ago. It's natural to panic, so just go with it. Next, you'll feel a slight dizziness as your brain is robbed of oxygen, at the same time the carbon dioxide builds up in your bloodstream. You'll start to lose your vision, and you may feel a little drunk. You also might lose control of your bodily functions, depending on the last time you urinated or had a bowel movement. There's nothing you can do about it, and the first responders are prepared to deal with it. Any questions?"

By now his eyes were practically bugging out of his head from fear. He was sixty-four years old, married (clearly not faithfully), three children (one who was blackmailing him), and a home with no mortgage (paid off by Slush Fund Man, in exchange for several pivotal votes on the Court). How could it be that a man who'd aced his three years at Harvard Law, clerked for a former Massachusetts Supreme Court justice, served nine years on the Court of Appeals for the Second Circuit and six more as a justice on the U.S. fucking Supreme Court, found himself in such a degrading predicament?

He'd made it to the pinnacle of a noble law career, and now this whore was aiming to take it all away from him.

"Why?" he asked her, his voice barely more than a breath. "What did I do?"

"It'll come to you," she told him, and then she gave a steady tug on the scarf that was tied around his neck, as if she were hoisting the main sail of a yacht on Chesapeake Bay. "And purely in the spirit of karma, it's not what you did but, in a sense, what you didn't do."

And it did come to him, right around the time his skull felt as if it were going to explode. She hadn't mentioned that part, and it seemed to confuse him. He couldn't breathe, could scarcely see, and his lungs burned. He fought to maintain consciousness, but his field of awareness was beginning to slip away. Then, just before he blacked out, he remembered it all: James Crittenden. East Chop. And a young girl named Lisa Fisher, who had disappeared one spring evening years ago and whose body was never found.

Chapter 10

"How we feel this morning?" asked the nurse who brought Monica breakfast. It was a different nurse, younger and more energetic than the one who had snapped at Brian Walker the day before. Also, she'd asked the question in English which, while less than perfect, was far more comforting than the food she'd delivered from the kitchen. "You sleep good, yes?"

Monica looked at the strange gruel on the tray and thought about bagels and berries and orange juice, and a cup of fresh ground coffee. "Fantastic," she replied.

For the first time in days she actually did feel fantastic, or as close to it as she could hope for. She had no idea how long she'd slept, but—except for the ghostly presence she'd felt in the middle of the night—it had been uninterrupted, something that hadn't happened in months and months. A blast of sun was angling through the window across the room, casting a broad trapezoid of light on the otherwise drab wall. Outside she could hear the distant street noises and rumblings of Islamabad, and she even thought she might hear birds chirping if she listened hard enough.

"You leave today?" the nurse asked.

"I'll know when the doctor gets here. Is he in?"

"Dr. Mugheri arrive at ten."

"What time is it now?"

The nurse checked her watch. "How do you say...half past nine. Finish breakfast, he visit you then."

Nine-thirty. She'd slept a good twelve hours, more than she had managed in years. She glanced over at the other two beds, both of them empty, and said, "Where are my roommates?"

The nurse looked at Monica uneasily. "Humaira is out for scan," she said. She hesitated a moment, glancing over at the empty bed next to Monica's. "Komal is with Allah."

"Allah?" she said, letting the implication settle in. "You mean—?"

The nurse lowered her eyes to the floor and shook her head. "I not should tell you, but in sleep she pass away."

Monica suddenly felt cold, felt as if she'd never get away from all this death and dying. Only when she heard the landing gear thump down on her descent into JFK would she be able to breathe a little easier.

Dr. Mugheri appeared just after ten, dressed in scrubs with a stethoscope loosely draped around his neck. He exchanged pleasantries with Monica, then proceeded to prod and poke her generously. He removed the bandages and unwrapped the gauze that was strapped around her, then touched her chest a little too liberally to simply satisfy medical curiosity.

"Very good," he told her when he finished. "There is nothing more I can do for you."

"What does that mean?"

"It means you are free to leave, as soon as we complete your discharge plan."

"I need to call the airline," Monica said as an odd euphoria swept through her. Euphoria at finally getting out of this room, out of this hospital. Or maybe it was the last of the pain meds working their way out of her system.

"There is no need, my friend," the doctor said with a smile. "I am told your passage to the U.S. has been arranged. You are booked on a flight to leave this afternoon, direct through London. The ticket is being held at the embassy, and an attaché—I believe you've already met him—will be around presently to take you there. A nurse will be in shortly to help you to dress."

This was everything Monica had hoped to hear. She grinned at the doctor, unable to hide her excitement. "Thank you, Dr. Mugheri," was all she found herself able to say.

The doctor dipped his head politely. "Go in peace, and may Allah be with you," he said as he turned toward the door.

"Wait...before you leave..." she said, stopping him. He turned, and she glanced over at the empty bed next to hers. "I understand one of my roommates passed away in her sleep—"

"Yes, very tragic. And unexpected." A look of bewilderment crept into his face, betraying his overall stoic nature. "Cardiac arrest, no warning at all. Strange. Very strange, indeed." Then he realized he shouldn't be discussing these matters with another patient, and tried to steer the conversation around to things more mundane. "I wish you safe travels, my friend. And if you desire anything—anything at all—please don't hesitate to summon one of the nurses."

Once he was gone, Monica slowly sat up on the edge of her bed. She slipped her feet to the floor and tried putting weight on her injured ankle. Not quite as bad as yesterday, and she spent the next few minutes poking around her room. She washed her face and tried to do something about her hair. As a gesture of friendship one of the nurses had given her a flowing yellow and red *salwar kamiz,* and for a brief moment she thought about wearing it on the plane. Instead, she elected to wear a pair of jeans and a pink shirt she'd found in her backpack, along with a hint of lipstick and rouge. When she finally dared look at herself in the mirror, she truly was amazed by the image that was smiling back at her.

A half hour later Brian Walker arrived to escort her to the U.S. embassy. He stared at her in awe, wondering how this could be the same woman who just yesterday had been draped in lifeless hospital garb, and whose hair had hung to her shoulders in stringy ropes.

"Monica Cross, your carriage awaits," he told her, pushing a wheelchair into her room.

"I have to ride in that?" she asked him.

"This may be Pakistan, but hospital policy is the same around the world," he replied.

She thought this over, then said, "Were you able to find my cell phone?"

"No sign of it anywhere. I'm terribly sorry."

A wave of disappointment welled up in her and she felt like crying. She'd come all this way and endured a series of horrific events just to get her cover shot, and she had nothing to show for it. Two people were dead, not counting the two jihadists she had killed, nor the passengers in the plane. She'd suffered twisted and broken bones and other agonies, and she'd stumbled upon the story of the decade, but had no photographic proof of any of it.

"Those pictures were one in a million. A billion—"

"We've looked all over for it." Walker tried to manufacture an empathetic shrug, then looked at his watch. "If it ever turns up, I'll make it my personal mission to get it to you. Meanwhile, your camera bag and equipment are being sent to New York via courier."

"I appreciate that," she said, but she knew her phone was gone for good. "Listen, we'd better get going if you're going to make your plane. It leaves at five o'clock local time, and the ambassador wants to speak with you."

Monica cast him a curious look and said "Seriously?"

"Just a formality," Walker told her. "Think of it as an exit interview. Here—let me help you into the chair."

She tried to make it on her own, but the sharp sting in her chest forced her to give in.

"You sure you have everything?" he asked her as he wheeled her out the door.

"If I don't have it, I don't need it," she replied, doing her best to seem encouraged. "By this time tomorrow I'll be home."

Brian Walker pulled the black Chrysler 300 up to a massive steel gate flanked by security guards and blocked by a barrier that retracted into the pavement at the push of a button. The morning was hot, the dictionary definition of oppressive, and the overworked air conditioning was complaining under extreme duress.

As the car edged up to the checkpoint, he offered his badge to a uniformed guard, who inspected it and his passenger closely before waving them through. Once inside the barricade, the vehicle glided up a driveway to the front of the concrete and glass structure that served as the U.S. embassy. It was an immense building, eight floors of what critics had described as post- modern Genghis Khan nihilism. Situated in the middle of a large compound, it was completely encased by a high wall designed to protect everything within from potential political unrest without. Islamic extremists had burned the previous structure to the ground in 1979, and the capture of bin Laden in 2011 not too far up the road in Abbottabad hadn't eased tensions much. While the Pakistani government grudgingly accepted the U.S. as a necessary geopolitical ally, many of its people regarded Americans as imperialist dogs who should be driven out.

"This is one of the largest U.S. ambassadorial outposts in the world, with twenty-five hundred employees," Walker told Monica as he pulled up in front of a set of granite steps. "What you see here recently replaced the one that was rebuilt in 1980, at a cost of eighty-five million."

"Our tax dollars at work."

He led Monica inside and escorted her in an elevator to the top floor. They stepped out into a large foyer with a pair of mahogany doors to the right. He pushed one of them open, revealing yet another foyer where a uniformed soldier was sitting behind a desk. Monica hadn't grown up in a military family and thus wasn't aware of what all the stripes and medals meant, but a nameplate on the desk identified him as Capt. R. Flores.

"The ambassador is running a few minutes late," the captain announced. "But he said to go into his office and make yourself comfortable."

Walker thanked him, then ushered Monica down a short hallway, where another set of doors much larger than those out front seemed to be standing sentinel over whatever diplomacy and secrets were discussed within. He touched a button and they swung inward automatically, revealing an expansive room paneled in deep teak or walnut or maybe some local variety of tree. The coffered ceiling was constructed from a matching wood and suggested an old-world ambiance, while the floor was covered with the largest Persian rug Monica had ever seen. One wall was filled with row upon row of books with frayed bindings, and the four windows that occupied most of another looked down on a garden that appeared to suffer from drought and State Department budget cutbacks. Yet another wall was cluttered with framed oil portraits of men and women whose significance was lost to history, but somehow contributed an aura of classical relevance.

Brian Walker helped her over to a soft leather couch set in front of a massive fireplace that appeared not to have been used since it had been installed. He invited her to make herself comfortable, then told her he would go and let the ambassador know she had arrived.

"I think I'm scheduled to drive you to the airport when you've finished your debriefing," he told her. He dipped his head politely, then retreated back through the door and closed it.

Debriefing? What could she possibly be debriefed about?

Monica glanced around and imagined herself sitting in some Jane Austen manor with a butler and footman and handmaids, perhaps a rakish duke striking an imposing pose near the fire while puffing on a pipe and quoting Winston Churchill or Descartes. Had Monica not been incapacitated by her injuries she would have wandered about, inspecting the artwork and the books and the rug. Instead, she simply sat at the edge of the leather couch, hands folded in her lap, itching to get on with whatever the ambassador had in mind. All she wanted was to be done with all this, once and for all.

Ambassador Boyar was equally inclined to be done with this young woman from New York who had wandered into his little corner of the world and caused such a ruckus. Wayward Taliban fighters and Kashmir rebels crossing the border into Pakistan were a constant part of his diplomatic oversight, but American tourists were not supposed to be the cause of international incidents.

As he pushed his way into the room, he appeared pressed for time and bothered by Monica's nettlesome presence. He headed straight toward the sofa where she sat, a manila folder in one hand and an unlit cigar clenched tightly between his teeth. It looked soggy, as if he had been biting it for some time.

He was a tall man, about six-two, but his height was more than offset by his girth which, while not tremendous, was enough to betray a fondness for fatty foods and rich sauces. His nose was crisscrossed by a roadmap of veins that suggested an affection for Scotch. A mop of silver hair hung in disarray from the top of his round head, framing a pair of dark, deep-set eyes that studied her keenly as he lowered his ample frame into an oversized Rococo chair positioned diagonally across from her.

"Please, don't get up," he told her as he extended her a hand. "You must be the infamous Monica Cross."

Monica certainly didn't feel infamous, nor would she have been able to rise from her seat had she been so inclined. "Pleasure meeting you, sir," she said.

He studied her clothing, her hair, her make-up. "I see you've refrained from the more feminine aspects of dress, without paying local customs any mind," he observed, speaking in a stiff vocal pattern she'd once heard described as Locust Valley lockjaw.

"I'm aware jeans aren't the accepted custom here," she said, trying not to sound defensive. "But, considering my injuries, I thought it best to address comfort rather than culture, since I have a long flight ahead of me."

Ambassador Boyar didn't respond right away. Instead, he removed a single sheet of paper from the manila folder, quickly read it, then slipped it back into the folder again.

"I know you have a plane to catch, so I'll be brief. From what I understand, you arrived in Islamabad twelve days ago, checked into the Serena Hotel that evening, and came here to the embassy the following morning."

Monica nodded politely, but felt a little on edge. Boyar was getting around to something, and she wished he'd travel in a straight line to get there. "I'm a photographer for *Earth Illustrated* magazine, in New York," she explained. "My editor—Arnie Kelso—notified your staff in advance that we would be coming."

"We?" The ambassador looked at her through squinty eyes.

"Yes. I was travelling with a colleague, Branson Dahl. He wrote the article that I was taking photographs for."

"This Branson, he was the American fellow you say was killed?"

"Yes, along with our guide. By the same butchers who tried to kill me."

"His body has yet to be found, and by now...well, we may never find him." The ambassador again consulted the single page, then looked up with a tight smile. "It says here that one of our consular officers advised you not to make the trip."

"Mr. Walker advised us of the dangers, yes. But the magazine had an article that required photographs, and I came here to take them."

"You made the trek up to the glaciers despite being told not to go," the ambassador pressed her.

"He never actually told us we couldn't go," Monica corrected him. "He just informed us about the risks. We thanked him for his concern, and that afternoon we met up with our pre-arranged guide and caught a bus to Gilgit."

"Let's fast-forward to the incident on that mountain pass," Boyar said. "The two men you killed were local Pashtun, and they were being sought by the Pakistani Department of Defense in connection with another attack."

"I guess I did them a favor, then."

"Unfortunately, the Interior Secretary does not see it that way," he informed her.

"But...those men tried to kill me. It clearly was self-defense—"

"Mrs. Cross, please," the ambassador said in a voice that tried to be low and reassuring. "I believe you. But you have to understand the sensitivities of this region—sensitivities that have existed longer than the United States has been a country. The area in which you and your colleague were hiking has been in turmoil for centuries. Over the last fifty years the locals have fought three wars between Pakistan and India, who have been battling for control of Kashmir. Forty years ago, they clashed for control over a glacier, if you can believe that. *A goddamned sheet of ice.* And now we've got Taliban coming across the border from Afghanistan like it's the Amtrak shuttle. Their philosophy is to kill first, ask questions later. Which is what they did in the case of your companions."

"And they would have killed me, too."

"Precisely. But they didn't, because somehow you were able to take them by surprise."

Monica felt a worrisome shiver that suggested the ambassador had yet to address the specific reason for this meeting, and she wasn't going to like it. "Is there some sort of diplomatic problem?" she asked.

"The problem, Mrs. Cross, is that you are a woman who appears to have bested two vicious brothers. As you can imagine in this misogynistic corner of the globe, that's an extremely embarrassing truth for the families of those involved. What I'm trying to tell you, and to make a short story no longer than it need be, is that certain factions in that region are calling for your capture."

"They...*what?*" Monica said, her eyes open as wide as her gaping mouth. She waited for him to respond but, when he didn't, she added, "You mean they want to *arrest me?*"

"Oh, I doubt very much they're interested in legal formalities," he replied, a grim darkness forming in his eyes. "The fact is, we're hearing a lot of chatter that a bounty has been placed on your head."

"That's freakin' crazy—"

"Of course it is," Ambassador Boyar quickly agreed. "And there's no need for you to fear a thing. Three hours from now you'll be on your way home, leaving all this behind. Once you're out of the country you'll be out of harm's way, and these families will eventually let it go."

Monica felt a little better, but not much. "You're making this sound like a major international conflict," she said, rubbing both temples with her hands.

"Actually, I'm trying to keep it from becoming one," he explained. "And believe me, it would be wise of you to keep a low profile until you touch down in New York."

"All I plan on doing is get on that plane, have a glass of wine or two, and sleep all the way to London," she assured him.

"Good thinking," the ambassador assured her. "I just need to make you aware that your discovery of that airplane up in the mountains has become quite a sensation. A global news story, in fact. Here and in London and in New York, you may be approached by pariahs of the fourth estate who will ask you about your experiences up in the mountains. For national security reasons, and your own safety, I ask that you not provide details of what you did or saw up there."

Monica brushed a strand of hair away from her face, then folded her hands back in her lap. She stared intently at the ambassador, whose brow was creased in a glum look of diplomatic dismay. "What I saw was the wreckage of an old crash, and evidence that everyone on board had been shot. That's all."

"I'm aware of your statement, what you claim you saw," he said. "That's not what our official investigation shows."

"Well, your investigation is wrong. I saw it with my own eyes. I took pictures."

Ambassador Boyar raised his hand to indicate silence. "We'll see, if and when we ever locate your phone. Meanwhile, all that is immaterial. What we are asking in return for your safe passage out of Pakistan is that you refrain from discussing what you believe you saw up there in the mountains. We don't want you arrested. Or worse."

"But—"

"But nothing, Mrs. Cross," he said in a voice that suggested some *mansplaining* was coming. "You found the wreckage of a plane that crashed six years ago. All the bodies were badly decomposed, and you elected not to look too closely at them. End of story."

"You're asking me to lie," she said.

"All we're asking is that you tell a little less than you think you know." The ambassador chose his words carefully, one of the requirements for anyone who had spent a career as a diplomat. "This world is far from perfect, and its inhabitants are not infallible. What is right or noble is not easy to define, and the truth is far from absolute."

Monica remained silent. She let her eyes focus on a space halfway between herself and the floor, then finally drew her gaze back to the ambassador.

"Just get me out of this country and you'll never hear a word from me again," she said.

"Done," the ambassador replied, his negotiations with this young woman finished. "I'll have a car brought around immediately, and Mr. Walker will drive you to the airport."

Then he was gone. Monica remained seated on the broad leather couch, wondering what had just gone down. She was having great difficulty imagining herself a fugitive, her life possibly in danger from local radicals who were out for her blood. She had even a harder time grasping why the ambassador seemed intent on keeping her quiet about the bullet holes she had seen in the five crash victims. Why could it possibly matter whether they'd been shot, asphyxiated from the high altitude, or died upon impact?

Chapter 11

Phythian covered the first three miles on foot. Then fate smiled on him and a Toyota Town Ace bounced up behind him in a torrent of dust. The vehicle was the color of rust, no hubcaps, tailgate missing, rear glass replaced with a sheet of carboard duct-taped to the chrome frame. The pick-up bed held several burlap bags of unknown contents, most likely sorghum or millet.

He recognized the vehicle and knew the driver. His name was Andwele Dourado, a local farmer who scraped a living out of the earth, growing whatever the unpredictable seasons would allow. He also fixed almost anything that had a small engine, dabbled in electrical repairs, and mended small plumbing leaks. He and his extended family—wife, two daughters, mother and mother-in-law—lived about twelve miles east of Phythian's camp, and because of the narrow dirt road that passed by both properties, over the past four years they had come to almost be friends.

"*Asubuhi nzuri, rafiki yangu,*" Andwele greeted him, leaning across the seat and opening the door as an invitation. He was thin but every ounce of flesh on his bones was muscle, and a good guess would put him in his forties. His black skin glistened in the heat, and a faded John Deere cap was perched on his head. Visor in the front, the way it was meant to be worn under a punishing sun. "*Unaenda wapi?*" Where are you going?

"Terrat," Phythian replied, never one for using more words than absolutely necessary.

"Where's your truck?"

"Flat tire," Phythian lied in Swahili. The truth was, he didn't want to drive his own vehicle into town, leaving it to the elements—both human and natural—for an indeterminant amount of time until his travels permitted him to return.

"I take you," the man said in English, welcoming him inside with a sweep of his hand.

The two men had established a polite camaraderie over the years, but they rode mostly in silence on the thirty-mile journey into town. Dourado spoke very little English and, similarly, Phythian had acquired just a thin grasp of Swahili. Each of them occasionally would try out the few words or phrases they'd picked up from the other or, in Phythian's case, from the English-to-Swahili translator on Google. But the result was little more than an awkward language exercise that lasted a few seconds, and eventually led to more silence. This morning he had too many things on his mind to converse idly about *ng'ombe wa ng'ombe* (the cattle herd), *mazao ya matunda* (fruit crops), or *bei za mboga* (vegetable prices). Dourado eventually got the hint.

Five years ago, when Phythian purchased the two-hundred-acre plot of land and began to renovate the decaying buildings, he was pleasantly surprised to find it was blanketed by digital high-speed Wi-Fi, courtesy of a Silicon Valley multi-billionaire whose idea of a grand, charitable gesture was to bring the internet to every home in Africa. Coverage tended to be sporadic, but on good days, which here on the eastern fringe of the Serengeti seemed to be most of the time, Phythian occasionally fell victim to his deepest curiosities and connected to the outside world.

That's how he'd learned yesterday of the wreckage that had been found in the mountains of Pakistan. He'd never known the precise location where the aircraft had come down, since he'd bailed out of the cabin not long after it had crossed back over the Lebanese coast. As he drifted down to earth, the broad nylon canopy billowing above him, he kept an eye on the towns and roads below. He knew there was always a risk that he would come down in unfriendly territory, but fate was with him that day, and he landed in a field about two miles east of Ain El Jaouzeh, dangerously close to the Syrian border.

As he'd gathered up his chute, the King Air 350 was already well on a course that would take it thousands of miles beyond where the G3 had expected it to hit the water. By the time the flight was reported missing over the Mediterranean, it would be cruising at twenty thousand feet above Iraq and Iran, an altitude it would maintain until its twin turboprops sucked every drop of fuel out of its tanks. With its rear door gone the constant drag of wind would cut its range, but Phythian didn't care.

Nor did he care how long it might take for the wreckage to be discovered. Perhaps years, most likely decades. Thus, he was surprised to learn from the BBC last night that a photographer from a glossy pseudo-science magazine had literally stumbled upon the site in a region of Pakistan where almost no one ever went, and where nothing ever should have been found.

Phythian's first instinct was to remain disengaged. This was no longer his business, and he wanted no part of it. The wreckage was but a remnant of his former life, one that he'd managed to tuck away in a dark corner of the past where he was sure it would lie, forever frozen in the permafrost of time. He'd managed to free himself from the vicious tentacles of the Greenwich Global Group and had made a clean break, even though he'd had to escape to the far reaches of Africa to do it. There wasn't a country on any continent in the world where the motherfuckers didn't have eyes and ears, and if they had even the remotest suspicion that he'd liberated himself from their clutches and was still alive, they would hunt him down wherever he might be. The fact that no remains of the plane or the victims were ever found would cause them to wonder, but they'd never know with any degree of certainty.

Not unless—or until—the wreckage was found.

Four months into his newfound freedom he'd found the abandoned safari camp in the Manyara region at the edge of the Tangarire River ecosystem. It was located in the ancient wash of an alkaline lake bed that had dried up thousands of years ago, but which thrived on an ample supply of groundwater that fed several year-round springs. While it consisted mostly of dry grasslands, the seasonal rains nourished groves of sycamore fig and quinine and mahogany, and attracted untold species of migratory birds and mammals.

The property consisted of a main structure fashioned from trees originally harvested on the property, perched on a knoll with three-sixty views that allowed him to see any cloud of dust in the distance that indicated someone was approaching. He'd torn down eight insect-infested wood platforms that, years before, had held the glamping tents where tourists would awaken to the sight of giraffes and bushbucks and Thompson gazelles. Where they once stood, he now tended a sparse garden of beans and potatoes, but he'd never had much of a green thumb and his efforts mostly were futile. The only outbuilding he'd kept intact was the brick cooking hut located fifty yards from what now served as his residence, which he'd learned during the renovation could be accessed by a reinforced tunnel four feet in diameter through which prepared food for safari guests could be transported via an old trolley. Apparently, it was to keep the predatory lions, leopards, and jackals from getting too close during human feeding time.

All land in Tanzania legally was the property of the government, with citizens granted rights of occupancy renewable for up to ninety-nine years. As Phythian quickly discovered when the camp's rights-holder attempted to transfer the parcel into his name, foreigners were only permitted to hold land for investment purposes. Official negotiations were set to break down until the District Commissioner for Lands, Sub-leases, and Licenses—a self-important and dreary man in the equally dreary town of Babati—curiously found himself granting a rare exception to this oddly persuasive American.

Once the official signed and stamped the proper documents, Phythian set to work, finishing his renovation project just weeks before the December rains began to fall. The newly refurbished compound was a rustic example of African paradise accessible only by the dusty, two-rut trail that doubled as an animal path, which fed onto a wider lane before intersecting with the road to Arusha. One autumn night, after realizing he hadn't thought of the G3 once in well over twenty-four hours, he decided to name the place *Utuliva*, the Swahili word for serenity.

"*Amerika inaonekana kama mahali kama kijinga*," Andwele Dourado said this morning, out of the blue.

Phythian grinned, just as he always did when the cattle farmer and gracious entrepreneur mentioned the latest stupid thing that came out of the U.S. "*Ndiyo sababu nilihamia*," he replied, his standard response whenever politics came up in conversation: That's why I moved.

An hour later they rolled into Terrat. Dourado pulled his truck into a spot of shade under an acacia tree in front of the post office. It was a low-slung wood-and-clay structure with a sun-bleached canvas awning beneath which, it seemed, most of the village's business was conducted. A half dozen men either sat on rickety chairs or squatted on the ground, sipping chai tea or coffee or, like one young man this morning, a can of

Kabisa. Phythian thanked his friend for the ride and wandered inside, his watchful eyes warily drifting right and left as he focused on anything out of the ordinary. Old habits die hard, even out here in the African Serengeti.

A fan churned in a corner of the dusty room. Flyers flapped where they'd been pegged to a bulletin board, and a framed photo of the nation's authoritarian president hung above a doorway. A young woman with a child in tow was munching on a candy bar, backhanding a swarm of pesky flies as she wandered back out into the sweltering heat.

When Phythian was satisfied that all was right with the world, or at least his small corner of it, he approached the postal worker standing behind a chipped laminate counter. "*Asubuhi nzuri, rafiki yangu,*" he greeted him. "*Barua yoyote kwa ajili yangu?*" Any mail for me?

"*Samahani, si leo,*" the young man said, shaking his head. His name was Elimu Juma, and he was dressed in a short-sleeve cotton shirt and khakis, head shaved close. Teeth that offered a massive grin, large black eyes that always seemed to welcome the world, including, as a subset of that, everyone who came into his post office.

"*Nataka kununua tikiti ya Arusha,*" Phythian told him. Besides being the place to get one's mail and refuel on the daily update on local gossip, the post office also served as Terrat's bus station. Since the village was located many times removed from the beaten path, there were only three transports a week that made the tedious, dusty journey to the city of Arusha which, for his immediate purposes, happened to have an international airport—of sorts—that could put him on a different continent by evening.

"*Njia moja au safari ya pande zote?*" Elimu replied. One way or round trip?

This was the question Phythian had been pondering ever since he'd made the decision to leave the serenity and security of *Utuliva.* He knew as soon as the plane wreckage was found that the overbearing Chairman and his officious sidekick Diana Petrie—in fact, the entire G3 executive board—would be on high alert and out for his blood. Their little mission to blow up the plane and kill him had failed miserably, and confirmation of that failure now was the lead topic of the global *intelegraph,* which was his term for the spymaster whisper mill.

Fingers would be pointing, heads would be rolling, and deputy directors would be calling for Phythian to be found and dragged in before...well, before what? The Hague? He couldn't be arrested, couldn't be tried. He couldn't be convicted, and couldn't be allowed anywhere near the press. He knew too much, and that knowledge made him a real threat, someone who could shift the balance of power around the world. Making matters worse, he had proof of the G3s numerous deadly transgressions, and that proof was known as Equinox.

Should that single device find its way into the wrong hands—any hands, in fact—the repercussions could be cataclysmic. In a world where information translated to power, Equinox was the Holy Grail, and the G3 would be furious that it had gone missing. The empty Faraday case investigators would have found in the plane wreckage was evidence of that, and the G3 would correctly assume only two people in the world could know its possible location: Rōnin Phythian, or the photographer named Monica Cross.

That meant her life was in grave danger and, through his actions of six years ago, he had put it there.

So, to answer Elimu Juma's question, would he be needing a return ticket to Terrat?

"*Njia moja, tafadhali,*" Phythian told the inquisitive postmaster as he counted out fourteen thousand Tanzanian shillings. One way, please.

Chapter 12

After being safely escorted from the U.S. embassy by a uniformed security guard, Monica once again was seated beside Brian Walker in the black Chrysler. They were in light traffic heading south on the Kashmir Highway toward the new Islamabad International Airport, heat rising in ripples from the parched asphalt. She kept mentally replaying her conversation with the ambassador, her temper simmering like a pot of stew. Advising her not to talk to reporters about her experience was one thing, but trying to convince her that her eyes had deceived her about what she had seen... well, that was another matter altogether. She'd taken photographs of the bullet holes, for Chrissakes—photographs that had disappeared, along with the mobile phone she'd used to capture them.

Despite protocol to the contrary, Monica had demanded to sit up front. They drove with the windows closed to keep out the noxious aroma from the ubiquitous waste bins that seldom were emptied, once again the air conditioning struggling to keep up with the heat. Located near the northern edge of the Pothohar Plateau and at the foot of the Margalla Hills, Islamabad was unbearably torrid during the summer, and the temperature inside the Chrysler had climbed to well over ninety.

They arrived at the airport a good two hours ahead of Monica's scheduled departure. Walker pulled the car with diplomatic plates into a "no parking" zone and defied the local authorities to do anything but look in contempt at American privilege. He grabbed her backpack in one hand and used the other to assist her inside the terminal.

Dr. Mugheri had wrapped Monica's ribs tightly, and she experienced a pulsing throb of pain when she moved. Walker accompanied her to the ticket counter and lingered while an agent familiar with English checked her through London to JFK. While they waited, Walker dug into his jacket pocket and pulled out a cell phone, one of the later models but not one of the pricey brand-new ones.

"This is for you, in case you run into any snags during your layover," he told her. "My counterpart in London, a guy named Cliff Broward, has already been alerted that you're coming. His number is pre-programmed into it, so give him a call if you need anything."

"Thank you," Monica said as the ticket agent returned her passport and handed her a printed boarding pass. "I appreciate all you've done, especially for not saying 'I told you so.'"

"No need to heap any further insult on top of injury," he observed. "I'm just glad you're alive and on your way home."

"Me too," she said.

They started to move toward the security queue, but at that moment a swarm of passengers pressed past them. One member of the pack—a dark man with a bushy brow and a single dark eye, with an empty socket where the other once had been—seemed to be heading on a collision course toward her. At the last second Walker grabbed her arm and yanked her aside, eliciting a groan of pain as the man's elbow dug into her ribs. She did not notice the sharp nib of the fountain pen that had missed her skin by mere millimeters as it stung Walker on the hand.

"Who the hell was that?" she gasped, once the angry-looking man disappeared into the crowd again. She stared after him, then turned back to Walker.

"He...tried to attack you," he mumbled, the words barely forming on his lips.

Monica had no idea what had just happened, didn't comprehend what he was telling her. Instead, she said, "Mr. Walker...are you all right?"

"Get to...your gate," he rasped as his legs buckled and he collapsed to the floor.

She instinctively bent down and stared at him blankly, not grasping what was going on. One second he'd tugged her out of the way of something she hadn't seen, and the next he was lying flat on the polished concrete.

Then his mouth moved, and she snapped back from the brink of despair. "Get...on... that...plane," he ordered her, his voice now no more than a breath.

"But…I can't just leave you—"

Passengers kept brushing past them, and no one seemed to pay any mind to what had just happened. Then Ambassador Boyar's words came back to her—*a bounty has been placed on your head*—and a new round of questions began to bounce around her brain.

"Go," Walker muttered again. "Now."

How could Monica abandon this man who had been so kind to her, even if he had been evasive and cagey? He required help, but he told her to make her flight. Insisted, in fact. What else could she do?

"Leave…me," he urged her, as if reading her mind. Then his arms and legs fell limp and his eyes rolled upward, dull and lifeless.

It was at that point that the truth hit her: the one-eyed man had meant to kill her. And somewhere in this crowd of passengers cueing up to file through the security gate, she knew he was watching her. She couldn't see him but she sensed his presence somewhere close, as sure as she had felt the same dark evil invade the gloom of her hospital room last night. He had struck so swiftly and precisely that not one of these people standing here had even seen it happen.

She cast Brian Walker a glance of unspoken apology, labored to hoist the pack onto her back, and limped up to a man dressed in a uniform and a badge who was standing near the security gate. Despite the language barrier she was able to point out the very ill man lying on the floor across from the departure screens. The guard was slow in understanding what she was saying, but eventually realized what was going on and called for assistance. When Monica was convinced Brian Walker was getting the medical attention he required, she hurried to the security checkpoint and fed her carry-on into the X-ray machine. As she was waved through the metal detector, a roiling flood of relief and guilt churned through her.

She felt like crying, but she just didn't have it in her.

Chapter 13

Vice President James Crittenden was an early riser, typically feeling refreshed and recharged, but tonight he'd barely been able to grab a wink of sleep.

He rarely fell into bed before midnight, and usually only required five or six hours to feel fully rested when he was in residence up in Washington. Fortunately, President Mitchell had made it clear he wasn't a vital aspect of the administration, which meant his presence wasn't required in the nation's capital on a daily basis. While he carried a full agenda of bridge openings and political speeches and ribbon-cuttings, it was all ceremonial bullshit that left him plenty of time to play golf and think. And most of the time he was thinking, it involved conspiring to replace Mitchell in the White House. The VP was, after all, next in line in U.S. constitutional succession, as well as the anticipated front-runner when term limits put the widely anticipated two-term president out to pasture five years from now.

When he wasn't required to be in DC, Crittenden preferred to be in his private residence just a half hour's drive outside his boyhood home of Biloxi. Set squarely in the middle of twenty acres, Raven's Rest was listed on the National Register of Historic Places, and recognized as one of the finest examples of antebellum authenticity in all of Mississippi. When he'd purchased the residence sixteen years ago its bones were tired and creaky, just like the former cotton magnate who had sold it to him. After committing to a complete overhaul to bring the place back to its slave-era splendor, Crittenden had given his wife free reign to fill it with artifacts culled from every corner of the Old South. No expense was spared, and the homestead once again played host to dignitaries, politicians, magnates, and tycoons.

But this morning—four o'clock local time—there were only two people inside the six-thousand square-foot residence. The live-in housekeeper and manservant had their own quarters over the eight-car detached garage, where they kept watch over a collection of Cadillacs that dated back to 1959. And the vice president's Secret Service detail similarly was holed up in the guest cottages that surrounded the Romanesque pool and sculpted topiary garden.

Crittenden's wife Raeanne was up in Natchez for some sort of prayer event, and their two children were off at college. Daughter Valerie was in her senior year at Amherst and son James III was a sophomore at Harvard, just as his daddy had been. The craven northerners had brought the Confederacy to its knees but damn, they did have exquisite institutions of higher learning.

No other relatives, friends, guests, or interlopers occupied the eight bedrooms or were wandering the halls, which was critically important. Important because this morning the VP was entertaining a slippery and unscrupulous individual named William Raymond Tate, whose presence in the house easily could have given rise to a great deal of unwanted conjecture. Known in the political trade as a facilitator, Tate was a corrupt and shady reprobate whose scurrilous and vulgar tendencies made him one of the most feared yet effective operatives in the darkest corners of American politics. And, thus, one of the most sought-after.

"He's definitely dead?" Crittenden asked as he rubbed his palms with a dab of hand sanitizer, the fourth time he had done this since shaking hands with his visitor. They were seated in the private pub in the basement of Ravens Rest, designed to resemble the Tap Room at Pebble Beach, where the then-governor had once made par on the twelfth hole. "You have proof?"

"I received the text when I landed," Tate assured him, tired from his last-minute flight. "Three photos in all."

"Do I want to see them?"

"If you choose, but let me warn you…they're pretty graphic."

Crittenden thought on this, weighing a ghoulish curiosity against plausible deniability. Despite the early hour, he took a sip of the Johnny Walker Blue he saved for special occasions—such as this morning, even though he had a speech to give in four hours. A fundraiser breakfast for the man who had replaced him in the governor's mansion three years ago, and who had just revealed his plans to run for four more years.

He savored the smooth flow of the Scotch going down, then glanced at Tate.

"Graphic, as in bloody?"

Tate had declined the offer of expensive Johnnie Walker, and was sipping from a can of sparkling water instead. "More like compromising," he said. "And totally destructive to the man's reputation."

The vice president nodded, since he fully understood the existential threat of professional extinction. Which was the reason for Tate's presence here tonight, and delivery of the news that would lead to the man's imminent departure. "I think I'll pass, then," he replied. "When will it hit the news cycle?"

"Figuring in the time for housekeeping to discover the body, and the authorities to arrive and identify it, and then to determine the proper protocol to report it, I think we're looking at a little after ten until word gets out."

"Eastern time."

"Of course, Eastern. The police commissioner and his sycophants will dither a bit about how to handle it, Wheeler being a Supreme Court justice and all. But Washington leaks like a syphilitic dick, which means no later than ten-fifteen. That's a little over five hours from now."

"And you're certain he's dead?"

"Jesus fuck," Tate cursed, then whipped out his phone and thumbed up one of the photos Adam Kent had sent him an hour ago. "Here—see for yourself."

The vice president didn't want to look, but curiosity got the better of him. He studied the shot a few seconds, then handed it back. "Gay pedophilia? Really?"

"Homo-autoerotic asphyxiation," Tate clarified as he slipped his cell back into his pocket.

Crittenden seemed distracted, the true implication of the photograph sinking in. Wondering what people might think if he were to be found in the same kind of compromising position. His wife Raeanne would be devastated and ashamed, and his kids would be humiliated at school. They'd drop out, go into hiding. Maybe even leave the country. No one survives that kind of public ridicule and disgrace without incurring a lot of lasting damage.

"It's going to be hard on the children," he said absently.

"A destroyed legacy," Tate said. "Exactly what you paid for. Speaking of which—"

Crittenden realized what his fixer was getting at. He took another sip of Scotch and wandered over to a wooden case that was affixed to the far wall of the barroom. Without hesitation he pulled open the double doors, exposing a circular cork board with darts lying in a slotted tray. Inside was a manila envelope, as broad and thick as a Tom Clancy novel, and handed it over.

"You can count it if you want," he said.

"No need; I know where to find you." The envelope was far too large to stuff it anywhere on his person, so Tate just gripped it in his hand as he turned to go. "You took care of the contractor fee separately?"

"Another half million in bitcoin already transferred," Crittenden told him.

"Then we're all done here."

"Not quite," the vice president said. "There's another matter we need to resolve. Something that should have been taken care of six years ago."

Tate knew where Crittenden was going, and waved him off with his hand. "I'll tell you now what I told you back: no one will ever be able to pin the disappearance of that airplane on you."

"I don't give a damn about the fucking thing, or the people who were in it. All that matters is what's on that hard drive."

"I'm on it," Tate assured him. Succinct, to the point.

"I chipped in a lot of money to get rid of that goddamned thing," Crittenden said, continuing his tirade. "That money was a guarantee that the past remains in the past, and it's up to you to make sure it stays that way. I haven't come this far to be fucked over by some twit with a camera."

"She's been under tight watch since she arrived at the hospital, and they're releasing her today. And when they do, well—" Tate gave a quick glance at his watch, then added, "—I should be getting word of her demise any time now."

"Fan-*fucking*-tastic," Crittenden said as he drained the last of his Scotch. "Let me know when that happens. Meanwhile, find that Goddamned drive."

"Yes, *Mr. President*," Tate replied, appealing to the VP's malignant narcissism and unyielding ambition. He squeezed the envelope in his hand, and finished his mineral water. "Now, if you don't have any more business to discuss, I'll show myself out."

Chapter 14

ISLAMABAD
9:08 AM GMT, 12:08 PM LOCAL

"Miss, your luggage—"

Monica Cross snapped out of a spell of gnawing anxiety when she realized the short man who stood at the end of the security check-point was speaking to her—in English. She glanced down and saw that her backpack was obstructing other bags exiting the X-ray unit.

"Oh, I'm sorry," she apologized.

She lugged it off the steel rollers, then slipped her shoes back on her feet. She attempted to blend in with the rest of the crowd pressing up a rampway toward the international gates, but the persistent pain caused her to move slowly. Several times she glanced over her shoulder, not only to try to catch a glimpse of the one-eyed man who had brushed way too close to her, but also to see if Brian Walker was receiving the medical attention he badly needed. A small crowd had gathered around him, but the array of metal detectors blocked her view. She felt dreadful for abandoning him where he fell, but instinct told her there was nothing she could do. Now her only thought was to escape this damned hellhole and just get back to the good old U.S. of A.

By the time she reached her gate the Airbus A330 was already boarding its first class and elite passengers. A small mob pressed forward as the ticket agent rattled off boarding instructions, first in Urdu, then in English. Monica pushed her way into the center of the human horde, stealing a nervous glance over her shoulder to see if she could spot the man who had tried to kill her. If he was out there, she couldn't see him.

She felt a need to use the ladies' room, but she decided she could wait until she was aboard the plane. Safety definitely came in numbers, and she had no desire to separate herself from the crowd. When it finally was her turn to board, the gate agent studied her flight documents and passport carefully.

"Have a nice flight, Mrs. Cross," he finally wished her as he handed them back.

She said nothing as she hobbled down the long jetway toward the plane, fighting back every urge to take one last glance at the milling crowd. What was it the ambassador had said? *"Certain factions in the region are calling for your capture."* That was it, of course: the family of the two men she had killed had sent one of their own down to Islamabad to avenge their deaths. She could hear Boyar's words now, coming out in that erudite upper-crust cadence: "We believe it would be wise to keep a low profile until you touch down in New York. In fact, we'd like you to forget this entire trip, and everything that happened during it."

As she took her seat an alternative truth hit her. Maybe this had nothing to do with pride or shame or provincial misogyny. Maybe it was the wreckage of the plane she had stumbled across, and the five bodies she'd been told not to talk about. They'd all been shot in the head, twice. She knew what bullet holes looked like, for Chrissakes. She'd even taken photographs which, very conveniently, had disappeared. Along with her phone. What was it Ambassador Boyar had told her? *You found the wreckage of a plane that crashed six years ago. All the bodies were badly decomposed, and you elected not to look too closely at them. End of story.*

Then a person standing in the aisle next to her said, "Excuse me, ma'am. I believe I'm in that seat."

Monica snapped her head around and stared up at a young woman who had addressed her in a polite British accent. She was in her early thirties and had a full head of hair that Redken would call blended caramel. Dressed in a striped tunic and loose-fitting white pants, a white cotton hat perched on her head. A purple rollaboard and an overstuffed purse lay at her feet.

"This is row eighteen, right?" the woman added. "I'm tired of dragging this bloody bag all over the airport."

"Here, let me get out of your way." Monica slowly edged out into the aisle, after which her new seatmate squeezed the wheeled suitcase into the overhead bin. Monica attempted to help, but a sharp stab in her chest caused her to wince.

"Oh, please...you poor thing. I can get it." She flashed a sympathetic smile, then used both hands to lock the bin firmly in place. "By the way, my name's Fiona Cassidy. And damn, am I ever glad to get out of this place."

"Monica Cross," Monica introduced herself in return. "And the sentiment's the same."

"Pleased to make your acquaintance, Monica Cross," Fiona said, and instantly Monica knew she had found a friend she could trust.

Both women made themselves comfortable. Fiona opened her purse and fished through it for a box of Peppersmith mints. She popped one in her mouth, then offered one to Monica, who eagerly accepted.

"What a relief...at least this time I know I'm not going to be hit on the entire flight," Fiona said, then gave Monica a guarded glance. "You're not going to hit on me, are you?"

"Not my type," Monica said with a grin. "You on your way home?"

"Bloody right." Fiona replied. "Can't wait to get back to London. That's where I live right now, but I'm originally from Warwick, and Manchester after that. I'm a travel agent, but I rarely see a chance to get out of the office."

"I didn't think they had travel agents anymore," Monica observed. "The internet, and all that."

"We're definitely a dying breed. But I work for a company that sells adventure experiences for people who are crossing things off their bucket lists. Here's my card."

Monica glanced at it, the words "Britannia Travel" embossed at the top, then slipped it into her pocket. "Sounds like a great gig," she sighed as she relaxed in her seat.

"The pay is lousy but the perks are great," Fiona said as she stole a glance out the window beside her. "To tell the truth, I could have done without this little junket, but the company's thinking of offering a guided tour of the glaciers. 'An experience of a lifetime,' is what they call these things."

"That's why I'm here."

"Really? For the experience of a lifetime?"

If you only knew, Monica thought. "Work," she said instead. "I'm a photographer."

"Really? That is way cool. Do you work for a company, or are you freelance?"

"I'm with *Earth Illustrated* magazine. I don't know if you have it in the U.K.—"

"Are you kidding?" Fiona gushed. "I love that magazine. The agency subscribes to it, and I read it cover to cover every month. That's why you're here, taking pictures for the magazine?"

"The Baltoro Glacier, in fact," Monica confirmed, leaving out the dismal details. "I was assigned November's cover shot. We work months in advance."

"And now you're going home?"

"New York," she nodded. "I never thought I'd say this, but I can't wait to get my hands on a pretzel from a street cart."

"I went to New York once, when I worked for a different agency. Fun place to visit, and great theater. But tickets are so expensive, it's scandalous. Hey, would you like to borrow some lipstick, maybe a little eyeshadow?"

Monica blinked at the sudden change of subject, but went with it. "I look that bad?"

"Well, I certainly can understand wanting to dress down around this place, not attract attention," Fiona encouraged her. "But you'll be landing in London in nine hours."

Monica hadn't even thought about make-up in over a week. "Maybe after we get airborne," she replied.

At that moment the plane shuddered as the flight attendant at the front of the cabin closed the door and turned the lock. The lights flickered and the Airbus jolted once more as the ground crew began to push it back from the gate.

Until this moment Monica hadn't given the actual flight a moment's thought. She had been so preoccupied with getting out of the hospital that she had no idea what time it would be when they landed in London. One thing she did know: just a few more minutes and the plane would be in the air.

She glanced over at Fiona, who had fallen silent and was gripping the armrest.

"White knuckles," she explained before Monica could comment. "I know they say it's a lot safer to fly than to drive, but you should see me behind the wheel."

Monica didn't want to talk about how safe it was to drive. Not a day had passed since Phillip's death that she hadn't thought about the last few seconds of his life, how his car had somehow spun out on a patch of black ice and flipped over before slamming into a tree. Sure, it had been snowing all day and the road was slick, but he was a careful driver and she knew he wouldn't press his luck given the weather. He owned a Tesla, one of the larger, heavy models with a wide body and excellent traction, and investigators concluded he was driving under the speed limit when he careened into the woods.

The plane shuddered again, and another spasm caused her to grimace.

"Are you all right?" Fiona asked.

"Just a flesh wound," Monica replied. "I met with a bit of a hiking accident."

"What did you do, fall off the glacier?"

"Pretty close," Monica told her. "I took a little spill down the side of a mountain."

"Ouch...that must have hurt," Fiona replied. "Were you traveling alone?"

"No, I was with someone from the magazine."

"But you're flying home alone?"

"He had some business to clear up," Monica said.

It was then that she realized the plane wasn't moving. It was just sitting there on the tarmac, engines idling, the passenger cabin slowly warming under the blistering June sun. The air conditioning ductwork had already been disengaged from the jet's belly, and circulation was nil. Then the pilot's voiced cracked over the microphone, in English.

"This is First Officer Farris from the flight deck," he said. "I'm sorry to tell you, but we are having a minor technical issue that is forcing us to return to the gate. Please keep your seats while we're moving. As soon as we pull up to the jetway, the flight attendants will open the main cabin door and you are to disembark the plane immediately. Please leave your carry-on bags where they are; you will be reunited with them when we re-board. When we arrive at the gate you are to proceed to the terminal in an orderly fashion, and remain there until you receive further instructions. Thank you, and we're very sorry for the inconvenience."

Monica's heart bottomed out. This couldn't be happening, not now. She closed her eyes and fought back a rush of all-too-familiar tears. How could she possibly get off this plane and venture back inside that airport, where undoubtedly her would-be killer was waiting for her.

Then it struck her. This was no coincidence; this emergency had to be *his* work. The one-eyed man hadn't been able to get to her before she got on the plane, nor was he able to board it himself. Instead, he'd somehow had the flight turned back. She felt a twinge of paranoia chewing at the back of her brain, but her sense of logic told her she was right.

"Dammit," she cursed, her voice barely more than an angry whisper.

"Ditto," Fiona Cassidy agreed. "I don't have time for this shit. I have to get back to London tonight."

"And I need to get home to New York. I wonder what the problem is."

"Probably a faulty gauge or a cabin light that will take them hours to figure out," Fiona grumbled as she glanced out the window.

Monica suspected otherwise, but kept her thoughts to herself. It was safer for her and Fiona that way. After all, she was the one with a bullseye on her back.

The plane started moving back toward the gate. It was a short trip, maybe a hundred yards, and it ended with a jarring lurch as the pilot hit the brakes. A bell chimed and several hundred passengers scrambled to their feet and started collecting their belongings.

"Please leave the plane immediately, do not take any carry-on luggage with you," a flight attendant reminded them. "That means everyone."

Monica and Fiona tried to edge out into the crowd that was beginning to press up the aisle toward the exit, but it was no use. "Let 'em go," Fiona said. "The plane's not going to explode in the next two minutes."

All of a sudden Monica understood. The one-eyed man must have called in a bomb threat. The airline was emptying the plane in order to search it, inch by inch. And while the passengers waited around the terminal for the "all clear," which could take hours, she would be right in his crosshairs.

"That's it," she said to herself.

"What's it?"

"Nothing—just thinking aloud," Monica replied. This was getting more dismal every minute. She stood in the aisle and assessed her options, trying to get a line on a plan. Finally, she found a dim ray of hope, and said to Fiona, "Bring your purse with you. I think I'm going to need your help with something."

"A little make-up?"

"A big make-over," Monica replied.

They waited until the rush of passengers had subsided. Then Monica moved out into the aisle and opened the overhead bin. She knew she wouldn't be able to get her entire backpack off the plane, but there were a few things in it that were vital to her survival. She rummaged through the front zippered pouch and dug out the *shalwar qamiz* that the nurse had given her. Then she stuffed her passport, wallet, and a few assorted necessities into the rear pocket of her jeans.

"There's something going on that I should know about, isn't there?" Fiona asked suspiciously as she grabbed her own bulging purse from under the seat.

Monica chose not to answer the question, not at that very moment. Instead, she told her new friend, "Just in case we get separated, meet me in the ladies' room in five minutes."

Fiona nodded and followed Monica out of the plane. The male flight attendant at the door began to protest Fiona's removal of her handbag, but she simply ignored him as they both walked up the jetway.

As they emerged from the gate, Monica focused her eyes on the crowd, but there was a planeload of disgruntled travelers milling about that prevented her from seeing much. Her assailant could be anywhere, but she didn't have a clue where. She felt as if this scenario might never end, but kept her frustration to herself.

"Rest room dead ahead," Fiona told her, nodding toward the edge of the passenger area. She grabbed Monica's hand and tugged her through the restive mob. "Follow me."

Monica saw him then, hovering at the perimeter of the concourse. Tall, dressed in loose-fitting linen jacket and faded denims. Jet-black hair, lips curled up in a permanent sneer: empty eye socket. He appeared anxious as he looked about, searching for a woman in western denims and a pink shirt. But Monica had already draped the shawl over her head, and in a few minutes, she would emerge from the restroom an entirely different woman.

"Okay, what gives?" Fiona demanded once they were safely inside the lavatory. "What the bloody hell is going on?"

A Pakistani woman was washing her hands at the sink, and Monica waited until she was gone before she began her story. She told it quickly, selectively editing as she went and, when she finished, she didn't know whether she'd been at all convincing. Fiona had said nothing during the entire tale, and didn't reply for a good ten seconds after Monica was done. Then she slowly shook her head and reached out with both arms, wrapping them around her new friend.

"You poor thing," she said, her words swollen with compassion but not pity. "You've been to hell and back."

"I'm not back yet," Monica sighed. "Not by a long shot. But I think you can help me."

"What do you have in mind?"

"Whatever you can scrounge up in your bag of tricks."

"I'm sure I have something that can do the job," Fiona assured her. She fumbled through her cluttered purse, taking out a handful of lipsticks, mascara, eye shadow, several shades of rouge, and an engraved brass compact. "Before I got into the travel business, I worked in a beauty parlor. I'm Level Three-qualified, so just relax and let me have a go."

Ten minutes later Monica stared at herself in the cracked mirror over the row of sinks. She felt like a changed woman as she studied the work of art her new friend had just created. Her eyes carried a thick, smoky hue, while her lips were a deep red and her cheeks were a pale rust that hinted of a high mountain sunburn.

"You're a true miracle worker," she gushed as she stared at the mirror.

"You should see what I can do when I have all my stuff," Fiona replied with a broad grin of satisfaction. "Anyway, I don't think you'll have a whole lot of trouble now."

"Think I can pass for a local?" Monica said, her doubts lingering.

"Enough to keep that arsehole from recognizing you," Fiona said with a touch of pride. "Especially if you wear that."

"It's a *shalwar qamiz*. A nursed at the hospital gave it to me this morning."

"He'll never know."

"Hope not," Monica sighed as she felt a wave of relief wash through her. Maybe she'd beat this bastard at his own game after all. "I think we're going to have to separate until we get back on the plane," she said. "Wouldn't make sense for a local woman to be hanging around with a travel agent from London."

"What about safety in numbers—?"

"Not this time. I'll keep to myself and be just fine."

Fiona hesitated a moment, then said, "See you back at the gate, then. Or on the plane."

"Count on it."

Monica remained in the restroom a few more minutes, but she knew she couldn't stay in there forever. She was gripped by an unyielding fear of the man with one eye, and plagued by her dismal chances of getting out of Islamabad anytime soon. How long would it take security crews to search an entire Airbus for a bomb, if that's really what the hold-up was? An hour, maybe? Two? Longer than that?

The more she thought about it, the more she realized she couldn't simply entrust her life to fate. She hadn't done that when she'd beaten the odds up on the high-mountain trail, nor when she'd discovered the twisted wreckage of the airplane. She'd survived both incidents by drawing on her inner strength, her wile, and her smarts. And she would do that now.

Acting purely on impulse, she retreated to one of the stalls and locked the door. The cell phone Brian Walker had given her just minutes before he'd been struck down was one of the newer models, refurbished but functional enough to connect with the airport's free Wi-Fi. She found a modest signal, which allowed her to access one of the more popular travel websites listing airfares and accommodations around the world. She selected "one-way flights" and entered "ISB" for Islamabad, followed by "JFK" for her final destination.

The search turned up three flights leaving that same day, including the one-stop through London on which she was already booked. Mentally crossing that one off her list, she studied her other two choices: a single stop direct that had more than a twelve-hour layover in Abu Dhabi, or a two-stop with plane changes in Istanbul and Frankfurt. While she hated to land and take-off twice, the entire flight time was six hours less than the alternative. Plus, it was set to start boarding in less than twenty minutes, whereas the Abu Dhabi flight departed later that evening.

Without thinking twice, she booked the second of the two, paid the airfare with the credit card she'd snagged from her backpack, then downloaded the QR code for her boarding pass into her phone. She hated to run out on Fiona this way, but she could explain later, if and when she got the chance. Right now, it was a simple matter of survival.

Monica waited in the ladies' room until just before boarding time, then kept her head down as she exited in order to avert eye contact. She shuffled off in search of her new gate, trying not to attract attention, certain that with every step she was putting more distance between herself and the one-eyed man.

Then she almost bumped right into him. He was standing beside a concrete pillar that supported the buttressed ceiling, his eyes appearing desperate and determined. He looked down with disgust at the Pakistani woman who had brushed by him, and cursed her clumsiness. Monica mumbled something and straggled off, keeping her head down and trying not to limp. Could he be the same man who had crept into her hospital room the night before? The man who had taken the life of the poor woman who had switched beds with her?

She blended into the crowd at the gate where her flight to Istanbul was boarding, and kept to herself as she slowly edged forward with the rest of the passengers filing onto the plane. When she got to the head of the line the airline agent scanned the code on her screen, glanced at her identification, then waved her through the jet bridge door.

The aircraft was another Airbus, and Monica hobbled down the aisle, looking for the seat designated on her phone. She finally found it, relieved to see it was in the rear at the window. There was no one for her to crawl over, which allowed her to just squeeze in and pull the edge of her headscarf up around her face.

Finally, she was safe. Or maybe just *safer*. She exhaled a deep breath she'd been holding in her weary lungs, almost for fear that it might be her last. All she had in her possession was her passport, her phone, and her wallet with a single credit card in it—no toothbrush, no comb, not even a change of clothes. But for now, none of that was important. All that mattered was that she was on this plane, while the one-eyed man remained out there in the terminal, searching for her.

And, by the time he realized he'd run out of options, the plane would be out of Pakistani air space and she would be on her way home.

Chapter 15

The dented Peugeot pulled to a stop in front of the Hotel Salvador on a side street two blocks off *Carrer Prat de la Creu* near the center of Andorra le Vella. The capital of the tiny but wealthy Pyrenees nation was nestled snugly in the mountains between Spain and France, its claims to fame being its ski resorts, tax-haven status, and duty-free shopping.

The summer evening held a bit of a chill, and a gentle breeze trickled down through the rifts in the mountains to the north. The sulfuric essence of mineral springs and sap from trees that lined the ragged slopes hung in the air. The same full moon Phythian had viewed from the deck of his camp in the Serengeti just last evening was lurking behind a thin veil of alpine mist, occasionally peeking through in all its lunar splendor.

The flight from Nairobi to Barcelona had been an hour late taking off, but the pilot made up for lost time and actually touched down twenty minutes ahead of schedule. Phythian was traveling light—just a small backpack that could be slung over one shoulder—and he'd quickly caught a bus as far as Cardona. From there he'd hitched a ride; even at such a late hour finding a willing driver hadn't been difficult, his unique powers of persuasion being what they were.

He'd found the two-star Hotel Salvador on an app on his phone, and had asked the driver to let him off there in order to keep his true destination a secret. Chances were good that the security cameras at Barcelona-El Prat Airport had picked him up at some point between the gate and the exit, and right now a computer algorithm somewhere in the world likely was analyzing minuscule touchpoints of his face in the crowd. If one of those software programs happened to score a hit on his biometrics, the G3 would know within seconds that he was in Spain and—best guess—headed toward the landlocked country of Andorra. When questioned, the driver of the Peugeot could only truthfully say that he'd dropped him off in front of a no-frills hotel with rates equal to that of a bare-bones youth hostel, and which had mostly poor ratings on TripAdvisor.

A small storefront just steps up a narrow stone alleyway off *Av. Princep Benlloch* billed itself—in large letters painted on the front glass—as *cerrajería veinticuatro horas*. In smaller lettering the sign further read, *Hablamos Catalán, Castellano, Francés, e Inglés*. While the sole proprietor—a proud French nationalist named Martin Beaudin—was, indeed, a certified locksmith who spoke four languages and whose services were available in emergencies twenty-four hours a day, his services rarely were called for and he generally kept to himself.

On the other hand, his father had been a renowned resistance fighter and devoted intelligence officer during the war, and was a widely heralded recipient of the Legion of Honor, Order of Liberation, Military Medal, and *le Croix de Guerre*. It was during a ceremony bestowing one of these awards, after the fall of the Third Reich, that the elder Beaudin had met an enterprising young British spy named Thaddeus Stone. After much cajoling and a good deal of wine, the impassioned agent had persuaded the French war hero to join forces with a small cadre of like-minded loyalists who were taking it upon themselves to hunt down the post-war Nazi scourge. In this capacity, the fearless *beau ideal* was to become one of the architects of the clandestine Greenwich Global Group, and had served briefly as its chairman until a stroke dropped him to his knees on the Champs Elysees in the center of his beloved Paris.

The young Martin Beaudin had been unaware of his father's covert activities until shortly after the old man's death in the early nineties. Following a hero's funeral held with highest military honors at Ablain St.-Nazaire French Military Cemetery, Mr. Stone—the organization's new Chairman and last living co-founder—personally traveled to Andorra La Vella to recruit the young man into the fold. Again, after much conversation and fine wine, Beaudin Jr.—who only recently had departed his native France for the clean, cool air of the Pyrenees—pledged his fealty to the G3. Which, he was only to learn later, had long ago shifted its mission from one of justice and valor to a more duplicitous aspiration of net yield and profit.

While Beaudin—aka *Le Serrurier*—occasionally did grind new keys and replace old locks in the small yet bustling Andorran capital, he spent a disproportionate amount of time serving as the G3's Director of Records and Archives. It was a position in which he kept track of every extralegal mission the Group ever engaged in—past, present, and still in the pipeline. These records were stored on a proprietary cloud server in an unidentified building on a nameless street hundreds of miles away in Luxembourg, and dated all the way back to the group's first successful mission, which involved the fatal shooting of three former SS officers in a dance hall in Salzburg in early 1946.

Since that first operation more than seven decades ago, the G3 had successfully completed four thousand, eight hundred sixty-one life-ending assignments, and it was *Le Serrurier*'s responsibility to guard the details of every one of them. The latest entry was the autoerotic death of Supreme Court Justice Colin Wheeler last night in Washington and, if all went according to plan, the next would be the execution of Monica Cross later today in Frankfurt. Inexplicably, the intrepid photographer had eluded her assigned killer in Islamabad, a mid-level freelancer with local connections who had been engaged at the last minute to poison her as she was leaving Pakistan. His failure to complete his task had been dealt with quickly and permanently, per the G3's sworn covenant with its independent contractors.

Le Serrurier was home, no question about it. Phythian sensed him upstairs, asleep in his bed on the third floor. *Good*. Alone, which also was good. Furthermore, his brain indicated he was in a non-rapid-eye movement sleep, which indicated he wasn't dreaming. Even better news, since Phythian found it easier to penetrate a sleeping mind that wasn't cluttered with the baffling layers of disorientation that characterized the common REM dream state.

Five seconds later, Phythian had extracted from the slumbering locksmith's dormant memory the six-digit code to the push-button lock to the side door, as well as the four numbers that deactivated the security alarm. Keeping his senses alert in order to detect whether the brain upstairs suddenly lurched awake, he entered the numbers into the keypad and pushed the door inward on hinges that had been oiled recently. He then turned off the motion detectors and cameras, and made his way to the staircase that led to the bedroom three flights above.

A thick carpet runner muffled his ascent, and when he stepped onto the top landing, he stealthily made his way to the master chamber door. It was cracked open, just enough to circulate some of the refreshing mountain air, and Phythian gave it a gentle nudge the rest of the way.

He stood in the darkness a moment, absorbing the geography of the room and once again assessing the sleeping man's brain waves. Then he said, in a voice barely more than a whisper, "*Heure de se réveiller, Le Serrurier.*"

"*C'est quoi ce bordel?*" the aging Frenchman grunted, half-asleep and wondering if he might be dreaming. Which, of course, he hadn't been.

"*Bonsoir, Monsieur Beaudin,*" Phythian replied, an unnerving sharpness in his voice. "Or should I say, *bonjour,* given the early hour?"

"*Qui es-tu par Dieu?*" Le Serrurier asked, blinking his eyes in the dark. "*Qui diable ates-vous?*"

"You know who I am, Martin. *Donnez une minute.*" Give it a minute.

The aging son of the dead French war hero did just that, and Phythian sensed the electro-chemical reaction crackling in his brain. He could have helped the old locksmith out with a mental nudge—pushing the correct answer into his head—but he wanted Beaudin to figure this out on his own, however long it took.

It took a while, given the disorientation from being jolted out of a deep sleep and the worrisome presence of a stranger lurking in his dark room. But eventually Beaudin, who by this time was sitting up in his bed, the lights still out, whispered, "*Mon Dieu, tu es* Phythian—"

The name came out like an icy filament of dread, an unease that accompanied the mention of a dark entity of whom one dared not speak, an enemy one had hoped was long dead but feared someday would show up to exact unspeakable revenge.

Phythian lowered himself into a Queen Anne chair in a corner that seemed darker than the rest of the room, only the vague outline of his figure visible in the gloomy shadows. "Give the Frenchman a cigar," he said.

"But...why have you come here?" Beaudin asked, this time in English, which seemed appropriate since the lettering on the window down at the street mentioned it was one of four languages spoken within. "Are you going to kill me?"

"That choice is entirely up to you," Phythian replied.

Martin Beaudin shook his head briskly and pleaded, "Just tell me what you want, *s'il vous plaît.*"

"Surely the brilliant locksmith and keeper of all G3 secrets doesn't fear a specter who pays an unexpected visit in the middle of the night."

"I'm not a fan of ghost stories," Beaudin informed him with a noticeable shudder. "And whatever you think you know of me, you are mistaken."

"I know that you are a dispirited man, no friends to speak of, no future other than to fix locks and drink wine in this peculiar mountain town. And to keep the secrets of the dead."

"I like my life here in Andorra just fine."

"You can tell yourself that, but I sense a deep melancholy about you tonight. A deep-rooted feeling of apprehension and discord."

"Feeling of *what*? What the devil are you talking about?"

"Melancholy. *Ennui.* Perhaps you're even growing a touch suicidal."

"What? *Mon Dieu, non.*" But as soon as the words were out of his mouth, he realized a deep sense of despair enveloping him like a cloud of bees swarming around their queen. "I…I'm feeling nothing of the sort," he insisted.

Phythian didn't respond; didn't have to. Instead he mentally gripped the Frenchman—who was wearing nothing but cotton briefs with blown elastic around the waist—and caused him to sit up in his bed. A moment later Beaudin was on his feet, crossing the dark room to an antique wardrobe in the corner, opening the double doors and reaching into the darkness. His hands fumbled through a mound of winter sweaters piled on an upper shelf, and finally pulled out a Luger P08 Pistol, manufactured at the Royal Arsenal at Erfurt, Germany. It was the same gun that had been acquired by his father from a dead Nazi that wintery night in Salzburg not long after the war, and used in a half-dozen subsequent assignments in the years since.

Without hesitating, and clearly without thinking, he put the gun to his head and slipped his finger across the trigger. He held it like that for a good five seconds, then five more before Phythian released his mental grip and Beaudin finally lowered the weapon to his side. He shook his head as if emerging from some sort of trance, then let the firearm clatter to the floor.

"Are we feeling better?" Phythian asked, a purely rhetorical question that drove home just how lethal he could be.

"*Mon Dieu*…you…almost killed me," Beaudin said with a stammer he hadn't experienced since his famous father had died.

"Correction," Phythian replied. "You almost killed yourself. I'm sure you're familiar with my file, so you know what I'm capable of."

Le Serrurier stood there, his underwear hanging off his buttocks, perspiring even though the room was chilled. A slight hint of fear hung in the air, or maybe that was just sweat from the near-death event he had just survived. He could see the Luger on the floor by his feet, and he made a motion to bend down to pick it up.

"Leave it," Phythian suggested. "Best not to give temptation a second chance."

Beaudin nodded and left the gun on the worn carpet, turned to face him. "So…what happens now?"

"Now you put on something a little more respectable and we go down to that lovely drawing room I passed on the way up the stairs. If I'm not mistaken, you have a very inviting Leroy Chambertin Grand Cru 1990 in the cellar hidden behind the bookcase, and we're going to share a glass."

"*Pour l'amour de Dieu*—they only produce seventy cases of that wine a year," Beaudin said. "It cost me thirty-five hundred Euros at auction—"

He caught himself mid-complaint, just as he sensed Phythian's grip start to hijack his brain again. He fought off another wave of depression and a growing urge to again reach down and pick up the gun, place the barrel in his mouth and savor the taste of oiled steel on his tongue. Then, just as quickly as it came, the sensation of despair disappeared and he felt a baffling surge of bliss.

"On the other hand, wine is a gift from God to be enjoyed with friends," he acquiesced. "And the bottle of which you speak should be right at its prime. Follow me."

The summer evening—or morning, as the clock on the mantle would have it—was too warm for a fire in the wood stove insert. In fact, Martin Beaudin continued to perspire from his near-suicidal experience upstairs, so he pulled open a pair of double glass doors to reveal the iron railing of a Juliet balcony and let in some of the fresh mountain air.

The thin mist that had filled the night a few hours earlier had dissipated, and a flush of light from the moon far above the darkened peaks filled the room. Phythian had taken a seat in a leather chair, well-worn oxblood with brass tacks, lumpy padding that seemed to have coagulated in the seat over the decades. Beaudin chose a gilded parlor chair with blue upholstery, set diagonally across an antique cocktail table fashioned with inlaid wood and mother of pearl. An open bottle of wine, covered with a thick layer of dust and faded label, sat in a hammered silver dish in the center.

"Tell me, to what do I owe the pleasure of this unexpected visit?" the locksmith asked his guest. His nerves had settled a bit, sensing that Phythian had not come with the express purpose of killing him. Not yet, at least.

Phythian studied the wine in his glass: a rich red, the color of the currants his mother used to turn into jam on crisp autumn afternoons. He raised it to his nose and gently inhaled the rich tannins and fruity, complex aroma. "Maybe I just wanted to finally make your acquaintance, after all these years," he eventually said.

Beaudin appeared to take pleasure in swirling his wine absently in a wide-bodied glass, but he had not yet tasted it. At fifty Euros a swallow, the anticipation was just as valuable as the drinking. "Not a likely scenario," he said. "As you surmised, I'm familiar with your file. You're here because you want something."

"And you, the locksmith, can provide me unlimited access to what I seek," Phythian confirmed with a minimal nod. "Willingly, or under duress. Your choice."

The Frenchman pressed his pudgy lips together in a resolute frown. "Not much of one, but I don't wish to quarrel. Just tell me… where do we begin?"

Since this was not Phythian's bottle of *Cote de Nuits* and he had not been the one to pay such a ludicrous price for it, he took a long sip, noted what might be described as plums, earth, and sweet spice; and the currants that had come to mind previously.

"It's always good to begin with an understanding," he said.

"Then tell me—what is this the beginning of?"

"I could say 'a beautiful friendship,' since you're a weaselly little Frenchman and I'm an American ex-pat on foreign soil. But that's an over-used movie line, even if it is a classic. Also, I don't make friends, beautiful or otherwise. Let's just say this is the foundation of a *quid pro quo* arrangement."

"This for that," Beaudin said. "So…if I give you what you want, what do I get?"

"If you're smart, perhaps a few more years to live," Phythian replied with a tight grin.

Le Serrurier considered this a moment, finally took that fifty-Euro swallow. Unlike Phythian, he found the taste dusky yet palatable, well worth the wait. Cherries, cocoa, even a lingering hint of the Gitanes he'd smoked earlier, before he'd turned out the light and headed upstairs, three hours ago, now.

"Fair deal," he said. "Tell me, Monsieur Phythian: exactly what have you come to my little corner of the Pyrenees in search of?"

"Three things. Provide me with the answers I seek and I'll leave you be."

"How do you know I won't alert the G3 as soon as you walk out my door?"

"Knowing them, I'm quite confident they already know I'm here," Phythian replied, with a dismissive wave of his hand. "In fact, I'm kind of counting on it."

"I see," the Frenchman replied, his skin appearing to tighten in fear.

"Shall we get on with this, then?"

"Whatever you say. What information do you seek?"

"First: tell me about the flight from Haifa. The one designed to kill me. Who paid for it?"

Le Serrurier gulped, his Adam's apple visibly rising and falling in his throat. Anyone who had ever served the Greenwich Global Group in any capacity had sworn a loyalty oath never to divulge any of its business or its secrets. When The Chairman had approached him in the early nineties and asked him to join the fold in an executive capacity, he'd personally had made clear the mortal consequences of violating this sacred vow. Beaudin understood the stakes here, knew that if he even considered betrayal, he'd be dead within days. Then again, if he defied Phythian, he might be dead within mere seconds.

"It was a pool party," he finally said, averting his eyes to the floor. Feeling the burn of shame for not enduring even a flicker of torture before caving to his fears.

Phythian knew the term, how it worked. At times a contract was too expensive for one customer to pay full freight, and the cost was spread around to a pool of interested parties.

"This pool party—how much, and who attended?" he asked.

"Twelve million for the full job," Beaudin told him. "CIA, MI6, Aussies, Germans, and SVR. All the major players wanted a stake in it."

"And the buy-in?"

"Two million each."

"Two times five is ten," Phythian pointed out.

"There was a private investor, as well. An *Américain* millionaire with political aspirations to protect. And a dirty little secret he wanted to keep buried at all costs."

"Would I know him?"

"If you follow American politics," *Le Serrurier* said.

"And I was the target?"

Beaudin couldn't stop his betrayal of the G3 and The Chairman even if he wanted to. Phythian's eyes were boring into him, and behind them was the incredible power of a highly persuasive mind molded by the best strategic psy-ops trainers in the world.

"Everyone on that plane was a pigeon but yes, you were the primary mark." He wanted to ask why Phythian had shot them all, since that was not part of his official mission, but worried that such a question might lead to unnecessary pain, for which he admittedly had minimal tolerance.

"For what gain?" Phythian asked. "Why such drastic measures?"

"The G3 doesn't like it when its employees color outside the lines," Beaudin replied. "In your case, they were troubled by that *ad hoc* incident involving the Vatican."

This brought a nod of comprehension, and a hairline grin formed on Phythian's lips. "The cardinal was a pedophile and serial rapist," he said. "You may believe that Jesus died for your sins, but that prick definitely died for his."

"The Holy See was a good, repeat customer. What you did to him didn't sit too well with the board."

"They were afraid I'd start taking matters into my own hands."

"*Tout à fait exact,*" *Le Serrurier* confirmed. "You were too lethal to let you go rogue, and our partners were starting to get nervous. What if one of them unwittingly crossed you and became a target? You could control their minds, make them do whatever your whim dictated."

"The world needs checks and balances," Phythian said with a shrug.

"So noted," Beaudin said as he found himself pouring another four hundred Euros' worth of wine into his guest's glass. "In any event, the G3 weighed *les avantages et inconvénients*, and a decision was made. Your value to them was immeasurable, but your elimination would be worth the loss. In the end it was agreed that you had to be removed."

Beaudin confirmed what Phythian already had concluded: In those last few weeks before the flight from Haifa, he had begun to feel a personal sense of moral outrage, both for all the lives he had taken but also toward the organization that compensated him generously to take them. It was this outrage, in part, that had caused him to precipitate the untimely death of Cardinal Allessio Giudice as he stepped in front of a truck while crossing Via Gregorio VII in Rome. Such extracurricular measures were neither condoned nor approved by the G3, and he'd quickly perceived there was a unified call to have him terminated. It was a fact that at first had infuriated him but which, over time, he'd come to appreciate as a gift.

"Clever move, hiring me to ditch the plane over the Med," he replied after considerable thought. "While at the same time bringing in an unconnected third party to blow it up, with the intention that I wouldn't get wind of it. Blame the terrorists."

"There's always a group eager to take credit for such things."

"And everything would have worked if I hadn't found the Gruyere in the galley," Phythian said. "With a Slovakian detonator embedded in it."

"I didn't know the details of the plan until long after the fact," Beaudin said. He would have liked to take another sip of wine, but fear was causing his hands to tremble too much to hold the glass without shaking. Any second he expected a volley of gunshots to rip through the windows of his house, killing them both. The G3 could work fast when it had a collective mind to do so, and he personally knew that at least two *mécaniques* lived within an hour of Andorra de Vella.

Phythian sensed the paranoia simmering in *Le Serrurier*'s head, but knew for a fact the G3 was nowhere nearby, at least not within a thousand yards, the outer limit of his mental range. "No need to worry," he consoled him. "We're safe here for at least little while longer."

Beaudin detested Phythian's ability to pick through his brain, afraid more than anything what other stray memories he might find in there. In an attempt to distract and deflect, he again pondered a question that had been bothering him ever since he'd learned about the *femme photographe* who had found the wreckage in the mountains of Pakistan. This time he decided to mention it.

"What point was there in shooting them?" he asked. "All those people on that plane?"

"I couldn't run the risk of someone on board playing hero and try to land it after I bailed out," Phythian said. "Also, shooting them would make it impossible for anyone to declare their deaths accidental if they were ever found. Rest assured; there was no torment and no one suffered."

After thirty years of dedicated devotion to the G3 cause, *Le Serrurier* had ceased to give much thought to human suffering and torment. It was a residual hazard of the job, as worrying about such things tended to play tricks with even the shallowest of consciences, and led to a lack of focus and concentration.

"So that's it?" he asked as he finally ventured another sip of wine. "That's what brought you here to my corner of the Pyrenees on this beautiful summer evening?"

"Not quite. There's still the matter of Equinox."

If Beaudin had seemed visibly stirred from the mention of the plane crash, he was clearly shaken by the reference to the G3's darkest secret. "*C'est quoi ce bordel?*" he blurted out as he squirmed in his chair, his pretense of calm abruptly replaced by a very real feeling of dread.

Phythian gauged the sudden shift of fear but said nothing to assuage it. Instead he unzipped a pocket in his money belt and pulled out a black device about the size of a smart phone. The corporate logo of its manufacturer was embossed on it, and it affixed to it was a label that read:

EQUINOX

He gave it a cursory glance, then handed it over.

"*Baise moi,*" the Frenchman uttered under his breath as he held the hard drive in both hands. "*Où as tu trouvé ça?*"

"It was on the plane, in a Faraday case," Phythian said. "And please, let's keep it to English, shall we?"

Beaudin nodded but seemed not to hear. He turned the device over in his hands, slowly, staring at it in great wonder. He examined the power slot and twin data ports in the back, then reluctantly handed it back, gently, as if it were a Faberge egg.

"*Vous n'avez aucune idée de ce que c'est*," he muttered, his words no more than a sigh.

"I told you, *English*," Phythian reminded him. "And yes, I do know what this is. It says right on it. And to answer the next question you're too afraid to ask, yes, I have fully examined its contents."

"*Nique ta mère*," Beaudin said as the color drained from his face. "If you've seen it, then why ask about it?"

"I want to know how the G3 could have been this sloppy. Allowing its entire archives to be hacked and copied onto a drive that then fell into the wrong hands. How are you even alive after a breach of security like that?"

"A thorough internal review determined that the lapse, as monumental as it was, was the direct fault of a former executive board member. He was terminated—with extreme prejudice, I might add—and replaced."

"The same way I was thought to be terminated with extreme prejudice?"

"I had nothing to do with that decision," Beaudin assured him, his trembling hands causing his wine to ripple in his glass. "*S'il vous plaît croyez-moi.*"

"I have no reason not to believe you," Phythian assured him. In fact, he'd already downloaded a significant amount of data from the locksmith's brain that verified what Beaudin was saying. It also confirmed that the terminated board member had been replaced by a government wonk named Adam Clayburn, whom Beaudin had never met and apparently did not think very highly of. "And all the same, the Equinox drive ended up on that plane—*my plane*—inside a protective bag, along with five innocent people who were targeted for me to kill."

"A job you took—and completed—quite willingly," Beaudin reminded him, the words slipping out before he could stop them.

"The devices of the wicked lead only to treachery," Phythian said, the chill in his gray eyes returning.

Le Serrurier inhaled a deep breath, certain he was committing suicidal treachery of his own, convinced that The Chairman somehow would learn of this wine-fueled chat within hours: probably knew about it already, listening in with high-tech surveillance devices, even though this residence and the storefront downstairs were swept every couple of days.

"Within the G3's singular frame of reference, it seemed easier to clean up the entire mess with one discreet mission," he explained.

"And eliminate me in the process," Phythian replied.

"Win-win, as you Americans call it. And like I said, not my decision."

"But you know the details. The Equinox drive contains the particulars of every sanction the G3 assigned since its inception. Executed presidents, billionaires, religious quacks, reporters, actors. A conspiracist's wet dream."

"What do you want from me?"

"The files on this drive were downloaded three weeks before I got on that plane, when the main server in Luxembourg was hacked. That means the details of my pool party—as you so aptly put it—aren't on it. I want names, dates, everything."

Mon Dieu, he knows about Luxembourg? Beaudin did his best to neither confirm nor deny what Phythian apparently already knew, but ultimately it was a lost cause. "That might take hours," he said, doing his best not to glance at the clock on the mantle.

Phythian picked up the bottle, which was half full. Although this fussy Frenchman who overpaid for wine seemed to be the sort of pessimist who would perceive it as half-empty.

"I'm in no hurry if you're not," he said, as he poured himself another measure.

Chapter 16

"You're going to think I'm nuts, but I'm writing my next piece on Justice Wheeler."

Carter Logan announced this as he poured half a splash of pinot noir into his glass. At twenty-two dollars a bottle it was a bit pricey, since he could buy the same wine for six-ninety-nine at the Trader Joe's on 25th Street. But he'd just received his biweekly check from the publishing syndicate, which convinced him he could afford a few extra dollars and go out for dinner.

"Seriously?" asked the woman seated across the table from him. Her name was Raleigh and she was, as the name suggested, from North Carolina—Apex, actually, about ten miles west of her namesake city. She was the reason they had come to this restaurant tonight, a trendy neighborhood joint at the edge of Kalorama called Dixie's and locally famous for its mac and cheese and collard greens. You can take the girl out of the country, but not the other way around. "Why would you want to put yourself through that?"

"You sound skeptical," he said as he raised his glass to his lips.

They were well into their meal—Dutch treat—and Raleigh was finishing a bite of her shrimp tacos. She swallowed, then replied, "What's there to write about? The pervert died while waxing his carrot and watching kiddie porn."

Logan almost spit out the wine, managed to swallow it without choking. "I can always trust you to provide solid visuals," he said with a laugh.

"Don't get me started," she replied. She was an intense woman: dark, penetrating eyes, strong cheekbones, mocha skin that a former artist

119

boyfriend had described as Pantone 161. She was the first child of an infamous interracial marriage that had helped to kill Jim Crow in her home state, and now she captivated a broad, multi-ethnic cable audience throughout the Washington metro viewing area. "The jokes have been circulating through the newsroom ever since the story broke. Unless this different angle of yours really is different, I'd drop it."

"I appreciate your concerns," Logan assured her as he took a bite of fried chicken that was too good to be anything close to healthy. "But I've done a bit of digging, and I've got a different angle on the case."

Raleigh bit her lower lip and studied him intently. "A different angle?" she said.

He raised his glass, almost as if in a toast. "A theory no one else is looking at."

Two years ago, Carter Logan and Raleigh Durham—*yes, her parents had actually done that to her*—had been an item; not a protracted item, nor one that was particularly intense or impassioned. *Passionate*, yes, and at times even romantic, but only for a few weeks, until they both realized they were using each other to soften their own respective rebounds. She had just broken up with the artist boyfriend, and Logan continued to make the mistake of calling out "*Katya*" at the most inappropriate moments. Blurting out your deceased fiancé's name during a heated session of sex might be excusable the first time, but doing it repeatedly is grounds for having your shoes hurled at you in the dark.

Fortunately, Carter and Raleigh reached the same conclusion at roughly the same time and decided it was best if they pulled back on the romance and focused on being friends. It was a word that rarely went over well during a break-up but, since they weren't really breaking up and the feeling was mutual, it was more respectable. And it allowed for certain extra-friendly benefits if and when the mood struck.

Tonight probably wouldn't lead to such benefits, since Logan was more focused on the article he was writing than he was on her.

"What is it?" she asked him. "Your theory, I mean."

"I'm not sure I should tell you."

"You think I'm going to steal this wonderful, crazy idea of yours?" she replied, pretending to be offended.

No, he didn't think that at all. In fact, he was worried that Raleigh—

whom he loved and respected in many and varied ways, past and present—might come to think he was a complete moron.

"I believe you're going to look at me as if I've totally lost my mind."

"Why should tonight be any different?" she said with a grin. "But go ahead—try me."

Rubber, meet road, he thought. It was time to either go all in, or change the subject. Too late for that, of course, and besides: he actually welcomed her opinion. What he really wanted—*needed*—was for her to hammer him from every angle, logical and plausible and otherwise, see if his idea could withstand all her journalistic pummeling. And Jesus, was she a damned fine journalist, two local Emmys and a host of other awards during her eight years on the air here in Washington, before jumping ship to cable news.

"I think Wheeler was murdered," he told her. "Framed to make it look like he was choking the chicken."

She said nothing for the longest time, as if she were struggling with telling him she thought he had lost all credulity as a journalist. In fact, she'd been about to take another bite of taco, but she set it back on her plate and then actually cocked her head. She leaned forward, fixing him with those brown eyes that reminded him of Hershey's kisses, and said, "There are so many problems with that theory that I don't know where to begin."

"You think I'm delusional?"

"Well, there's that," she replied with an endearing chuckle. "But I'm talking about all the facts of the case."

"Which facts?" he asked, shoveling a forkful of mac and cheese into his mouth.

"Let's begin with the murder scene itself."

"See? You're already admitting it was a murder—"

"I'm just pacifying you," Raleigh told him. "But I'll start again. Let's begin with the scene of the crime—and remember, suicide is a crime. Justice Wheeler was alone. Locked in his room. No one else was there. No forced entry, no sign of a struggle."

"He knew the person and let him in. Or her."

"How did he end up naked, in a chair?" she asked.

"Wasn't hard to convince you, last time," he reminded her with a wink.

"That was different. But okay, smarty-pants. Let's go that way. What was he doing in that hotel suite?"

"You already know the answer to that," Logan replied. "He regularly reserved it under an assumed name every six weeks or so. You reported that tonight."

Raleigh chewed the last bite of her taco, the spicy sauce of which dribbled down her chin while she spoke. "But remember: his wife was out of town. He could have just stayed home."

"Which makes sense, if he was just going to beat his own drum," Logan agreed. "But a hotel room would be much more discreet if he expected someone to show up."

"Then let me ask you, Cart." Her nickname for him, which had stuck even though he hated it, because it's what his older sister had called him since he was four years old. "Wheeler had hundreds of pictures and videos on the laptop that was found in his room. *His laptop.* Each one of them downloaded on different days, over a three-year period. How do you explain that?"

Logan trickled some more wine in his glass, eyed the level to make sure he wasn't taking more than his share. "I have to admit, that had me stumped, too. But then I talked to a friend who told me there's a lot of software on the market that can permanently modify the time and date a file was created, or last opened. Comes in handy for law firms or political campaigns that need to cover their tracks."

She studied him intently, and he could see her mind going to work on what he'd just told her. Finally, she said, "There's got to be something on the hard drive that would allow a forensic investigator to find the original 'create date'—"

He nodded and said, "As my friend told me, FBI analysts can determine the true history of file date/time changes, as set by the computer's internal clock. But not always, if the software that was used was advanced or proprietary. Especially if no one suspects murder in the first place."

"You think Wheeler just sat idly by while the perp entered the room and set up this elaborate scheme to kill him and destroy his reputation?"

"No. I suspect he was drugged with something that acted fast and then dissipated just as quickly. Another friend—an EMT out in Fairfax County—told me there's these things called neuromuscular blockades, usually used in ambulances and emergency rooms, that can knock a person flat for about six or seven minutes. Enough time to perform a tracheotomy, that sort of thing. The person blacks out and is completely submissive and compliant, and the drug dissolves quickly in the bloodstream. After a few hours it leaves little to no trace at all."

"You've really thought this through," she observed when he'd finished. "You're really going to do this."

"I'm already well into it," he confessed. "Look: we already know the who, what, where, and when of Wheeler's death. Hotel suite, autoerotic asphyxia, the night before last. What we don't know is the why. Or how much it cost."

"And you aim to figure that out." It was a statement, not a question.

"You're not even a tiny bit curious?"

"Look, Carter." *Carter* this time, not *Cart*. "You know I admire the hell out of you, your sense of ethics and justice. You go places no one else cares to go, and sometimes it takes you out on a limb that could come crashing down, with you on it. That takes a special type of person."

Logan picked up the remains of his fried chicken but didn't take a bite. Raleigh had never been condescending in the past, and he chose to believe she was just being truthful, in her own endearing way. He looked her in the eye and said, "I write a syndicated blog that pays shit. I drink cheap wine, and I have to re-use my coffee grounds just to get some caffeine into a cup. I have no budget for serious research, no assistants who can do the legwork for me."

"You're saying I do?" She could have been offended by his insinuation, but their friendship was the kind that stood up well to criticism, implied or inferred.

"I'm saying that I can't prove Wheeler was murdered other than suggesting basic 'what-ifs,' but someone else—with the correct tools— might have the nads to dig a little deeper."

Raleigh Durham chewed her lower lip, as if it were part of her last taco. Eventually she moved to her upper lip, until she had lipstick on all her front teeth. "Don't take this as anything other than a statement from one friend to another, okay? Promise?"

"Whatever it is, I promise."

"And as you may recall, I don't have gonads."

"The lack thereof being a prime cause of physical attraction."

Even though she rolled her eyes, she was reminded that it was his aberrant sense of humor that had drawn her to him in the first place. "This piece you're writing—I want you to show it to me when you finish it."

"Then you think I'm on to something?"

"I'm not saying that," she clarified for him. "But I do have resources, and I do have assistants who enjoy doing legwork. I might be able to convince someone to take a look, if I see a strong enough case to do so."

"I knew I loved you for a reason."

"Down, boy. I did say 'might' and 'if.'"

"And I did use the past tense," Logan told her, offering her an appreciative grin. "Any event, that's why you make the big bucks."

"My contract is up for renewal at the end of the year, so we'll see how that goes. And I think you're ignoring something else entirely. Actually, a big thing."

"And what is that?" he asked.

She fell silent again, as if deciding the best way to get into it. Then she said, "Well, if you're right about this—and that is a big if—whoever pulled it off isn't going to like you poking around their shit."

"I appreciate the advice, and I'll keep that in mind."

"And there's something else," she then said.

"I knew there had to be a shoe dropping somewhere," he replied. "What is it?"

"I want you to promise—if I ever find myself sleeping over at your place again—that you will never, ever make a pot of coffee with yesterday's grounds. That is beyond disgusting."

"Deal," he agreed, clinking his glass to hers. "Which begs the question, what are you doing for breakfast tomorrow?"

"Is that an invitation?"

"It's one of the benefits of having a beautiful friendship," he told her.

"So is saying 'no' on a work night."

Chapter 17

After polishing off the bottle of pricey Grand Cru 1990 and coming to a mutually agreeable accord that spared his life, Martin Beaudin had eagerly offered Phythian the use of his Citroen C4. After a perilous pre-dawn drive down the treacherous Port d'Envalira Pass switchbacks of eastern Andorra, he'd parked it in the long-term lot at the Toulouse-Blagnac airport. How it would find its way back home to Andorra was not his concern.

Their conversation had ended on a cordial note, influenced by the wine and the subtle reminder of death that seemed to linger in the shadows. By the time the last drops of *Cote de Nuits* trickled down their respective throats, it seemed as if they were long-lost friends reunited by chance in the Pyrenees. Of course, both men assumed they now were targets of the G3: Phythian for having the stones to return to Europe after pulling off the flight to nowhere, and Beaudin for hosting him and presumably giving up the organization's closely held confidences.

The earliest nonstop flight from Toulouse to Frankfurt was via a cheap no-frills airline with advertising plastered on the overhead bins and coin-operated locks on the restroom doors. *Fifty Euro cents to empty one's bladder or bowels.* Since there were no first-class seats on this plane, Phythian had been forced to fly in the crowded main cabin, jammed against a window in row eleven and next to a spongy man who clearly had no sense of personal hygiene and whose overwhelming fetor was intruding on his personal space.

No food was served on the flight, but Phythian had purchased a croissant at *Le Panorama* near his departure gate. He picked at it now as he sipped a cup of watery coffee the flight attendant had brought, his mind drifting back to that defining morning years ago when his life seemed to have reached a vital juncture that set his path at a right angle to everything that had happened up to that point. He'd recently severed his ties with the Marines, accepting the general discharge that was being offered rather than face charges stemming from an incident in Okinawa that was not of his doing. Military brass didn't want to prosecute him, nor did they wish to have him within their ranks any longer than necessary. A mutual agreement between judges advocate had been reached, and Phythian had been set free to do his own thing—as long as he never spoke about the incident involving one Captain Harding, nor the reconstructive surgeries that followed.

Phythian had saved a good chunk of his military pay and set off on a spiritual journey that took him to India, Myanmar, Bali, and Vietnam. He visited temples, lit lots of incense, prayed with priests and monks. He grew his hair and didn't shave. At various times along this mind-adjusting journey he'd meditated with gurus and shamans, and evaluated the fantastical magical mystery tour his life had become.

One December morning in California changed all that.

Like many other men and women and misfits of all stripes in search of divine guidance or altered consciousness, Phythian had found himself in San Francisco following his metaphysical wanderings across southeastern Asia. He'd done all he could in his quest to make peace with the cacophony of voices that had constantly droned in his head ever since he was dragged out of the icy water that lifechanging day as a child. Voices he came to understand were the actual thoughts of people around him, that he somehow could hear even though there was no sound. At first, he thought he was going insane, or that some sort of psychosis had set in with the onset of puberty, maybe schizophrenia, but more likely all of the above.

He'd landed at SFO two days ago, and was crashing at the home of a woman friend he'd made in Hanoi, who had succumbed easily to his mental nudge for sex, but with whom he'd also ended up having a remarkable time wandering along the shore of *Hồ Hoàn Kiếm*, exploring the shops and restaurants of the *Ba Dinh*, watching the *Múa Rối Nước*.

Her name was Annette Houston, pronounced like the Texas city and not the Manhattan street, and it was the first time in many years that he'd felt comfortable inside his own skin. By his standards she was beautiful, with auburn hair and pale skin spotted with a full constellation of freckles and eyes that caused the word *cerulean* to come to mind, framed by retro glasses that looked like they came from the donation box at Lenscrafters. She was fun and spirited, and toward the end of their eight days together they began talking about *after*. After this unexpected Asian escapade ran its course, after they returned to their previous lives.

Even in Hanoi things cost money, and Annette's ran out first. She went home, lots of goodbye kisses at the airport and promises to stay in touch. Ten days later he'd found himself shelling over the remains of his savings for a one-way ticket, and twenty-four hours after that he was knocking at her door in Oakland. He was broke but, given his aptitude for mental persuasion, that had never been a concern. It was interesting how many people gladly would hand over their last dollar to a stranger when they suddenly had a perplexing yet overwhelming compulsion to do so.

The government first initiated contact with Phythian three months after the Twin Towers had come down. Two weeks before Christmas on a particularly chilly morning in the Bay Area, he found himself riding the BART red line from the Ashby station near Berkeley into San Francisco. Annette was crazy for *The Nutcracker*, so he'd purchased half-price tickets for a matinee performance and they'd arranged to meet in front of Macy's at Union Square at noon.

The NSA spook had boarded the train at the West Oakland stop, and moments later he'd taken a seat across the aisle from Phythian. He wore a black overcoat and a fedora that looked like the hat Frank Sinatra wore on the Christmas album Phythian's parents played when he was a kid. The man pretended to read a copy of *Sports Illustrated* and did not glance up at his mark as he casually skimmed the pages of the magazine.

Thirty seconds after the train pulled out of the station Phythian nudged the man with the toe of his weathered loafer and said, "Why are you following me?"

The man pretended to ignore him and kept reading, causing Phythian to bump him with his toe again. "What do you want with me?" he asked.

Several passengers cast nervous glances at him, as if someone was always doing something strange on BART. "Look, mister," Phythian said, his voice louder and more direct. "Or should I say *doctor*? We both know why you're here, so quit the fucking games."

The man put the magazine down and folded his hands in his lap. "I'm sorry, young man, but I don't know what you're talking about—"

"Of course, you do, Dr. Segal. *David*. You arrived last night from Washington on American Airlines. Business class. The seats next to you on the plane were empty, because people are a little skittish about flying these days. You have a return ticket for tonight, the red-eye, landing tomorrow a little after five in the morning. How am I doing?"

The man, who really *was* a doctor named David Segal, started jiggling his left foot—an old habit when he started to get excited about something. It was clear he was trying to decide how to play this, how to deny what Phythian had just said. And it was equally clear that he knew there was no point, because Phythian was already several moves ahead of him.

"You're good," is what Segal finally said. "Exceptional, I might say, since you haven't had any formal training at this."

"Are you going to tell me what *this* is about? Why you're following me?"

"You're wrong about that," Dr. Segal replied. "You were already on the train when I boarded."

"You had someone at the Ashby station call you on that phone you have in your pocket. A woman, five-feet-seven, short blond hair. Jillian, spelled with a 'J.' She told you I got on the second car."

David Segal said nothing, just nodded in awe of Phythian's ability. He glanced out the window at the dark tunnel wall, mindful that they were now beneath San Francisco Bay, not a comforting place to be, given the global threat of terrorism at the time. Eventually he looked back at Phythian and said, "You got all that from my head?"

"Low-hanging fruit. So, Doc…are you going to tell me why you went to all this trouble to deny meeting me?"

"Operational assessment," Segal told him. "It's what we prefer to do with first contact."

Phythian studied the man a moment, eyeing the old shaving scars on his cheeks and the remains of a blister on his upper lip. "Are you going to tell me who this 'we' is, or do I have to pull that out of your head, too?" he finally asked.

"I'm not authorized to do that," Dr. Segal explained, his left foot jiggling now like Buddy Rich pounding a base drum riff. "My role is strictly one of clinical observation."

"This observation—how's it going up to this point?"

"Better than expected, I must say."

Phythian fixed his eyes on Segal's, stared at him until the government shrink felt an electrostatic tightening inside his skull, which was followed by a chill not dissimilar to a brain freeze one would get from biting into a rock-hard ice cream bar.

"Are you feeling all right?" Phythian asked, almost goading him.

"I…you…what the fuck are you doing?" Dr. Segal asked him, as he tried to break free from Phythian's mental grip.

"An observational assessment of my own."

Phythian glanced around, spotted an elderly black woman at the far end of the car immersed in a copy of *The Life of Pi*, which he had read while in Thailand just weeks before. She was heavyset and wore a red hat with a small cluster of dried flowers stuck in a band of purple. A mischievous look came to Phythian's face as he looked back at the doctor, then closed his eyes and pushed hard with his brain.

A momentary look of panic caused Segal's eyes to open wide. Then, without saying a word, he rose to his feet and gripped the grab bar to steady himself in the rattling car. Two seconds later he was making his way down the aisle, coming to a stop directly in front of the woman with the hat.

"Excuse me, ma'am, but you are a truly dazzling specimen of pure beauty," he told her. "I would very much like to touch your breast."

With that he leaned down and planted the palm of his hand on her ample bosom, at which point Phythian released him from his mental grip. At the same time the woman in the hat slapped him hard across the face and jumped to her feet.

"Pervert!" she screamed. "Get away from me! Sicko!"

Segal appeared to be frozen in place, then said, "I'm sorry, ma'am. I…I didn't mean to…I mean, oh, never mind."

All eyes in the car were on him as he made his way back up the aisle. The woman pulled out her flip phone, but she saw that there was no signal in the tunnel. A college kid with a molting soul patch looked as if he were considering attacking him, then thought better of it.

"That was cruel and uncalled for," Segal said to Phythian when he had settled back into his seat. "She could get me arrested."

"She won't," Phythian assured him. "I have everything under control."

The doctor glanced over his shoulder at the woman, who appeared to have forgotten the entire incident and was buried in her book again.

"The people I work with totally underestimated you," the psychiatrist said, his heart pounding from his unstoppable indecent behavior. And from the incredible talent he had just witnessed in the flesh. Phythian didn't seem like a particularly likeable guy, but he'd never met a raw recruit who was.

"So, are you going to tell me about this thing called The Farm?" Phythian had asked him. "Or do you think should we attempt another observational assessment?"

Chapter 18

Diana Petrie stepped off the elevator into the twenty-first-floor hallway. It was early, just before six in the morning, and she could have used a few more hours' sleep after dealing with the headaches that continued to mount from the Pakistan situation. But the Chairman had sent her a text thirty minutes ago demanding that she be in the office by the top of the hour, so here she was, punching numbers into the digital keypad, turning off the alarm system, and deactivating an array of defensive measures designed to ensure the security of the facilities within.

She could have spoken with him by encrypted phone from any room in her apartment, each of them with a view of the park, and all of them cozier than this dark, dusky office whose grass-paper walls and consignment furniture dated back to the seventies; maybe even the sixties. But The Chairman—who considered himself a technophile even though in reality he remained very much a luddite—was a stickler for protocol. *His* protocol, which dictated that Code Red conversations be conducted in the executive conference room, no exceptions. Thus, when he said "jump," people jumped. Not with the same results as when Phythian mentally issued the same command, but with enough gravitas to make one fear for his or her job security.

He was waiting for her when she entered the conference room and coaxed her computer screen to life. "Petrie," he greeted her with his raspy voice once she turned on the two-way videoconference relay. "My apologies for waking you up."

"You can't wake up what never sleeps," she replied. She wished she'd been able to pick up a cup of coffee on the way, but nothing was open this early in the morning. "What's this all about? Your text didn't say."

"Too sensitive," he replied. "But to answer your question now that you're here, Phythian has surfaced in Europe."

"He *what*?"

"Your boy appeared in facial recognition about twelve hours ago. Arrived in Barcelona on a nonstop from Nairobi. Cameras picked him up."

"Nairobi, as in Africa?" Petrie inquired.

"Unless they moved it," he said, his nose wrinkling as if he'd passed gas. "But it's the Barcelona part that gives us cause for concern."

She thought on this for about two seconds as his words sank in. "It's the largest international airport near Andorra," she said.

"Correct," The Chairman confirmed. "Our erstwhile friend paid a visit to the locksmith."

"What makes you think he went to see Beaudin?"

"It's predictable, and Beaudin himself sent a text to personally alert me after he left."

Which means he compromised us and is sucking up to you, she thought. "Did he say what Phythian wanted?" she asked instead.

"Information," The Chairman said. "He mostly asked about his last assignment, and who issued the kill order to take him out."

"We should have dispatched someone to run interference," Petrie lamented.

"Andorra's tucked away pretty tightly, only two roads in and out. Never would have gotten there in time."

"Did he say whether Phythian has a plan? Why he flew all the way from Africa—where I presume, he's been all this time—to visit the little locksmith in the Pyrenees?"

The Chairman didn't respond for a few moments, appearing on the screen as if he might collapse under the weight of his illness. Or perhaps it was just the weight of an unfortunate situation that seemed to be going from bad to worse. Eventually he said, "He apparently was particularly interested in the twit who stumbled upon the plane in the mountains."

"Monica Cross."

"He wanted to know our plans to terminate her."

"If he asked that, he knows about Equinox," Petrie surmised.

"How do you figure?" The Chairman countered.

"He believes we'd have no interest in her if she hadn't possibly been exposed to that hard drive. Which tells us he knows it was on board that plane, as well. Beaudin didn't mention it?"

"Not a damned word, but I sent a debriefing team to follow up." A euphemism that needed no clarification. "Should be at his place in a couple hours."

Good, Petrie thought. *Saves me the effort.* "Did he happen to mention what he told Phythian?" she asked him. "About the Cross woman, I mean?"

"The truth," The Chairman replied. "The first leg of her flight home from Islamabad to London was delayed on the ground. Fake bomb report. Clever little twit booked another flight, this one to Frankfurt, and she's due to land—" he checked his watch "—about forty minutes from now."

"We should have dispatched her when she got to Istanbul," she said.

"Our closest contractor was in Cyprus and we couldn't get him back in time," The Chairman said, making a low rumble in his throat. "We need to finish this as soon as possible."

"Consider it done," Petrie assured him, already a step ahead of him. "I have things in place, all set to go." *Things not even Beaudin knew about,* she thought as she ended the call.

Chapter 19

Phythian had finished the croissant and his second cup of coffee-flavored water well before the budget flight from Toulouse to Frankfurt began its descent over the German countryside.

The man seated beside him had relocated himself to the back of the plane, the result of mentally causing him to believe a host of loathsome things about Phythian: he was a sex offender recently released from a ten-year prison sentence, a fleeing psychopath who had just butchered his wife and daughter, the world's most dangerous paid assassin, come back to exact revenge on those who tried to kill him. Maybe he was all of the above.

He stared down at the patchwork quilt of farms below, stitched together with two-lane roads and larger byways that connected small towns with larger cities. The Rhine River bisected it all, and he managed to make out the Quadrate of Mannheim below to the right, the peculiar layout of streets dating back to the early seventeenth century, when Frederick IV of the Palatinate laid the foundation stone for the city and created its checkerboard pattern.

That pattern now caused him to think of the calculated moves in a world-class chess match. A casual player of the game when he was young, he'd schooled himself on the world's top contests of the day—Morphy vs. Allies, Byrne vs. Fischer, Geller vs. Euwe. He knew he could never achieve their level of excellence and, even when he'd acquired his aptitude for peering into another person's mind, he found he was not masterful enough to plan far enough ahead to plot out the end game.

The confrontation on the BART red line in the tunnel under San Francisco Bay changed everything.

Ten weeks after that encounter with Dr. Segal, Phythian was picked up by a limousine in front of a hotel in Pentagon City, across the river from Washington. The air was cold, the skies gray, the streets slushy from yesterday's snowfall. The driver deftly pulled to the curb, checked Phythian's name and identification, and stowed his duffel bag in the trunk. He then instructed his passenger to climb into the spacious backseat, where he was given a set of instructions: no phone calls, no recording devices, no cameras. No contact would take place with friends or family, and never, ever was he to talk about where he was going or what he was about to do.

The limo took him about ninety minutes west of the city, into the Shenandoah Valley, past the town of Strasburg. A bulletproof glass partition had been rolled up between the front seat and the rear compartment, presumably as a security measure. But Phythian understood it for what it was: a feeble attempt to keep him from probing the driver's brain and extracting any more information from him than he'd already been given.

"The less you know the better," was what Petrie had told him the day before, when they'd met at a sleazy lunch joint off New Hampshire Avenue in Foggy Bottom. "We want you to arrive at The Farm as if you'd stepped right off the boat. No pretense, no advance warning."

The Farm was exactly what the name implied. It was a training facility operated by an organization whose name he was not told but quickly determined was the Greenwich Global Group. It, in turn, was funded in part by a clandestine Senate Intelligence sub-sub-committee and buried so deep even the red-tape worms couldn't find it. Located on an old homestead three miles east of the West Virginia state line, it was defined by a large brick house with white federal columns that stood at the end of a long tree-lined driveway. Rolling pastures of lush, green grass were partitioned with freshly whitewashed board fencing, and Phythian counted a dozen thoroughbreds grazing in the fields, despite the late February chill. It was a perfect pastoral setting contrived such as not to draw attention, and the comings and goings of fancy limousines and supply vehicles wouldn't give anyone a moment's pause in millionaire horse country.

Phythian was driven past the large brick house to a red barn standing a hundred yards beyond it. The limo pulled directly inside the structure, where Petrie greeted him with a firm but stiff handshake. She wore no expression on her face, which looked as if it had been carved out of the same rock as the presidential monument in the Black Hills of South Dakota.

"Good to see you again, Mr. Phythian," she'd told him. "I fully expect your time here to be worth your while, and ours." At that moment he'd sensed a futile attempt to block him from tapping her true thoughts, which went something like: *If I'm not mistaken, and I never am, you are going to prove to be an incredibly valuable asset. And I'm the lucky one who gets to shape your abilities.*

Then she turned and left him in the care of an African American man in beige khakis and a brown jacket, collar turned up against the winter cold. He led Phythian up a flight of stairs and down an exposed landing that overlooked the interior of the barn below. Even though he didn't introduce himself, Phythian knew the man's name was Dwight Andrews, married, two kids, and a steep mortgage and college tuition that hounded him in the middle of the night. The girlfriend on the side only added to his worries and woes.

He was a senior-level shrink on loan from the Pentagon, and he was growing weary of research candidates who were able to guess simple images on playing cards at a rate only slightly better than chance. No one in the entire history of the project had ever done better than that, but if Phythian could do what Petrie said he could, it would buy another three years' job security and possibly a boost in pay.

They stopped outside a door marked "E," and Andrews opened it.

"Your quarters," he explained. "Your bunk mate has already arrived."

This was the first time Phythian had heard anything about a bunk mate, but he wasn't surprised. *The less you know, the better this entire experience will be for all concerned,* Petrie had explained. The Marines had prepared him for that, and he didn't really mind as long as the guy didn't talk too loudly, or think too much.

Phythian stepped into the room and set down the single duffel he was allowed to bring with him. A man dressed in military garb was standing near the window, and he'd turned around when the door opened. From the stripes on the uniform Phythian could tell the man was a major—British Army, not American.

"Richard Thompson," the major said, extending his hand to Phythian.

Phythian shook it, felt a firm, hard grip, but nothing bone-crunching. "Thompson," he repeated. "Do you spell that with or without the 'p'?"

"How the fuck you think?" the major said, tapping the plastic government-issue name badge reading "Maj. R Thompson" that was affixed it to his shirt.

"British midlands," Phythian told him, correctly identifying the clipped consonants and the softened vowels.

"Birmingham," the British officer conceded. "And you are?"

"Rōnin Phythian."

"Fith-what?"

"Phythian. P-h-y-…"

"I don't give a shit how it's spelled," Major Thompson said with a snort. "No one's giving us a bloody test at the end of this."

Phythian didn't need to tap his innate intuition to detect the deep sense of raw anger in the guy. "What are you here for?" he asked.

"Beats the hell out of me," the major shrugged. "One day I'm in Kandahar shooting at ragheads, and the next I'm landing at Dover with orders to come here. How 'bout you?"

"Experiments, is all I've been told," Phythian said, trying to keep things vague. Just as Petrie had suggested.

"No shit. That's all they do here at Greenwich, is experiments. Why the fuck are they gonna be experimenting on you?"

"Remote viewing, intuitive imaging, that sort of thing."

Major Connor shook his head in disbelief, said, "You mean ESP bullshit?"

"It's more like I can see what's going on in other people's heads. What they're seeing, what they're thinking."

"You're telling me you can read minds?"

Phythian didn't need the overt stiffening in the British officer's body posture to know what was going on in the head of Major Richard Thompson, with a 'p.' "They don't call it that, but that's what they're going to try to assess while I'm here," he replied.

"Bollocks…they give me a bloody mind reader for a roommate," he said, almost under his breath. "Okay, show me what you can do."

"I don't think that's a good idea," Phythian replied.

"I think it's a great fucking idea, unless you can't. Unless what you really are is a snake oil salesman. A total fraud."

"Trust me. You really don't want me going through your brain, finding stuff you don't want found."

"I'll tell you what I don't want found, you bloody poof," the major snapped at him, his eyes sizzling with a cocktail of adrenaline and testosterone. "C'mon…give me your best shot."

Phythian had known from the start this was where the conversation was going, just as he knew how it was going to end. That's why he really was here, after all: to learn how to define and structure his extraordinary abilities, and maintain reasonable control over them. Until then, his skills were crude and his technique lacked finesse.

"Okay," he said with a casual shrug.

"'Okay' what?" Major Connor pressed him.

"Okay, I'll tell you what's going on in your head," Phythian clarified. "But be forewarned, you're not going to like it."

"You think I give a shit what you think I like? Lay it on me."

So Phythian went for it, laying it out like a prosecutor going up against a hostile witness. Which, in effect, Major Thompson was.

"You're here because of anger issues," he began, raising a hand when the British officer took a step toward him.

"No shit," the major scoffed.

"It was triggered by the incident with Colonel Courtright, Third Mechanized Division," Phythian said. "But your issues actually go way back, and the Greenwich people have convinced your higher-ups they can help you channel your rage in a purposeful direction. In fact, you're here as part of an intervention program. You came here to get your issues under control and, if you're successful, the court martial goes away."

"What the bloody hell do you know about that?"

Major Thompson glanced at Dr. Andrews, who had not moved from where he was standing in the doorway. Observing this exchange with morbid curiosity and guided by a hands-off policy that required him to stay put and see how this confrontation resolved itself.

"The rage began when you were a kid," Phythian continued. "Six, maybe seven. You don't really remember it, which is probably a good thing. Your father sold office products for a living, but he died in a car crash near the town of Coventry. Your mom got married again, to a Welshman named Uther. She was in love with him but you saw your new stepdad for what he really was. A sorry-ass bastard who was just there to take advantage of your mom, drain her of what little money she had. His attacks on you started out small. He stepped on your feet when he walked by, rolled your fingers up in the power windows of his Rover. Little things that turned into big things. Before long he was smacking you around, first with wet towels and socks filled with bars of soap, ensuring they wouldn't leave marks—"

"That's enough—" Major Thompson snapped, his voice almost a snarl.

But it wasn't enough, because once Phythian got started he had a hard time shutting down. Another reason he was here at The Farm, to learn how to mete out his extrasensory brainpower in moderation. "When you were about ten, he started to beat you. On the bottoms of your feet, the back of your head, places where bruises wouldn't be noticed. Then one day he came at you with a golf club. A putter, actually, with a brass-colored head, and you finally took action. Swift and final. In fact, Uther disappeared that day, didn't he? Just walked out on your mom, no note, no explanation. Except he didn't walk out, not really. No, if someone were to dig down about two feet under that row of old yellow roses in your mum's garden, they'd find him. Parts of him, anyway."

That's when Major Richard Thompson completely lost control. Without any warning he charged at Phythian, with the intention of knocking the intuitive senses out of this bloody psycho, teach him good not to drill into his brain like that. A place no one had ever gone, and where no one was wanted. His stepfather was the first man Richard Thompson had killed, but he had not been the last. And Phythian very likely would be the next.

But Phythian had sensed Thompson's opening move. In fact, he had experienced the Brit's entire thought process as it was unspooling in his head. As easy as *queen's pawn to d4*, a classic opening gambit.

Twelve years' in the Marines had exposed him to many different stages of aggression, and he'd picked up a few defensive moves in boot camp, and afterwards. He was out of fighting shape and his movements were jerky and unpolished, while Major Thompson looked quite the scrapper he thought himself to be. A fist fight would not end well for Phythian, making it necessary to take the man down without a punch.

The nose dive from the second-floor landing fractured the Brit's skull and dislocated his shoulder. Dr. Andrews noted the injuries in his file and later, under prolonged questioning, Major Thompson insisted he had not intended to jump. An abrupt sense of deep melancholy had suddenly engulfed him and he'd taken a running header out the door and over the inside railing. He didn't remember a thing about the entire incident.

Phythian never came in contact with Thompson again during his entire tenure at The Farm, although he'd heard the British officer remained on the grounds somewhere. He'd also heard that the G3 had managed to channel his anger in a way that made him a useful asset on the battlefield of covert operations.

Chapter 20

Frankfurt, Germany
10:52 am GMT, 12:52 pm Local

The night was black and cold. Monica Cross crouched low behind a garbage dumpster, hiding from the man with one eye. He'd been chasing her for what seemed like hours, but in just the last few minutes she seemed to have finally eluded him. He was gone and she was free, and she could go home.

Then, almost out of nowhere, a young girl called to her from the kitchen window behind her. It was her daughter, the one she and Phillip would never have. The girl had her face pressed to the glass and was about to blow her cover. Monica motioned for her to hush when someone grabbed her by the shoulder.

"Mom...mom...you'll have to butcher seal pups."

Damn: they'd caught up with her at last.

Then her eyes flickered open and she woke up.

"Ma'am, ma'am...you'll have to put your seat up," the flight attendant repeated, releasing her hold on Monica's arm. "We're about to land."

Monica glanced around the cabin and couldn't help giggle as a wave of relief washed away the fear. The last thing she remembered was her refill of Bordeaux an hour after lifting off from Istanbul, before she curled up against the window and drifted off to sleep.

"Frankfurt?" she asked, rubbing her eyes with the heel of her hand.

"Yes, ma'am," the flight attendant confirmed with a smile. "Your seat back, please—"

Monica nodded and pressed the button. Immediately the seat lurched forward, and she realized her ribs didn't feel quite as bad as they had when she'd left the hospital. Maybe she was on the mend. Maybe it was the wine. And maybe today would be better than yesterday.

Then she remembered the little girl in her dream and felt that same familiar veil of grief descend on her, like a blanket enfolding her on a cold night; remembering the plans she and Phillip had spent hours talking about—a girl and a boy, a house with a yard and a treehouse, schools and family vacations. But all of that came to an abrupt end that night right after Christmas, with a single phone call from an officer with the New York State Police.

"Mrs. Cross...this is Captain Jay Utley...there's been an accident... terribly sorry."

Even now she could hear his voice ringing in her brain, and she physically shook her head to make it go away.

This morning she was sitting on the aisle, which gave her no view of the city below, no sense of altitude, no reference point to gauge how long before the plane touched down. With all the chaos back at the airport in Islamabad she hadn't realized her layover in Istanbul was almost four hours, and she'd endured a long line at customs before being waved through. The entire time she was in the terminal she'd kept her eyes open for any sign of trouble. In her mind she was a target, and everyone was a suspect. But no one was paying any special attention to this woman dressed in the brightly colored *shalwar qamiz*, no one coming at her with a deadly needle or a knife or a gun.

Now, as she waited for the thump of wheels on the tarmac, she pulled the *dupatta* from her hair and realized her make-up was running from nervous anticipation. She considered making a mad dash for the rest room, as if she were going to be sick. At least there was water and soap in there, and she could do a passable job on her appearance. But at that moment the landing gear thudded into place and Monica knew she'd have to wait out the descent and find an airport lavatory as quickly as possible after she got off the plane. She wiped what makeup she could from her cheeks and eyes, then wrapped the *dupatta* around her hair again and drew the edges close to her face—just in case someone was in the terminal waiting for her.

The Airbus touched down forty seconds later. As the brakes squealed and the engines reversed, Monica sensed a sudden release of tension throughout the plane, followed by a swell of impatience as the aircraft taxied from the runway to the gate. Passengers grew restless with the slow pace, passing the time by unbuckling their seatbelts and dragging their carry-ons from under the seats in front of them. The senior flight attendant came over the P.A. system and told them to stay put and be patient, as the plane would be moving for a couple minutes yet.

An eternity later the lumbering aircraft pulled up to the jetway and a bell chimed. The weary international travelers jumped to their feet *en masse*, yanking bags from the overhead compartments, eager to get out of the flying sardine tin. Monica waited until all the others had disembarked, then edged out of her seat.

"Have a wonderful stay in Frankfurt, or wherever your travels take you," the flight attendant at the front of the aisle said in both German and English.

Monica flashed her a smile as she left the plane and slowly made her way up the ramp into the international terminal. It was a massive structure designed in the post-Bauhaus style of concrete, steel, and glass, and seemed the size of a small city. Just to the left of the gate she located the departure screens and smiled giddily when she saw the words "on time" next to her flight number. She had just over two hours to make the connection, which gave her more than enough time to scrub her face, change out of the *shalwar qamiz*, and wind her way through passport control.

She scanned both sides of the long corridor, finally found what she was looking for: a door with a universal sign showing a stick figure wearing a skirt. She started to follow several other women inside, then noticed a separate doorway with a picture of a unisex person changing a baby. *Even better.*

The room was empty and held a toilet, sink, and a fold-down table for dealing with soiled diapers and wipes. Monica peeled the grimy *dupatta* from her head and dumped it in the trash bin, then turned on the tap and started scrubbing her eyes and cheeks. Once she was rid of the makeup, she straightened out the jeans and shirt she had pulled on early yesterday morning. She would have liked to put on some new underwear and a clean bra, but those would have to wait until she got home to New York.

Damn, that sounded good…New York City.

Home.

At that moment the door opened and a woman slipped inside. "Oh… excuse me," she announced as she entered. In English, with a thick accent that seemed decidedly more French than German. "I didn't know this room was occupied."

"Come on in," Monica replied. "I'm just tidying up."

"Thank you so much," the woman said. "I just had the most dreadful flight."

She appeared to be in her forties, athletic build, with a rugged yet handsome face. White skirt and green blouse, a leather belt cinched around her waist. Her mushroom blonde hair, almost silver, was bunched up in a messy bun, a wooden peg driven through it to hold it in place.

Monica gave her face another careful glance in the mirror, gently rubbing a finger on the skin under her right eye. The swelling seemed to have gone down, as had the bruising. Satisfied, she turned to go and pulled on the door handle, but it wouldn't open.

"I locked it," the woman said in a voice as cold as the Arctic tundra. She was letting her hair down, combing out the tangles with her fingers, holding the wooden peg between her teeth as a snarl formed on her lips.

"Locked it?" Monica asked. "Why?"

"So you can be a good girl and we can get this over with."

She took the peg from between her teeth and removed what appeared to be a small plastic cap on the end. Monica only caught a glimpse, but that was more than enough time to notice a sharp point no larger than a thumb tack protruding from one end. Prior to yesterday her first reaction would have been to freeze like a squirrel in the middle of the street, but she'd learned a lot about herself since her encounter with the rebels on the mountain trail.

"Bitch," she seethed as she instinctively let loose with her foot, aiming at the wooden peg. A spasm shot through her ribs, and her ankle screamed in torment.

The unexpected response surprised the woman, who had been assured her target was disabled from the injuries suffered in her fall. She yelped as Monica's foot missed the needle but caught her wrist. Monica heard something snap, and the peg went flying across the room.

"Motherfucker," the woman wailed in anger and pain. "You're dead."

Monica lunged toward the wooden peg on the floor, but her opponent grabbed her good ankle and brought her down with a resounding crunch. She wrapped the crook of her elbow around Monica's neck and began to squeeze, the constricting pain almost too much for her to bear.

"I should've killed you...the second I came in," the woman grunted as she pressed Monica's chin down against her chest, while her arms were doubled behind her neck.

Monica squirmed and kicked out with her legs, but the woman was too strong and experienced to get tangled in a mass of limbs. Running out of air and options, Monica drew her head as far forward against her breast as possible, then snapped it backward with all the force she could muster. The base of her skull caught her assailant squarely in the mouth and caused her to loosen her grip, allowing Monica to slip from her clutches. Blood was pouring from her assailant's gums, and she attempted to stanch the flow—and the pain—with her hand.

Once more, Monica scrambled for the wooden peg, and this time she was able to wrap her hand around it. She was careful not to stick herself with the sharp point; she was certain it was coated with the same deadly compound that had stricken Brian Walker. At the same moment the woman came rushing straight at her, head lowered, weight thrown into her attack like a bull charging through the streets of Pamplona. All Monica could do was slide low to the floor and allow the woman to crash headlong into the unforgiving wall.

The room shuddered with a resounding thud. Monica scrambled away, then pivoted back around to face her attacker. "Who the hell are you—?" she snarled.

Her assailant cradled her jaw in her hand, a deadly look of vengeance etched in her face. She closed her eyes, and for a moment Monica thought she might have died. Then they blinked open again, inflamed with rage, and the muscles in her face seemed to tighten, as if preparing for yet another attack.

"You are so going to die, you mother—"

Monica sensed where this was going, but she didn't have the patience. Rather than wait for the woman to finish her threat, she plunged the needle into her neck. "Nighty-night," she whispered as the woman's eyes rolled upwards and she wilted on the hard tile.

Monica slowly rose to her feet, her hands shaking almost uncontrollably as a shot of adrenaline punched through her veins, which helped to dampen the throbbing in her ankle and ribs. Without thinking, she wiped the hair peg on her shirt and deposited it in the trash, then checked her own appearance in the mirror. Not bad, considering. And much better than the dead woman lying just a few feet away.

Satisfied that she didn't appear to be a major wreck, she turned the knob and stepped as calmly as she could back into the bustling terminal.

She limped to the departure screens and brought up the digital boarding pass on her phone one more time, then glanced at the overhead monitor to double-check her departure time.

That's when her heart sank.

Phythian's flight from Toulouse touched down eight minutes after Monica's, and pulled up to the gate at the other end of the enormous Terminal 1.

The G3 had tried but failed to kill Monica Cross while she was in Islamabad. Lacking the resources to set up a follow-up ambush in Istanbul, Frankfurt appeared to be the Greenwich Global Group's next best hope. He'd learned this from Martin Beaudin, both through normal conversation and threads of information he'd mentally pried from his brain. As he'd expected, the G3's interest in her stemmed from the disappearance of the hard drive known as Equinox. She'd taken a photograph of the Faraday case, which was empty when investigators found it in the wreckage. Had she removed the device, they wondered, or had it been empty when she'd found it? Her belongings had been searched thoroughly and her phone confiscated while she was in the hospital and, while there was no sign of the device, the fact that she even knew of its existence—let alone its name—was a major threat to global stability. And, more important, to the G3's very existence.

Subjected to further questioning, Martin Beaudin readily had provided Phythian with Monica Cross' updated itinerary, which he was able to access from the G3 cloud servers via his laptop. Once Phythian had what he needed, he elected to leave the Frenchman alive, shivering from the Pyrenees chill that was blowing the sheer balcony drapes like the tendrils of a mournful ghost. He also was trembling from the thought of what the G3 would do to him once The Chairman learned of this late-night incursion by an assassin long thought dead.

"Best to strike first," Phythian had advised him as he stood to go, examining the empty bottle against the dim bulb of a glass lamp with dangly pink crystals that looked as if it had come from a cheap bordello.

Le Serrurier had flashed him a worried look, said, "What does that mean?"

"Give him a call," he replied. "Tell him you led me into a trap in Frankfurt."

Beaudin had brightened at the suggestion; not a bad idea. "That might work," he'd agreed. "For a time, at least."

"To long life, then," Phythian had said, toasting his empty glass to the locksmith before disappearing into the night.

Now he pushed his way through the mass of humanity crowding the concourse, past hustling businessmen and tourists and weary parents with whining kids that squealed and threw tantrums on the hard floor. The commotion was enough to drive him mad, and the mental blather only made it worse.

Phythian did his best to tune out the noise as he studied the row of ceiling-mounted video screens. *Le Serrurier* had confided in him that Monica Cross had a modest layover in Frankfurt before her connecting plane to JFK took off, same terminal and airline as this one. But when he checked the list of "Departures" he saw the notation "Cancelled" next to her flight number.

Cancelled? How could that be? Just before he'd lifted off from Toulouse, he'd checked her itinerary on his phone and saw the plane was expected to leave for New York on time. But that was over two hours ago, and a lot could happen in a short amount of time—especially when the G3 was part of the mix.

The arrival monitor told him that Monica Cross' plane from Istanbul had already landed. He could sense her now, a couple hundred yards down the long structure, several dozen crowded gates in between them. He attempted to zero-in on her, probe her mind to get a fix on what she was thinking and feeling. He'd been out of the game for years, but it had come back to him quickly when he'd stood below *Le Serrurier*'s window just a few hours ago in Andorra La Vella and mentally extracted the code to the push-button deadbolt.

Phythian turned away from the departure screen and locked his brain onto hers. She was somewhere down the hallway, in a restroom of sorts. Not your typical ladies' room, but a place where parents wiped shit off their babies. He felt what she was feeling: intermittent fear, yet an element of relief. Pain yet freedom. Apprehension yet confidence. Peeling off her Pakistani outfit, scrubbing away a layer of hastily applied makeup. (Thank you, Fiona Cassidy.) Using the toilet. (Lousy sheets of TP that feel like wax paper, but they'll do.)

Then he sensed an unexpected stab, followed by a rough kick. There was a brief moment of silence, followed by a thrust and a reflexive jab.

Someone was attacking her.

Phythian hesitated about half a second, abruptly shifted his cerebral energy from pull to push, the way he'd been taught all those years ago at The Farm. Instead of gently pulling thoughts and feelings from the woman named Monica Cross, he now pressed hard to get her to act. Fight back and attack. *Kill or be killed.*

She did, as his mind picked up a quick snap that resulted in a nasty crunch, then an instinctive lunge that ended with blood. And death.

The bedlam lasted mere seconds, and in that span of time he'd lost his mental connection. He feared the worst, that maybe Monica had been killed, but a second later he picked it up again, sensed an overwhelming tremor of panic and bone-penetrating dread. She was still alive, despite some kind of horrific fight to the finish. Against a woman, with a clipped French accent. Luxembourg, actually. And then it hit him, just as her last dying thoughts dripped from her parietal, occipital, and temporal lobes: *La Duchesse de la Mort.* The Duchess of Death. Also known as Simone Marchand, career intelligence operative and—at one time—extraordinary field agent for the Directorate-General for External Security in France. Highly trained in hand-to-hand termination techniques and invaluable in several off-the-books operations, she'd been furloughed following the botched burglary of the hotel room of a Chinese CEO on French soil.

Three months after that monumental blunder, an official within the French Ministry of Defense had wired the G3 five hundred thousand Euros to terminate her. Preferably an automobile accident similar to the one that had been staged in the *Pont de l'Alma* tunnel in Paris ten years earlier, but considerably lower profile. Instead, a recruiter from the Greenwich Global Group by the name of Diana Petrie confronted her in a car park and offered her a lucrative position. Given no alternative, Marchand had accepted on the spot.

Two days later the contracted vehicle mishap occurred anyway, a single car crash on the *Peripherique.* The driver behind the wheel died instantly and her body burned beyond recognition. Dental records were involved, bitcoin changed hands, and no one was the wiser.

Fucking Greenwich bastards weren't taking any chances, Phythian thought now as he sensed Simone Marchand's brain fade to black. *Sending one of their best and deadliest to kill Monica Cross.*

And even though they had failed—again, and against all odds—he knew they would not give up until they succeeded.

Chapter 21

Adam Kent was pretending to proofread a position statement he had pretended to write for Vice President Crittenden regarding the Colin Wheeler scandal.

A career policy wonk who had served as the covert liaison between Langley and the G3 for half a decade, he easily had fallen into his cover role as Deputy Chief Strategist for the Vice President. It was a convenient ruse that allowed him to function deep within the executive branch without attracting the suspicion of fellow staffers, and it allowed him top secret access to matters of significance to the G3 executive board.

Given his highly sensitive intelligence background, he understood and appreciated the value of an independent organization that could handle certain tasks deemed too dirty for any government to undertake on its own. The CIA had been placed under a Congressional microscope back in the seventies for its alleged wet work, causing the then-U.S. President to warn that "no employee of the United States government shall engage in, or conspire in, political assassination." That executive order had been a boon for the Greenwich Global Group, which proved to be a trustworthy partner capable of functioning below official scrutiny, and essentially removed all American complicity in such matters. Even though a few knee-jerk presidents managed to make ill-conceived pre-emptive decisions in the name of expediency, the G3 remained the go-to partner for extralegal activities.

Operating out of a fourth-floor office in the Eisenhower Executive Office Building just west of the White House, Kent deftly served as the back-channel intermediary between the Director of National Intelligence and The Chairman. One critical and necessary aspect of that function was arranging sanctions of select individuals who were determined to pose a threat to America's national interests. Unchecked foreign ministers, rogue diplomats, unscrupulous businessmen, and arms traders on the come: no one was outside the reach of the black hat company known as the G3.

This morning he'd been dealing with one of those pending sanctions—the termination of an unsuspecting photographer named Monica Cross—when one of his three cell phones rang.

"Yes,'" he answered, having expected the call.

"How's the lid?" rasped the voice on the other end of the line.

Despite the two-way audio scramble that diluted the signal during its 128,000-mile journey up to two separate satellites, as well as all the encryption software, the abrasive rattle emanating from The Chairman's throat was audible. It was the sound of Death, and it made Kent's skin feel almost reptilian.

"Vacuum-sealed," he assured the old man. "Totally hermetic."

"Total certitude is certified folly," The Chairman hacked.

The team of doctors in Milan that was being paid a small fortune to keep the old man alive had explained five weeks ago that he would not live to see the new year. He could have remained in his villa in Varenna on the shore of Lake Como, but he had a particular fondness for the twenty acres of granite that protruded like the back of a whale from the depths of the Scottish sea. He had acquired it thirty-six years ago from a family that had owned it for twelve generations, in exchange for twenty thousand pounds cash and lifetime fishing rights. The locals regarded him for what he was—a foolish blueblood with too much money and time on his hands—and in private they ridiculed the old man for paying such a high price for a chunk of useless stone.

The island was infested with termites and windswept pines and timbers from shipwrecks, and likewise was peppered with curious remnants of ancient folklore. The place reportedly was haunted at times by the ghost of a Norse woman abandoned on its rocks by her Viking husband who wished to preserve her maidenhood. And, on dark winter nights when the moon was gone, the pathetic cries of a stranded whaling crew could be heard rising up from the icy depths.

This mythology was all bullshit to The Chairman, who had reconstructed the main house from blocks of stone shipped in from a quarry near the

Isle of Skye. The structure squatted atop the highest point on the island, ninety feet above mean high tide, and it had a clear view of the sea in all directions, as well as the mainland eight miles to the south. Before the Chairman had bought it, the place was named *Eilean Taibhse*, but now it simply was known as Gray Rock. Salt water was distilled through a reverse osmosis system, while a diesel generator provided ample electricity to power the house and four outbuildings. A pair of satellite dishes replaced the ancient telephone cable that years ago had been washed out in a gale, providing secure Wi-Fi phone and internet service. A granite L-shaped quay extended out from the leeward side of the island and afforded ample deep-water dockage for vessels up to eighty feet in length. Aside from the monthly delivery of diesel fuel, however, few boats ever paid a visit.

A half dozen signs that read No Trespassing: Violators Will Be Shot probably had something to do with it.

On this fine morning The Chairman was sitting alone on the west veranda, sipping a mug of coffee with a dribble of Scotch in it—or maybe a dram. The ocean was calm and flat, and a gentle breeze was seeping in from the southwest. A few high clouds lumbered across the cornflower sky, and for a moment he watched a distant jet ply its way westward over the Atlantic while listening to the comforting chug of a fishing boat working the fog-shrouded shore.

"The common curse of mankind is folly and ignorance," Kent assured him, drawing on his knowledge that The Chairman had dabbled in Shakespearean theater while attending University College in London, and was particularly fond of the bleak *Troilus and Cressida.* Then, to steer him away from the inquisition he knew was coming, he asked, "If you don't mind me asking, sir, how are you feeling this morning?"

"Like a piece of atrophied liver," came the raspy answer. "How's the Wheeler thing playing over there?"

"As expected," Kent replied, resigned to the interrogation he knew was coming. "Shock. Confusion. Disbelief. And, of course, the embarrassment that was intended."

"No one suspects anything?"

"Not that I can see."

"I can hear a 'but' in there."

Kent shifted in his seat. His throat suddenly felt parched, and his mouth tasted as dry as beach sand, with bits of sea glass thrown in. "Actually, sir,

I've heard a rumor about a rumor that someone's poking his nose where it doesn't belong."

"Does this someone have a name?" the Chairman hacked.

"Carter Logan. Worked for the *Washington Post* until a year ago. Now he writes a syndicated blog."

"What's his interest in Wheeler?" came the gruff response.

"So far, just talk. He's been asking around about computer hacks, Wheeler's rulings, personal background. General shit."

"I don't like general shit."

"Neither do I, sir. We're keeping track on what he's up to. Word is he has a bit of a booze problem."

"Which could make him a loose cannon."

"Or an easy mark," Kent pointed out.

"Whatever you need to do," The Chairman said.

"Yes, sir."

"And I want this Pakistan thing taken care of. Both the photographer and Phythian, as soon as practical."

"Both targets arrived in Frankfurt within the last hour, as expected. I'm waiting for confirmation of their respective terminations as we speak."

"You are not to fail at this, Kent. I hand-picked you for this role because I knew you were reliable and thorough."

"I appreciate the confidence," he said. He waited for The Chairman to end the call, so he could get on with his day.

But the nonagenarian former war cryptologist living on a rock eight miles off the Scottish coast was not finished. "There's something else you need to know," he rasped through a throat clogged with phlegm. "And by 'need to know,' I mean it's highly confidential."

"You're talking about the thing that appears to be missing from the plane."

"You know about it?"

"I wouldn't be doing my job if I didn't," Kent replied.

Over the encrypted phone The Chairman seemed to grunt, and Kent could swear he heard the sound of liquid gurgling—like someone pouring Scotch into a mug of coffee.

"Then you saw the pictures," the old man finally said. "The shots that photographer took with her Goddamned phone."

Kent thought it interesting that The Chairman could not call her by her name, just her profession. Much less personal connection that way which, in this line of work, was a prudent idea.

"I have," he said. "Mangled wreckage, bullet holes, empty briefcase—"

"And that's the crux of our problem."

"May I ask why?" Kent replied.

"Because the device you refer to as a *thing* contains every detail of every mission the G3 ever conducted, up to six years ago."

"When you say 'every detail,' exactly what are we talking about?"

"I'm talking who, what, where, when, why…and how much. Photos. Video surveillance. Bank accounts, numbers, transfers. Everything. Every job."

"Damn." He considered the enormity of The Chairman's words, then said, "How the fuck was this allowed to happen?"

"Short version is someone on that plane hacked our server, we believe with the intention of selling the download to the highest bidder. Right under the nose of your predecessor, which is why he's no longer with us and you are. Fortunately, the data was digitally watermarked and we were able to track its path to Israel."

"Mossad?" Kent's immediate and natural response was to think of Eitan Hazan.

"All indications point to no, but you never know who you can trust in this business."

"If you knew where it was and who stole it, why not just steal it back?" Kent said, now that The Chairman was filling in the gaps in his own intel.

"It was decided that the simplest plan was to simply destroy it, along with the people who hacked it."

"The five passengers on the plane."

"They were all part of a scheme to compromise us, each in their own way."

Buy the ticket, take the ride, Kent thought. "And now we know it wasn't destroyed at all," he ventured.

"Precisely. Our people looked everywhere, but Equinox was nowhere in the wreckage."

"Which means someone took it. Either—" he was about to say *Monica Cross*, but caught himself "—the photographer who snapped the pictures, or Phythian when he bailed from the plane. My money is on Phythian."

"Your money isn't at issue here, Kent. What's at issue is the twelve million dollars paid by our partners to make sure that drive never, ever gets into the wrong hands."

"Of course, sir."

The Chairman inhaled a dusting of salt air that drifted up from the barnacle-encrusted rocks below, then ended the call without saying another word. He shuffled to the edge of the veranda, his knees stiff from psoriatic arthritis, and stared out at the horizon, where the veil of fog was beginning to lift. The sky above it was a brilliant blue, almost the same shade that, as a young man who had joined the fight against the Germans, he'd imagined the birds to be as they returned to the white cliffs of Dover, when the world once again would be free from fascism and the Nazi scourge.

Every day and night since the grim diagnosis from the doctors in Milan, he was reminded of the vast void that awaited him, and how he would never live long enough to come to terms with life's true meaning. The real purpose of seven billion befuddled humans composed of complex molecules and genomes, wandering aimlessly around an average-sized planet orbiting a medium-sized, banal star at the edge of one of billions of galaxies scattered across the infinite reach of the universe.

The thought made him feel small and mortal and insignificant, enough to bring him to tears. But he had not cried in decades, and he saw no need to engage in the useless practice now.

Chapter 22

Twenty minutes ago, Flight 72 to JFK had been on time. Now the screen said "cancelled."

"No frickin' way," Monica said as she read it again.

It seemed as if the terminal floor had dropped out from beneath her feet, and she was falling into a deep abyss. She fought off a wave of panic, and a tightness this time gripped her heart rather than her ribs. How could her flight be cancelled? These things just didn't happen.

The rational part of her brain told her she was wrong: flights are cancelled all the time, for any number of reasons. Weather, mechanical issues, union shutdowns. Bomb threats. But an intuitive sense she could not explain told her this was the work of whoever had sent that bitch from France, or wherever, to murder her. Someone intent on making sure she didn't leave this airport alive. They'd failed to kill her in Islamabad, and her abrupt change of plans meant they hadn't had time to organize any sort of plan in Istanbul. Maybe hadn't even known she was headed there. But Frankfurt was another matter: there had been ample time to coordinate with airline computers, then target her before she even had time to get to her next gate. The attempt on her life in the changing room had been deliberately planned, even though it had failed. Whoever was intent on killing her had no idea she would fight to the finish.

To hell with them, whoever they are, she thought. *Hell with them all.*

She was going to fight back with her fists or her wits, whatever was required to survive.

Right now, what she needed was to get out of there. A woman lay dead in the changing room just yards from where she stood, and her body would be discovered any second. There would be a scream, airport police would be called, people would panic. It would only take seconds for word to get around that a killer was on the loose, and surveillance footage would be reviewed to see who had used those facilities. Analysts would isolate a few frames showing the dead woman pushing her way inside, followed a minute later by Monica hurrying out.

When that happened, chaos would erupt. Armed guards would block the exits, passengers would be questioned, flights would be delayed. Immigration would be locked down. The media would arrive and reporters would start talking about terrorists, radicalized extremists, violent fringe factions. Within minutes the incident would be transmitted around the globe, and a manhunt for the savage Frankfurt Airport killer would be mobilized.

No time to waste. Farther down the corridor Monica spotted a large sign declaring *Passkontrolle*. A steady stream of travelers—some of whom had just gotten off the same flight as she had—were riding an escalator down to a lower level. Monica fell in with them, occasionally glancing over her shoulder to see if there was any commotion back near the restrooms.

So far, so good, she thought.

At the bottom of the moving stairs the passengers split into several groups. She followed some of them into a line designated "Non-EU Nationals," where she stood on her pulsing ankle until a control officer flashed a light and waved her forward.

"*Welcommen*," he said to her as she stepped up to his window.

"*Bitte*," she replied, handing him her passport. Forcing a smile, following up with just about the only German phrase she knew. "*Wie geht es dir?*"

"Very well, thank you," he said in English. "What brings you to Frankfurt on this beautiful June morning?"

"Just connecting through to New York," she replied. "From Istanbul."

"I see, I see." He studied the photo in her passport, flipped through the pages, then fed it through a digital scanner. "What flight are you on?"

She told him the airline and number, hoping beyond hope that the immigration computers didn't receive up-to-the-minute departure updates.

Evidently they didn't. No bells rang, no sirens went off. Instead, the customs officer stamped the passport and handed it back to her. "Have a wonderful journey home," he told her.

Not until Monica had made it safely out to the main passenger terminal did she fully grasp the enormity of her situation. She had just killed a woman, and she was on the run from forces she did not understand. Her body was a mass of pain, like a boxing bag that had just endured an hour-long workout. For some reason she had become a target, but not for the reasons that Ambassador Boyar had given her about martyred rebels and family revenge. This was Germany, for Chrissakes: no way did Pakistani political influence extend this far and, if it did, they wouldn't have sent a woman with a French accent to kill her.

One thing was certain: if she was going to get out of here with her life, she wouldn't be able to just buy another plane ticket out of Frankfurt the same as she'd done in Islamabad. Whoever was behind this plot clearly had the power to cancel her flight to JFK, which meant their tentacles extended far and wide. As soon as her name went into an airline computer she would be flagged, and *they* would know where she was going. She felt an ache of helplessness building inside her, but surrendering to her fears and desperation wouldn't get her anywhere. She'd almost surrendered after Phillip had died, every day feeling as if her life were draining out of her, and there was no reason to go on. But she *had* gone on, in fits and starts, ups and downs, blacks and whites: yoga and *tai chi*, even a couple beginner classes in *jiu-jitsu*. She was determined not to be ambushed by this setback—not this one, and damned sure not any others that might be thrown at her.

Monica's German was virtually non-existent but, as she glanced around the terminal, she recognized the universal icon for rail travel. She followed the signs in the direction of the *Bahnhofe*, the railway station that served both commuter- and long-distance destinations. Not as efficient as flying, but at this point she felt she had no choice. As long as she was moving she felt safe, and she wanted to put as much distance as she could between herself and the dead woman. She was fully aware that wherever she went she'd face the same problem of booking an airplane ticket, but for now she was okay with just delaying the inevitable.

One thing at a time, she thought.

Her immediate question was what other city would be best to try to book a flight home to New York. Her best options were Paris or Amsterdam, or maybe London. Paris was closest—a digital monitor said the trip took only four hours by rail—and it was where she and Phillip had honeymooned five years ago. They'd fallen in love with everything about the City of Light: the museums and gardens, the romantic Latin Quarter jazz club that made them feel like soul mates falling in love for the first time. Even some of the *bona fide* tourist traps, like the Eiffel Tower and the Louvre. At the end of their nine days they'd vowed they would return someday, maybe with children in tow. They would rent an apartment near the Seine, nibble croissants in the *Rue Cler*, sip wine at their favorite bistro in the Latin Quarter.

On the other hand, while Amsterdam was a greater distance, it carried no emotional baggage. There was no history with Phillip, no memories of the past or promises of the future. Same as London, which was the shortest distance between the two final points: eight hours from Heathrow to JFK. Plus, they spoke English. Problem was, there wasn't another train headed there for another ninety minutes, and she wanted to get out of Frankfurt as soon as possible.

She started to punch her route info into an automatic ticket kiosk when she noticed a man in khaki slacks and a lightweight linen jacket approaching her from across the terminal. Their eyes met, and she had no question that he knew who she was, why she was here. He appeared to dip his head in a slight not of recognition, then slipped a hand inside his jacket as he continued toward her. His eyes fixed on hers as he moved forward, slow and determined. She felt her blood chill and, and once again she was reminded of just how easy it was to die.

Then another man, this one dressed in black jeans and a tweed sport coat, changed all that. He seemed to appear from nowhere, viciously charging at her would-be attacker and knocking him to the concrete floor. As part of the same continuous motion, he unleashed a harsh kick to the stomach, then rushed up and grabbed Monica's elbow. Ignoring his victim's groans and the travelers around her who were whipping out their phones and shooting video that would go viral within minutes, it was the last thing she wanted.

"Monica Cross?" he asked her in a hurried voice.

How did he know her name?

"Mrs. Cross, you must come with me." Regional accent of some sort, German or maybe something else. *Israeli*? "I'll explain later."

She blinked, then stared at him. "Like hell," she said.

"Look, ma'am. You stay here, you're dead, as I'm sure you've already figured out."

"What do you know about that?"

He wasn't accustomed to answering questions, and he wasn't about to start now.

"You come along with me, you'll live to be the lovely old lady you deserve to be."

The injured man on the flatform continued to groan in pain, but she knew he'd be staggering to his feet within seconds. "Who the hell are you?" she demanded.

"German Consulate." He tightened his grip on her elbow and began to forcibly guide her toward the terminal exit. She started to resist but found she didn't have the willpower. "I'll explain later, when you're good and safe. Away from all this."

Monica drew one more, quick glance back to the man on the floor of the train station, struggling to rise to his feet. His eyes focused on hers, his lips trying to say something, but his words only coming out in ragged gasps.

"Move…now!" the man in black and white ordered her.

Monica wrestled her arm free and said, "I'm not going anywhere with you—"

"You must. He was trying to kill you."

They're all trying to kill me, she thought. The man who claimed to be from the German Consulate had hurriedly steered her down a corridor that appeared to lead outside the station, but she wasn't going one step farther unless she knew what the hell was going on.

"How do you know my name?"

Good question, and he had an even greater answer prepared for her. "When your flight from Islamabad to London was canceled, we got word that you'd rebooked through Istanbul and Frankfurt. Your ambassador—I forget his name—"

"Boyar," she said.

"*Ja, ja.* Boyar." He glanced over his shoulder, in the direction of where he'd just attacked the man in khaki slacks and linen jacket. Who, he noticed, was no longer there; a disconcerting predicament that made him nervous. More than nervous, in fact: he was frightened. An emotion that a figure—*legend*—of his ego could not accept, much less admit. "He called your embassy in Berlin, and they called us. And right now, I need to get you away from here."

"Let me see some ID."

He was prepared for this, as well, and pulled out a leather wallet that held a card with his photo and official identification on it. Monica examined the badge, saw that the image matched the face and the card came from the German Consulate.

"Erich Rohm," she said, reading his name slowly.

"That's me," he explained. "And now we really do need to go."

The woman was Monica Cross; Phythian was certain. She'd been standing there studying the railway departure screens, just as the police began to swarm the station, with no idea what to do or where to go, afraid she'd be arrested for killing Simone Marchand. Although there was no way the police could have connected her to the crime that quickly.

Phythian only had a general idea of what she looked like, based on the low-res image he'd downloaded into his phone while waiting for his flight in Toulouse. But he knew it was her and, likewise, she seemed to have recognized something in him as their eyes had locked. She'd been staring right at him, as if she realized he'd seized her mind just a few moments before, and had mentally guided her through the deadly fight in the restroom.

Then Eitan Hazan had interfered. Even though the ID he'd shown to Monica identified him as Erich Rohm.

How curious that they would send him, Phythian thought. *The master planner behind the colossal fuck-up that had failed to kill me six years ago.*

Then again, it made a certain sort of sense. Ten years ago, a covert fiasco within the Israeli intelligence community caused Hazan to be kicked up to a desk job and stripped of his many commendations. One day a woman named Diana Petrie from the mysterious Greenwich Global Group paid him a visit, and presented him with an employment offer that was too attractive to turn down.

Four years later, when Petrie had sought the services of a skilled artisan with a unique set of competencies, she'd read Hazan in on Mission 4,826. With her *carte blanche* blessing, he had leased the King Air 350 XER, devised a failsafe plan to ensure that Phythian would be at the controls, and identified a specialist who would create a bomb and make it look like a block of cheese. He then found someone else—totally independent of the G3—to place the device in the galley of the aircraft.

Hazan had thought of all details, considered all the anomalies and possible permutations and loose ends. He mentally reviewed every aspect of the plan, and ran as close to a dress rehearsal as he could while not involving another soul who had any ties to Phythian. He'd even hired a third-party subcontractor to sever the cords on Phythian's parachute as an additional layer of insurance. A motorcycle accident on the *Okef Krayot*, however, had delayed her arrival at the airport, and that component of the operation had been scrapped.

Our wills and fates do so contrary run, that our devices still are overthrown, the Player King had said in Hamlet, and nowhere was that more evident than the moment Hazan had spotted Phythian on the train platform three minutes ago.

And vice versa.

The fact that Hazan had been allowed to live—much less promoted to the G3 executive board after the botched mission—remained a mystery. The Chairman should have terminated him after such an unacceptable failure but, as Martin Beaudin had explained as their conversation had neared the bottom of the bottle, the Israeli legend—at least in his own mind—had been given one more chance. Hazan's directive this morning was to remain outside the perimeter of Phythian's mind and terminate him, before the mind-reading freak ever sensed he was there. Yet for some reason, he'd hesitated rather than complete his task. Equivocation had never been Hazan's weakness in the past; no matter his target, he'd never dithered, never faltered. And, except for Mission 4,826, he'd never failed.

But this time was different. Phythian had caught sight of him and, in that fleeting moment, his past errors had reminded him of all his faults and deficiencies.

Monica Cross leveled a hard glare at the man who had identified himself as Erich Rohm. "Where do you intend to take me?" she asked him.

"Someplace safe," he replied, without telling her anything, wishing he'd put a bullet in her the moment he'd had the chance, finishing what Simone Marchand had not. But the sight of Phythian had shaken him to the core of his being.

"Why should I trust you?" she demanded, and it was at that moment that she realized she *didn't* trust him. Didn't buy his story one bit.

"I have a car," he insisted. "There's a safe house—"

But Monica was tired of lies, tired of deception; even tired of civility. If she'd had time to isolate all the individual elements that were influencing her thought processes right now, she might have realized her mind was being shaped by an external force—a force that convinced her she had to do something this very minute, or she might not live to see the next.

Without warning she struck out and planted her foot firmly and swiftly in Rohm's groin. He doubled over in pain and unleashed a string of German expletives that faded behind her as she hobbled to the escalator that descended to a lower concourse. She kept one eye over her shoulder as she limped through the hive of passengers buzzing to wherever they were headed. Three uniformed officers with military-style guns rushed past just a few yards away, reminding her just how dire her situation was. Thirty full minutes had elapsed since the fight in the changing room, and soon the railway station would be swarming with armed *Polizei*. She suspected she was safe until witnesses stepped forward or surveillance video was reviewed, but time was ticking by. She couldn't get out of Frankfurt fast enough.

Finally, she spotted an automatic ticket kiosk. The digital timetable on the screen said the train to Amsterdam was scheduled to leave on time, so she selected it as her destination and inserted her credit card. Within seconds the ticket had printed out and she was on her way.

Testicles are densely packed organs with thousands upon thousands of sensitive nerve endings, more than virtually any other part of the body. Eitan Hazan was experiencing the painful truth of this biological fact, feeling the impact of Monica's shoe clear up into his abdomen.

Her kick had been hard and swift, and caught him totally off guard. He was curled up in agony, hands between his legs, trying not to attract attention on the main level of the station. Not since a secret mission in Beirut fourteen years ago had his genitals been so pulverized, by a trained operative for the Lebanese Special Operations Command. Hazan had killed him two days later, but only after full functionality had returned to both legs.

This morning he'd been so involved in his attempt to coerce Monica Cross to leave with him, to the point that he'd momentarily overlooked the fact that she'd somehow managed to get past Simone Marchand. *La Duchesse de la Mort* had driven in from Paris in plenty of time to set herself up in Terminal One before Monica's plane touched down, but he hadn't heard a word from her for over thirty minutes. He had no love for the woman—she was a self-absorbed, complicated *hure*—but the fact that she wasn't answering her phone told him she had not fared well.

Complicating matters even more was the appearance of Phythian.

Hazan had been briefed on his unexpected presence in Europe just hours ago, and had readily volunteered for the job to kill him. It was the least he could do to remedy his past mistakes, and it was just a one-hour hop from Berlin to Frankfurt. During that time he'd mentally reviewed a number of ways that he might take his old nemesis—the object of his greatest failure—by surprise. And then kill him.

The key was not to let Phythian know he was there, and to do that he would have to elude detection until he got a good, clean shot at the bastard.

As prepared as Hazan thought he was, he'd been momentarily distracted by the appearance of Monica Cross on the railway platform, studying the timetables. She should have been dead and, indeed, she looked as if she'd just gone ten rounds with a grizzly bear. But she was very much alive and visibly shaken by the events she had just experienced, and seemed to be frantically looking for the best way to disappear.

How could The Duchess of Death have fucked up such a simple job?

It was in that same moment that Hazan also had spotted Phythian. He'd been walking toward her slowly, studying her intently, no doubt attempting to penetrate her mind with his creepy neuropsychic power. Hazan had stood there and watched them both, two ghosts who should have been dead: one at the hands of Simone Marchand in the airport terminal, the other in the disappearance of a twin turboprop six years ago.

Now, as he waited for his testicles to decompress, he cursed himself for not killing them both when he'd had the chance. Should have marched up and plugged them both with the SIG Sauer he'd checked through from Berlin via diplomatic pouch. Failure rarely permitted a second chance, and he'd needed to make good on this opportunity The Chairman had offered him.

Yet he'd let both of them slip through his fingers. They were here in the railway station, somewhere close, and he couldn't afford to let either of them get away again. First priority was to kill the Cross woman, then somehow override Phythian's near-mythic abilities, and shoot him dead.

Chapter 23

Over the past three years Vice President Crittenden had found myriad reasons to loathe his official residence at the Naval Observatory in northwest Washington. To begin with, it was over a thousand miles from his beloved home in Mississippi, measured by how the raven flies. Second, its original construction dated back to before the Civil War which, to him, represented an era when elitist Yankees were invoking fractious rhetoric toward the South and its agrarian economy, one that was increasingly dependent on slave labor.

Plus, the Union Navy itself had been instrumental in the defeat of the Confederacy, even if the H.L. Hunley had managed to sink one of its treasured ships. To be living in its official observatory in the heart of the Union capital was the height of irony, an afront to all the Mississippi boys and men who had laid down their lives to preserve the ideals of southern sovereignty and the confederacy for which is stood.

But the real reason he had a distaste for the place was the security; tighter than tight, as if he were a teenager who'd just been grounded. When he was at home in his cherished Raven's Rest outside Biloxi, his Secret Service detail respected his privacy and allowed him significant latitude within the gates of his own home. Most days they'd be in their bunker behind the main residence, poring over row upon row of surveillance monitors, but the rooms inside the mansion were safe from prying eyes and ears. At least, that's what he'd been told—so he believed he enjoyed a modicum of privacy.

The residence at the Naval Observatory was a different matter altogether. The white three-story Queen Anne-style house, with a traditional turret and dormer windows, featured an asymmetrical floor plan that made Crittenden's OCD wife uncomfortable. The master suite was located on the second floor, along with another bedroom, a study, and a den that Raeanne had instantly claimed as her sewing nook. At one time the attic had been used as servants' quarters, but over the years it had been divided into four bedrooms, two of which were used by their children during their infrequent trips home from college.

It was the protection detail itself, however, that he abhorred the most. Fucking guards were on him like shit on a shoe. They were everywhere on the grounds, often hovering downstairs in the living room or in the basement kitchen. He'd heard that past VPs even had a problem with them washing their clothes in the family's private laundry room.

All this protection and concern for the man who was "just one heartbeat away" made it difficult to arrange this morning's face-to-face follow-up with William Raymond Tate, who had called him on his secure mobile phone around an hour ago.

"There's a rumor circulating that could prove troubling," Tate had said when Crittenden answered the phone. The VP had flown back up to DC last night for an *ad hoc* meeting with the president later today, but his wife remained down in Mississippi. "We need to meet."

"Gonna have to make it early," the vice president had replied. "I've got a full schedule today."

"I only need two minutes. Your golf game can wait."

Now, seventy minutes later, they were seated in the second-floor study down the hall from the master bedroom. Crittenden had updated it in dark wood paneling that echoed the private pub in the basement of Raven's Rest, albeit half the size. It was warm, almost hot, the AC unit not strong enough to adequately pump enough cooled air up from the condenser to chill it with any efficiency. Thus, an oscillating fan created a breeze that just barely kept both men from perspiring, even at this early hour.

"You assured me this was a slam-dunk," Crittenden said, sipping from a cup of coffee into which he'd surreptitiously dribbled a little bourbon... and then a little bit more. "Full court press, I think you said."

"I despise basketball, and all the cultural allusions that go with it," Tate replied. No coffee, no mineral water this morning. "What I said was, it'll be a home run."

"Whatever," Crittenden said, dismissing the crossed sports metaphors with a roll of his eyes. "Point is, you insisted Wheeler's death would be a sure thing, the evidence would be conclusive. 'Incontrovertible,' is the word you used. No one would have reason to question it. And now you tell me that some two-bit blogger is turning over rocks to see what's under them?"

"First, he's not just a blogger. He's won a lot of awards in his career, caused a world of hurt for a lot of people. *Our people.*"

"Then why isn't he still with the *Post*?" The vice president uttered the word as if it carried a vile taste, like cloves or the fried kale Raeanne had such a taste for.

"Budget cuts," Tate replied. "That was the official story, at least. Unofficially, there was some alcohol involved, put him on the purge list."

"What do we have on him?"

"Give me twenty-four hours," Tate said. "I just put two of my men on it. All I know is the boozing started when his fiancé died six years ago. Damned near flushed him down the crapper."

"Shit follows the path of least resistance," Crittenden said.

"Maybe. But this shit carries its own stink, and that worries me."

Crittenden didn't like the wrinkled brow or the darkness that seemed to have fallen over Tate's eyes. "All right, I'll bite. Why the concern?"

"Does the name Katya Leiffson mean anything to you?"

"Should it?"

Not to a sociopath who has absolutely no empathy for another living soul, Tate thought. "That was his fiancé's name," he said. "The blogger."

"Good to know," Crittenden responded with a shrug.

"She was one of the five passengers who died in the crash."

The cocky confidence in the vice president's eyes abruptly faded, replaced with a flicker of alarm. "Don't fuck with me," he said.

"I fuck you not," Tate replied.

"And now he's looking into Wheeler's death?"

"That's what I'm hearing. Questioning the videos and pics on the computer, the silk noose. The whole autoerotic thing. He's even calling for the M.E. to conduct an in-depth tox screen, see if there's some sort of fast-acting anesthetic in his system."

"Is there?"

"You don't want to know. Point is, he's asking the right questions, and one of them might land him the right answer."

"You can't let this lead back to you," Crittenden reminded his trusted friend and fixer.

You, not *us*, Tate noticed. "I'll make sure it doesn't," he said.

"You promised me results, not problems, Billy Ray. Twice, in fact. I don't need to remind you what's at stake here—"

"No, *Mr. President*," quipped the man who was being paid handsomely to expedite Crittenden's ascendance from this ratty old residence in northwest Washington to the mansion at 1600 Pennsylvania Avenue. As quickly as possible, if all things played out as they were planned.

"Speaking of which, how is our succession strategy progressing?" Crittenden inquired.

"All is proceeding according to plan," Tate assured him.

"We're still looking at that fucking media thing?"

That fucking media thing was the annual White House Media Dinner on Saturday evening, tomorrow night. It was just another of the many things Crittenden despised about this town, a sophomoric farce of ribald humor and racy innuendo that one had to endure in order to appear affable and self-deprecating. President Mitchell played the game like a seasoned pro, but Crittenden considered it Sodom-and-Gomorrah burlesque of Biblical proportions.

In years past he'd been loath to go anywhere near it, but this one he wouldn't miss for all the world. It was pre-destined not just to be the event that changed his life, but one that changed the course of history for all time.

"Everything's locked and loaded," Tate assured him.

"Lots of eyewitnesses."

"Eight hundred and four of them, at last count."

Crittenden nodded at the mental image, then said, "And you'll take care of this reporter?"

"Blogger," Tate corrected him. "You'll read about him in the papers. Armed mugging gone horribly wrong."

"Do you think we can risk that? People might put two and two together—"

"News of Mr. Logan's demise will be mitigated by a much larger story," Tate replied as he rose from his chair to leave. "Less than forty hours from now you'll have just been sworn in as the next leader of the free world."

Less than a mile away, Raleigh Durham stared at the computer screen, holding her mug of donut shop roast in both hands as she read. Trained to articulate every syllable of every line on a teleprompter five nights a week, her eyes went over every sentence word for word, each one of them ratcheting up her intrigue even further. When she came to the end of the story, she didn't take a sip of her coffee, which was getting cold. Instead she stared intently at Carter Logan and said. "This is friggin' unbelievable. If it's true."

Logan was leaning against the kitchen counter, nibbling on a cinnamon bagel, watching her reaction. "I have sources and evidence to back it all up," he assured her.

"Did you pull an all-nighter on this?"

"Nothing but time on my hands."

"But...how did you get access to those pictures? I mean, that has to be the most guarded laptop in this entire city—"

"The value of a secret is that it remains that way," Logan told her, revealing nothing.

"And you actually were given access to his room?" Raleigh asked him. "The crime scene at the hotel?"

"Sources and secrets often are one and the same."

"And the medical examiner?"

"She remembered a piece I wrote a few years ago," Logan explained. "A defense attorney dragged her through the fire on the stand, made her look as if she buried forensic evidence in a high-profile trial. I checked into it, found that the defendant's lawyer paid someone to tamper with it. The article I wrote pretty much saved her career."

"So, she owed you," Raleigh said.

"Magic markers." He took another bite of his bagel, washed it down with a swig of orange juice right from the carton. "But overall, you like it?"

She blanched as she watched him put the container back in the fridge. "I'm never going to drink OJ here again, but yes, I like it. Again, if it's true."

"Every word of it. So, I want you to say it."

"Say what?"

"That I'm not delusional."

"Never thought you were."

"I want to hear you say it anyway," Logan replied.

"I don't think you're delusional," she assured him. "And I want to remind you what you said when you pitched this idea to me."

"I didn't pitch it," he corrected her. "I just told you what I was working on."

"Semantics," she huffed, with a flip of her hand. "You implied that I might be able to convince someone—one of our producers—to piggyback on this, if there was a strong enough case to do so."

"That's not exactly how it went, but yeah, I remember."

Raleigh took a sip of coffee, which she had brought with her rather than take a chance on Logan's second-hand grounds. "Anyway, what's the chance you could hold off on submitting this to your editor?" she asked. "Just a couple hours, to give me time to check out a few things?"

"You'd better get moving," Logan told her.

"You're kicking me out?"

"*Au contraire*. In fact, I think we should take a little stroll into the bedroom and bat for the cycle, as they say in the big leagues. But in the spirit of full disclosure, I need to tell you that my editor is going to post it this morning, as soon as he runs it past the corporate lawyers."

Raleigh practically leaped out of her chair, splashing coffee on the already-filthy laptop keyboard. "Dammit, Carter. You promised."

"I told you I'd let you read it when it was finished. That's why I called and woke you up, why you agreed to stop by on your way downtown."

He was right, of course. He hadn't promised her anything when he'd pitched—*synopsized*—the story to her last night at dinner. But if Logan had the sources and evidence he claimed to have, he knew she'd want in on it. It was his story and he deserved the credit, but she was ambitious and determined, and had been looking for a way to scrabble up the ladder to the roof. Which, in this case, meant the network.

"How much time do the lawyers have?" she asked him.

"As long as it takes," he said. "But as you saw, it's only six hundred words."

"Crap." Raleigh grabbed her purse, which she'd set on the floor near the door. "I appreciate the lead time," she said, heavy sarcasm, kissing Logan on the cheek.

"And I appreciate whatever back-up you can give me," he replied.

She started to turn the knob, then stopped, her eyes burrowing into his. "There's another thing we talked about last night, remember?"

"Last night we said a great many things, and you said I should do the thinking for both of us—"

"Dammit it…now's not the time for *Casablanca* quotes," she scolded him, even though she still giggled. "What I mean is, I told you that if it turned out you were right about Wheeler's death being murder rather than suicide…well, whoever pulled this off is going to go full ballistic if the truth gets out."

Chapter 24

The departure platform was one level down. Monica figured the man who called himself Erich Rohm would guess she'd be heading there, boarding a train bound for some destination that would get her incrementally closer to New York. Despite the pain in his groin, he would go through the same mental process she did, study the various timetables, eventually narrow the choice down to two. Paris or Amsterdam. And eventually he would select the latter, simply because it left the soonest: just eleven minutes from now.

Her first instinct was to hide in the tiny lavatory until just before the doors closed, a tactic that had not worked well the last time she'd tried it. Also, because Frankfurt Main was an air and rail hub serving all of Europe, trains didn't just make quick stops as they rolled through. Many remained at the platform for a long while allowing as many passengers as possible to board, whether they were headed toward Brussels or Munich or Nuremberg. Or Amsterdam, by way of Cologne. That meant she was a duck on the pond until the doors closed and the wheels started turning.

At a sundries shop that sold magazines and souvenirs she purchased a black sweatshirt with the word *Deutschland* emblazoned on the front in Germanic *Fraktur* lettering. She yanked off the tags and pulled it on over her head, then capped off the look with a baseball hat with a red, black, and yellow flag on the front. No sunglasses, although she did spot a cheap yellow pair left over from last autumn's Oktoberfest in Munich. She liked them, but figured they'd make her stand out in this indoor crowd. She checked her look in a mirror, felt confident she would blend in and attract neither the attention of the police nor the man named Rohm.

As she limped toward the escalator that would take her down to the railway platform, she passed a crowded cocktail lounge packed with travelers enjoying lunch and a beer. They all seemed to be watching the newscaster on the giant television mounted near the ceiling, a split screen with the right half showing flashing lights and wild commotion inside the Frankfurt airport terminal. Far worse, the left half showed a still frame of a woman who appeared to have just left the baby changing station in Terminal One. A caption at the bottom of the screen read: *Möglicher Verdächtiger bei Mord am Flughafen identifiziert.*

Monica's German was almost nil, but her panic returned as she realized her face—grainy and dark as it was—was already out in the news media. Every police officer in the country probably had a bulletin, which explained their heavy presence here at the station.

She tugged the bill of her cap further down over her forehead and kept moving. She riveted her eyes to the floor, except for an occasional nervous glance around the platform. Her train was already standing at the edge of Platform 3, the doors wide open, waiting for passengers to climb aboard. She inserted her ticket into the turnstile and edged through, then took one last glance over her shoulder as she made a beeline for the nearest second-class car.

The Cold War that dominated the last century's political mindset indisputably created an almost Strangelovian paranoia which, in turn, led to the development of knee-jerk government programs that served little purpose other than ratcheting up suspicion and fear. And, ultimately, they wasted hundreds of millions of taxpayer dollars.

Rattled by the discovery in the 1970s of a Russian program to weaponize the human mind, the American intelligence community devised a parallel project to study and identify a full spectrum of heretofore discounted paranormal experiences. Funded by monies funneled through the CIA and DIA, the venture dabbled in neuropsychic transmission, extrasensory mind control, and remote viewing influences. In applicable terms, the clandestine enterprise probed the alleged abilities of select individuals who claimed they could "see" events, locations, or images from a great distance. Within months, investigators at the newly founded Project MINDGAZE reported startling success in their para-psychic research and, at the direction of their intelligence community overlords, began to foster creative approaches through which they could apply their findings to covert operations, both theoretical and practical.

Over the years, close to one billion dollars were invested in the venture. The program's truest devotees claimed incredible results, although no one outside the inner circle was permitted to see the evaluations and analyses. Since taxpayer dollars were involved, clandestine as they might have been, a team of Congressional bean counters was engaged to investigate the investigators—and analyze their findings. Many of the amazing results were debunked by these outside auditors, MINDGAZE was stripped of its funding, and the entire thing was folded into an obscure entity overseen by the National Security Council. A fraction of its original size, the project continued to explore the power of the human mind and paranormal perception, with limited success. Once again, independent researchers were brought in and, after a thorough probe that cost millions more, they concluded the data was neither compelling nor reliable enough to be used for any sort of military or intelligence actions. The recommendation was that the entire program be scrapped.

Officially, it was. Unofficially, MINDGAZE was integrated—through a series of shell companies and dummy corporations—into the Greenwich Global Group. In the early years the rejuvenated operation produced results that were interesting but not spectacular, which meant that each year the doctors in charge of its longevity were forced to justify their existence. Each year the G3's executive board voiced renewed skepticism that the program's eight-million-dollar annual budget was a wise allocation of finances, and each year it reluctantly renewed its funding on the last day of December.

Then Phythian came along.

The doctors and researchers at The Farm conducted multiple MRIs and SPECT scans, which showed that parts of his brain were lit up in ways that defied description. They floated all sorts of theories and pseudo-scientific lingo that might explain his innate abilities, all of which tested way off the charts. Gone were results that were just slightly above the random odds of chance. Phythian aced everything that was thrown at him, beginning with guessing four different shapes—square, circle, star, diamond—on the reverse side of a deck of cards. Perfect score. The experiments then graduated to standard playing cards: fifty-two out of fifty-two, each and every time. Next came random images of horses, trees, billboards, automobiles. One hundred percent.

The researchers were ecstatic almost to the point of orgasm. Not just because they finally had found the test subject they'd been seeking for decades; they also now had reason to ask—*demand*—that their annual funding be doubled. They also found something both peculiar and fortuitous during their experiments: Phythian's success relied entirely on the presence of another human mind. He was able to "visualize" an image or a concept only if it first was filtered through another person's brain, which he then quickly "hacked." A deck of the same cards without a researcher present was useless.

The true breakthrough came when the program shifted from passive remote viewing to active mind control. Whether it was the result of his being submerged in the icy quarry all those years ago or some other unexplained event, Phythian proved himself to be adroit not only at *reading* minds, but *pushing* thoughts into them, as well. The incident with Dr. Segal on the BART train in San Francisco was the lynchpin of this new realization and, within weeks of his arrival at The Farm, the euphoric scientists determined their new research subject was the star pupil they'd been waiting for since the project began all those years ago.

Months of government-funded training allowed Phythian to sharpen his skills to such an edge that, at the train station at Frankfurt Airport, he almost knew what Monica was going to do before she did it. Same thing with Hazan, whom he'd met years ago and had already established a lasting extrasensory shortcut. That was what terrified the Greenwich Global Group more than anything: his flawless capacity to know what anyone within a thousand-yard reach was thinking, *if he put his mind to it*. The closer his physical proximity to the target, the better the "connection"—which, he now knew, was why the G3 had made sure there were almost infinite degrees of separation between themselves and the handful of operatives who were directly involved with planting the bomb in his airplane six years ago.

In any event, it was this close proximity—Monica had been standing no more than thirty yards away from him on the platform—that had turned her brain into easy pickings. Eitan Hazan, too.

Chapter 25

Diana Petrie was sitting on a concrete bench, staring at what she considered the ugliest deformity New York City had offered to humanity in the last half-century. It was a towering monstrosity known as The Vessel, a structure of crisscrossing and zigzagging stairs that she suspected would have made M.C. Escher weep in dismay. Billed as the centerpiece of the Public Square and Gardens, the bronzed steel and concrete sculpture was a money pit that had cost one hundred fifty million dollars to construct and offered nothing beneficial in return. A stairway with no destination, to Petrie it epitomized the futility of human endeavor and the misplaced priorities of a civilization that had lost its way.

Yet here she was, staring at it, drawing on its emptiness to fuel the fury that was building inside her. Fury because she had just seen the police photos of Simone Marchand sprawled on the floor of the airport restroom, her bruised and lifeless body crumpled against the subway tile wall. Not all that different from the people who had jumped to their deaths from the hideous eyesore before her, which was why it again was closed to tourists.

"How the fuck did this happen?" Petrie whisper-yelled into her cell phone, which was encrypted and scrambled, per usual. "My instructions were clear and simple: surprise, attack, kill."

"This'll have to wait," Eitan Hazan barked at her. "I'm busy."

"Where are you?"

"Frankfurt *Flughafen*." He was staggering through the second level of the railway terminal, keeping an eye open for Monica Cross. He did not need this interruption and almost had not answered, but he knew better than to avoid a call from the Dragon Lady.

"What's that?"

"The train station at the Frankfurt airport. Everything is under control."

"Under control is a dead target. Two dead targets. Yet you're telling me they're both alive, and Simone is deceased."

Hazan wasn't about to explain that one of the targets, Monica Cross, had just obliterated his testes, nor that he'd blown his surprise attack on Phythian. "I'm on it," was all he said.

"You are not authorized to make flash decisions in the field."

"Copy that."

It was morning rush hour in New York, not quite eight o'clock in the morning. Seething with anger and frustration, she had wandered downtown to Hudson Yards to gaze at the one thing that could be worse than the total failure of the double assignment she had put in play—although not by much.

"We'll discuss Simone later," she told him. "Right now, your job is to take care of Cross and Phythian."

"So noted."

"I want proof of death," Petrie said. "Incontrovertible."

She ended the call and looked up. *Dear God*, she thought: the ugly architectural was still there, the bronze stairs glinting in the morning sun, winking whimsically as if the damned thing had been in on the joke from the start.

Chapter 26

Monica's train departed Frankfurt *Flughafen* one minute late, something she could easily live with. A steady rhythm seemed to settle into her body with each revolution of the wheels on the tracks, and by the time her car cleared the far end of the platform she began to feel as if she'd left her problems behind.

The station had been overrun with police and soldiers carrying heavy artillery and two-ways radios. They'd been watching every passenger who boarded the train, and asked to see her passport when she approached her car. Fortunately, they didn't seem to know who they were looking for yet, most certainly not this young woman dressed in German national pride, even though she was American. She received just a cursory glance as she stepped up from the platform, and no one paid her any attention when she took her seat and tried to look as unobtrusive as possible.

This had been hard to do, since less than an hour ago she had killed a woman with her bare hands. Self-defense, wholly justifiable, but it rattled her to the core of her being. Not just this particular fight to the finish, but also the death of the two jihadists—or whatever they were—on the narrow mountain trail. Less than a week ago she never would have imagined herself as someone who could take a human life, yet now she was sitting on a train in Europe wondering how she had turned into a cold-blooded murderer.

The events of the last few days caused her to revisit the past, recalling weekend trips with Phillip to their favorite stretch of sand at Mastic Beach on Long Island, watching the autumn foliage turn aglow up in Vermont, hunkering down over a long Christmas weekend in a borrowed cabin on a lake in Maine. They had no heat, no electricity, but plenty of blankets and a fireplace that flooded the place in a romantic blush, embers that popped and crackled well into the night.

Now, with each turn of the wheels, the rhythm of the rails and the blur of countryside lulled her into a gentle slumber. For the last twenty-four hours her brain felt as if it were filled with numbered balls bouncing around inside a lottery machine, but it seemed someone had unplugged it and they had become inert…just like her mind.

Sometime later she awoke as a conductor's voice announced their pending arrival at *Limburd Sud*. It was the only stop the high-speed made between Frankfurt and Cologne, where she had to change trains for Amsterdam. Monica's timetable told her this was just a brief stop, and when the brakes lurched to a halt, she ventured a glance out the window. Even here there were police on the platform, but not as many of them and none of them appearing as attentive as they had been back at the airport. Her fold-up route map indicated they only stopped here for two minutes before moving on.

A mere flicker of time, but Monica counted every one of the hundred-twenty seconds.

Just as she got to one-hundred-ten, a man slid into the seat next to her. She opened her eyes a notch and studied him as he fussed with an overnight bag. He was a few inches under six feet, a few pounds over average. He wore wire-rim spectacles that made him appear in his fifties, and a dark suede jacket with leather elbow patches that looked as though it might not have been laundered in weeks… and smelled that way, too.

Something about her demeanor must have attracted the man's attention, because he smiled at her apologetically and said to her, "*Verzeihung, bitte.*"

Monica lifted her shoulders in a polite shrug. "*No sprechenzie Deutsch,*" she replied in one of the few clipped German phrases she knew.

The man thought for a moment, searching his brain for the English translation. "Please, do forgive me," he said as he adjusted his glasses on the bridge of his nose. "I did not mean to wake you."

"No trouble at all," she told him, realizing that her hands were clenched in tight fists. Just in case she had to use them.

"I do apologize, *Fraulein,*" he said. "I was seated in the car in front of this one, but it was too loud."

"Well, don't worry," she assured him. "I won't talk if you don't."

He seemed to get the hint and settled into his seat. Monica noticed he had a paper bag that read *Schweinske* on the side, and grease spots were starting to form from whatever was inside. He pulled out a sandwich wrapped in paper, opened it on his lap as the train again began to pick up speed. The man took a bite of his meal and said, "I hope you don't mind me eating."

"Not at all," Monica replied. "And I hate to inconvenience you, since you just sat down, but I need to use the restroom. I'll be back in a flash."

She wouldn't be, of course. There were six second-class cars as part of this train, and she could find another seat on any of them. She hated feeling paranoid, but she'd sensed a sudden need for a change of scenery. Every mile that took her closer to home, she felt that much more relieved, more reassured. Although a dark feeling nibbled away at the back of her brain.

Monica found an empty seat two cars forward from hers. There were two of them, side-by-side, which allowed her to spread out without worrying that someone might encroach on her space, maybe stick a gun in her ribs or wrap a garrote around her neck while she was dozing.

And doze she did, as the steady metronome of the rails kept pace with the beating of her heart.

She awoke an hour later to the call of nature. She got up and shuffled down the aisle, found that the lavatory in her car was occupied, two more passengers hovering in the aisle waiting to use it. Monica felt an ankle cramp coming on, and she decided to exercise her joints rather than join the queue. She made her way through the vestibule into the next car, then the next one, where she finally found a restroom that wasn't in use. She turned the knob and gave it a nudge, but it barely moved. The sign on the door indicated it was vacant, so she pressed against it with greater force. This time it opened just a crack before catching on something. She knocked politely, just in case someone inside didn't know how to throw the latch, but there was no answer. Finally, she leaned her full weight into it, and just barely managed to squeeze inside. The door slammed shut behind her, as if driven by a spring-loaded mechanism, the sudden motion activating a light over the aluminum sink.

What she found in there almost made her scream.

Erich Rohm was slumped on the floor in a corner of the tiny compartment. The door had caught one of his shoes, which was why

Monica hadn't been able to open it at first. His head was tilted back on his neck, his mouth open, his eyes lifeless—lifeless because of the single hole in his temple, blood and brains sprayed across the wall.

Monica clutched her hand to her mouth and felt herself grow dizzy. She stared at those dark eyes, the pudgy nose, blood dripping from his head and pooling dangerously close to her shoes. His finger was on the trigger of the gun that had fired the fatal shot, still gripped in his right hand on the filthy lavatory floor. Had he taken his own life?

Her first instinct was driven by panic. She yanked the door open and stumbled out of the tiny restroom, then doubled over, gasping for a breath of air that took forever to arrive. She inhaled several ragged gulps, none of them filling her lungs, and felt as if she might faint.

And then she saw *him*.

The man who had been approaching her at the airport when Rohm had interfered.

Rather, she saw the back of him, standing at the other end of the aisle. He was peering through the glass door that opened between this car and the first class one in front of it. His hands were cupped around his eyes and he appeared to be looking for someone. *For her*.

She pushed her way back inside the restroom and turned the lock. The overhead light flickered on again, casting an eerie, green glow throughout the compact space. She tried not to look at Rohm, but couldn't ignore his stunned face staring up at her from where his bloody head sagged against the wall. Or the gun, which seemed massive because it had one of those sound things screwed to the end. *A silencer*. She felt as if she was a spectator intruding on this most private of moments at the end of a person's life. But his body also reminded her of what she herself might look like just a few short moments from now, if she didn't take care.

Ten excruciatingly long minutes later the train came to a stop. An automated voice announced from an overhead speaker that the train had pulled into Cologne, and Monica waited for the sound of shuffling feet out in the aisle to subside. Once she sensed the crowd of passengers had thinned, she gingerly pushed the door open and peered out.

A few stragglers were milling about in the aisle, collecting their belongings from the floor in front of them. She gave one last glance at Erich Rohm, wondered what his orders had been. Was he a good guy or a bad guy? Was there really any discernible difference anymore? Had he really been at the airport to help her, or was that just a ruse to get her alone and then… well, *then what*?

More and more questions swirled through her head as she slipped out of the lavatory. She still had to pee, but nature would have to wait. Right now, she just swallowed her fear, held her breath, and stepped down onto the platform.

Chapter 27

One of the perks of being vice president of the United States was that few people noticed how often you played golf.

Crittenden knew that would change when he moved from his current address down to Pennsylvania Avenue, but it was an inconvenience he could live with. For now, he and his Secret Service detail could hit the links three, sometimes four days a week, without anyone paying attention to where "Heartbeat" was at any given moment. *Heartbeat* being the unofficial nickname his agents had assigned him, on account that it was the factor that separated him and the highest office in the land. For the record, his official code name with the Treasury Department was Raven, bestowed upon him because of the name of his Mississippi homestead.

At the moment he was on the second fairway of a private club in Potomac Heights, located just thirty minutes north of his residence on the Maryland side of the river. It was a glorious expanse of neatly trimmed zoysia and bentgrass, designed with devious bunkers and treacherous lakes whose muddy bottoms were littered with expensive Callaways and Taylormades and Titleists.

The right side of this particular fairway was home to a stand of majestic oaks that seemed adept at reaching out and snatching a well-hit ball on the fly. That's what Crittenden was tending to now, as his tee shot had hooked into the trees, then bounced off the trunk of a massive elm. He was deciding whether to use a five wood or the new nine-iron lofted hybrid that a Japanese financier had presented to him after they'd played a particularly difficult—and embarrassing —round back in April.

He gauged the distance from where his ball lay in the tall crabgrass to the pin, eventually figured the five might be best suited to get back on the fairway. He moved farther back on the ball—one of a dozen monogrammed Bridgestone Tour RXs that had been gifted to him by the defense minister of Taiwan—and set his stance—feet just wider than his shoulders and parallel to his intended line of flight. He was not a natural at the game, which meant everything he did on every swing was by the book—posture, grip, address, takeaway, backswing, downswing, follow-through—followed immediately by a string of cuss words as the ball took off at a wide angle and landed on the other side of the fairway in one of the demonic sand traps that the VP swore the course architect had placed there to annoy him personally.

"Fuck you, Nicklaus," he cursed as he marched over to where he'd parked his cart.

He thrust the club into his Founders Club golf bag—a personal gift from Scotland's cabinet secretary for health and sport—and yanked a deerskin cover over its titanium head.

Instantly a shiver coursed through every nerve ending in his body, and suddenly he was twenty years old again, finishing his junior year at Harvard—not Old Miss, as his mother had urged him, nor Rice, which was where his father had earned his undergraduate degree. *Harvard*, a northern college in a northern city that violated virtually every tenet of the Crittenden family code, and was considered a slap in the face to all the sons and brothers and fathers who had laid their lives down in defense against the Union invaders.

Fact was, Crittenden had liked Harvard and, despite its Yankee affectations, enjoyed the city of Boston—not the snow and ice so much, but the people were friendly and weren't obsessed with manners or social veneer. Rarely did he hear someone say "yessir" or "yes ma'am," nor did he miss the forced pretense. Sweet tea wasn't readily available for lunch in Cambridge, but beer was. The barbecue was dry and bland, but he quickly developed a taste for lobster and clam chowder. And Catholics turned out not to be the devil in disguise, as his Aunt Esther always claimed, since they went to church every Sunday, the same as Baptists.

Six weeks before finals that junior year, James Crittenden and a handful of his classmates were invited to spend the weekend at a frat brother's summer home on Martha's Vineyard. The only thing the future vice president knew about the island was that Senator Ted Kennedy had driven off a bridge there and drowned the girl who was riding with him. There had to be something sexual going on between them—after all, he was a Kennedy—and the mishap had not only killed her, but destroyed any future presidential aspirations he might have. Crittenden had no intention of following him down that road. *No siree.*

There had been a party that night, and significant quantities of alcohol were consumed. The blowout spilled well over into Saturday morning and, after a few hours of sleep, the festivities started up again. More bottles of hard liquor turned up on the bar, as did an anonymous baggie of weed. By now some of the younger locals had learned of the bash out in East Chop, and a few of them came out to investigate.

Three of the uninvited but very welcome guests were the Fisher sisters, ages nineteen, sixteen, and fourteen. Lori was a checker at the fish and meat market in Edgartown, while the younger Leah and Lisa were high school junior and freshman, respectively. Their parents were off-island that weekend and with nothing better to do—and just coming down off a blustery winter void that brought the island to the brink of depression—the girls were ready to let loose.

The booze and the pot and an adolescent brain temporarily located at the junction of his legs caused young Crittenden to be drawn to the fourteen-year-old. Through any set of eyes, she would be described as jailbait, although to a Harvard undergrad with a passing interest in literature, the more appropriate moniker was *Lolita.* Within minutes of spotting her across the pine-paneled sunporch of the frat brother's beach house, he felt the same surge in his loins as Nabokov's Humbert must have sensed in his.

"You don't sound like you're from Harvard," she had said to him, her blue eyes gleaming with youthful innocence.

"Mississippi, actually," he explained. "Land of magnolias, cotton, and mockingbirds."

"And slaves."

"Not in over a hundred fifty years, Sugar. Do you like bourbon?"

She flashed him a smile that was sweeter than a glass of fresh-squeezed lemonade. "Why, I don't believe I've ever tasted it," she replied, in a mock southern accent.

"Well, there's always a first time for everything. Try a sip of mine."

She hardly gave his offer a second thought as she swallowed a hefty gulp. "That burns," she said. "Can you get me a glass?"

Something deep in his brain screamed *Kennedy*, but another part of his body heard an entirely different calling. He poured her a shot, and then another one, and an hour later they found themselves on a narrow stretch of beach out near Farm Pond, a bottle of Ten High wedged into the sand. Crittenden had thought far enough ahead to bring a towel, which he had stuffed into a drawstring trash bag that now was bunched up beneath their clothes and shoes. Lisa was lying on her back on top of the towel, clad only in her panties and a small training bra. He was on top of her, their lips locked, his trousers unzipped but at that moment still up around his waist.

No-no-no, his head was screaming, but the rest of him was chanting *go-go-go*.

More kissing ensued, then more drinking, and more touching. A lot more touching, until he again heard the words "no, no, no"—only this time it wasn't the voice in his brain.

It was fourteen-year-old Lisa Fisher who, even through the haze of eighty-proof bourbon and several hits of weed back at the beach house, had realized what was about to go down.

"I'm not ready," she told him, trying to push him off her.

"Ready for what?"

"This. Tonight. *You*."

"What are you talking about—"

"I don't want it to be like this."

"Be like what?" he asked.

"Just stop. Please. *No*."

"Fuck," Crittenden said. He could hear the pleading in her voice, and some fear. Panic, too, but mostly what he heard was self-loathing and disgust, and he felt a surge of darkness wash through him. He kissed her again, but she pushed him away.

"No," she said again, louder this time.

Reflexively he slapped a hand over her mouth and snarled, "You know you want this."

She shook her head and tried to wriggle free, but the weight of his body held her down. She tried to scream, but he reached out and fumbled for the garbage bag that had held the towel. When his fingers finally found it, he opened the drawstring and then pulled it down over her head. He wasn't thinking, of course, just reacting to the events of the moment and an almost empty bottle of Ten High.

She had fought him, but he was stronger. And, in his mind, he had more to lose. She struggled for a full minute, kicking and thrashing on the towel before her body went limp beneath him. Then the moon came out from behind a cloud and he saw that her bra had come partially askew, exposing the round edge of one tiny nipple.

When it was over, Crittenden sat back and slowly climbed off her, brushing grains of sand from his trousers. He stared at her lifeless body, just fourteen years old, a girl whose parents were out of town, a girl who had tried bourbon for the first time only hours ago. He glanced around, saw a mound of driftwood near some beach heather or poverty grass or whatever the hell grew out here on this damned island. He ran over to it, sank to his knees, and threw up—not because he had just killed this girl named Lisa Fisher, but because he had killed his future—before it ever got off the ground.

Then he began digging.

Now, thirty-six years later, as he yanked the deerskin cover over the carbon fiber driver with the titanium head, he shook the filament of memory from his brain. He dropped his ass behind the wheel of courtesy golf cart and touched his toe to the pedal. The electric vehicle jumped into motion, taking him toward a sand trap—this one a much lesser threat than the beach in East Chop—on the other side of the fairway.

Just then, the cell phone in Vice President Crittenden's pocket rang, the incoming call signaled by the opening riffs of Kate Smith's "God Bless America." The official rules of the exclusive country club mandated that cell phones be turned off while playing the course, but matters of national security allowed for an exception. It wouldn't look good if something happened to the President and Heartbeat couldn't be located, just because he was going for par on the ninth green.

Such a putt by Crittenden was highly unlikely on this or any other hole at the Potomac Heights club. He weighed answering the call against making the eight-foot shot but, when the screen told him it was William Raymond Tate, he announced, "Sorry…it's the White House. I have to take this."

He turned and walked off the green, keeping several strides ahead of a Secret Service detail that was desperate to keep him in check.

"What?" he snapped at the phone. "I'm in the middle of something."

"I know where you are," Tate replied. "I'll be brief. The article went up an hour ago."

"What article?"

"The one I warned you about. The blogger, speculating about Wheeler's death."

Motherfucker works fast, he thought. "Have you read it?"

"Of course, I've read it," Tate said, almost spitting out the words. "It's mostly hat and no cattle. No facts, plenty of conjecture. But somehow, he got to the medical examiner and the metro police. Drilled down far enough to find some inconsistencies in the evidence."

"Does he say who he thinks did it?"

"He does not. In fact, he speculates it probably was someone who had a beef with one of Wheeler's court positions, either past or upcoming."

"Is there any way this can be traced back to you?"

There it was again: *you*, not *us*. And definitely not *me*. "No chance," Tate assured him. Despite his outward confidence, he personally was furious at how sloppy the G3 hitman—hit*woman*—had been in dealing with the Supreme Court Justice, and he'd leveled both barrels of venom at Adam Kent just two minutes ago, before calling the vice president. "You're clear. We all are."

"Make sure it stays that way," Crittenden snapped. "The past remains dead and buried."

Dead and buried was how Lisa Fisher had remained after the party in East Chop. Local and state cops, even the FBI, had seemingly scoured all of Martha's Vineyard for three weeks, but turned up nothing. Not a shred of clothing, not a drop of blood, not a fingernail or a print from her size six sneakers. This was back in the infancy of DNA analysis, which meant they hadn't looked for that, and the twenty-year-old Harvard junior named James Crittenden covered his tracks with immaculate deniability.

Over the first few days the police grilled everyone who had been at the party. That meant twenty-four persons of interest, including the two remaining Fisher sisters. Everyone had been either too inebriated, stoned, or involved in their own intimate interludes to notice where the fourteen-year-old girl had gone. Crittenden swore he'd passed out on the living room couch long before midnight, a half-empty bottle of bourbon on the floor beside him. Several frat brothers vouched for him, either out of Greek loyalty or drunken disregard.

Wary of his precarious situation in the matter, Crittenden appeared genuinely concerned for the girl's whereabouts. He'd welcomed the detectives' questions, eager to help but not to the point that he might cross that fine line between witness and suspect. Yes, he had spoken with Lisa Fisher earlier, and he had given her a sip of his drink. Then he'd told her she looked too young to be at a party where alcohol was being served, and shouldn't she run along home and watch TV with her parents? His words had angered her and she'd stormed off—presumably, he told them, to get something to drink on her own, or find someone with fewer scruples who would get it for her.

"I didn't know her folks were off the island at the time," he'd insisted, and the cops had believed him. "Those kids sort of crashed the party, but no one really thought to kick them out."

After the initial search, life returned somewhat to normal. The Fishers grieved and blamestormed and did their best to pester the police, who claimed they were doing their best to find their daughter. Accusations were hurled and gossip was spread, as family and friends pointed fingers at the Harvard boys and castigated the media for insinuating that Lisa's disappearance could in any way have been her own fault, or that of her parents. Some loose-lipped locals fueled rumors that Mr. and Mrs. Fisher were swingers, and their daughters were overly promiscuous. Fights broke out at bars over the course of the summer, and one man tried to run another man's car off the road because of something that was said at the hardware store.

As summer evolved into fall and then winter, the tragedy fell from the public consciousness, as tragedies often do. The Fisher story faded into local lore and, eventually, became little more than an asterisk in Vineyard history.

The following May, James Crittenden had walked from his rented apartment on Hammond Street to the Harvard Book Store in Cambridge. He was taking a break from studying for finals, which he wasn't taking too seriously because he'd already agreed to join his father's property development firm down in Gulfport, meaning he could afford to coast. For months after Lisa Fisher's death he'd felt like Marley in Dickens' *A Christmas Carol*, hauling around a heavy chain he had forged from his brief encounter with a girl that was far too young for him, and whom he had accidentally killed. Except there was nothing accidental about it: he had suffocated her deliberately, and then buried her deep beneath the driftwood mounded at the edge of the sand.

Honestly, he'd expected her body to be found by now. For almost a year he strolled the campus thinking sirens and blue lights would show up any second, he'd be hauled in, denied bail, and tried for murder—all because of one small indiscretion. The governor had recently vetoed a bill that would have reinstated the state's death penalty, but the prospect of being cooped up with killers and rapists for the rest of his life haunted his dreams.

When he walked into the book store that Wednesday in May he was surprised to find his old frat brother, the one whose parents' beach house had been the site of the party, seated at a table alone, a cup of coffee in his hand. Crittenden had nodded at him, uncertain whether he should walk over and chat it up or go about his own business, which was to try to find a gift for his new girlfriend, a beautiful young woman named Raeanne he'd met over Christmas break and who was due to graduate from Ol' Miss that month. But the frat brother, whose name was Colin Wheeler, waved him over and used his foot to push out the chair across from him.

"Sit down, Jim," he'd said. Pleasant and cordial, but cold and detached at the same time.

Something told Crittenden he should leave, but Wheeler insisted he take a load off his feet. He was a year older and was just finishing up his first year of law school, taking a much-needed break from his own studies. *High achievers, those Harvard men.*

Wheeler didn't ask if Crittenden wanted a cup of coffee, and Crittenden was feeling anything but social. Even though he'd eagerly attended the party in East Chop, he didn't particularly care for this Yankee blue blood who wore his arrogance on his crimson sleeve and was convinced his shit didn't stink. After a few moments of aimless small talk, a thin smile crept into Wheeler's smug face and he said, "I saw you, you know."

Crittenden's heart constricted a bit, and he said, "Saw me? What do you mean?"

"That night last spring. At the beach."

"I'm sure I don't know what you're talking about—"

But Wheeler had raised a hand, signaling him to stop. "I was there, too. Shouldn't have been, and I won't tell you why. Anyway, I saw what happened."

"I really don't know—"

"Yes, you do. But don't worry. I'll never say a word, unless you give me cause to."

"Are you threatening me? Trying to blackmail me?"

"Please…stop with the Dixie indignation." Wheeler lowered his voice, sounding almost conspiratorial now, and added, "I saw you pull the bag over her head and kill her."

"I…don't…"

"No worries, my brother." The smile remained etched into his face, a smile Crittenden would see in his dreams until the day he died. "A man does what he has to do."

"Look, Colin…whatever you think you saw—"

But Colin Wheeler didn't care to continue the conversation, didn't care to know what Crittenden believed he'd seen. Instead, he waved him away with the back of his hand, like a horse flicking away a fly with its tail.

"It is what it is," said the first-year Harvard law student who, twenty-six years in the future, would receive a presidential appointment to the U.S. Supreme Court. "Now, you run along and have a good life. And if I were you, I'd stay away from little girls."

Chapter 28

The Dupont Circle escalator serving the north end of the DC metro station was one hundred eighty-eight feet in length. It was not the longest in the city's underground system, but one of the steepest as it descended into the thick metamorphic subplate beneath Massachusetts Avenue.

Carter Logan could have walked north from his small apartment to the red line stop at Woodley Park, but this time of year it was packed with tourists headed to the National Zoo. Plus, it was in the opposite direction of where he was headed, which was Gallaudet University in the northeast section of the nation's capital.

Twenty minutes ago, he'd received a text from Dr. Ralph Finley, an assistant professor who had read Logan's blog earlier that morning. The syndicator's lawyers had given his article their tacit approval, and it had gone live shortly after Raleigh had left his apartment. As a computer scientist—and, Logan suspected, a rather proficient hacker—Finley had claimed some knowledge about altering the date and time of origin of digital files on a computer.

Logan had not intended to dive down the rabbit hole any further than he already had. He was merely a blogger rather than an investigative journalist, and his *modus operandi* was to raise the specter of suspicion and doubt, then watch as other news media, pundits, and talking heads piled on. This time, however, he felt something gnawing at the back of his brain, a manic sense that Wheeler's death was connected to something darker and more sinister than a closet pedophile taking care of business... or pleasure, in this case.

He'd agreed to meet Dr. Finley on the steps of Hall Memorial Building, the center of the university's Information Technology Department. He had stopped at an ATM along the way and retrieved a paltry forty dollars, just enough to get him through the upcoming weekend, if he budgeted wisely.

His preoccupation with finances was why he failed to notice the woman who leisurely had followed him down Connecticut Avenue from the steps of his apartment on Wyoming Avenue. She had done her best to look drab and mousy, baggy jeans and olive-green T-shirt, gray baseball cap without a logo, canvas bag slung over her shoulder. Maybe mid-thirties, although she was highly skilled at appearing almost any age she set her mind to—such as the other night, when she'd knocked on Justice Wheeler's door and he'd eagerly let her inside his comped suite at the Franklin Pierce Hotel.

After Logan stopped at the cash machine, he momentarily glanced at the cover of *USA Today* in a street box, then took the escalator into the musty bowels of Dupont Circle. The woman tailing him didn't want to follow him down there—being below ground was the one thing that truly terrified her—but today she had no choice. When she was a young girl, she'd regularly been chained to a support post in the basement of her childhood home as punishment for the smallest infractions that would set off her drunk stepfather: leaving her books on the kitchen counter, forgetting to bring in the mail, not wiping the spoon tray on the stove after dinner. One violation and down she would go into the dark cellar, and there she would remain for hours until the motherfucker called for a beer and remembered why she wasn't there to fetch it for him.

Her target this morning was moving with a distinct purpose, as if he had an appointment with what he probably thought of as his destiny—somewhere along the Red Line, which meant she would have to go down into that gloomy tunnel if she were going to keep an eye on him.

She would then figure out her best strategy to have him die a death—one that would earn her a one hundred-thousand-dollar bonus—that ultimately and irrefutably would be ruled natural.

See you tonight in Samarra, she thought as she closed her eyes and timidly set her right foot on the top step.

Dr. Finley was already waiting outside the main entrance to Hall Memorial Building, a four-story brick-and-glass structure that Logan figured had been designed during the architect's austere period.

As with many of the faculty and students at Gallaudet, the professor suffered from a hearing impairment that was medically diagnosed as moderately severe. Listening and speaking were difficult but, if Logan was patient and had sufficient time to spare, Finley had promised the meeting should prove valuable to his research on Colin Wheeler's death.

The associate professor recognized Logan from his blog photo and approached him even as Logan was walking down Lincoln Circle toward him. They shook hands, and then Finley sent him a text:

Mr. Logan...thank you for coming.

I'm glad you contacted me, Logan texted back. *And please call me Carter.*

Then I'm Ralph. Let's go in out of this heat.

Text messaging without question has changed the way people around the globe communicate with each other, but nowhere has it had a more profound effect than within the deaf community. Finley had already expressed this to Logan prior to this meeting, and they had agreed that using their phones to conduct a conversation would be much more practical than trying to use sign language or scribbling notes on index cards.

Follow me up to the lab where we can chat, Finley texted, motioning "up" with his thumb.

Show me the way, Logan replied.

Finley was a slight man, hair cut close to his scalp, black skin that glistened with perspiration from just a minute's exposure to the DC summer sun. He wore tortoise shell glasses with thick lenses, and hearing aids were nestled in both ears. Logan wondered if he'd been born with impaired vision and hearing, or if he'd suffered through a childhood disease, something like meningitis or encephalitis. Either way, he knew it would be impolite to ask, and not germane to their pending discussion.

The lab was located at the end of a hallway on the third floor. Since this was the university's information technology learning center, he wasn't surprised to find himself in a room full of keyboards, computer servers, external drives, and monitors. It was cold and carried a slight electrical smell, the byproduct of all the voltage buzzing through cables and surge protectors, and the air conditioning itself. Lighting came from overhead tubes, the old-fashioned kind that flickered and buzzed when the ballast was giving out. Sanitation seemed to be a low priority, since food wrappers and empty coffee cups covered most flat surfaces.

This is where the magic happens, Finley texted, adding a smiling emoji with sunglasses.

Please don't try to saw me in half, Logan replied.

Finley laughed when he saw the response, then typed, *No rabbits, no hats. Please sit.*

Logan pulled out a wheeled office chair and lowered himself into it. Finley did the same, then rolled himself over to what appeared to be the main computer console. His fingers flew across the keyboard in a flurry of movement and, when he finished, he texted:

As you might guess, deaf people aren't big on small talk. Shall we begin?

Logan didn't bother to text back, just nodded his response.

Good. As we discussed earlier, I believe you are right about the Wheeler porn jpegs. Dates were modified to look like random downloads.

Logan nodded again, and replied, *Easy to do, if you know how. Which I do.*

Finley proceeded to walk him through the process of modifying both the creation dates and most recent modification times of a half-dozen image files. The process took all of thirty seconds, and when he finished, he turned to Logan and wrote, *This is what I think they did to Wheeler's laptop.*

Another nod from Logan, who then replied, *Who is they?*

This caused the professor to smile, then tap his finger to his head. Smart thinking.

We'll get to that in a minute, he texted. *First, let me show you something.*

The IT professor tapped a few more keys and the six images disappeared from the screen, replaced by browser pages that digitally stacked themselves one on top of the other. Each appeared to be a webpage from various media outlets or wiki organizations committed to exposing global conspiracies and evil cabals.

What are those? Logan texted.

Reports of other autoerotic deaths that appear to be suspicious. Take a look.

Finley wheeled himself aside, allowing Logan to read the first headline on the digital stack, which dated back to the previous summer:

State Legislator's Death Reportedly Due To Autoerotic Mishap

Logan clicked on the page beneath it and found a similar story, titled:

Controversial Pastor Killed By Bungled Solo Sex Romp

And beneath that, three more:

Labor Minister Dies By Own Hand During Sex Game Gone Bad
Autoerotic Asphyxia Death Ruled An Accident
College Professor's Death Was "Sexual Misadventure"

There were ten stories in all, but Logan got a strong sense that this represented just the tip of whatever iceberg Finley thought he'd found.

Think they're connected? he asked.

Rather than respond directly, Finley brought up an Excel spreadsheet titled Correlations Between Autoerotic Deaths. It contained a good thirty rows, each of them containing the name of a deceased victim, and five columns spaced evenly across the screen. These were identified by headings that included "date," "location," "victim's livelihood," "images present," and "possible motive." Data had been filled in for each of the identified victims, with a simple "Y" or "N" indicating—Logan presumed—whether incriminating images had been found at the death scene.

It was the fifth and final column that caught his attention. Finley clearly had done some extensive—and impressive—research, providing a solid reason why someone might wish any of the thirty individuals dead. Adverse court rulings, revenge, gambling debts, embezzlement, abuse, power: every one of the victims had a possible motive entered in his final column.

Logan studied the spreadsheet line for line, then pushed back from the screen.

Interesting? Finley wrote

Very. Is this research or speculation?

Both. And admittedly imprecise.

How long have you been at this? Logan wondered.

Eight months, was the response. *Ever since my brother died.*

I'm terribly sorry, Logan wrote back. *I had no idea. Is he on this list?*

Finley gave a doleful nod, pointed at one of the names halfway down the screen. Korey Wright. *Half-brother, really. He died last winter.*

Logan looked at the screen again, saw that Korey Wright's occupation had been Army MP. The cause Finley had given for his death was "whistleblower."

What sort of whistle? he asked.

Something he saw in Turkey. Reported it, and ten days later he was dead.

Logan noticed that a "Y" had been included in the "Images Present" column next to his half-brother's name. What sort of images? he inquired.

Finley averted his eyes to his lap, clearly embarrassed by the question—

and the answer. Even though he obviously didn't believe any of this bullshit, the doubt lingered.

Little boys, he texted.

An almost imperceptible nod was the only appropriate response. Then: *If this is true, who do you think is behind it?*

It is true, and I don't think...I know.

The answer took Logan by surprise, and he studied Finley to gauge his mental balance. Behind those thick lenses he found certitude and conviction, no sign of doubt or hesitation at all.

Are you going to tell me?

Finley nodded, then texted: *Yes, in case something happens to me.*

Sounds sinister. Do you have proof?

No. But these people definitely exist, although they weren't easy to find.

Show me, Logan requested, giving him a nod of encouragement.

Finley didn't reply, just took up his position at the keyboard again. He opened a program from the index, typed in a series of commands, then hit enter. Finally, he followed up with a quick text that read: *Welcome to what we call the deep web.*

Chapter 29

Monica glanced at the digital read-out on the phone Brian Walker had given her: almost four o'clock local time. The video departure screen in the *Köln Messe/Deutz* station said that her connecting train to Amsterdam would depart in twenty-three minutes, which meant she would have to make herself scarce until it pulled up to the platform and she was able to board it.

Understandably, she'd acquired a new aversion to restrooms, so that option was out. On top of that, armed police officers were clustered in groups of two at the exits. She didn't know if that was a regular thing, since a number of European cities had experienced terrorist bombings over the past few years. Or maybe security had been ramped up because authorities were continuing to look for a suspect in the airport murder down in Frankfurt.

Either way, she couldn't just hang where she was. The dead man who had identified himself as Erich Rohm almost certainly had known she was on the train to Amsterdam, and either had been keeping an eye on her or, worse, was there to do her harm. Her sense of paranoia was becoming validated hour by hour, and now only confirmed that she needed to exert extra caution in everything she did.

The departure screen told her that a train to Brussels was leaving in twelve minutes. Not a high-speed express; this one was a local that appeared to stop at every small town between here and there, but it would get her there in under two hours. The city was not one of the destinations she had originally considered, but it was a major air hub and would have plenty of flights to JFK. And no one could possibly know she'd changed her mind, until she bought her ticket.

The problem was, it departed from *Köln Hauptbahnhof*, a four-hundred-meter hike across the Hohenzollern Bridge over the Rhine. Cologne was one of Europe's largest railway centers, with long-distance railway lines running into the city along both sides of the river. Monica's route from Frankfurt had arrived on the eastern side at *Köln Messe/Deutz*, and that was where her connection to Amsterdam would be leaving from. If she were going to shift destinations, she would have to hustle, not easy for a woman with a badly sprained ankle and injured ribs.

In the end it was an easy decision. She located an ATM that accepted her plastic and spit out two hundred Euros, which she then used to purchase a second-class seat to Brussels. It would be harder to track her movements that way, and she liked having some extra cash. She glanced at the ticket, then the route map: sure enough, her departure terminal was across the bridge, so she began to hoof it.

Phythian was one step ahead and two cars behind Monica when she stepped down to the platform at *Köln Messe/Deutz*. He'd been in the last second-class car of the train, four behind where she'd seated herself upon leaving Frankfurt, and had zeroed in on her brain waves the moment the train had pulled out of the station. Eitan Hazan had slipped aboard at the last minute, correctly surmising that she would choose the train heading to Amsterdam. Anticipating this move, Phythian had made sure the former Mossad agent had seated himself in the same car as his, just four rows in front of him.

Not long after the train had departed *Limburd Sud*, Hazan abruptly had stood up and walked up the aisle, pushing his way into the next car. If his target was on this train—and he was betting his career and life on that fact—now was the time to find her and kill her. He assumed she had changed her appearance back in Frankfurt, maybe bought a scarf and some make-up. All he had to do was wait until the train had almost pulled to a stop, and shoot her with the SIG Sauer he kept inside his sport coat, confident that the sound suppressor would muffle the shot to a soft *phffft*.

Then he would deal with Phythian, whom he knew had to be on the train somewhere.

Phythian had given Hazan a head start, staking him a half-car lead. As the train began to pick up speed he rose from his own seat and trailed after him, taking great care as he moved up the aisle to appear like a passenger casually looking for the rest room or the dining car. He clearly had the advantage: he was behind his target and still possessed the mental finesse that at one time had made him such a deadly human threat. Hazan, on the other hand, was standing at the front of the car, frustrated that he hadn't yet found the Cross woman.

Then Hazan had turned, and the mere sight of Phythian unwound him like an old clock spring. It was clear that Phythian had retained the skills that had made him such a threat at the peak of his career, and he knew how lethal that made him. Was the fucking freak reading his thoughts right now, tapping into the very real and overwhelming fear that was causing him to freeze right where he stood? Was he already determining Hazan's fate, deciding the best technique to employ on this high-speed train hurtling through the German countryside?

There were many answers to his questions, but the one that was most critical at that moment was that yes, Phythian continued to possess a full range of intuitive capacity. And, like an underestimated old geezer playing pick-up chess in a city park, he'd already thought this one through to checkmate. He knew Hazan was here to kill Monica, who was three cars in front of them. He knew about the P230 automatic stashed inside Hazan's coat, and he likewise knew Hazan would not hesitate to fire through a railcar full of passengers, none of whom had any idea that two paid killers were preparing for a shootout in their railway car. Not unlike the true event that had inspired a Clint Eastwood movie several years back.

He knew all these things, yet he did not act. Instead, he simply stood there in the aisle as Hazan felt an unmistakable mental grip on his skull, realized he was being drawn into a plan he could neither fight nor flee. The mental pressure began with just a feeble uptick in his pulse, but quickly intensified until he was overcome with an acute feeling of dread. Within seconds the undulating folds of depression engulfed him, and in that moment of despair and desolation he knew there was only one way to put himself out of his own misery.

With Phythian guiding his actions, Hazan pulled open the door of the restroom beside him and stepped inside. After the door clicked into place there really wasn't much decision involved: just point and shoot. The length of the gun with the silencer attached was a bit problematic in such a confined space, but he managed to contort his arm enough to touch it squarely against his temple.

The sound suppressor muffled the shot, but Phythian knew Hazan was dead the instant the slug tore into his brain. It was as if a wall switch had been flipped and a lamp suddenly extinguished. No white light appeared to guide the dead Israeli's path to eternity, no deceased relatives reached out to welcome him into the vast ethereal afterlife, no *Sheol*. His passing was marked only by a flawed soul taking flight in a smelly rest room on a high-speed train slicing through the German countryside.

Here one moment, gone the next.

Monica settled deep in her seat, keeping her face below the windowsill as she considered life's random echoes, the concentric ripples that form when you throw stones into a pond and then collide and change course over time.

Case in point: she wouldn't be on this train if she hadn't listened to her sister, hadn't accepted the assignment to photograph the Karakoram Mountains. Or if she hadn't fought off two vicious rebels, and hadn't tumbled into the wreckage of a plane crash. Or if the man with one eye who had followed her to the airport had not called in a bomb threat and forced her off her schedule.

If only one of those things hadn't happened, she might be home by now.

Home: the thought suddenly warmed her, then chilled her just as quickly. She missed Phillip terribly, the warmth of their bed and the way he would snuggle up against her back and tuck himself in like a set of spoons, and let her subtly know that she had aroused him in his sleep. She missed the way he had made coffee for her every morning, even though he didn't drink it, and the way he let her pick his ties, and the way she let him fasten her bra when he asked politely. She missed the champagne he would buy for no reason, not expensive but symbolic because it was the same *domaine* he had brought her on their first date. She missed the way he eased the cork out so gently that it uttered only a quiet sigh. She missed all of him: his smile, his eyes, his ears, his touch, his kiss. His very life.

Forty minutes after departing Cologne, Monica decided to call her sister. What harm could there be in a two-minute conversation from a train in the middle of Belgian farmland? How many times had Kathleen phoned her at two in the morning, frantic over some stupid thing she had done or was thinking of doing? Well, this time it was Monica's turn.

Kathleen answered on the second ring, and Monica could tell from the sound of her voice that she was worried. "Monica...where the hell *are* you?" she demanded. "I've been worried sick about you."

"If it's Friday, it must be Belgium," Monica quipped.

"What are you talking about? Belgium? What's gotten into you?"

"I figured as long as I was over here, I might as well try the waffles. Or the endive."

"Seriously?"

Monica hesitated a moment, taking a deep breath. She felt both drained from the pace and uncertainty of the last twenty-four hours, yet oddly invigorated by the overall experience.

"It's a long story," she said. "My flight home was cancelled, which led me to make alternate plans. I'm on my way to Brussels now and, with any luck, I should be home this time tomorrow."

Kathleen started to say something, then hesitated. Monica thought she heard a voice in the background—a male voice, that said something like "...almost got her."

"Kath...is someone else there with you? I heard a voice—"

"That was Patrick," her sister said, a little too quickly. "He hasn't left for work yet."

Possible, even probable—but that voice did not sound like Patrick's. And what was it he'd said? *Almost got her*? What the hell did that mean? And, if it wasn't Patrick, as her sister had said, who the hell was it? She pondered the words a moment, and then she knew.

"Kath, I've gotta go," she said.

"Hold on, Sis...not yet—"

But Monica wasn't about to hold on, not another second. She ended the call with a quick stab of her finger, then sagged against the wall of the railway coach.

Someone was there with her sister. Tapping the phone. Keeping her on the line long enough to trace it. She wondered how quickly today's computers could pinpoint a transmission to a cell phone on a train barreling through Europe. The old standard in the movies was sixty seconds, but that was back before satellites and virtual switches and fiber optics, on a phone that had been provided to her by the U.S. embassy in Pakistan.

And what would it matter in the long run? Monica had already mentioned she was on her way to Brussels, and had actually made a joke about Belgium. *How stupid could she be?*

She settled back in her seat and tried to recall every word of the conversation, but she was scared—damned scared—and running out of ideas. If someone was listening to Kathleen's phone calls, the government must be involved. They knew where she was going, and would be there waiting for her. She fumed, thinking of the choice words she would deliver upon her sister when she got back to the states. *When*, not *if*. But anger was not what she needed right now; she needed a plan.

For a fleeting second she thought about Arnie Kelso, her boss. She really should call him, but hadn't yet found the opportunity or the time. Brian Walker had told her that he'd been notified of her plight, and her pending arrival back in New York. She owed it to him; after all, Arnie had been the one who told her to take as much time as she needed after Phillip's death. Her job would be waiting for her, whenever she returned.

But that would have to wait, because just then the front door of the railway car slid open and two uniformed officers pushed their way inside.

Chapter 30

Sixteen years after killing Lisa Fisher, James Crittenden hired the Global Greenwich Group to help him eliminate a problem.

During his first campaign for the Mississippi State Senate, he'd run into a spot of trouble in the form of a letter that had arrived at his home in Biloxi—not Raven's Rest, but the five-bedroom residence he'd recently constructed on the shore of Mullet Lake, after a modest investment in one of the first casinos on the Gulf Shore turned into a cash cow. The envelope had been hand-addressed in block lettering using what appeared to be a felt-tip pen, no return. Postmarked at the central post office in New York City, as generic and untraceable as a letter could get. Inside was a note, typed on plain white paper in what appeared to be ten-pitch Courier, almost identical to the font ball on his own IBM Selectric III in his own office at the time.

The letter was brief and got right to the point:

> *Kokytos—*
> *She would have turned 30 today. Just to let you know, in case your conscience might be bothering you. Not likely, after all these years, but you never know how (and when) the past, present, and future collide.*
> *Horus*

There was no question whom the letter was referencing. The Fisher girl had been fourteen the night of the party in East Chop, making the math easy, as was the mental leap that told Crittenden that whoever sent this missive knew what had transpired that evening on the beach across the road from Farm Pond. Five of his classmates had been at the shindig that weekend, and all of them had covered for him, whether they had known his whereabouts or not. So had Colin Wheeler, the officious prick who had been sitting in the Harvard Book Store that day in Cambridge and had implied that he knew the truth, the whole truth, and nothing but.

It was the same Colin Wheeler who now was a judge for the United States Court of Appeals, second circuit, with a wife and two children who lived just a short train ride from Manhattan.

Crittenden had sat on the letter for three days, contemplating the timing and other aspects of the cryptic message. First, of course, was *why now*? Why send him a reminder of that horrific night, sixteen years after the fact? What would he—*or she*—hope to achieve? In the days and weeks after Lisa's unfortunate transcendence—he could never bring himself to use the word *murder*—he'd conveniently shifted blame for her death from him to her, where he'd convinced himself it truly belonged. He had not been responsible for her fate; it was just the unfortunate outcome of an awkward situation that had been remedied in a less-than-perfect way.

Of course: the timing had to relate to Crittenden's political ambitions. He'd just announced his candidacy for the fiftieth district senate race, and was considered the front-runner against two other primary candidates. Could the letter-writer—and the more he thought about it, the more he believed it had to be Wheeler—be aware of his political aspirations? Maybe this was the start of a blackmail ploy, or one of his Harvard classmates was trying to gaslight him.

The note was sent to a person named Kokytos by someone who claimed to be Horus. Had Crittenden paid attention during his Classics lectures, he would have remembered that Kokytos was the god of the underworld river of tears and despair, while Horus was the ancient Egyptian sky god whose right eye was linked to Ra, the sun god. While the *Eye of Horus* was thought to protect the pharaoh in the afterlife, it also was as an all-seeing symbol that witnessed and warded off evil. Was the writer of the letter insinuating that Crittenden was heinous and corrupt, or simply that he personally had seen what had happened that night?

On the morning of the fourth day, he showed the letter to a particularly callous and merciless knee-capper for a local crime ring that had just been shut down by the FBI. The young thug's name was Billy Ray, although his birth certificate listed him as William Raymond Tate, a bagman for backroom card games long before the state legalized them in 1990. Tate had recently helped Crittenden deal with a gambler who had run up a sizable blackjack debt and then had bloodied one of the priciest suites in the hotel after beating up a call girl. Crittenden believed problems were best dealt with swiftly and harshly, to send a message that neither he nor his casino were to be messed with.

"What do you think?" he'd asked, after Tate had read the note twice.

"What I think is, I don't want to know who *she* is, or what happened to her."

Crittenden didn't want to go there, either. "I just want to know who sent it," he replied.

"Could be just about anyone," Tate had replied. "Any ideas?"

Crittenden almost blurted out *Colin Wheeler*, but quickly caught himself. If Wheeler had been stupid enough to send it, he could be dealt with the same way Tate had dealt with the delinquent gambler. But if Wheeler *hadn't* sent the note, Tate's brutal interrogation methods might inflame some long-smoldering memories in his old frat brother that could come back to haunt him, especially since Tate wasn't known for his tact or finesse.

"No one I can think of," he'd said. "That's why I showed it to you."

"I'll look into it," was Tate's response.

It had taken two months but Tate finally tracked down the culprit. It turned out to be a seasonal resident of Martha's Vineyard, a classics professor at Columbia—*made sense*—who had driven up from Bronxville that May weekend sixteen years ago to take care of a plumbing issue at his summer house. He'd happened to be sitting in his glassed-in sunroom late that night, finishing a shot of Scotch—one of many—and had happened to look out his window just as Crittenden and the Fisher girl had sneaked through his yard, their faces caught in the glow of the moon.

Why had he waited all this time to make contact? Tate had questioned hm. Under great duress involving an icepick and tin snips, he'd confessed that the plumbing issue he'd been dealing with actually involved a weekend tryst with one of his undergraduate students. His wife believed he was giving a guest lecture at the University of Chicago and, if he'd spoken with the cops at the time, the whole charade would have crumbled. So, he'd pulled his BMW into the garage, turned out the lights, and pretended not to be home.

Why now? Because he'd recently retired, his inevitable and expensive divorce had just been finalized, and he figured it was time to come clean—clear his conscience and admit to past sins, both committed and witnessed. Plus, he'd recognized Crittenden's face from the internet, and couldn't believe the charlatan who had killed the poor girl was now entering politics. He'd even had the balls to cite the call of God for his decision to run, the concepts of "hypocrisy" and "blood guilt" clearly not troubling him at all.

Tate had said he'd understood, and quietly left the man's office. When he got back to his hotel room—a seedy but cheap place at the edge of Hell's Kitchen—he dialed a number that rang a phone just six blocks away, in the austere offices of an obscure hat company in a building next to Grand Central Station. Two weeks later the retired PhD was found lying on a sidewalk on the Upper East Side, his wallet missing and a deep gash in his carotid that had caused him to bleed out.

All this had gone through the vice president's mind as he waited in the outer Oval Office, shifting his weight from one foot to the other. The motorcade had whisked him to the White House directly after his triple-bogey putt on the ninth green, and he'd barely had time to change back into his pressed blue suit, pale yellow shirt, red tie—and flag pin, of course. He'd also managed to clip on the monogrammed cuff links the CEO of a Silicon Valley tech firm had given to him, the ones carved from fresh ivory smuggled out of Tanzania.

The first-floor anteroom had a splendid view, but Vice President Crittenden was not there to look at the sterile blooms in the redesigned rose garden. Nor was he looking at the president's secretary, a young politico named David Downs who, like the commander in chief, was from Pennsylvania. Instead, he was eyeing the bright red briefcase on the floor that was the trademark of Maggie Brown, the two-term governor of Iowa who was considered one of the party's rising stars.

Thirty seconds passed, then sixty, before the door between the two rooms opened. Governor Brown seemed to almost dance through it, light on her feet and a confident glint in her green eyes. In her late forties, she was a strikingly attractive woman, especially since none of her polish or enchantment was the result of supplements, implants, or scalpels.

"Good morning, sir," she said as she pumped his hand. "Always a pleasure to see you."

Bullshit, he thought as he watched her gather her briefcase from the floor. "The pleasure is all mine, governor," he said in a mellifluous accent, as if King Cotton himself were speaking. "Here on state business, I presume?"

"The President is always about business, and always about the state," she replied with her usual homespun charm. "You have a good day now, you hear."

Crittenden wished her the same, then lingered in the anteroom until David Downs gave him the signal to enter the Oval Office.

"James," President Mitchell greeted him from behind his desk—the same Woodrow Wilson desk that had been used by Nixon and Ford, cluttered with a pile of folders and loose documents. A model of a split rig schooner occupied one corner of the polished surface, and a brass clock encased in a glass bubble was set on the other. The president's profile was backlit from the light streaming through the large south-facing windows, lined with blue draperies. He did not stand when Heartbeat entered the room.

He was in on the Secret Service joke, too.

Crittenden walked over and sat in a chair in front of the desk, his customary perch whenever the two men met one-on-one, which fortunately wasn't all that often, since they had practically nothing in common. President Mitchell was a political enigma from Pennsylvania, socially moderate but fiscally careful, and he'd required a strong southerner on the ticket in order to swing two states that had shifted into the toss-up column after the last election cycle. Mississippi was not one of those states, but Crittenden had been his go-to man nonetheless.

"Good to see you, sir," the VP said. "I just ran into Maggie Brown." Getting right to it.

"She had some sort of interment at Arlington this morning, stopped by before heading back to Des Moines," the president explained. "Hope I didn't interrupt your game."

"It was just the front nine," Crittenden replied, the man's overt sarcasm not lost on him. "Your message said this was a matter of utmost importance. And discretion."

"That's what I've always liked about you," Mitchell told him, interlacing his fingers in front of him. "Right to the point. I know a lot of people from your neck of the woods who can chew your ear off for hours, but not you."

"Life's too short to kill time, being that time itself is what kills you in the end."

"Did that come from somewhere?"

"Some playwright," Crittenden replied with a shrug. "And I'm pretty sure I mangled it. What's this about?"

The president inched his chair closer to his desk, folded his hands on the wood surface that had been buffed and polished to the point that he could practically see his reflection in it. "Tell me, James...what do you think of change?" he said, focusing his eyes directly on Crittenden's.

"I don't have any snappy quotes about it, if that's what you're asking."

"It's not, Jim. In fact, I think we both have a good idea what sort of change I'm referring to here."

Yes, Crittenden had a suspicion, and he'd been expecting the hammer to drop at some point before the start of the re-election campaign. Despite the buddy-buddy façade, it was no secret these two men had differing personal mindsets and political agendas. And when Maggie Brown waltzed out of here not three minutes ago, the VP's suspicion had been confirmed. Still, he was not going to acquiesce without putting up some sort of resistance, so he replied, "American voters aren't very comfortable with change, sir. That's why our party is in office."

"Indeed, it is," President Mitchell agreed. "But demographics *are* changing, as are the voting blocs that get you to two hundred seventy."

"I'm not sure I'm following you," Crittenden said.

"I'm talking about women, Jim. They make up over half the electorate of this nation, and they're increasingly gaining power across the country."

"Which is why you have five women in your cabinet."

"Exactly. But our pollsters tell me that we face a woman problem next election, and we need to address it head-on."

"Sir?" the vice president said, no doubt in his mind where this was going.

"I've been approached by the chairman of a very large Dow thirty firm that wants to talk to you about becoming their next CEO," Mitchell said. "A professional courtesy, giving me a heads-up about their interest before they approach you directly."

Crittenden had been anticipating a possible shift in the ticket, but not a request for his resignation. Since this was late June—just over sixteen months before the next election—he figured the politics of the matter would move at a snail's pace, give him some time. However, it was obvious that an arrangement was already in the works, a carrot-and-stick deal that probably paid many millions of dollars a year, plus stock options and bonuses.

As the major shareholder of the largest gaming company east of the Mississippi, Crittenden had no need for a high-paying corporate job. He'd been forced to put his assets in a blind trust upon taking office three years ago, but his advisers assured him he personally was netting two million a month, after taxes. Which he'd found a legal way to rarely, if ever, pay.

"You want me to step aside," he said, keeping his fury in check.

"It would be for the benefit of the party, and you would be rewarded handsomely," the President explained. "Much more than shaking hands and delivering eulogies at funerals."

"When would this be expected to happen?"

"To be frank, we're looking at an abbreviated time frame," Mitchell replied. "My advisers tell me it would be best to have a new vice president in place by the end of the summer, giving us a seasoned incumbent who's up to speed on matters of state by next year's convention."

"And Maggie Brown would be that seasoned incumbent," Crittenden finished for him.

"She's immensely popular and very well liked in her home state. And the Senate. Easy confirmation—possibly even unanimous—because no one in either party wants to upset the *status quo* in Iowa."

The vice president now glanced out the east door to the rose garden, where he had played second fiddle during more official photo ops and press events than he cared to count. Standing off to the president's side and smiling at the periphery while Mitchell lulled the media and America to sleep with his empty platitudes. All that was about to shift, forever, although not exactly in the way the president anticipated.

"Wise political decision, sir," Crittenden said, choking back his desire to reveal what he really thought. "You've always been a pragmatic leader and a shrewd campaigner. As I said at the beginning of this wild ride, I serve at your pleasure."

"I'm glad you see it that way," Mitchell replied, with a gentle nod of his head. "Like I said, it's all best for the party. And the country, of course."

"Absolutely. What sort of timing are we looking at, if I may ask?"

"I'd like to begin the transition at your earliest convenience," the President told him. "We jointly announce your departure this coming Monday or Tuesday, giving the rumor mill a few days to start grinding before I float Maggie's name next Friday. That gives her two full news cycles and the Sunday morning talk circuit before the Senate takes up a speedy confirmation."

It was totally thought through, always with political expediency the top priority. "Again, very wise strategy, and I completely concur," Crittenden said. "So, when do I meet the chairman of this Dow thirty firm that's looking to hire a new CEO?"

Thinking, *by Monday morning you won't even be sitting in that chair, you fat fuck. I will.*

Chapter 31

Monica kept her head against the window, pretending to sleep, keeping one eye open just a sliver. The two uniformed officers were walking up the aisle slowly, studying each passenger one by one, paying close attention to the women and totally disregarding the men. Every second they inched a bit closer to where she was seated, trapped against the window. Could the call she'd made to her sister have been traced that fast, and Interpol or some other law enforcement agency had determined she was on this train?

They stopped, spoke briefly with a woman whose hair was tied loosely in a kerchief. After asking a few questions they deduced this was not the person they were looking for. They moved on, ignoring the man seated behind her. Then they glanced across the aisle at a young red-haired girl who looked too young to be the mother of the child sitting beside her. They addressed her in French, the young woman answering with a noncommittal shrug as the little boy playfully reached for the nearest policeman's gun. In a flash the officer had it out of its holster and aimed point-blank at the little boy's head. From the look on the officer's face Monica could tell this was not a drill.

"*Tu viens avec nous*," the policeman with the gun commanded the young woman. His partner said something to him, but the policeman vehemently shook his head. Using his weapon as an extended finger he motioned for the woman to stand up. She started to grab her boy and the policeman said, "*Oui, amenez-le aussi*" as he indicated for them both to move out into the aisle.

Confused by all the commotion, the little boy started to cry, and the policeman yelled at him to shut up. Then he led them both up the aisle and through the door into the next car.

Monica exhaled long and slow, realizing the police had not been there to arrest her. They had to be working an entirely different case altogether, possibly a domestic spat, the red-haired woman maybe snatching her son and trying to make a run for it. She settled back against the window and inhaled several deep, relaxing breaths designed to slow her heart and take the edge off her anxiety. *Pranayama.* The gentle vibration of the glass melded with the pulsing of her heart, and she began to feel a sense of control as she let the past—distant and recent—slip away.

Three cars forward, Phythian sensed Monica freeze at the abrupt appearance of the two policemen. A quick mental scan of their brains, however, told him it had nothing to do with her, and the red-haired woman they'd apprehended was wanted in connection with an illegal baby-adoption ring in Ghent. He continued to be impressed with Monica's endurance and fortitude; rarely had he encountered a person—target or otherwise—who possessed the ability to sense danger and make flash decisions that would avert trouble. Certainly, he had helped her out in Frankfurt when she was most in need of a mental nudge, but mostly she had proven herself cool and nimble when pushed to the brink.

Yes, she had made a blunder by calling her sister in New York, but not for the reason she believed. Whether the conversation was being monitored or not, the real threat likely lay in the phone the attaché named Walker had given to her, the one into which a call monitoring app and GPS tracker had probably been installed.

Other than his late-night visit to *Le Serrurier*, which he knew would raise a red flag, Phythian had managed to remain under the G3's radar. The locksmith's call to The Chairman would reveal his interest in Monica Cross and, likewise, that he was headed to Frankfurt. This had given them time to figure out his intention and his motivation, and then come after him. Which they had done.

So depressingly predictable.

Six years ago Phythian had made a clean break. Not even *Le Serrurier* knew where he now called home, and he was determined to keep it that way. But when he'd returned to *Utuliva* after killing the Russian *podonok* who was set on bagging one of nature's most magnificent creatures, he'd learned of the discovery of the wrecked plane. He'd barely slept that night, assessing how the Greenwich Global Group would deal with the reality that their plot to blow up the Beechcraft King Air had failed. It had not fallen in pieces into the Mediterranean, all the passengers had died from gunshots to the head, Phythian was likely alive, and the Equinox drive was missing. A worst-case scenario, and they would not stand down until they dealt with the wayward photographer who had discovered the wreckage and, in their collective mind, possibly knew secrets she should not have known. Theirs would be a blunt-force approach, particularly if they even remotely believed Monica Cross had the device in her possession. Possession was nine-tenths of the law, and execution was the last.

In his previous life, none of that would have mattered. He'd lost count of how many lives he'd taken during his years in the employ of the Greenwich Global Group, and his conscience had further hardened with each successful assignment, like wood petrifying over the eons. Every death had separated him from his own *vijñāna*, as a Buddhist monk in Thailand had once defined it. At some point along the way, he'd become indifferent to the pain and suffering he'd brought upon his victims.

Utuliva had changed all that. There, the light and grace of the universe fell upon the Serengeti every morning, and expanded in all its grandeur until the stars and distant galaxies filled the heavens at night. Call it the work of nature or the Supreme Being, the sheer beauty of life began to flow back into Phythian's world, drop by drop. This was the same way the African rains began with a trickle from the sky each winter, and continued until the plains were soaked and the rivers ran full and the animals came from miles around for the annual rite of renewal.

When he had learned about the photographer named Monica Cross who had stumbled upon the wreckage in Pakistan, he knew what awaited her. The G3 would make absolutely certain she did not make it home to the states. The mere fact that she had seen the inside of the plane, let alone stumbled on the empty Faraday case that had contained the Equinox drive, was enough reason to sentence her to death.

And she didn't have a clue.

Monica's train pulled into *Bruxelles-Midi/Brussel-Zuid* station in the center of the city right on time. Her travel map told her the airport was only eleven kilometers away, and she'd developed a plan she believed might get her on a plane and out of the country before computer algorithms even knew she was gone.

But the phone call with her sister had really spooked her, as had the two police officers who had escorted the red-haired woman and the boy off the train in Liege. Plus, she remained rattled by the sight of Erich Rohm's body in the cramped restroom, blood and brains on the floor and walls. She was convinced he'd been on board the train because of her, although she did not know how or why.

She also knew she'd stayed alive this far because she'd made decisions that didn't fit into the character of a helpless woman who somehow had stumbled into an international incident. Some of her success of the last few days had been dealt by the hand of fate, but others occurred because she'd made deliberate choices along the way. She sure as hell wasn't about to stop now, even though her ticket told her Brussels was the end of the line.

Three cars forward, Phythian remained impressed with her headstrong impulse. What she did not know was that two independent hitmen were waiting in the shadows of Platform 5, as well as a back-up operative at the top of the escalator, standing by just in case. All of them American, all on temporary loan from their respective acronym employers. Word of Monica Cross' elusive nature had spread through the ranks, and no one was taking any chances.

The final stop for this train was the French town of Calais, the European port of entry for the Chunnel that ran beneath the English Channel and connected the continent with the U.K. A quick check on her phone told her the trip from there to London would be leaving just eight minutes after this one was scheduled to pull in. That would be calling it close, considering she'd have to navigate her way through yet another railway terminal and purchase another ticket with cash. No way was she going to make the mistake of using her credit card, giving *them* yet another way to track her movements.

Her plan also involved making one more phone call, but she didn't dare use her cell. No telling what sort of software the American embassy might have installed on it to track her movements. Brian Walker had mentioned contacting a man named Cliff Broward if she ran into trouble in London, but she had no intention of doing so. Instead, she dug through her pocket and pulled out the embossed card Fiona Cassidy had handed her on the plane in Islamabad.

Monica never thought she'd have reason to actually look her up, certainly not this soon. But after all she'd been through, she realized she needed a friend and, possibly, a secure place to crash for the night. Given the hour she'd be arriving in London, she'd be faced with renting a hotel room, which might prove difficult if she didn't use her credit card. And she had almost hit her daily limit on ATM cash withdrawals. Since Fiona was a travel agent, maybe she could offer some professional advice, or arrange a place to stay at a company discount.

Monica was positioned next to the window, and no one was seated next to her. But across the aisle was a young man with a shaved head and tattooed neck, a ring through his nose, studs the size of nickels inserted in holes in his ear lobes. He'd attempted polite conversation earlier, speaking English but with a continental accent, then spent an hour playing video games on his phone. Now he was reading a graphic novel, and he'd stuffed the mobile device into one of the many zippered pockets of his oversized trousers.

She put on her nicest smile and leaned across the seat beside her, attracting his attention with a wave of her hand. "Excuse me," she said. "I'm sorry to interrupt you, but would it be at all possible to borrow your phone a minute?"

Tattoo looked up, and she realized how green his eyes were. They almost matched the lizard scales inked on his skin. "My phone?" he repeated.

"I know it's an imposition, but mine installed an update earlier and now I can't make any calls. It would be quick—"

"No problem," the kid replied. He was ten years younger than she was, almost a child, not a likely candidate for Interpol agent or CIA ringer. He dug the phone out and handed it across the aisle to her. "Don't worry about the charges…it's on my parents' bill."

"Thank you," she told him. "You have no idea how much I appreciate this."

"No problem," he said again with a disinterested shrug, then went back to his book.

Monica punched in the number on the business card, hoping she got the international codes right—not something Americans tend to worry about, but a big thing in Europe. She waited, and then a few seconds later she heard the call clicking through.

"Britannia Travel and Leisure…this is Fiona," a tired voice announced on the other end, and instantly Monica felt a tsunami of relief flow through her.

Chapter 32

The woman alternately known as Linda or Sylvia or Beatrice, or any of a dozen other names, emerged from the metro station and walked north up Massachusetts Avenue.

She was still tailing Logan, who remained too preoccupied to notice her at the far end of his metro car on the ride back from Gallaudet. He'd spent forty-two minutes with the deaf computer science professor, while she had remained outside the building, sitting in the shadow of an elm tree and performing a quick mobile search of Gallaudet's Technology Information faculty. She'd found the guy quickly: Ralph Finley, age forty-six, tenured professor. Taught two classes in advanced computer programming, office hours were Monday, Wednesday, Friday from ten o'clock to noon, a nice gig if it you could get it. He also was involved in post-graduate research in cyber security and digital subversion, and had written several books and dozens of articles on the dark web, black market commerce, and deep state conspiracies. Publish or perish, as the old academic adage went.

Well, maybe publish *and still* perish, she'd thought with a bemused grin.

Forty-two minutes was a lot of time, and she did a lot of digging. Turns out Dr. Finley was a contributor to a number of websites that dealt with network enumeration, vulnerability analysis, and ransomware overrides. He also was a known "white hat hacker"—someone who broke into corporate security for legitimate reasons, usually to test a company's firewall or conduct penetration tests. Additionally, he'd testified as an expert witness in several high-profile cybersecurity lawsuits.

But the Google hit that snagged her attention as she sat with her back against the trunk of the elm tree was a story she'd found on the twelfth page of a Google search. It was a listing for one of the many conspiracy sites that fueled the misbeliefs of a troubled populace, everything from the Malevolent Masters of the Planet to the Reptilian Elite to the Fluoride Plan. Dr. Ralph Finley was mentioned only once on the web page, but it was the context that bothered her:

Gallaudet University associate professor Ralph Finley claims to have identified a deep web organization responsible for the systematic murder-for-hire of hundreds, possibly thousands, of innocent victims in the U.S. and around the world. He says the loosely knit group operates from an office somewhere in New York, but thus far he has been unable to pinpoint its exact location.

While waiting for Carter Logan to reappear she dispatched a quick text, which then was forwarded twice more. Within a minute she received a response, which read:

Follow Logan. Leave Finley to us.

Confirmed, she'd texted back, punctuated with one of her favorite emojis: ☥

Just then Carter Logan had emerged from the main door of the lab building, headed back to the red line station. Linda *et al* slipped her phone back in her Army-drab satchel and fell in behind him thirty yards back.

Raleigh Durham's office was on the third floor of a building at the corner of 18th and L, less than a two-block walk from the Farragut North metro. She was right down the hallway from the main studio, which in the morning housed the set for *American Daybreak*, and in the evening was the headquarters for *Eye On DC*, her sixty-minute cable newscast. At the moment it was dark, although some tech-looking guys were in there fiddling with the cameras or the lighting system.

Logan knew the way to Raleigh's office, but the cable news facility was a heavily protected operation in today's environment of protesters, hackers, and terrorists. The security guard on duty recognized him, but insisted on escorting him down the corridor to Raleigh's office anyway.

"I Googled your guy, Ralph Finley," she said as soon as the guard left them alone. No "hello" or good to see you," just straight to the point. She was chewing a bite from an egg white sandwich she'd gotten from a nearby coffee shop. "He's a bit loopy, you ask me."

"I admit, Finley's a bit on the paranoid side," Logan replied. "But maybe that's what makes him good at what he does."

"Or maybe what he does is what makes him loopy."

Logan had talked in circles with Raleigh before, and he knew it got him nowhere fast. "The thing is, he understands how to navigate the cybersecurity world," he said. "And he told me this wasn't the first time the autoerotic thing was used in the death of a big-wig. Far from it."

"He provided you examples, I presume?" she asked.

He dug into his pocket and handed her the print-out of all the names Finley had showed him earlier. "Turns out he's been following this particular sort of thing for months," he said. "Didn't know who to share it with until he read my story."

She accepted the single page with skepticism and unfolded it carefully, as if it might contain a new strain of coronavirus. "All these people died from autoerotic-induced asphyxia?" she asked after she'd glanced through it.

"If you believe Dr. Finley," Logan replied. "And I do."

Raleigh said nothing, just studied the names. Her eyebrows lifted several times, as if she recognized one or two. When she was finished she said, "Do you mind if I make a copy?"

"Knock yourself out."

She spun around and placed the creased sheet of paper on the glass of her copier and hit a button. Five seconds later she handed him the original, hanging on to the duplicate.

"Now, about this murder-for-hire organization with deadly tentacles that reach around the globe," she said. "The firm you mentioned on the phone."

"The Greenwich Global Group. G3 for short."

"You want my honest opinion, it's a little far-fetched," she told him.

"On the surface, yes," Logan admitted. "Maybe even loopy, as you said. But Finley is convinced they're behind Wheeler's murder, and it could be he's on to something."

"It's more likely his roof ain't nailed down real tight," she pointed out. "Look—you go and do your Edward Murrow thing, keep me posted."

"Just remember: Murrow made his name by following the dots wherever they took him."

"So did Geraldo Rivera," Raleigh shot back. "And like Gloria Swanson said, I'll believe it if I see a there, there."

"Gertrude Stein," Logan corrected her. "And she was talking about the city of Oakland, not some dark cadre of butchers killing people in cold blood."

"Have you ever been to Oakland?" she said.

"In fact, I have. It gets a bad rap."

"Okay, okay. I can see it in your eyes: woe to all who stand in your way and keep you from the truth."

"What else is an indigent, downsized blogger to do?"

She grinned at that, said, "Just be careful and watch your ass, Cart. Your guy may be one fry short of a Happy Meal but, if he's not, you might find yourself so far up the creek you might hear banjoes playing."

William Raymond Tate detested limousines for precisely the same reason many politicians in DC loved them. They were conspicuous, they were public, and they tended to reduce the time spent going from one tedious appointment to the next. Tate preferred to drive his own car—a black Porsche 911 GT4 with the full carbon fiber interior—so he could take time strategizing the day's events, plan tomorrow's business, and work out his frustrations on other drivers.

Adam Kent had called ahead to say he'd be at Tate's condo—at the Watergate Hotel, of all places—at ten-forty to pick him up. The limo—actually a black GMC Yukon—had arrived right on time, and the political fixer was in fine form, having already earned a hundred thousand dollars that morning on a situation he'd made go away for a client in Belarus.

"I understand Crittenden met with the president this morning," Tate said as he climbed into the back seat. Much of his own professional and financial fate was linked to Crittenden, and the next thirty-six hours would prove to be critical in the lives of both men.

"Word gets around," Kent replied, not the slightest bit surprised by Tate's question.

"Was it the news we anticipated?"

"Mitchell is predictable, if not premature. Crittenden's resignation is expected Monday."

"Which means we only have a narrow window of opportunity," Tate pointed out.

Kent gave this the slightest of nods, then said, "Narrow is more than we need. Let me assure you, everything is in place for tomorrow night."

"Just like you assured me that Wheeler's death would be locked up tight?"

"If you're referring to the blogger—Carter Logan—you have nothing to worry about."

"You read what he wrote this morning—"

"I did, and we have it all under control. You just make sure you keep your dog on a leash for the next twenty-four hours, and leave the logistics to me."

Tate grunted a reply that was barely audible. He was meeting a contact at the National Institutes of Mental Health, a drive he would have preferred to make on his own, whipping his throaty Porsche up Wisconsin Avenue rather than taking the Parkway the long away around. But the matter at hand was critical, and best discussed in privacy—and brevity. Hence the limo ride with Adam Kent. Which made him feel like a squirrel trapped in a wire cage.

"You'll have to drop me at the gate at South Drive," he said as the black Lincoln rolled down old Georgetown Road. "Security is tighter than a noose at a lynching."

Kent blinked at the metaphor, but said nothing. *Southern boys.* "I've got clearance. I can take you wherever you're going."

Tate didn't want Kent to know exactly where on the NIMH campus he was headed, lest he figure out why he was there. Instead, he said, "Doctor says I need to walk whenever I can, and I'm learning to enjoy it."

"Suit yourself," Kent replied. He communicated new instructions to the driver, who deftly edged into the left lane so he could make the turn into the institute's main entrance.

There was a long string of traffic coming the other way, which meant they were forced to wait. After a few seconds, Tate said, in an almost-offhand way, "I'm assuming your people have our photographer issue under control."

"*Fait accompli*," Kent said. Under normal circumstances he hated to lie, but he despised this unctuous little prick even more. "All is quiet on the eastern front."

Which, of course, couldn't be further from the truth.

Chapter 33

Monica felt almost home now. When the train emerged from the Chunnel on British soil, she felt yet another layer of tension ease, and for the next fifty minutes she drifted in and out of a welcome slumber as the train sped toward London. Once again, the window served as a hard pillow, and she welcomed the escape—temporary as it was—following two days on the run.

A sudden blast jolted her awake. Trembling from the sudden punch of panic she glanced around, realized none of the other passengers in the car was even slightly alarmed or frightened. The abrupt burst had simply been the horn from the engine up front, signaling the train's approach into St. Pancras Station.

Named for its location in St. Pancras parish and the fourth-century Christian boy martyr Pancras of Rome, the gargantuan terminal is sited at the southern end of the London Borough of Camden. At the time of its construction in 1868, Londoners boasted the massive steel-and-glass structure held the largest unsupported arched roof in the world, one of the great wonders of Victorian architecture. All Monica was concerned with at the moment, however, was the presence of any police officers or plainclothes investigators from Interpol or MI6—anyone who might have an interest in detaining her as soon as she stepped down from the train.

But there was none of that. No cops, no spies, no assassins lying in wait. She stood on the platform, absorbing the signs and all the choices she had now that she was in London. She knew she could take her chances and figure out the best tube route to get her out to Heathrow. Or she could wait a minute to exhale, give her mind a chance to reboot and see if Fiona actually had managed to hoof it all the way from her office to meet her.

And there she was, a look of wonder and awe in her eyes. Monica started moving toward her and, when they met, they each slung their arms around the other, as if they were long-lost friends. Other passengers jostled them as they rushed by, but neither of them cared.

When they finally pulled apart, Monica said nothing for a long moment. It took Fiona to break the silence, as she shook her head in amazement and said, "Monica Cross...as I live and breathe. You actually made it to London."

"You have no idea how wonderful it is to be here," Monica sighed. She felt as if she might cry simply from the relief, if not the sheer exhaustion of the journey. "I hope I'm not intruding—"

"Intruding? My God—it's just so awesome to see you. When you didn't get on the plane... well, I thought the worst. You must tell me everything that's happened to you—"

"It's a long story," Monica said. She glanced up at the station clock above her, then at her watch. "What time is it here, anyway?"

"Quarter of eight," Fiona told her. "The night is young."

"That's funny. I set my watch to Greenwich Mean Time when I was in Brussels, and it says it's six forty-five."

"We're on British Summer Time right now," Fiona explained. "It makes no sense and there's talk of rolling it back, but things work slowly this side of the pond."

"Sounds no different than our side," Monica replied.

Fiona studied her new friend again, then said, "I just can't believe it's you. What the dickens have you got yourself into?"

"One giant misunderstanding, but nothing I can't get myself out of." The last thing Monica wanted was to scare her newfound BFF with stories of mysterious strangers and hired killers. "Like I said on the phone, I need your help, one more time."

"Of course, of course. Whatever you want."

"And you swear you didn't tell anyone I called?"

"What would I tell them?"

"Nothing, I guess," Monica said with a shrug. "But I promise I'll fill you in when we have a chance to talk."

Fiona Cassidy glanced up and down the platform, then gently turned Monica around and gave her a gentle nudge toward the far end. "Come... let's go and get you a drink."

"I really could use a glass of wine right about now," Monica admitted.

"Well, there's a great little place I know around the corner. Better yet, let's go back to my place. This may take most of the night, and I have a huge couch you can crash on."

"I can't begin to tell you what I've been through," Monica told her fifteen minutes later, after they'd emerged from the Covent Garden tube station. They were walking on Cranbourn Street, past a Japanese Restaurant and a shop that sold pricey sunglasses. Despite the gloomy skies and the threat of rain, she felt calm and at peace with the world—or at least her little corner of it, right now in this moment.

"When you didn't show up at the gate back in Islamabad, I was scared something bad had happened to you," Fiona said. "There was nothing I could do, and then they loaded us back on the plane and we took off."

"I freaked," Monica replied. "I couldn't just wait around, worried that some man with one eye was going to sneak up from behind and kill me. I did what I had to do, and bought another ticket."

"I was hoping it was something like that."

"There was a flight to Istanbul that was leaving in thirty minutes, and I got a seat on it. I apologize if I caused you any grief."

Fiona nodded at that, seemed to accept it. "No worries," she said. "I don't know that I would have thought of that, but it got you out of there."

"And brought me here," Monica replied, leaving out the trouble in Frankfurt. "How 'bout you? When did you get home?"

"Early this morning," Fiona told her. "Barely got any sleep, and I wanted to take the day off. But my boss is a total wanker and said 'no way.'"

Once again Monica's mind went to her own boss at *Earth Illustrated*, and how she still hadn't called him. It was the middle of the afternoon in New York; maybe she could catch him once she arrived at Fiona's place. Then again, if his phone was tapped, *they* would know right where she was.

"Your boss sounds like a real prince," she said.

"We already have enough of those around here," Fiona replied with a chuckle. "When do I get to hear this great tale of yours?"

Fatigue was beginning to take hold, and all Monica really wanted was to slip into a deep sleep. But she had gone to Fiona for help, and she felt she owed her some sort of explanation.

"Wine first," she said, delaying the inevitable.

Fiona's place was a tidy one-bedroom flat on Tavistock Street, a second-story walk-up with no elevator. White walls, large windows, oddly contemporary, it retained many of the original features that gave it a period feel. Fireplace, crown molding, refinished hardwood floor, framed prints of modern art on the walls.

Monica was comforted to see the double locks at the front vestibule downstairs and three more upstairs on the apartment door. Once they were safely inside, Fiona went into the kitchen and proceeded to slice the metal casing off a bottle of sauvignon blanc with a Swiss Army knife.

"Old boyfriend gave it to me," she explained. "The knife, not the wine."

She pulled out the cork, then poured a healthy measure for both of them and carried the glasses out to the adjacent living room. Monica curled up in a corner of an old couch that looked as if it had been passed down through multiple generations. Fiona sat in a chair facing her, with her feet tucked up beneath her.

"So…what's going on?" she asked. "Tell me everything."

Monica took a sip of wine, the crisp taste of green apple and peach flowing over her tongue. "What's going on is this," she finally said, then launched into her tale of the last thirty-six hours. She skipped over the dead woman in Frankfurt, but managed to fill in enough grisly details so that, when she finally finished with stepping off the train thirty minutes ago, Fiona was staring at her with wide, incredulous eyes.

"This is just so…so unbelievable," Fiona said when she'd finished.

"You don't believe me—?"

"No, no…I mean yes. Please—don't get me wrong. I just mean that… well, this sort of thing just doesn't happen. Not to me, at least. Like, I live an everyday life. I catch the eight o-clock tube, and I get to the office at half-past. I book everybody's fabulous holidays, Africa and India and the South Pacific. And I stay inside my own little world, my own shell of a life."

"You went to Pakistan—"

"How romantic," Fiona said, her mouth turning down in a frown. "You know what I mean. I want adventure."

"I'd be happy to trade," Monica replied as she finished her wine and set the glass down on the table.

"Can I talk you into a refill?" Fiona asked her.

What she really wanted now was sleep, about twenty hours of it. For the first time in days she felt relatively secure in the knowledge that no one had followed her here, no one could trace her to this apartment. She hadn't used her bank card since Cologne, and she'd turned off her cell phone way back in Brussels. She didn't know if it could be tracked if it were powered down but, short of tossing it in a rubbish bin, it was the best she could do.

"Just a little," she said, holding her finger about an inch from the bottom of her glass. "And then maybe we can use your laptop, there, to book an early flight out of Heathrow."

"Whatever I can do to help," Fiona assured her as she wandered into the kitchen alcove with the glass.

Monica fought to keep her eyes open, a battle she knew she would lose within minutes. The rush of adrenaline finally was starting to subside, and when her body realized it was beyond recall, sleep would come. How wonderful it was to finally be off the hamster wheel and relax without worrying that death was lurking right around the corner.

She must have nodded off a second, because she barely heard Fiona say something to her out in the kitchen. She blinked her eyes open, saw her new friend standing there, gripping a gun in both hands, the barrel aimed directly at her chest.

"Don't you bloody move," Fiona said, her eyes as dark and menacing as any storm cloud Monica had ever seen. "Should've killed you when I fucking had the chance."

Chapter 34

Israeli Foreign Minister Lior Eichorn's nonstop from Berlin touched down on runway 1R/19L at Washington's Dulles Airport almost four hours late.

The eleven-hour flight had been delayed taking off from its layover in Frankfurt, due to some sort of commotion resulting from a reported fatality in one of the terminal restrooms. The excitement had caused temporary runway closures, which then postponed the arrival and departure of dozens of flights for a good part of the morning. Fortunately, Eichorn's plane was already out on the taxiway, second in line for take-off. The Airbus had been pushed back from the jetway eight minutes before the murder was estimated to have occurred, which meant there was no way the suspect could possibly be on board.

For this trip he was traveling with two members of Shin Bet, the Israeli internal security service. Since the State of Israel did not own a private aircraft for transportation of its government officials, heads of state—except for the prime minister—were forced to fly first class via regularly scheduled commercial airline. First preference, for obvious reasons, was El Al, not only because it was Israel's national airline, but because of its near-impeccable safety record and its on-board missile defense system. There was no direct service via El Al from Berlin to Washington, however, which meant Eichorn and his party were forced to share the crowded skies with a plane load of tourists, businessmen, and noisy German exchange students on their way to America for the summer.

When the plane landed at Dulles, it taxied directly to a guarded gate, where armed security agents cleared the three Israelis through a private immigration checkpoint. They then were escorted to a waiting convoy consisting of three black Chevy Tahoes and two motorcycle cops. Eichorn sat in the back of the second vehicle, flanked by his two protectors, each of whom was handed a weapon as soon as they climbed inside. Before the short procession pulled away from the private arrivals curb, an attaché from the Israeli Embassy handed the Foreign Minister a manila envelope that was closed with a metal clasp.

"Your itinerary, sir," the attaché told him. His name was Benjamin Covitz, mid-thirties, born and raised in Tel Aviv except for six years of college and graduate study in Boston.

"What about the invitation for tomorrow night?" Eichorn inquired.

"You are the personal guest of the president at the annual media dinner," Covitz assured him. "Private reception at six o'clock. Your suit will be pressed, shoes polished."

"I wish my wife could have joined me for this," Eichorn lamented. He and Alina had been married thirty-nine years, but three months ago she had been diagnosed with stage three cervical cancer, and was undergoing treatment at Chaim Sheba Medical Center in Ramat Gan. When doctors had first presented her with the grim news he had offered to stand down from his post, but she had absolutely refused. "Who else is on the guest list?"

"The usual suspects, sir. Mostly members of the White House press corps looking for a free meal and bottomless champagne. Some senators and cabinet members, a cadre of lobbyists, and the usual Hollywood types."

"And the vice president?"

"He'll be seated on the dais."

"Should make for an interesting evening," Eichorn observed. "Americans do have some peculiar customs."

"Self-effacing humor is considered honorable, I guess."

"Particularly among thieves," Eichorn replied with a chuckle.

He settled into his seat, the two burly special forces types sitting on either side of him. As the small motorcade got underway his mind drifted back to the multitude of texts that had downloaded into his phone when he'd switched it out of airplane mode. He felt a deep sense of remorse for the confrontation he'd had with his cousin at the Berlin embassy, the threats of violence and the crazy display of the gun. He'd sent Eitan Hazan an apology, but had received no word in return: very unlike him, unless he was royally pissed—or something else.

Setting his immediate concern aside, he scrolled through his messages and found one that left him more encouraged:

Shipment arrived. Delivery scheduled.

Excellent, Eichorn thought. *Everything is working according to plan.*

The motorcade pulled onto the Dulles Access Road and headed eastward toward Washington. He eased back in his seat, ignoring the banal and tedious architecture that had sprouted across the suburban Virginia landscape. He had first come here thirty years ago, when much of this terrain was lush forest and rolling hills. Now it was all just formless buildings squatting on the land, a tedious sameness punctuated by cell phone towers and asphalt and automobiles clogging the roads. How he missed the arid hills of Israel, and his wife Alina, who was being looked after by a cousin while Lior was out of the country, *again*, on state business.

Most of all he missed his daughter Avigail, whose death he still grieved as much today as he did six years ago when her plane vanished into thin air.

A dark feeling settled in as he wondered for the tenth time in as many minutes, *Eitan—where are you, and why haven't I heard from you?*

Chapter 35

London
7:41 pm GMT, 8:41 pm Local

At first Monica thought she'd drifted into a dream, one from which she had yet to awaken. This was so bizarre and freakishly weird that it couldn't possibly be real.

"Fiona—" she managed to say.

"I told you, don't fucking move."

Monica didn't think she'd even twitched, except maybe to blink back to full alert. *What the hell was this all about?*

"Put your hands where I can see them," Fiona snapped at her. "Now."

Both of them were already in her lap, but she raised them—*very slowly*—so Fiona couldn't possibly miss them. "What's going on—?"

"Shut the bloody fuck up," Fiona said as she edged closer, out of the kitchen. "You have no idea how much trouble you've caused."

"Me? I'm just trying to get home."

"Not happening."

Monica's mind was racing, part of her brain insisting this was part of an hallucination. "Please…what is this?"

"The end of the line. On your feet."

"What?"

Fiona made a threatening gesture with the gun, as if she could make the situation any more terrifying than it already was. "I said, stand up."

Monica did what she was told. Almost crying, thinking she'd come this far, but not quite home. All because she'd evidently trusted the wrong person in the wrong place at the wrong time. "Can you please just tell me—"

…*who you are and what this is about?* was what she was going to say, but she never got the chance. At that moment the front door burst open

228

and slammed against the inner wall. In the same instant a man charged in from the hallway, instantly assessed the situation, and put three bullets into Fiona: two in her chest and one in her head. It took about two seconds, and there was almost no noise, since the SIG Sauer he held in his hand was fitted with a suppressor. The bullets made only a *thwitt-thwitt-thwitt* sound, soft little shots, and then it was over.

Fiona Cassidy didn't stand a chance. She blew backward from the force of the flying lead and collapsed against the wall, the resulting smear of blood and brain matter almost matching one of the modern art posters hanging on the wall. An abstract print by Joan Miro that had an abundance of red.

Within the same two-second period, Monica dived into the corner of the sofa on which she'd been sitting when she'd been ordered to stand up. Then a combination of exhaustion and shock restricted the flow of blood to her brain, causing her to crumple to the floor.

Phythian gently kicked the door closed and set his gun down on a small table that was used for mail. It wasn't really his gun, since he'd lifted it off Eitan Hazan in the restroom back in Cologne after Monica had stepped off the train—much easier than trying to obtain one in Amsterdam or Brussels or London, wherever she ultimately decided to go.

Once he was sure the situation was under control, he made his way to the couch, where he straightened Monica out and elevated her feet to improve her circulation. Within seconds her eyes flickered, then opened a crack and stared up at him.

"Who the fuck—?" she started to say, but he put a finger to her lips and mentally nudged her not to say another word.

"She was MI6," he said. "She had orders to kill you."

"You *shot her*—"

"The quick and the dead rarely ride the same horse, until after fate intervenes," Phythian told her.

"What kind of bullshit is that?" Monica seethed, as a wave of outrage overcame her. "You were at the airport. Frankfurt. I saw you. And then on the train. You killed that man in the bathroom."

"He killed himself," he told her. "And he was there to kill you."

Monica coiled herself into a defensive ball, arms hugging her knees to her chest, then said, "And are you going to kill me, too?"

"No. I'm here to make sure you stay alive and get home to New York."

"How do you know about that?"

"I know a great deal about a number of things," he said. "Don't move."

Phythian motioned with his finger to stay put, then crossed the room to where Fiona lay slumped against the wall, the pistol lying on the floor beside her. He touched a finger to her blood-slicked neck, waited to make sure there was no pulse, then picked up the gun. When he was absolutely certain she wasn't going anywhere, he turned his attention back to Monica.

"Here's what we're going to do," he said.

Chapter 36

Diana Petrie rarely handled clients personally; too much risk, putting an actual face and a voice to the Greenwich Global Group and the nonexistent hat company that served as its front. Negotiations generally were conducted online with what was called an onion router, cybercurrency, and extreme anonymity, deep beneath the scrutiny of intelligence agencies and enterprising hackers with malevolent intentions.

But Georgy Sokolov was no ordinary client. He was a repeat customer, having used the services of the G3 several times since his fortunes had shifted following the end of the Cold War. A former KGB officer whose work had covered all five sections of the Second Chief Directorate, he'd reinvented himself during the Yeltsin years and wrested control of several oil fields during the country's transition from communist rule. Refineries and pipelines and trade deals followed, and over the next three decades his net worth had climbed to well over eleven figures and three commas, in U.S. dollars. He was one of those oligarchs who regularly was seated at the Russian president's elbow during state dinners and ministry meetings, and a decade ago his American assets had been frozen by the then-president as part of wide-ranging sanctions put in place following the annexation of Crimea.

That had posed a bit of a personal hardship for almost a year, until the tragic death of the U.S. Commerce Secretary's son quickly resulted in those sanctions being lifted. Sokolov then liquidated his real estate in New York and Palm Beach, and relocated his equity holdings to countries that were less prone to exerting financial pressure on foreign nationals.

The G3 had been involved with the direct resolution of that situation, and Petrie had warned Sokolov never to contact her personally again. There were proper channels for such dealings and, as with all its clients, she expected him to abide by the rules. They were there for a reason, foremost of which was protection and invisibility for all parties concerned. But, since he was Russian and rich and a former KGB thug, rules did not apply to him.

Sokolov had called this meeting yesterday, and he'd verbally beaten Petrie down until she reluctantly agreed to meet with him personally. Because of a pending assault charge stemming from an incident in Las Vegas, he dared not enter the U.S. under any of his four passports. Likewise, he chose not to conduct business via digital communications, even if they were encrypted and scrambled with foolproof proprietary software. The meeting had to be in person, which was why Petrie was seated at a table in a corner of the Loskins Bar in the Leif Erikson terminal at Iceland's Keflavik International Airport.

She had touched down in Reykjavik twenty minutes ago, and the arrivals screen had told her Sokolov was going to be fifteen minutes late coming in from Latvia. They had mutually agreed on this location for their meet, and she was nursing a vodka with ice, both of which were in plentiful supply in this city just south of the Arctic Circle.

Sokolov had selected the island nation for its proximity to their respective continents. It was just a brief sit-down, no more than ten minutes, barely enough time to enjoy a quick drink and conclude a deal. The price he was willing to pay would make the journey worth her time, and he was prepared to add a hefty surcharge if she could expedite the assignment, same as last time, when the adventurous son of the Commerce Secretary had base-jumped off El Capitan in Yosemite and his chute inexplicably failed to open.

Sokolov approached the cocktail lounge from the gate where his Baltic Air flight had just pulled up. He was a large man, about six-feet-two, two hundred thirty pounds. A heavy coat was slung over his arm and a black fedora with white band was perched on his head. The G3 database listed him as sixty-six, born in Apraksin, a town not far from St. Petersburg. He had advanced degrees from Moscow Institute of Physics and Technology State University, with a career track that took him to the Soviet Army and then to the Committee for State Security. Married with three children, although the computer had indicated that one of those children—his oldest son, and a senior engineer in his oil empire—had recently been killed during a private safari in Tanzania. Petrie had a strong suspicion that's what this meeting was about.

Sokolov sat down at the corner table where Petrie was already seated, indicated to the cocktail server that he would have what she was having. Then they got right to it, no small talk, because the circumstance that had brought them together from far reaches of the globe was anything but small.

"I need sniper," he said. Passable English, much better than her Russian, although she could get by if she was pressed to use it.

"Your son?" she asked. "Vasily?"

He nodded at her words, leaned forward to lower his already-hushed voice. "I make worth it," he assured her.

"I know you will," Petrie told him. "Why a sniper?"

"Is how he died. Eye for eye, measure for measure."

"You know who it was who shot your son?" she asked.

"I have resources, too," Sokolov replied with a wry grin. "I not know name, but know where he live. You have sniper?"

Of course, Petrie had a sniper, several of them, in fact. None of them came cheap, but no one did in this line of work. She ran through a short mental list of contractors who might fit the bill, a killer who could get into whatever country was involved, with the equipment required to take the shot, then exfiltrate immediately.

"What range?" she asked him.

"Mile, mile-and-a-half. Your choose."

She didn't ask, nor did he volunteer, why he wanted the shot taken from that distance. It was a difficult but not impossible feat. In fact, several years back a Canadian special forces marksman had killed an ISIS militant outside Mosul with a bullet fired over two miles away. Such perfection required not only the best rifle in the world, but an ability to correctly assess the wind, the light, the angle, the effect of gravity, even the curvature of the earth. The bullet had been airborne almost ten seconds before plunging into its target, but the marksman had pulled it off. He even got a medal for it—discretely.

The Canadian in question was not on the G3 payroll, despite several attempts to incentivize him. Killing an ISIS militant with a lust for beheading infidels was one thing, but murdering faceless persons just for a seven-figure payout apparently insulted his principles.

Petrie had several qualified shooters in mind but, as she took a healthy sip of vodka, she devised an alternate plan that no one ever need know about.

"It won't be cheap," she told the oligarch.

"Like I say, money not object. Motherfucker killed my son, he die."

Petrie had learned years ago not to allow conscience, ethics, or morality affect the hard edges of her job. If a client was willing to pay top dollar for an assignment, her role was to facilitate its execution while maintaining a healthy distance between herself and the actual mission. In her mind she served as the means of destiny, or maybe even the hand of God, exacting infinitesimal changes in the fabric of history. And, over time, she'd convinced herself she was playing a fundamental, even indispensable, role in the historic course of the planet.

She forced Sokolov to sit impatiently while she mentally calculated the business aspects of the job—compensation, travel, incidentals, overhead— and then quoted him a price. He didn't blink, even though it was twice what the mission should actually cost. She knew he was emotionally invested in the outcome, and it was best to hook him before a level head took over.

"Done," he said, as he slid a thick envelope across the table. "Here is gift."

Petrie didn't open it, just slipped it into the Christian Louboutin purse that hung from the back of her chair. Then she said, "Always good to do business with you."

"*Da*," he replied as rose from the table. "I have plane to catch."

"Have a good flight back," she told him, and then he was gone.

Chapter 37

The Kalorama neighborhood in northwest Washington near Carter Logan's small apartment was dotted with pricey gin joints, pubs, and saloons. The Embassy was particularly noted for its apple martinis that rang up at eighteen dollars a pop, while The Corner Office served up an amazing flight of six India Pale Ales for twenty-one. If one wanted the best Moscow Mule in town, with a touch of watermelon juice, Tolstoy's Attic was the place to go. Eight ounces of delicious froth served in a hammered copper mug that was listed on the menu at thirteen hundred rubles or, depending on the current exchange rate, about twenty dollars U.S.

With Logan's bank account nearly depleted and his rent coming due in five days, he couldn't afford any of these places. His go-to joint when he didn't want to drink alone in his apartment was a corner tavern called Hobo's, where happy hour beer was three bucks a mug, and a glass of house red would set him back seven. More expensive than drinking a bottle of TJ's cheapest by himself, but at Hobo's the company was better and he didn't have to worry about selecting the music. An ancient Seeburg jukebox was pressed into service from the start of happy hour to last call, and there was always something playing for everyone.

Despite his uninspired finances, he decided to celebrate tonight. Most evenings he sat around his place and watched a little TV, had a glass of wine, watched more TV, drank more wine. But tonight, he felt he had reason for optimism. Three reasons, in fact. First, Professor Finley at Gallaudet had pretty much validated his thesis that Justice Wheeler had been murdered, rather than succumb to a creepy autoerotic death. He'd even taken it a step further by identifying the organization he believed was behind the staged death, a dark web entity known as the Greenwich Global Group. Logan's own subsequent Google search had turned up nothing, and he was too intimidated to travel down the wormhole to the dark web on his own laptop. No telling what he might find there, or who might find him.

Second, Raleigh Durham had confessed that his theory wasn't as crazy as she'd first thought and, in fact, there might be some substance to what he'd written in his blog.

Third—and infinitely more important—was the sheer number of voicemails he'd listened to when he'd left Raleigh's newsroom at the corner of 18th and L. There were fourteen in all, including three network reporters, one news anchor in New York, and a half dozen newspapers that included the *Times* and the *Globe. Plus,* a cable news network wanted to schedule a live six-minute segment, if he was available.

On top of that, his old boss at the *Washington Post* had called to set up a meeting as soon as possible Monday morning—even over the weekend, if that was convenient for him. His name was Hilton Clark, and he'd left three phone numbers, making it sound important and urgent.

Logan could have played stubborn, insisting he couldn't go back to his old job when he was in forward motion. But he was neither stupid nor pigheaded, and thus had returned the call while walking up Massachusetts Avenue, tracking him down at the Old Ebbitt Grill on 15th Street.

"Fascinating piece," Clark had praised him above the din of the lunch crowd. "I assume you have sources to back it all up?"

"I do," Logan had told him. Not entirely accurate, but hey, this was Washington, DC, the seat of American government, and the progenitor of untruths and deceit.

"I'd like to talk to you about it."

"What do you have in mind?"

"We'll have to talk about that," Clark had replied. "A desk just opened up in Metro. Figuratively speaking. Not the same deal as before, 'cause budgets are tight. But if this turns out to be what you seem to think it is... well, when might you have time to meet?"

"I'll be honest with you, Hilton," Logan had said. "My dance card is a little empty right now. You name a time and place, I'll be there."

He heard some shouting in the background, followed by a drunk gang singing "Happy Birthday." Then Hilton Clark said, "I'll tell you what. I have an extra pass to tomorrow's White House Media Dinner, and I think we have time to vet you with the Secret Service. Unless you've become a Russian provocateur since you left here."

You mean, since you summarily handed me a cardboard box on a Friday afternoon and told me to clear out my things, words he felt like saying, but didn't. In addition to being the mother of invention, necessity also was a great reason to keep one's mouth shut.

"I can do that," Logan told him. "See you there."

"Great. Mayflower Hotel, as usual. Cocktails start at six, but security will be tight. Come to my room when you arrive."

With that carrot dangling in front of him, Logan had stopped at Hobo's for a seven-dollar glass of wine. Over the six years he'd been coming here he'd often wondered, as wordsmiths were wont to do, if the tavern was actually owned by a Hobo, and therefore the apostrophe indicated a possessive, or it had been put there by someone who simply didn't know any better.

Halfway through his glass of wine he sensed someone edge up beside him, to his right, someone wearing a fragrance that a parfumier might describe as "a unique blend of green tea, bergamot, jasmine, freesia, and orchid." He glanced over, saw a woman standing behind the empty stool next to him, shrugging a light wrap off her bare shoulders.

"Is anyone sitting here?" she asked in a slow and relaxed voice—no discernible accent, not that it mattered because he was instantly distracted by the cascade of blonde hair that fell past her shoulders. She had large blue eyes, full lips painted the color of Bing cherries, smooth skin, a billowy lace dress that exposed an ample amount of flesh in the most provocative of ways. More curves than the jogging trail that ran through Rock Creek Park, and probably a lot more fun.

Happy hour had ended just over thirty minutes ago, and the place had thinned out considerably. That meant most of the stools at the bar were empty, including the one to his right.

"Be my guest," he said to her, straightening his posture in an attempt not to look like a disheveled schlub. He typically recognized most of Hobo's patrons—paralegals and executive assistants, government employees who could afford to live in the neighborhood, softball teams that came in to celebrate a victory, or drown a defeat. Occasionally someone would walk in, order a drink, pound it alone, and leave. But mostly this was a neighborhood joint with a clientele that lived within a ten-block radius, especially on a Friday night at the start of a long D.C. summer.

"What's your name?" the woman asked him as she settled her shapely bottom on the Naugahyde stool.

"Carter," he told her as he lifted his wine glass from the counter, but did not drink from it. "New to the area?"

"Do I look new?"

She looked much more seasoned than new, but his mental filter told him not to go there. "I just haven't seen you in here before," he said. "What's your name?"

"Giselle," she replied with a smile. "And yes, I just moved into a place a couple blocks from here, on Wyoming Avenue."

"That's where I live. I guess that means we're neighbors."

"Well, glad to meet you, neighbor." Since she didn't have a drink yet, she picked up a dish of limes from the bar and clinked his glass in an improvised toast. "Tell me...what's good in this place?"

"The prices, for one thing. Although you missed happy hour."

"Well, that doesn't mean I can't still be happy," the looker named Giselle pointed out. She leaned forward and studied the bottles lined up against the far wall, and when the bartender sidled up in front of her she said, "What's your best cocktail that no one ever orders?"

The bartender, who was from Miami and whose name was Ramon, grinned. "The one I'm going to make for you right now, if you're into surprises."

"I love them," she told him. "Go ahead and surprise me."

While Ramon went to work with bottles and shakers and fresh juice, Giselle placed her purse on the counter, then turned slightly to face Logan. "I take it you come here often," she said, a twist on an old opening line.

"More often than I should," he replied. "It's a nice place to get away to when you work from home."

"Really? What do you do that allows you that luxury in this town?"

"I'm a writer," he said, past experience assuring him that women were fascinated by the romantic notion of a lonely hermit locked away in a cold, dark garret churning out words. "And it's a lot more about discipline than luxury."

"Well, I think it's *très* cool. What sort of things do you write?"

"I'm an investigative reporter, freelance, which allows me to set my own hours." He decided to leave out the novel he'd been working on for three years, forty-five thousand words, but was beginning to think would never get around to finishing.

Just then the bartender set a highball glass in front of Giselle and said, "Presenting your very first Across The Aisle. As in, reaching across the aisle to work together. Something very rare in this town these days."

She studied the drink, which somehow seemed to have red and blue clouds billowing in it, a slice of lime and a plastic mermaid perched on the edge. The rim was covered with a brown dusting of something that looked like cinnamon. "What's in it?" she asked him.

"Silver tequila, Kentucky bourbon, blue Curacao, grenadine, and a sprinkle of chili salt," he told her. "Enjoy."

Enjoy she did. Halfway through her third round she had kicked off her shoes and edged her stool closer to Logan, who was breaking his drinking-out rule and was well into his fourth glass of house red. Not a good thing, considering he had a lot of follow-up research to take care of tomorrow before crashing the White House bash at the Mayflower. Hilton Clark did tell him the Mayflower, right?

A little after ten o'clock Giselle seemed as if she might topple off her stool. She gazed at Logan with eyes that seemed focused on the wall behind him, while telling him a story that seemed to have no point except to go on and on. She emphasized the narrative at times by squeezing his knee, or straightening his collar, once even giving him a quick peck on the cheek.

Eventually she said, "I think it's time I go home."

Logan was thinking the same thing, not knowing exactly what she had in mind.

She fumbled through her purse for her wallet, then handed several fresh bills to Ramon. "Tonight is on me," she told him. "Whatever is left is yours."

"No…please, let me," Logan protested, not too vigorously. He could barely afford his own tab, let alone the specialty cocktails she'd consumed. Not as expensive as the extortionate watering holes along Connecticut Avenue, but enough to severely strain his credit limit.

"I insist, neighbor," she said with a smile. He continued his protest a couple more seconds, finally relented as she raised herself from her seat and lurched to her feet. "I think I might need…a little assistance."

"The good news is, we're both heading in the same direction," Logan told her. "Just give me your arm and I'll show you the way."

"I will follow…wherever you lead," she replied, with a hiccup.

He guided her to the door and out to the sidewalk, where the warm breeze of a June Potomac evening caught the hem of her dress and caused it to lift up around her legs…almost like Marilyn Monroe when she stood over the subway grate in *The Seven Year Itch*, but without Billy Wilder there to order another take.

"This way," he directed her, crooking his elbow so she could insert her arm through it.

"Thank you, kind sir," said the woman who was called Giselle. Or Linda. Or Sylvia or Beatrice, or any of a dozen other names, subtly checking her purse for the Spyderco Civilian ATS 55 knife with the folding steel blade, fabricated specifically for cutting through the toughest leather—and the flesh and bone beneath.

At the same time Logan felt his phone vibrate in his pocket, half a second before he heard the tone notifying that a text had come through. Instinct told him to let it go; he could check it out later. But the nature of his job told him there was no time like the present, and when he checked it, he found a message from his source at the Franklin Pierce Hotel. An image, and eleven words that probably saved his life.

This woman was on Wheeler's floor around the time he died.

The accompanying photo was a still taken from color surveillance video that appeared to have been taken outside an elevator, a clear shot of the very same chick who had sat down next to him and told him her name was Giselle—the one who three minutes ago had left Hobo's with him, her arm wrapped through his elbow—and who now had an evil darkness in her eyes and some kind of object in her hand, something with a sharp edge that glinted in the glow of a distant streetlamp.

He pulled away, spun beyond her range just as her hand thrust past his throat. She stumbled, then abruptly caught herself and whirled around. By that time Logan's brain—as soggy as it was from too much house wine—registered what was going on, and instinctively he jumped between two parked cars.

She'd come at him again, the blade arcing toward him as she lunged. Without thinking, without pro-conning the consequences, he'd shot his fist into her face, knocking her ass-over-sphincter onto the sidewalk.

Then he ran.

Chapter 38

The first hint of a new day was beginning to appear in the east, gray and damp. Monica was leaning against the car door, her arms folded across her chest both in contempt and defiance. The man behind the wheel, who had identified himself only as Phythian, had shot and killed Fiona last night in cold blood. Then he'd fed her some bullshit story about how the woman was a foreign operative—well, not foreign, since MI6 was a British agency and this was London—who had been tasked with executing her, as if she were some sort of global bad-ass hoodlum. Which, in a sense, she was, since German authorities were looking for the suspect who had killed an unarmed woman in the Frankfurt Airport.

Then, after explaining all this, he'd drugged her with something he'd found in the bathroom medicine cabinet, enabling her to get a good night's sleep.

"You're going to need it," he'd explained as she'd found herself swallowing the pills with a sip of sauvignon blanc, even though the label said not to take them with alcohol.

"Just tell me what this is about," she'd pressed him.

"It's best if we wait until morning," Phythian had told her, as she drifted off into a deep, unencumbered slumber.

Everything had happened with such speed that Phythian had almost been taken by surprise. He'd been downstairs in the front foyer when he'd perceived a distinct shift in Fiona's brain waves, sensed her reach into a drawer and grab the gun, then turn and aim it at Monica from where she was standing in the kitchen.

He'd had to take the stairs three at a time to get there before she pulled the trigger. In those few seconds he'd determined she was SIS and, unlike when she'd first run into Monica at the airport in Pakistan, her standing orders now were to shoot Monica on sight. Her handlers hadn't appreciated that she'd allowed Monica to slip through her fingers and, when Monica had called her from the train, she'd resolved to take swift and deliberate action. On her own; she would contact her superiors at Vauxhall Cross later, let them know she'd taken care of their collective problem.

That was ten hours ago. After helping Monica to bed, he'd taken up position inside the front door, just in case someone from headquarters came looking for her. But no night visitors appeared, and no calls rang through to Fiona's two cell phones.

Just before dawn Monica had blinked her eyes open to find him rummaging through Fiona's belongings, selectively pulling out her passport, credit cards, and a little more than one hundred Euros in various denominations. Her body remained where it had fallen last night; he hadn't even bothered to cover her face with a blanket.

"Preserving evidence," Phythian explained when she questioned him about it.

"Evidence? You fucking *shot her*."

"Let the investigators figure it out," he told her. He grabbed two dish rags from the kitchen and handed her one. "Wipe down everything you might have touched, and do it quickly. We need to get going."

Despite her outward fury she felt a peculiar sensation of calm percolate through her. It was as if she were being guided by a force outside her own self.

"Going where?" she asked him.

"You have a plane to catch. And I'm driving you."

Now he was jammed in behind the wheel of Fiona's Mini Cooper, knees almost pressing against the wheel as he ground through the gear shift on the left-hand side. Monica was in the passenger seat, her confidence in— and animosity toward—this man named Phythian swinging back and forth, like a pendulum. It was something she couldn't explain, and she sensed her emotions somehow were being played, like a puppeteer pulling the strings of a marionette.

"You killed her," she said again.

"That woman was not who you thought she was."

"She helped me get away from someone in Pakistan," Monica insisted.

"Fiona Cassidy was MI6," he told her again. "British Secret Service. She was sent to Islamabad to get close to you."

"Why didn't she kill me then, rather than wait until she got me alone in her flat?"

"Her rules of engagement had changed," Phythian explained. "You were never supposed to get out of Pakistan. Killing you was someone else's job. The one-eyed man."

How could he possibly know about that? Monica wondered as he steered the tiny car along the A4 through Chiswick. "You murdered the man on the train, too," she accused him then.

"I'm sorry you had to see that," he replied, momentarily taking his hands off the wheel and raising them as if in surrender. "You're welcome, by the way."

"I'm supposed to thank you for something?"

"Yes...you woke up this morning."

A long silence followed, as she tried to separate fact from fiction. She didn't have much to go on, except that this man who had taken Fiona's life hadn't killed her. *Not yet.* And what kind of name was Phythian? *FITH-yun.* She ran it over her tongue, several times. Eventually she asked, "What happens when we get to Heathrow?"

Phythian had followed her thought process, and was prepared with an answer. "You go one way, and I go another."

Monica studied his eyes, which she always believed were the mirror to the soul. Trouble was, she was having difficulty finding much life in them—a dismaying truth that Phythian had come to grips with years ago. "I'm not getting on that plane until I know what the hell this is all about."

He glanced up in the rearview mirror, something he'd been doing regularly since they left Fiona's apartment. He pulled to the left to allow a lorry pass him, keeping a wary eye on the driver as the vehicle edged by. "What this is about is saving your life, and righting a grievous wrong. Many of them, in fact."

"I appreciate the help, but right now the details are scant."

Another silence as he listened to her thoughts, and collected his own. "I suppose the best place to start is the wreckage you stumbled on in the Karakoram Mountains."

"What do you know about that?"

"It was inevitable that someone should find it," he told her, as if he hadn't heard her question. "At the time I didn't consider all the chaos it would create."

At that point a grim reality began to sink in, and Monica felt a wave of nausea building in her stomach. "You were the pilot," she said. "You crashed that plane."

"It was in my contract."

"You killed those people. All of them." All of a sudden, she unlatched the car door at ninety-five kilometers an hour and began to unfasten her seatbelt. Phythian instinctively grabbed her arm and yanked her back inside.

"Let me go—" she screamed.

"Close the door."

"Go to hell. Let go."

But he did not let go. Instead he squeezed her arm, hard and steady, until she realized she was powerless against him. She flashed him a look of fury, but the intensity she saw in his eyes told her to do what he said. As if she had a choice. Reluctantly she pulled the door closed, but remained as far away from him in the little car as she could.

"You're nothing but a...a cold-blooded killer," she whimpered, shivering with fear.

"My old job description." Phythian conceded. "Truth is, I've been retired for years."

"When was the last time you killed someone?"

"Not including your so-called friend?"

"Okay, I believe you about that. She was going to kill me. I mean before then."

"The man on the train, as you said. And before you get all self-righteous, you need to look at the bigger picture."

"Then tell me about it," she said. "This big picture of yours."

A sign at the side of the road told Phythian he had about ten minutes until they reached the main exit for Heathrow. He'd either have to talk fast, or do some selective editing. Even then, he'd probably have to use his unique powers of persuasion to assuage Monica's fears if he was going to get her on her plane.

"What I did to those people in that plane is something I've had to live with for six very long years," he began. "But it's in the past, and I can't bring them back."

"You can pay. You could go to jail."

He could have laughed at the suggestion, but that would have sent the wrong message. Condescension, maybe arrogance. "There's no such thing as jail for men like me," he explained. She started to interrupt, but he raised a hand, signaling her to let him continue. "Can you imagine me standing up before a judge or jury—if I was even allowed to get that far—and explaining that I functioned at the behest of the same governments that were trying to string me up?"

"What are you talking about?" Monica asked.

"Politics is an acutely hypocritical beast, Mrs. Cross," Phythian said. "Throughout the ages there have been people who do the dirty work so others may keep their hands clean. Slaves built the pyramids and chopped cotton, and chambermaids emptied the shit pots."

"But you kill—*killed*—innocent people. Have you no conscience?"

Phythian didn't wish to get into a Socratic debate over morality or ethics or the social imperative. He'd struggled with those concepts most of his life, ever since he'd killed the two bagmen who had thrown him into the frigid quarry back in Rhode Island. Something the G3 sure as hell didn't include in its lengthy dossier bearing his name.

Instead he replied, "Conscience is the window of our spirit, evil is the curtain."

She considered his words, then she said, "Who do you work for now?"

"I told you, I'm retired," he reminded her. "And until I read news of your discovery of that plane, I was content to remain that way. I'm here because of you."

"By coincidence or design?" Monica asked.

"All of life is one simple incident following another," he replied. "Circumstances, on the other hand, are those things that modify or influence a particular event. Cause and effect. There is a difference."

They sped past another sign, this one announcing the exit for Heathrow Airport was coming up in five miles. "Look...we'll be there soon," Monica said. "Talk."

Phythian knew he would have to engage Monica Cross in a meaningful dialogue before he could ever convince her to do what he had in mind, and he would have to do it without influence from his mental skillset.

"Does the word Equinox mean anything to you?" he asked her.

He detected a slight mental hitch at the mention of the word, but she recovered quickly. "Something about the alignment of the sun on the first day of spring and fall," she said. "I think Stonehenge was built because of it."

"That's not what I'm talking about, and I think you know it."

She stared at him blankly from where she was sitting, pressed tightly against the door. No response, but he didn't really require one.

"You found a black case in the wreckage of the plane," he continued. "A case that was labeled EQUINOX."

"How do you know about that?"

"You even took pictures of it. Pictures that conveniently disappeared. Right?"

The question brought an even greater look of bewilderment. *How could he possibly be aware of these things?* Then she remembered that Brian Walker had questioned her about the very same thing, and a thousand-watt bulb flicked on in her head.

"Oh my God," she said. "What you're saying is, whatever was in that case, someone thinks I took it."

"Exactly," he replied. "And they're terrified of what you might do with it."

Eight minutes later Phythian pulled Fiona Cassidy's Mini Cooper into a space in the short-term car park near the Terminal 5 departure entrance. He turned off the engine, opened the door, and unfolded his large frame from the driver's seat.

"Let's go," he told Monica, leaving the keys in the ignition.

"You still haven't told me what this is all about," she said, even though she sensed any sort of protest was futile.

"I'll explain inside," he told her. "You have a plane to catch."

"What about the car? We're just going to leave it here?"

"Fiona won't be needing it, and the authorities won't find it for days. By then you'll be in the wind."

In the wind. He made it sound like some sort of spy movie starring

Liam Neeson, before he got all soft and cuddly. "Where are we going?" she asked.

"Where I'm going is none of your concern," he said. "You're going to Washington."

"Washington? You said I'd be home in New York by dinnertime."

"And you will be. But first, I need you to make a little detour."

"But…" She stopped, realizing that whatever she said, it would have no effect on the outcome. He seemed to have that sort of influence on her. "Why Washington?"

"I need you to take care of an important matter for me," Phythian told her. "Once you've completed it, you just hop on the train and go home."

Monica was tired of trains. Planes, too, and she quickly identified a problem with his plan. "You're forgetting something," she said. "As soon as I check in for my flight—any flight—my name will be in the airline computers."

"Not your name—Fiona's."

She glanced at the ticket he'd printed out, back at the apartment. Sure enough, it was in Fiona's name, not hers. "I don't look a thing like her," she said.

"Which is why I'm accompanying you all the way through security to your gate."

"You'll need a ticket of your own to do that."

"That thought never crossed my mind," he said, an impish grin creeping into his face.

The agent at the ticket counter was an easy mark, a gullible brain like a four-pin lock, simple to pick. Phythian stood to the side as Monica handed over Fiona Cassidy's passport and explained she was on the next scheduled flight to Washington-Dulles, leaving in just over ninety minutes.

"No luggage?" the agent asked her.

"I'm traveling light."

"And you want a complimentary upgrade to First Class?"

Monica glanced over at Phythian, who gave her an encouraging nod but said nothing. "If you have one available," she said.

"We'll see what we can do," the agent replied. No surprise, since Phythian was staring at her intently, saying not a word but seeming to guide the woman's actions. She went to work on the keyboard, and thirty seconds later announced, "All set."

She then glanced at Fiona's passport and fed it into a digital scanner. Monica expected all sort of sirens and horns to go off, but the agent simply handed it back and said, "Have a pleasant flight, Ms. Cassidy."

Once they cleared the desk Monica couldn't resist asking the question that had been plaguing her for some time, and seemed ridiculous to ask. "You had something to do with what happened just now, didn't you?"

"First class is the only way to fly," he told her.

"What I mean is, you're able to influence what a person is thinking."

"A practical skill, but sometimes not a very virtuous one."

"You expect me to believe—" She stopped mid-sentence, as she suddenly came to grips with the last twelve hours. "You've been using it on me, haven't you? This practical skill?"

"Only when absolutely necessary. Which, I must tell you, hasn't been very often."

She said nothing to that, partly pouting but mostly trying to absorb—*accept*—what he was getting at. *Mind control? Mental manipulation?* She'd heard about—and scoffed at—things like coercive seduction and subjective persuasion, rumors about how the U.S. government conducted extensive experiments into it in the seventies and eighties. Hollywood had even turned it into a goofy movie starring George Clooney and a herd of goats.

"That's why I agreed to do this errand of yours in Washington, isn't it? Rather than go home to New York?"

"You agreed to it because you know there's a greater good," he explained.

"Horseshit. You've been messing with my mind."

"Nothing you won't recover from. And I'm simply making it easier for you to do something you'd readily agree to do without my assistance." Not the full truth, but more than she needed to know.

"Sounds like a crock of hypno-mumbo-jumbo," she said. "Makes it a helluva lot easier picking up girls, I'll bet."

"That falls under the 'not very virtuous' column," Phythian conceded. "Rest assured, you're safer with me around than you have been since you were rescued from the crash site."

"You really expect me to believe that?"

"Where do you think you got the moves to kill Simone Marchand in the restroom?"

"That was her name?"

"Also known as the Duchess of Death," he said, a wistful edge to his voice. "Originally from Luxembourg, but she always preferred Paris."

"You knew her?"

"She was one of us. *Them*. Recruited out of field work to management, but once you're in the life, you're never out of it."

"You make it sound like some cheap brothel on Bourbon Street."

"The world's two oldest professions," he replied.

The security line seemed to be an endless, serpentine queue, hundreds of impatient passengers shifting their weight from foot to foot as they inched forward, numbly checking their cell phones for some life-altering text. Eventually Phythian and Monica made it through, *sans* shoes and belts and everything in their pockets. Questions were asked by weary agents, body scanners indicated no weapons, and random tests revealed no trace of explosives. All of the protective measures being ironic, since Phythian possessed the deadly ability to turn any pilot in the airport into a weapon of mass destruction.

When they arrived at Monica's departure gate they sat near a window as far from other passengers as possible. Neither said anything for a couple of minutes; then she turned to look at him. "This matter you mentioned. Don't you think it's time to tell me what I have to do?"

He stood up and tried to be as inconspicuous as possible as he removed his money belt, the one he'd had to take off while going through security. He unzipped a pouch in back, and took out a letter-sized envelope that was sealed with a strip of tape. A name was carefully written on it in block letters.

"I need you to deliver this," he explained as he handed it to her.

She cast him a wary look as she took it from him, realized it contained a small rectangular object. She glanced at the handwritten name, said, "Who is Carter Logan?"

"No one you know," he assured her. "I just need to get it to him, and it would be best if you're the one to deliver it."

"What's in it?" she asked him.

"Nothing illegal, and completely harmless." This was not exactly true, of course, since it was a part of the reason the G3 had been chasing her from Islamabad all the way to London.

"Why can't you just mail it?"

"It's time sensitive, and highly confidential."

"So why me?"

Good question, with many good answers. Not one of which was relevant right now, but he decided to give her one, anyway. Something about tightening the bond of trust.

"His fiancé was one of the victims you found in the plane," he explained.

"*Oh, my God,*" she said. "For real?"

"As real as it gets. Just get it to him as soon as you can, and take the next train home."

"You make it sound easy."

"Far from it. In fact, there's a legitimate threat of danger. Eventually the people who are after you will figure out where you went. That means you have to be quick: hand over the envelope, and get out."

"Then what?" Monica replied, her mind flashing on her sister Kathleen. "I'm sure these people are already camped out in my hallway in New York, waiting for me to show up."

"Leave that part to me," Phythian told her, making it sound effortless.

She wasn't sure what he meant by that, but at that moment the gate agent announced her plane was about to start the boarding process, beginning with executive club and first-class.

"That's us," he said, rising to his feet.

"Us?" she asked, folding the envelope in thirds and stuffing it in a pocket of her slacks.

"We need to convince the agent, there, that you're Fiona Cassidy."

"How are we going to do that?" she wanted to know.

"You really have to ask?"

Chapter 39

The package had been waiting in Lior Eichorn's suite at the Israeli Embassy on Reno Road, just as the text had said it would be.

When he'd arrived from Dulles Airport earlier in the day, his security detail had carried his belongings upstairs to the visiting dignitaries' residence and had put everything away in the drawers and closets precisely the way he liked them. Same thing was done in the bathroom, where his toiletries had been laid out to the left of the sink, again with the desired precision: toothpaste, brush, floss, deodorant, razor, shaving creme. His five prescriptions made up a second tier toward the back...along with a bottle of ibuprofen just in case he drank too much gin.

And mixed in with all that, a pocket-sized vial of a brand-name hand sanitizer was sealed with a tiny bead of adhesive compound designed to keep the contents airtight, until it was broken and the cap was twisted off.

Eichorn dared not do that now. While the vial mostly contained the product listed on the label, it had been combined with a generous quantity of A-234, an organophosphate nerve agent developed by Soviet scientists and considered vastly more potent than its lethal predecessor, VX. One of several variants of Novichok, the selection of A-234 was deliberate and calculated. While one of the scientists who developed it in the nineties had long since defected to the west, Russia continued to be the only known manufacturer of the compound throughout the world. Its use in a high-profile killing on American soil not only would cause an international incident of the highest magnitude, but would deflect blame to the Kremlin and its former KGB president.

How Eichorn's source was able to procure even a small quantity at such short notice was a mystery, even to him. The Russians vehemently denied the existence of Novichok and its associated agents, as well as their involvement in any of the international killings attributed to them. But his fellow Israelis could be exceptionally enterprising, especially when it came to subterfuge, or just shifting attention from them to another player when political necessity dictated.

In Eichorn's case it strictly was a matter of retribution, the ultimate feat of political artifice, distracting the audience with the hands while the eyes were misdirected elsewhere. And, of course, there was the absolute need to maintain distance and deniability if the sky began to fall.

It was almost two in the morning when he got back to his room, seven hours earlier than in Jerusalem. He'd not spoken with his wife in three days, right after Eitan Hazan had confirmed his worst fears about their daughter. Her tears and wails had echoed those he'd felt in his heart for over six years, and had drawn down the curtain on a macabre tragedy that had begun when her plane had gone missing. They both had known in their hearts that she'd perished along with the aircraft but, as long as it remained lost, they'd been able to maintain a small fragment of optimism, as misplaced and futile as they both knew it was.

The discovery of the wreckage and the five victims had put a stop to all that. The pretending and dissembling of their daily lives finally could come to an end, replaced with a real sense of healing that permitted them to accept—even welcome—the grim face of truth. A different stage of grieving had begun, no more painless than the first, but much more final.

What made it all the more difficult was the guilt he felt for his complicity in Avigail's death. This was something he would have to deal with alone, until he finally took it to his grave.

He thought about calling Alina now. She'd be awake, probably out in the garden already tending to her lilies and irises. She'd gladly take his call, but he didn't want her to think that he'd stayed up this late, imbibing too much gin and flirting with pretty American women. Which was the truth and, no matter how much he might try to slur his way through an excuse, she would know. In the spirit of poet Ernest Christopher Dowson, he'd always been faithful to his wife, in his fashion. Now it was time for him to go to bed; he could call her tomorrow, when he was refreshed and ready to greet the morning.

Eichorn left the bathroom light on, gently closed the door until it projected a thin line across the floor. He usually preferred to sleep in total darkness, but tonight he seemed to need a visual reference point should he wake up. Or maybe it was just a need to keep half an eye on whatever evil might invade the room, a fear that remained from when he was a child and his mother would prop an ironing board against the front door of their small home. His father had been killed during the Six-Day War and, since they lived not far from the newly annexed West Bank territories, she had wanted to be awakened if intruders attempted to force their way inside.

He swept all the pillows and the duvet from the bed, slipped under the lone sheet. His head still spun from the events of the night, the drinking and the dancing, and especially the brief phone conversation he'd had with his assistant deputy in Berlin. But there was no word at all from Eitan Hazan, whose silence was growing more bothersome by the hour. It was foolish to think something serious might have happened to him: he'd fought at Entebbe and Morocco and Tunisia, and countless other hot spots over the years. He knew how to take care of himself. This was unlike his cousin, and he'd begun to grow concerned, if not outright worried.

His conscious mind struggled to cross the threshold into sleep. He bounced from one thought to another—events of yesterday, tonight, tomorrow—and once again his mind seized on the ampoule of hand sanitizer in the bathroom. It was just a simple matter, really: Mossad 101 training in its most elementary form. Essential tradecraft, and he'd mastered everything they'd thrown at him as one of the best in his class.

Problem was, riding a desk for twenty years can dull one's faculties, as well as one's confidence to use them. From a low-level intelligence recruit fresh out of university, Lior Eichorn had risen to one of the most powerful positions in the government, and he liked to think he wasn't finished yet.

Chapter 40

Washington
3:41 pm GMT, 11:41 am Local

More than eight hours after the fact, the woman who went by Giselle or Linda or Beatrice, or any of a dozen other names, was livid. She had failed in her attempt to kill Carter Logan, who now was aware his life was in immediate danger. She also sported a black eye where the cocksucker had punched her, right after he'd received a text on his Goddamned phone.

Only a few people alive knew her real name was Angela Wilde, and she'd made it a point during her thirty-six years on the planet to keep it that way. As long as she remained one step ahead of her past, remaining mobile and assuming false identities, her movements were virtually untraceable. Her prints were on file in a network of computers across the globe, but a rather painful acid treatment in Guadalajara had alleviated that problem for good—as had eleven rounds of plastic surgery, enough to fool all but the most sophisticated biometrics algorithms. She'd taken speech lessons that enabled her to switch accents from Boston to Texan to Australian in mid-sentence, and she spoke passable French, German, and Dutch, in addition to the Americanized English she was born into in Green Bay. Despite all her weapons and combat training—none of it provided by the military—she had all the appearance of your everyday Wisconsin cheese head.

The black eye, however, was a problem. It had darkened overnight, and the thick layer of pancake foundation she'd applied barely masked it—all because she had waited an instant too long, had failed to kill the damned blogger when she'd first approached him at the bar. Instead, she'd foolishly decided to play him while she walked with him up the street to the next block. She had already staked out a dark spot between streetlights, the precise spot where she could slash him with no risk of being seen. The red-and-blue specialty cocktails had been more potent than she'd anticipated, however, even though she'd developed a serious tolerance for alcohol. A convenient feat that came in handy the night she'd killed her drunk stepfather.

Angela stole another glance at her face in the fold-down visor mirror. *Damn.*

For the first time in her career, she felt distracted. Not since her very first mission had she felt like this, anxious and apprehensive that she might not be able to pull off a job. In less than eight hours she would face the biggest assignment of her life, one that would make the history books and force her into early retirement. She'd prepared for it for close to a month, run through the entire drill first on mannequins and then real people, none of the latter suspecting in the least what she was doing as she'd perfected her technique.

The G3 had already seen to it that she'd been thoroughly vetted by the FBI and Secret Service for her cosplay role: no prior arrests or brushes with the law, no contact with foreign nationals or terrorists or known criminals, and no bothersome family connections or college roommates with questionable pasts. Social media accounts had been created to reflect her indisputable support for the current president.

So why did she feel this agitated?

Because—in addition to her bruised eye, of course—the courier was almost fifteen minutes late. The Dragon Lady at the G3 personally had assured her that he was a true pro and would be there, on time and unobtrusive. He was cutting it close—too close—and Angela Wilde didn't like leaving anything up to the last minute. Or chance.

She also didn't like not feeling in control. Yet here she was, dependent on someone she did not know to come through with the appliance she required for the successful completion of her assignment. She'd been keeping her blackened eye open ever since she'd arrived almost a half hour ago but, thus far, she'd spotted nothing out of the ordinary. About a dozen cars were parked in the lot, many of them belonging to people who owned boats tied up at the Columbia Island Marina, across the Potomac from DC. Several vehicles had come and gone—all business as usual, she guessed—but no sign of the envoy whom she'd been told was unwavering in his punctuality.

Just then a kid on a skateboard appeared as if from another dimension, careening across the pavement as he charged toward her car. He jumped off just in time to avoid the collision, and his custom wheels rolled under the vehicle and flew up onto the grass on the other side. The kid—he looked no more than twenty—tumbled to the pavement as he tried to correct his balance, eventually coming to a rest against the rental Jetta's front left tire.

Fuck, Angela cursed to herself. *Cover blown.*

The young man dusted himself off and slowly rose to his feet. His helmet remained affixed to his head, and he adjusted it to make sure it fit snugly across his bushy crown of hair. And now that Angela Wilde really got a chance to look at him, she realized he was closer to forty, in her mind well past the age that any grown man should be riding one of those things.

"I'm sorry, ma'am," he apologized as he smiled at her through her open window. It was too warm to be sitting in a car without air conditioning, but running the AC with the glass rolled up on a muggy Washington afternoon would have been a dead giveaway. He glanced at the driver's side door and fender, then added, "Doesn't look like your car got a scratch, though."

"Are you all right?" she asked him, her detached voice lacking even a shred of empathy.

"Not a scrape. We're good?"

"Good?" she asked him.

"No cops, no insurance."

The last thing she wanted was for the local police to get involved. "Yeah, we're good."

"Fantastic," the kid said. He stuck out his hand for a quick shake, then circled around her car off to fetch his skateboard, which was lying upside down on the grass.

The entire incident had happened with such speed that he was gone before Angela noticed the tiny object in her lap: a pack of brand-name spearmint gum. She carefully opened one end of the sealed wrapper and pulled out the neatly sheathed sticks, one of them heavier and more pliable than the others. Plus, there was a silicon chip the size of a small toenail, as well as a bare wire that was no more than a half-inch in length.

Damn, she thought as she replaced the contents in the pack and slipped it into her handbag. The courier was already gone, but she looked in the rearview mirror anyway. *Vanished, without a trace.* She stole one more glance at her bruise, thinking, *looks like it might have already faded a bit.*

All of sudden she didn't feel quite as dispirited as she had just a minute ago.

• • •

The 747 touched down hard on runway 1R/19L—the same one Lior Eichorn had landed on yesterday—but Monica hardly noticed.

The problem with modern airports is that one can't just step off the plane and kiss the ground. This is exactly what Monica wanted to do now that she was back in the U.S., but she had to walk directly from the jetway to the stuffy, windowless netherworld known as Customs and Immigration. As the man named Phythian had impressed upon her back at Heathrow, she presented her American passport in her own name rather than Fiona Cassidy's, and breezed through the re-entry process without setting off any alarms.

She was eager to get outside into the fresh Virginia countryside, but first she had to make a call. As much as she wanted to wash her hands of this entire Pakistan mess and get up to New York, she had a task to complete and the man named Phythian had been alarmingly convincing. He'd also provided a solution to get her on an airplane bound for the U.S. without alerting any computers or tripping any alarms.

She waited for the phone to ring, but all she heard was a series of clicks spaced about two seconds apart. Eventually the clicks ended, and the phone went dead. She tried calling again, but got the same response.

"Damn," she muttered.

In Monica's dreams she had been able to call the number Phythian had given her, make the hand-off right away, then head to Union Station and buy a ticket for the next Amtrak to Penn Station—but not if no one answered.

She felt defeated and alone, and wanted to throw the phone against the wall. She was tired of being thwarted at every turn, as if someone was controlling her in a perverse game of tag and having great fun at her expense. More than anything she wanted to walk through the front door of her Manhattan apartment and gaze out at the modest view of the Hudson that had caused Phillip and her to choose it over the larger place near Central Park. Even though she would be alone, his presence and spirit were there every day—and that's what she needed the most now.

Her mind flashed back to one Saturday many years ago, when she had been about ten and her mother had taken her to a pet shop to buy a new leash for their dog. While her mother was trying to decide between blue and green, Monica had wandered off to a corner of the store and had been mesmerized while she watched a small python swallow a feeder mouse whole. When her mother finally located her, she was horrified at the thought that any shopkeeper would permit such a thing to happen in front of small children. She'd complained to the manager, but Monica had been fascinated by the spectacle, explaining later to her mother, "It's just the circle of life."

That's how she felt now: as if her life was being squeezed by a giant python. It was just a part of a bigger cycle of events, and there was nothing she could do but roll with it.

No one named Monica Cross, or anyone using her passport, had boarded a plane anywhere in Europe during the last twenty-four hours. She had fallen completely off the grid since she hadn't gotten off the train in Brussels.

To make matters worse, Eitan Hazan also appeared to be missing. He'd adjusted his assignment after Simone Marchand had failed at hers, and CCTV footage from *Frankfurt Flughafen* at the airport showed him boarding a train heading north to Cologne, the same with Rōnin Phythian, who seemed to be making no effort to mask his identity to the ubiquitous surveillance cameras.

That was the part Adam Kent found the most vexing. He was seated at his desk in the Eisenhower Executive Office Building, just a stone's throw from the White House. Described alternatively as an "architectural insane asylum" and "the greatest monstrosity in America," the structure now was home to an overflow of White House toadies and bootlickers. It was within these hallways of bureaucratic anonymity that he enjoyed great operational latitude, coming and going at all hours, no one questioning his role within the government. Which at the moment involved cursing the scant data that had been collected on Monica Cross. Three phones at *Earth Illustrated*, including the direct line to publisher Arnie Kelso's corner office, remained discretely bugged, as was the phone at her sister's house in Connecticut. Unlike the others, that one was legal, courtesy of the FBI, which had convinced Kathleen Butler that it was better to tap the residential land line than to reveal to her husband the intimate details of her steamy late-night phone liaisons with Lance Hendrix. Kent himself had ordered the telephone surveillance of Monica's apartment in New

York, as well as that of Carter Logan, whose location currently was not known, either.

Something that troubled him almost as much as the whereabouts of Monica Cross.

Shortly after noon Kent's mobile phone rang, just once. It was the dedicated cell that connected directly to Gray Rock, and foreshadowed a conversation he'd been expecting, and dreading.

"Fiona Cassidy," The Chairman wheezed.

"Excuse me, sir. Who is Fiona Cassidy?"

"A British MI6 rookie twit who apparently decided to go solo," The Chairman replied.

"And this affects us why?"

"Because we have reason to believe the photographer used her passport to board a plane to Dulles. Facial recognition confirms it."

"Shit on a stick." Kent didn't need this; not today, of all days. "Why are we just learning this now?"

"She had assistance."

Kent tried to follow what The Chairman was telling him, in between the man's bouts of hacking and expectorating. "What sort of assistance?" he felt obliged to ask.

"The sort that leaves Hazan Eitan dead on a train in Germany. His body was found yesterday, but authorities didn't release his true identity until an hour ago. Or how a three-fifty-seven slug found his right temple."

"It has to be Phythian," Kent said, seeing no other logical explanation. "How did these women know each other? Cross and the Brit?"

"They were seated next to each other on the original flight from Pakistan," The Chairman explained. "Fiona was planted there by British SIS to keep an eye on her, figure out what she knows about Equinox."

"Why didn't she kill Cross herself when she had the chance?"

"Above her pay grade, until things escalated."

"And no one noticed that someone purchased a ticket using this Cassidy woman's name, then used her passport to board an international flight?"

"SIS didn't program their computers to flag her," The Chairman explained.

Goddamned Brits, Kent thought. "When is her flight due to touch down?"

"It landed ten minutes ago."

"Shit on a stick," Kent said again. "You mean she's already here?"

"Why else would I be calling?"

A purely rhetorical question that Kent decided to leave alone. "Any intel on why the Cross woman is here, instead of home in New York?" he asked instead.

"None at all. And your job it to make sure whatever it is, never happens."

"What about Phythian?" Kent inquired.

"Surveillance cameras lost him at Heathrow," The Chairman hissed, like a venomous cobra hiding in the brush. "He was known to have a half dozen passports, so where he is—*who he is*—could be anybody's guess."

Chapter 41

At that very moment Rōnin Phythian was on board a small fishing vessel named the *Ceilidh* which, in Gaelic, roughly translated to "social gathering." The old wooden craft struggled against the bitter elements as it chugged out from the tiny village of Brodick on the Isle of Arran, an hour ferry ride across the Firth of Clyde from the town of Ardrossan. Phythian had arrived there an hour ago, following the bus ride from Glasgow, and he'd quickly found a captain willing to take him out for a cruise.

The *Ceilidh*—pronounced "kay-lee" by the locals—had plied these waters for thirty years and, barring any unexpected mishap, would be doing the same for the next thirty. Captain Urquhart—somewhat pronounced "urk-utt"—was the owner and master of the boat, and he'd assured Phythian of this fact before they set out on this charter excursion, as long as he paid full freight up front.

The sky was the color of charcoal, the sea a deep shade of pewter and running at six feet. A light rain was dribbling down upon the western Scottish coast, and the heavens were threatening to split open in a downpour. A wind was building from the northwest, blowing spray from the cresting waves across the bow of the boat.

"Thar she is," Urquhart said, peering through the now-driving rain at the gray horizon. He was a grizzled man, with a leathery face and gnarled knuckles. A mop of thick, black hair covered his scalp, and his chin was cloaked in a beard that carried streaks of rust and silver in it. "Lying off to starboard, thar," he said, pointing. "You can see her best when the chop lies low."

Phythian looked in the direction of the captain's gaze, but he saw nothing. He had never been in these waters before, and he did not know what he was looking for. Urquhart, on the other hand, had grown up in Lamlash, a few miles south of Brodick, and he knew the sea as if a nautical chart had been tattooed on the inside of his eyelids.

"Try these." He handed Phythian a pair of old British Air Force field glasses. "Look just above the horizon, there—"

This time Phythian did see it, but only briefly. At this distance it appeared as no more than a speck of stone protruding from the roiling waters, as gray as the sky and just as lifeless.

Gray Rock.

"The old man arrived middle of May, and he's expected to leave early next month," Urquhart said. "On account of he's not got a lot of days left in him."

"Are we expecting this storm to clear?" Phythian inquired.

"This is no storm, my friend. But we got a bloody fierce one moving in from the west, barometer's been dropping since midnight. Should be quite a blow."

"Can you put me ashore in weather like this?"

"It'll be rough, and you may have to jump the last couple feet," the captain said. "Gray Rock, she's a wild lass on a flat sea—and on a day like today, she's a true bitch and a bloody whore."

"Let's go have ourselves a look," Phythian told him.

Ten minutes later they had drawn within fifty yards of the rocky outcropping. The driving rain had turned into a ferocious squall, and the roiling seas had evolved into a wild, undulating swell.

Phythian peered through the tempest at the old stone quay; the water between it and the boat looked very cold. "There's the quay, there," he said.

"Any closer and she'll break apart." Urquhart said. "You going to pay for my boat if she goes down?"

"You said jumping distance."

"Bloody hell," the captain cursed. "I'll get you as close as I can, but I'm not losing my lady on account of a crazy man."

"Jumping distance," Phythian repeated, pushing the concept into Urquhart brain.

"You'd better be quick, then. I'm only making one pass at the bugger."

One pass was all it took, but not without the captain's steady hand on the wheel and his instinct for the sea. The lead-colored water pounded against the granite pier with five-foot waves, a constant eruption of salt spray washing over it and periodically obscuring it from view. The *Ceilidh* rocked and pitched as the captain eased the engine and came at it from an angle, closing from twenty meters to ten, then five. As he swung the vessel around, the surge began to roll the boat up against the old jetty, but he spun the wheel at just the right moment and yelled "Go."

Phythian went. He'd positioned himself along the starboard gunwale, a firm grip on the cabin top, and with one mighty effort he leaped across the heaving surf. At the same moment, the *Ceilidh* rocked seaward on the crest of an errant wave, hurling him into the side of the quay with the force of a catapult. The impact momentarily knocked the air from his lungs, and he started to slip into the numbing waters of the Firth of Clyde.

He clawed wildly at the rough stone and his fingers finally found purchase on a rock jutting out from the side of the quay. Then his foot found another small ledge, and he was able to steady himself as the boat chugged back out into the open water. Phythian heard the captain call out something to him, but the words were lost in the howling wind and the crashing surf.

A minute later he was standing on the top of the pier, shielding his eyes from the salt spray. His clothes were drenched, he was chilled to the bone, and he was being pelted by rain driven sideways from the force of the storm. Out in the depths of the gale he heard the engine of *Ceilidh* fading in the distance, as well as the occasional moan of a foghorn on the Isle of Arran.

Phythian knew from his evening with *Le Serrurier* that Gray Rock was a small knob of land twenty acres in size, the shape of a teardrop when viewed from above, or from Google maps. The main residence—a stone structure originally erected at the end of the nineteenth century—was nestled in the rocks at the highest point of the land, with a wrap-around veranda and a cupola providing a three-sixty view of the sea.

A narrow path led up from the quay through the dense scrub and grass that covered most of the island. The few trees that grew here—mostly cedars and alders—bowed at a precarious angle due to the constant sweep of the wind. As Phythian made his way to high ground he took great pains to look for booby traps and detection devices, but concluded none was to be found. Had The Chairman grown so arrogant over time to believe that no one would dare infiltrate his summer lair? Or was he saving his surprises—and his armaments—for when Phythian arrived at the top of the mount? Either way, he was going to find out soon. He'd followed the trail to the uppermost reach of the island, and now was crouched low beside a large fist of stone.

Thirty yards away stood the great stone house of Gray Rock.

Chapter 42

Monica Cross did what most travelers in a hurry did: she took the shuttle bus from Dulles Airport to the Wiehle-Reston Metro station, then rode the Silver Line a total of fourteen stops into the city. Along the way she tried calling Carter Logan five more times, each attempt getting the same series of empty clicks. Service in the tunnels was spotty and she kept losing signal, causing her frustration to mount with each passing station.

By the time she emerged from the Metro Center hub in the heart of Washington, her frustration had shifted to worry. The man named Phythian—he'd never given her his first name—assured her the number belonged to the blogger named Logan, but it wasn't ringing through. As she rode the escalator up into the steamy sump of summer, she punched the numbers in one more time, almost not bothering to wait for the irritating click-click-click.

To her surprise, this time it started ringing.

Just as she stepped off the moving stairs into the glaring sun a voice on the other end said, "Who's calling?" Suspicious and apprehensive, ready to hang up if given a reason to.

"My name is Monica Cross," she answered. "Are you Carter Logan?"

"Do I know you?" he asked, abrupt and testy.

"No. But I've traveled a long way to give you something." There was a pause on the other end, and Monica was afraid that Carter Logan—or whoever this was—might have hung up on her and not answer again if she called back. "I just got in from London, and I don't have much time."

"How did you get this number?" he demanded.

"From the man who gave me the thing I'm supposed to give you."

Another pause, then: "And who is this man?"

265

Phythian had told Monica was not to mention his name, not under any circumstances. The NSA operated a number of sophisticated eavesdropping systems—among them PRISM, ECHELON, and DISHFIRE—all of which were capable of monitoring virtually every phone call, text, email, or other digital communication. Best to keep his identity out of the surveillance system, he'd explained.

Instead, he'd instructed her to say: "It's about Katya Leiffson."

She heard a gasp on the other end, and then the voice became terse. Almost angry. "What do you know about her?"

"Just that the two of you were going to get married. If your name is Carter Logan."

"Who did you say you are?" he demanded.

"Monica Cross. I'm a photographer for *Earth Illustrated* magazine. I was in Pakistan until just a few days ago—"

"Holy shit. I know who you are. You found the plane."

"That's me," she conceded. "Like I said, I have something to give you."

"You—" He inhaled a ragged breath, then let it out. "You were there. You saw her."

"Yes, Mr. Logan," she replied, even though he had not yet confirmed his identity.

"You're sure it was her? Katya?"

"If she was on that plane, I'm sure it was. There were five of them."

"How...I mean, did she...what I want to know is, did she look like she'd suffered?"

"The crash happened a long time ago, Mr. Logan."

"Just tell me, dammit," he snapped. Not so much angry as impassioned.

"It would be better if we meet in person," she told him.

"We will, so you can give me whatever this thing is. But I need to know how she died."

Now it was Monica's time to regroup, take a deep breath. "She was shot, Mr. Logan," she told him. "All of them were."

Monica could almost hear the gears grinding in his head as thoughts churned and memories rose up from the deepest crevasses in his mind. She knew the signals: same thing happened whenever she thought about Phillip, which seemed to be just about every second of the day. At least until she'd been forced to run for her life; since then, she'd been focused on simply staying one step ahead of the triggerman.

"Where are you now?" he asked her.

"Metro Center. I can see a Macy's across the street."

"I know it. Look...I can't explain right now, but I think some people are after me. It's why I destroyed my old phone and just got this one. They gave me the same number, but all my contacts are gone. Six blocks south of you is the Museum of Natural History. Meet me there at two o'clock. South steps on the mall side."

"I remember it," she assured him. She spotted a sandwich shop that was part of a nationwide chain halfway up the block, and quickly formulated a plan. "I'll grab a quick bite and see you then."

Adam Kent was halfway through the crosswalk in the middle of 17th Street when his phone rang. He had a paper bag from a deli in one hand, and he had to fish the device out of his inside coat pocket. The June heat made it insane to wear a jacket in Washington, but he had an image to protect. Even though it was Saturday, the government never slept. And neither would he, until the immediate issues of the day were dealt with.

"What?" he barked, since it was not the phone The Chairman typically called.

"I'm told you're tracking an American target named Monica Cross," said an anonymous voice on the other end; southern accent, maybe north Georgia hills or eastern Tennessee. A dialect expert would know the difference, but Kent neither knew nor cared.

"Who gave you this number?"

"FYI, she cleared customs at Dulles forty minutes ago," the nameless voice continued, ignoring him. "And just four minutes ago she used a credit card bearing the same name at an address on G Street, just west of Metro Center. Place called Panera Bread."

By now Kent had reached the opposite curb. He glanced around, fuming that this was not like New York, where cabs were everywhere, even at lunchtime. It was not quite the same in DC. Hailing a taxi was not impossible, but those that were empty and looking for a fare tended to hang around the National Mall or outside Union Station. The curb in front of the Eisenhower Building was not a popular attraction on the capital tourist trail, which meant the chance of snagging a ride where he was standing was almost nil.

Two blocks east of him, however, was the White House, which was a different story altogether.

"I'll be there in five minutes," he said to this man he did not know. "She should still be there."

The cab driver was not happy to have picked up a fare that was only going six blocks, much less one who stunk up his vehicle with a nasty Reuben sandwich smothered with foul-smelling sauerkraut, and a side of pickles. But the twenty-dollar bill Kent handed him incentivized him to overlook life's immediate indignations, and there was always the possibility he might pick up another passenger at Metro Center. Which meant he wouldn't even log this in as an official ride, and could pocket the twenty.

The trip took all of three minutes, and Kent spent half that time contemplating the man on the phone. Clearly The Chairman had activated one of the NSA's security threads and was tracking Monica Cross via her passport and credit card. It had been a mistake for her to buy lunch with it, which suggested she either was low on American money, or had made a sloppy mistake. In any event, he was alarmed that she was in the middle of the city, probably killing time until she completed whatever task she came here to do. *Meet up with someone? Pick up something? Make some sort of hand-off?* The fact that Phythian was involved made the matter even more puzzling, and Kent didn't like puzzles.

The second half of those three minutes he focused on what he would do when he spotted her. For reasons he found un-fucking-believable, she had managed to make it all the way from the outer reaches of Pakistan to Washington, DC, leaving a swath of death and mayhem in her wake. Along the way two of the G3's finest enforcers had been lost, although largely because of their own hubris. Even worse, the thing called EQUINOX remained unaccounted for.

Most days Kent didn't walk the streets of Washington with a gun tucked into a holster under his jacket, and this was one of those days. His Kimber Micro nine-millimeter with Crimson Trace Lasergrips, white dot sights and sixteen-pound recoil spring, six bullet capacity, was locked in a briefcase under his desk on the fourth floor of the Eisenhower Building. Twelve years in the U.S. Army Special Forces and another eight as a Langley analyst—before he'd personally been tapped by The Chairman to fill a slot on the executive board—had caused him never to want to fire a gun again.

While he felt comforted to have one close by, he didn't need to have it on him unless events made it absolutely necessary.

But knives…well, they were another thing altogether. Adam Kent appreciated the close proximity and finality of knives, and a specially crafted case in his attic man cave held an extensive collection of them: filet and deboning knives, fixed-blade survival knives, Bowie knives, British commando knives—even the Marfione Custom Mini Matrix-R with a Nebula Damascus blade, Moku-Ti handle, and blued titanium hardware. That one was his favorite, for visceral reasons that had contributed to the dissolution of his marriage.

But not the folding credit card knife; that weapon, which fit nice and snug in his deerskin wallet, was not stored in the locked display closet. In fact, he carried that one tucked in his wallet inside his suitcoat pocket, where it was easily accessible at any moment.

Monica had ordered a Fuji apple salad and half a ciabatta roll, plus a large to-go cup of tea that she'd found too hot to drink. She was seated at a small table in the far corner of the restaurant, where she could keep an eye on her fellow diners.

She found it hard to believe she'd been released from the hospital in Islamabad only sixty hours ago. Three continents, four cities, and she didn't care to think how many people had tried to kill her since then. Until she delivered the envelope to Carter Logan—until she was safely back in her own apartment, sleeping in her own bed—she wasn't going to let down her guard, not for a second.

Most of the lunch patrons on this Saturday seemed to be tourists, with a few weekend office workers thrown in. T-shirts and sunglasses mingled with slacks and sundresses and ties. Monica enjoyed people-watching, and she found herself so engrossed in them that she almost missed the man in the summer suit who had pushed his way inside, studying the crowd rather than heading over to the "order" counter.

He seemed to be looking for someone, but Monica told herself not to be worried. There was no way anyone could know she was here in Washington, much less having lunch in this unobtrusive sandwich place. The guy had to be meeting someone, and he was simply checking to see if he—or she— had arrived. That's what she kept telling herself as she tried not to make eye contact, opting instead to focus on the contents of her salad.

The more he stood there, the more she didn't like his body language; impatient, almost in a hurry to get a job done. She picked at a leaf of spinach on her plate, saw him look in her direction, caught him reach inside his suit pocket for something.

Her heart leaped as she thought *gun*. But that was just her paranoia raging again, as the man pulled his wallet out of a pocket and plucked out a credit card. As he turned it over in his hand he caught her looking at him, and he shot her a tight grin that lingered longer than it should have. And much longer than made her feel comfortable.

Again, her brain told her *no way*, but the rest of her was screaming, *you're screwed*. And as one second ticked into the next, she realized she was. In her haste to keep an eye on the door, she had selected a table in a back corner, no escape route that would lead her to safety if someone figured out who she was.

A potentially fatal mistake.

They stared at each other for several seconds, and Monica sensed—correction, *knew*—he was here for her. In an instant he was pushing his way toward her, methodically weaving through the crowded tables, closing in. She had nowhere to go, nowhere to run. She felt like the fox who had managed to outrun the dogs for hours, and had become overconfident somewhere along the way.

"Monica Cross." Adam Kent said as he stepped up to her table, boxing her in. "I'm here to help you—"

"How did you find me?" Monica asked, her voice no more than a single strand of breath.

"Credit card," he said, quickly figuring there was no point keeping up the pretense. "Come with me."

"What do you want?" she asked, not budging from her seat. Her eyes flashed on his for half a second, but she couldn't bring herself to look at him longer than that.

"That depends on whether you cooperate," Kent explained, an arrogant smirk creeping into his face. "You've given us quite a challenge."

"What if I don't?" she said, a little louder this time. "Cooperate, I mean?"

The smirk turned into a sneer as he slipped a sharp, flat blade out of the object she had thought was a credit card. He exposed just enough of it to allow Monica a glimpse of the razor-sharp edge, "Come along without a problem, no one gets hurt. If you put up a struggle, you won't be around to see yourself on the evening news."

Monica hesitated a moment, as if trying to decide what to do. Kent waited patiently; in his mind she really had no choice. But Monica's mind was different, and she'd made a different choice the moment Kent had slipped the knife out of its black sheath.

She started to stand up, sighing with resignation, and Kent flashed her a smile of victory. "That's a good girl—"

But Monica had no intention of being good, nor did she consider herself a mere girl. Appearing resigned to her fate, she bent down to pick up a non-existent handbag, momentarily drawing his eyes away from where she was seated. And as soon as he wasn't looking at her, she grasped the paper cup of tea and hurled it at him.

The steaming liquid hit him squarely in the face. Instinctively he threw his hands up to his eyes and cursed at the same time. Monica gripped the edge of the small table and, with a great heave, pushed it over. It caught Kent just above the knees and tipped him backward, toppling him into a man seated directly behind him.

Monica wasted no time. She pivoted around Kent, who was clutching at his eyes and hurling a litany of cuss words at her. She stomped on his knee with all her might, driving a spear of pain into her ankle as she pushed past him and raced for the door.

The words "Stop that bitch" ringing in her ears as she hit the pavement.

Chapter 43

The great room in the center of the stone manor at the top of Gray Rock was a contrast in extremes. The storm that raged outside pelted the large glass windows, and visibility through the fog and sea spray was virtually zero. Inside, however, the flames in the massive fireplace with hand-carved granite mantel roared with the ferocity of Dante's *Inferno*, danseurs of light cavorting with the shadows of hand-carved chairs and grandfather clocks that had been crafted by artisans over a century ago; back in an era when pride and patience held more worth than paycheck and profit.

Warm and toasty, The Chairman lounged in a William IV reclining armchair, hand-finished mahogany with tulip legs in the front. He'd found the antique in a secondhand shop in Edinburgh twenty years ago, and had it packed and shipped to the island, along with a matching mahogany table that had been hiding in the store's attic.

This evening, a thick tartan blanket was draped over his emaciated legs, and he held a glass of warm Cuban rum in his equally skeletal hands. He was gazing through one of the windows as if he were remembering a time when most of his life was still ahead of him, and growing old and decrepit was just a feeble tease of a distant yet inescapable future. He had come to terms with his imminent demise several months ago, the same day the doctors in Milan had explained to him that his renal cell carcinoma was now the size of a grapefruit and was consuming far more calories than he was taking in. Especially since he had lost his appetite for most things, save for the thirty-year-old Don Pancho rum, a glass of which he held in his hand…and an occasional nip of the Balvenie Dark Barley twenty-six-year-old single malt he kept in the locked cabinet under the mother-of-pearl globe. He deeply inhaled the honey and nougat aroma, contemplating at what point in life a fading pensioner gladly switches his affections to rum and Scotch, and leaves women to the devices of younger men.

"We have a visitor, sir," came a voice from the doorway that opened in from the vaulted entry hall. It belonged to the old caretaker who had served the summer tenants of Gray Rock for over fifty years, long before The Chairman had taken up residence and renovated the stone structure. His name was Gordon but, like all his predecessors before him, he was known as Gordy. The nickname sounded a bit adolescent for a man in his late seventies but, because he liked his boss and the job paid well, he'd learned to let it go.

"Is that a fact, Gordy?" The Chairman said without turning around. "Someone braved the elements to come all the way out here on a day like this?"

"Does seems a bit puzzling, sir," Gordy replied. It was puzzling not because of the weather or the rough seas, but because everyone who lived in any of the villages on the Isle of Arran knew that travel out here was greatly discouraged. "What would you like me to do?"

The Chairman slowly pondered the question, more because his synapses were slow to fire these days than because he was giving it much consideration. Eventually he asked, "Where might our weather-beaten friend be?"

"At the southern edge of the clearing," Gordy answered. "He came up by way of the trail leading up from the jetty. Perhaps he got swept off a fishing boat."

"Are we certain it is a 'he'?"

"Just assuming, sir. Hard to imagine a lady foolish enough to venture out in this."

"I see your point, Gordy. Well, why don't you go fix a pot of tea? Better yet, fetch another glass for our visitor and welcome him in from the cold with a tot of warm rum."

The Chairman dismissed the caretaker with a wave of his hand, never drawing his eyes off the angry gloom roiling outside the window. *Fishing boat my ass*, he thought. No fisherman in his right mind would be out in a storm like this. One call to the mainland could get him that information, if he wished. He lived for information; it was the currency of the world—the great specie of power and wealth—and, judging by such standards, he was a rich man; very rich indeed. Information had its time and its purpose, but this evening there was no point in checking to see if any boats were late coming home from the sea.

For The Chairman had expected to receive company: perhaps tonight, perhaps tomorrow or the next day, but sometime soon, most definitely.

A most deadly adversary, he thought as a shadow fell upon the room. He peered through the dusky gloom as Gordy led his visitor into the library.

"Rōnin Phythian—can that really that you?" he inquired, squinting through eyes ravaged by age. "How many years has it been since our paths last crossed?"

"Nowhere near enough," Phythian responded. He'd already sensed The Chairman was aware of his presence on Gray Rock, desperately trying to determine the best method to deal with him. "Time has gotten the better of us both, I'm afraid."

"What's past is prologue," the old man agreed. "I must say, I never expected for us to meet again under circumstances such as these."

"You never expected us to meet again under any circumstances," Phythian reminded him icily. "Funny how our mistakes always come back to haunt us."

"The world is plagued by false starts and fickle turns," The Chairman agreed. "And since these starts and turns have brought you to my door, please: make yourself at home."

They were sizing each other up, much the same way fencers begin a match. Get a feel for the opposition: how he moves, how he thinks, what he feels—how he anticipates not just the next move, but the next five—and how he prepares for them all. *Lunge, parry, riposte. Passata sotto, counter-attack, remise, feint.* It was an art form defined by basic principles of competitive balance, mental acuity, and guarded sportsmanship.

"Thank you," Phythian said appreciatively. "Your house is my house."

Despite his confidence and bluster, The Chairman was finding himself unnerved by the confidence with which his unexpected visitor spoke. That Phythian was here at all was enough cause for concern, but the way he appeared to feel no sense of peril was disconcerting.

"Gordy, please pour our guest a glass of Don Pancho," he told the caretaker. "I do hate to drink alone."

"I'll pass, if you don't mind."

"A gentleman does not turn down the hospitality of another," the Chairman admonished him sourly. "Particularly when said gentleman has arrived without invitation or summons."

"Neither of us has fit the definition of 'gentleman' for a very long time," Phythian said. He continued to stand by the roaring fire, drying his trousers, making no effort to sit down.

"Care to elaborate?"

"I've always believed the term to mean a person with courage and honor in his heart. A man who is gallant and respectful and decent and, most of all, of high moral character. Gentlemen do not rape and plunder and kill at the expense of others but, unfortunately, both of us are forced to live with such sins."

"Hate the sin, love the sinner." The Chairman folded his hands into a steeple, the canonical irony apparently lost on him. "And I see no reason to anguish over actions of such little consequence when there's always been a greater objective to consider."

"The old 'ends justifying the means' excuse, is that it?"

"An elementary triviality that may not sound particularly civil, but sometimes one must consider the larger scenario. The greater good, as they say. At one time you used to understand that, my friend."

"What I've come to learn is it's a convenient way to expunge guilt and conscience."

"Let's not distract ourselves over lost scruples or dogmatic contrivances," The Chairman said. "Instead, please entertain me with why you have elected to visit my modest abode on such a dark and stormy night. Pardon the tired bromide, but I cannot resist. And Gordy, you are excused for the evening."

The caretaker nodded but said nothing as he slipped out of the room, leaving the two adversaries to their own devices. Once he was gone, The Chairman gathered up his glass of rum and let a trickle of the amber liquid flow smoothly over his tongue and down his throat.

"You're certain I can't interest you in a tot?" he asked.

Phythian thought for a moment how far he'd traveled in over the past three days just to get to this point. "I didn't come all this way to share the pleasantries of the day," he replied.

"Then what does bring you here, Phythian?"

"Monica Cross."

The Chairman narrowed his eyes and studied him warily, then said, "What about her?"

"Back off, or I shut you down."

The Chairman broke into a bony grin and shook his head with mock pity. "Shut me down? You're out of your bloody mind. You can't be so naive as to think you could set foot on this island and get away alive."

"What makes you think I intend to leave?" Phythian replied, returning the grin.

His words caused The Chairman to furrow his brow, which was abscessed and infected to the point that all that remained was a scraggy film that seemed the texture of onion skin. "You should have stayed wherever the hell you were," he said, his voice barely a thread above the crackle of the fire. "Left well-enough alone."

"Yet here I am," Phythian reminded him. "And my message is this: pull your dogs off Monica Cross."

"Why do you care?" The Chairman asked him. "Why does the fate of one insignificant woman matter in the overall framework of the world?"

Phythian had no interest in a pointless debate over existential philosophy or free will. His was a much more pragmatic reason for being there, and he got right to the point as he removed an object from his waterproof money belt.

"Do you know what this is?" he asked as he allowed the light from the fire fall upon it.

The Chairman had lost all vision in one eye years ago to glaucoma, and without his glasses he had great difficulty seeing out of the other. He squinted for a long time at the blurry object in Phythian's hand, then said, "That's Equinox—"

"You didn't think I'd leave it behind in the plane, did you?" Phythian said. "For just anyone to find."

"You were never meant to survive." The old man didn't even bother denying the mission he'd set in motion six years ago, in an attempt to rid himself of two big problems.

"The best-laid plans of mice and men often go awry," Phythian replied. "And if you don't pull your hounds off Monica Cross, I'll yank the plug on you and this entire operation. Beginning with the release of every bite of information that's on this drive."

"You're bloody crazy," The Chairman blurted, trying hard not to betray the signs of genuine worry mounting inside him.

"Perhaps," Phythian said as he glanced at the grandfather clock set against the wood-paneled wall. "Time's ticking."

"Humor me, for just a moment. Just how do think you'd pull off such a stunt?"

"'Golden lads and girls all must, as chimney-sweepers, come to dust.'"

"You think you're going to kill me." The Chairman said, almost laughing. "With a line from Shakespeare, no less."

"It would give me no greater pleasure," Phythian replied. "But pleasure and action make the hours seem short, which you would do well to realize. In the meantime, we have another, far more pressing matter at hand."

Chapter 44

Carter Logan instinctively knew he couldn't go home. The woman named Giselle, or whatever her name was, had known who he was and where to find him, which meant she also knew where he lived. Which meant others did, as well.

His apartment had probably already been tossed, his computer hacked and its contents downloaded, or stolen outright, listening devices and cameras installed, the whole nine yards. Her job obviously had been to kill him, leave him there on the sidewalk in what authorities would conclude was a mugging gone wrong.

His story on Justice Wheeler's death had to be the key to all this. Logan hadn't bought into the autoerotic asphyxiation ruse, instead using his syndicated column to raise doubts about the damning photos and videos, and other evidence. What was it Raleigh Durham who had told him?

Whoever pulled this off is going to go full ballistic if the truth gets out.

After his near-miss he'd walked for several hours as he tried to make sense of this new truth. Eventually he found an unlocked SUV, tucked himself into the back seat until the first glow of day appeared over the rooftops to the east. He'd slept fitfully, waking up at the slightest of noises, thinking the sleazebag with the knife might be prowling the streets looking for him. Or maybe the owner of the vehicle might show up and roust him with a squirt of pepper spray.

First order of business after wolfing down a breakfast sandwich was to get a new phone. Whoever was behind Wheeler's death—and his own near-miss last night—probably had cloned the old one, or placed some kind of GPS device in it that would signal where he was. Fortunately, he had an insurance policy that paid for a replacement if it was broken or stolen, so he walked to the phone store and waited until it opened for business. His monthly payment might go up a few bucks, but it was worth it if it prolonged his life.

The process took longer than expected, but seconds after setting up the replacement, he'd received the call from the woman who said her name was Monica Cross, who sounded as if she was in a big hurry, and insisted she had something to deliver to him regarding his late fiancé. After the events of last night, he'd been understandably suspicious, but she'd sounded convincing. She also admitted to being the photographer in the incredible story he'd seen on the evening news, the one who had killed two brutal jihadists and then had discovered Katya's body in the cabin of a wrecked plane. Even one of the Google alerts he'd received the night of his alcoholic bender had mentioned her name.

Improbable as her story had sounded, he'd agreed to meet her on the south steps of the Museum of Natural History sixteen minutes from now. Despite all that had happened over the last twelve hours, he strangely had a good feeling about this. *About her.*

Then again, he'd been mistaken before.

Minutes after catching a full cup of steaming tea in the face, Adam Kent was back in his office, unlocking the briefcase he routinely brought to work every morning, and took home every night. He had just retrieved his Kimber Micro nine when one of his phones rang.

"What?" he boomed into the pinhole microphone. The fury he felt from being bested by the Cross bitch was second only to the pain from hyper-attenuated nerve endings in his cheek and forehead—and his eye, which he worried might have some sort of permanent damage to the cornea—burned retina, possibly even ocular blindness. He'd wanted to chase after her as she stumbled out of the restaurant, but the thermal injury had forced him to flush his eyes with cold water in the restroom.

"You let her get away."

"She boiled my face, dammit."

"Witnesses said they thought she headed south toward the mall," the voice on the phone said, no empathy at all.

"We have to stop her." Kent checked the gun's magazine and slide, then stuffed it into his jacket pocket. "Wherever she's headed."

"We have a working theory on that."

"A theory? What kind of theory?

"We intercepted a call less than an hour ago. Her phone, the one she was given at the embassy. She may be heading to the Museum of Natural History."

"What business does she have there?"

"Carter Logan."

"The blogger," he said. "I want a team dispatched now."

"They're already in position, ready to go."

Monica was terrified. The man in the restaurant had been there to kill her. She'd seen it in his eyes, heard it in his voice, too. Even now that she was on American soil, her life remained in danger. Forget being arrested and questioned for the murder in Frankfurt; these goons were out to silence her, and they didn't care what they had to do to make that happen.

After fleeing the restaurant, she'd almost given up and gone home. The metro station where she had just arrived from Dulles was across the street, and she knew it was only a handful of stops to Union Station. *Amtrak. Safe and invisible.* To hell with the envelope, the man named Phythian, and whoever this Carter Logan was. She could call him later and mail it to any address he gave her. Right now, saving her own hide was all that mattered.

But she didn't take the escalator down into Metro Center, and she didn't go to Union Station. Instead she zig-zagged her way down to the Mall, going one block over, then two blocks back, the entire time making sure no one was following her. Her untrained eye told her no cars were tailing her, and she didn't see any evidence of stalkers on foot. Phillip had been a big fan of espionage movies, especially the Bourne thrillers, and she knew all about surveillance teams that traded off and circled around in order to keep fresh eyes on their target.

At least she thought she did.

She arrived at the Museum of Natural History fifteen minutes early. It was a warm afternoon on a Saturday in late June and the place was crowded, which could be both good and bad. Good because there was a lot of human cover, plenty of people to run interference should things go south. Bad for the same reason: how would she find Carter Logan among all these tourists? She had no idea what he looked like, and vice versa. Not a good set-up if he and she were to engineer a quick hand-off and make a hasty retreat.

Plus, someone could be hanging out in the crowd, waiting for the best moment to shuffle on by and put a bullet in her head.

Monica sat on the grass, facing the museum but not concentrating on it. Other people were lounging nearby, finishing lunch or soaking in the summer sun. A man was throwing a Frisbee for his dog, who seemed expert at catching it on the fly. A woman was feeding mashed food to a toddler, and a young child was running mightily, trying to get a kite into the sky.

At exactly two o'clock she rose from the grass and slowly strolled across Madison Drive, dodging cars and pedicabs as she edged toward the broad expanse of steps that led up to the museum. A steady stream of tourists was coming down them toward her; any one of them could have been Logan— or another assailant. But they all avoided her glance as they walked by, each one causing her to glance around nervously.

The steps were divided into two sets, separated in the middle by a broad terrace. She was halfway up the first set when she heard a voice behind her.

"Monica Cross?"

She wheeled around, half expecting to find the bastard from the restaurant holding that slick credit card knife in his fist. Instead, she found herself eye-to-eye with a man who seemed almost as nervous as she. Beads of sweat dribbled down his forehead, and his dark hair hung in clumps in front of his eyes. He appeared tense and jittery, like an addict in need of a fix, and he kept looking over his shoulder.

"Mr. Logan?" she said in return.

"Yes. You have something for me?"

"I do." She'd kept the envelope in her pocket since Phythian had given it to her at Heathrow, and now she took it out.

"Wait a minute," he said, gripping her hand tightly. "How do I know you're who you say you are?"

"How do I know you're Carter Logan?" she snapped, snatching her hand back. "Look... I've traveled thousands of miles to give this to you. Don't give me any shit."

"Who sent you?"

"Doesn't matter. Just take this—"

"You said it's about Katya?"

"That's what I'm told."

"We shouldn't do this here," he said. "You don't know who we're dealing with."

"I sure as hell do," she replied, pressing the envelope into his hand. "I need to go."

She turned to leave, but Logan gently grasped her by the arm. "Look... whatever this is, if it's about Katya, I'll never be able to thank you enough."

"You just did," she answered, a little too smartly. Then she turned and took a step up the stairs toward the stone terrace and the museum doors beyond.

As Monica moved forward a gunshot exploded and a small puff of dust rose from the granite in front of her, level with her head. Instinctively she wheeled around and pulled Logan down, just as another slug bit the stone barely an inch from where the first one had hit.

Someone was firing at them, and whoever it was, he damned sure wasn't going to miss again.

People on all sides of her shrieked and dropped to the ground. She heard screams of "shooter" and "gun" and "stop," tried to count how many shots she'd heard, a pointless exercise, since there was no fixed number of rounds a gun could fire these days.

Carter Logan dropped on top of her, covering her with his body. Then he gave her a gentle push and rolled with her, just as a third shot exploded off the very spot where they had been huddled.

She scrambled to get to her feet, but Logan grasped her arm and held her down. Another shot slammed into the step just below them. This time there was a loud pop, coming from somewhere nearby, and they both realized there was more than one gun.

"Run," Logan told her. "They're after me, not you—"

"Like hell they are," she corrected him. "They've been after me since I left Pakistan."

They looked at each other for a fraction of a second, almost too long. Then Logan pushed off and darted down the stairs in the direction of the pedicab stand. Another shot rang out as Monica headed the other way, up the steps toward the museum doors.

Her only hope was to blend in with the other tourists. Whoever was shooting at her was outdoors, and the Museum of Natural History was spread out across three levels and dozens of display rooms. With a modest head start she should be able to lose herself among the crowded exhibits, possibly even dash out the main entrance on the other side, onto Constitution Avenue.

She raced into the octagonal rotunda, past throngs of visitors staring at the massive African bull elephant that towered over the polished marble floor. It had been years since she'd set foot in this building, an eighth-grade trip to Washington that included all the major sights of the nation's capital. The Museum of Natural History was one of the highlights, and she had particularly liked the Hope Diamond and the cockroach kitchen. Things seemed to have changed a lot since then— some exhibits had been replaced and the elephant had gone through a long-overdue makeover.

Monica speed-limped across the rotunda and into the Ocean Hall, where a monstrous whale was suspended from the ceiling. She pushed her way through the clumps of people studying the bubblegum coral and a massive set of megalodon jaws. Once she'd navigated the crowd she continued in the direction of where she remembered the main doors opening onto Constitution Avenue would be.

But she was wrong. The main entrance was one floor below, down a set of steps to where the T-rex and the restaurant were located. *Damn.*

She hobbled toward a stairway to her right, taking the steps as quickly as she could, considering the biting pain in her ankle. Halfway down she reached a landing, and when she made the one-eighty turn to continue her descent to the first floor she felt her heart stop.

There he was, the bastard with the credit card knife who had tried to apprehend her at lunch. His skin remained a bright crimson hue, and a parboiled Muppet eye bulged from its socket. Somehow, *impossibly,* he was on the ground level of the Museum of Natural History, clearly looking for her.

How had he found her so quickly? It was a stupid question, one that took her half a second to answer. Someone must have been listening in to Carter Logan's phone, which meant that he'd been right: these people were after him as much as they were after her. Or: was it her phone, as she'd begun to suspect yesterday? Had it been bugged and infected with a GPS tracker that allowed *them* to keep tabs on her whereabouts?

All these thoughts tumbled through her brain in less than a second, enough time for her to spin around and speed-limp back up the steps to the second floor, just enough time for the man from the restaurant to spot her motion, and call out to her. "Give it up, Monica Cross," he said from below. "Game's over."

At the top of the stairs she hesitated, glancing at the exhibit halls to her left and right. Human Origins or African Voices? Or—*maybe*—the utility closet, which was across the corridor in front of her.

Stop running, you whore, Adam Kent silently swore, although the curse word in his mind actually began with "c." She was only a few yards ahead of him, and even if she veered off into one of the crowded exhibits, he would find her in a flash. But when he arrived at the top of the steps and glanced around, she was gone.

No way could she have disappeared that fast. She was tired and had to be on the verge of collapse. He knew she also had bruises and sprains and cracked ribs.

But she was not here.

His face continued to burn from her nasty stunt at the restaurant, and his eye was screaming in pain. He actually might lose it, all because of this crazy bitch. She deserved everything she had coming; his only regret was that he didn't have the Marfione Custom Mini Matrix-R knife that would allow him to treat her to the slow agony of death she so rightfully deserved.

He glanced right, left, straight ahead. No sight of her anywhere, his body sagged momentarily from disbelief and impending defeat. She couldn't have gotten away, but there was no sign of her—no sign of anyone moving with any speed at all, just dozens of tourists roaming about, studying the exhibits and reading the descriptive placards.

Kent stood at the top of the staircase and assessed his options. His Kimber nine was in his pocket, and Monica Cross was in the building. The Chairman was waiting for word that the target was finally down, case closed. The anonymous southern accent he'd heard on the phone could take care of Carter Logan; Kent's only concern at the moment was swatting a mosquito that had been an annoyance far too long. The question was, where was she?

Then he noticed the utility closet, and things suddenly began to look a little brighter.

Without hesitating he charged in, found her cowering at a slop sink in the far corner. She looked as if she might scream when he drew the cruel-looking gun from his jacket and pointed it at her.

"Make a noise—any noise—and you die right now," he told her as he slowly approached her. "Keep your mouth shut, maybe you buy a few seconds."

She decided to keep her mouth shut.

"You're good," he said, nodding at her appreciatively. "I lost money on you."

She started to say something, realized there was no point.

Kent studied her at length, now that he finally had time to look upon his prey. "You don't know what the hell is going on, do you?"

Despite his advice that she remain silent, she said, "Equinox."

The answer noticeably took him by surprise, and he recoiled as if she'd slapped him. "You're smarter than you look," he said. "Where is it?"

"I don't have it," she told him, her hands trembling like a seismic fault. "Never even saw the damned thing."

"But you know too much."

"Go ahead and kill me. By tomorrow morning the whole world will be reading all about this thing called the Greenwich Global Group and every despicable deed you bastards have done just to line your filthy pockets."

"Spare me the lecture."

"Or what? You'll shoot me?" Monica snickered. She was petrified beyond all belief, but it was time to play her hole card. "That would only be the start of your troubles."

Kent's nostrils flared and she could see fire in his eyes. "What the fuck are you talking about?"

"Phythian," was all she had to say.

Fuck. The murdering sonofabitch had turned up in the middle of the night two days ago in the middle of the Pyrenees, then had disappeared. As had the locksmith named Beaudin, something Petrie's termination squad had confirmed upon their arrival in Andorra. Hours later Simone Marchand had been killed in a restroom at the Frankfurt airport. Then, Eitan Hazan had been shot on a train in Cologne, and an MI6 agent named Fiona Cassidy was found dead in her London flat. Now Monica was here in Washington, delivering a parcel to the fucking blogger named Carter Logan. It explained a number of things, but it posed just as many questions as it answered.

Unfortunately, it was too late for questions. The Chairman had given im direct orders, and it was Kent's job to execute them. "Sleep tight," he said, as he pressed the gun to her temple.

Chapter 45

Resistance was useless, defiance futile. Despite the power he had allowed himself to believe he possessed over global affairs, The Chairman was just one more pawn whose boldness and bravado crumbled under the unconstrained influence of Rōnin Phythian.

For the past hour he had spilled secret after secret, name after name until his ancient mind was exhausted. His adversary—who should have been dead at the bottom of the Mediterranean six years ago—was relentless in his questioning, digging for the most seemingly insignificant minutiae. Names, dates, details, everything there was to know about the G3's most clandestine operations. The interrogation, demeaning in its scope and humbling in its process, jolted his dimming memory back to a time when good and evil were as clear as black and white, night and day. Nazis epitomized the darkness of humanity, and the Allied Forces who replaced oppression with freedom were hailed as the heroes of the time.

After the war, when he'd been approached with the promise of rooting out the Nazi vermin that continued to lurk in the forested crevasses of Europe, he'd jumped at the chance to become a custodian of liberty and deliverance. The pact that was consecrated at the Naval Observatory in Greenwich that winter of '46 was intended to rekindle the lights of truth that had been dimmed by the devastation of fascism.

Over the years, however, the G3's mission had shifted. What at first had seemed a righteous call to arms had evolved into a profiteering enterprise that cared not for whom the bell tolled, as long as the margins were healthy and net quarterly profits grew on a year-over-year basis. The Greenwich Global Group had been founded on the principles of rectitude and virtue,

286

but it had morphed into a lucrative killing machine—its aspirations not all that dissimilar to those of the tyrants that its founders had been hell-bent on exterminating.

What have I become? he asked himself, at the same time realizing it was not his own conscience that was posing the question. It was Phythian, who was working his mental sorcery on him from across the room, where he continued to warm himself in front of the raging fire. And he realized there wasn't a damned thing he could do about it.

Eventually the pensive introspection ended and an eerie silence filled the room.

"Are you damned well finished?" The Chairman asked, feeling as if every gram of his very spirit had been drained from his body.

"Almost," Phythian replied. "There's just one more thing,"

"And what the fuck would that be?"

"You're going to make a phone call."

For an instant he wondered if that was intended to mean something else, such as dialing into death…or meeting his maker. Was this how his life was going to come to an end, in a stone fortress atop a craggy piece of rock, at the hands of one of the most dangerous killers the world had ever known?

"And after I make this call?" he asked, his mind too paralyzed to say anything else.

"One thing at a time," Phythian told him, nodding at the mobile phone sitting on the mahogany end table that matched the ancient William IV recliner with the hand-carved tulip legs. "Tick-tock."

Resisting every instinct in his body, The Chairman found himself reaching for the phone. "You'll never get away with whatever you've got planned, you Machiavellian sonofabitch," he fumed. "You're crazy."

"As she has planted, so does she harvest," Phythian replied. "Such is the furrowed field of karma,"

"What sort of fucking gibberish is that?"

"The sort you should have considered long ago, when you still possessed a soul."

"You're no one to talk." The Chairman said, unable to take his eyes off the Equinox drive in Phythian's hand. "Whatever you intend to do with that thing, no one will believe you. It's just too fantastical."

"No one needs to believe a thing," Phythian explained. "The files on this drive are far too valuable to feed to the media or an online wiki site. As our little conversation of the past few minutes has so perfectly confirmed."

"Then what could you possibly hope to accomplish with it?"

"A slow but ceaseless reversal of fortune."

"You're talking gibberish again, you bloody tosser."

Phythian offered a thin smile and listed a shoulder in a shrug. "Equinox contains the details of every lethal operation you and your cohorts have ever engaged in," he said.

"And you're the leading player in a good number of them," The Chairman reminded him.

"Precisely why it's critical that it never fall into the wrong hands again," he agreed. "Fortunately, this little device—" he held up the black box just so there was no mistaking his reference "—is just a useless redundancy, a basic copy of everything that's on the main server in Luxembourg. Which, as you know, is a genuine Fort Knox of information, every byte just waiting to be monetized at the proper moment, in the proper way. Intelligence has become the world's currency, and it buys a world of goods."

"You can't just come in and steal a company out from under its board of directors. It just doesn't work that way."

"Excuse me, sir, but I've already done it."

With that, he edged over to the massive fireplace, opened the screen, and tossed the Equinox box inside. Hungry tongues of flames began to lap up around the sides, and within seconds the black plastic case was entirely engulfed.

"You've gone completely mad—" The Chairman sputtered, his voice just a bare wheeze of its former strength. "You'll never get into the cloud without the G3 password."

"*Cutty-Sark*," Phythian said as he watched the device shrivel into a molten lump. "You forget I had the assistance of a particularly cooperative locksmith in Andorra. Of course, it's been changed since then, just so you wouldn't be tempted to wipe the thing clean."

"*I am going to fucking kill you—*"

"Actually, sir, you should be much more concerned about your own survival. Considering all the bluster and bombast, you're weak and afraid."

"And just what am I afraid of?"

"What you have become, how you lost your compass somewhere along the way. You fear the end. A man who lives a full life is prepared to die, but the coward trembles as time grows near. But enough of all this: time to make that call."

"You are nothing but a fool and a dotard," The Chairman said.

"When the debate is lost, slander becomes the tool of the loser," Phythian replied as he rubbed his hands together before the roaring flames. The Equinox drive now lay in the glowing embers like a lump of spent coal. "Quit stalling and dial the number."

The Chairman made one last phlegmy grunt, then slowly punched out the digits on the phone he held in his hand. He glared at Phythian as the encrypted signal clicked through.

"Kent is an independent thinker," he told Phythian. "Confident and autonomous. He may decide not to listen to me."

"Just remind him where he was May 22, 2002."

The Chairman thought on this for a second, then said, "Rock Creek Park—"

"That date might not be in the cloud, but it will get his attention. And that of the FBI, if he tries to fuck this up."

"I suppose you're right," the old man said. Then, as if digital cell phone technology was some kind of miraculous novelty, he announced, "It's ringing."

Chapter 46

Anyone else and Kent would have fired first, answered later. But the ringtone indicated The Chairman was calling, and one did not violate the old man's penultimate order: pick up the damned phone as soon as it rings.

"Fuck," Kent snarled. He released the pressure on the trigger but kept the barrel of the gun pressed behind Monica's right ear. She was kneeling on the cold tile, insane with fear, but somehow at peace with her soul. Soon she would be in that same dark void where her husband had gone, and they would be together for all eternity.

If you believed in that sort of thing which, all of a sudden, she did not.

Phillip was dead, and she was alive. And as much as she had wanted to join him in rest ever since the accident six months ago, all of a sudden she did not want to die; not today, not tomorrow, not for a very long time.

Yet she dared not move.

"Yes," Kent snapped into the phone.

"Where the fuck are you?" The Chairman snapped back, his voice anxious and weary.

"With the target."

"Is she alive?"

"Yes, but that's about to change." He felt like pulling the trigger right then and there, just so the old man could hear him do it.

"Stand down," the Chairman said. "You are not to harm her, in any way."

"What the fuck?"

"I said, you are not to harm her."

"She's a lethal threat to the company—"

290

"Do not dare to question me," The Chairman barked. If he weren't so close to death his voice would have boomed, rather than rattled.

"He's there, isn't he? Phythian—"

"That is immaterial," The Chairman said. "Just do as I say."

"Put him on," Kent said. It was a demand, not a request.

"Who are you to tell me—?"

"I want to speak with the sonofabitch, now."

"That's not advisable, Adam. You know what he's capable of."

"He should be more concerned with what I'm capable of. *Put. Him. On.*"

There was a slight hesitation as the phone changed hands, thirty-four hundred miles away. Then Phythian came on the line and said, "Let her go."

"Fuck you. I'm calling the shots here, pardon the pun."

"I said, release her."

"You're not listening," Kent countered, just as he felt a tightness grip his skull. His brain started to feel light, as if he were about to faint. A sense of panic tickled his spine as he found himself lowering the gun. "What the hell—?"

"Tell her she is free to leave."

"Like hell—"

"You know better than to make me tell you twice," Phythian reminded him.

Kent almost snickered, but a sudden force squeezed his brain, as if he were wearing a helmet two sizes too small. For a second he thought of the ancient German torture device known as the *Schneiden*, designed to methodically crush a human head with the simple and gradual turn of a handle.

He winced at the pain, which he knew was not real but could not escape. Then he turned to Monica and found himself saying, "My business with you is finished. Go."

"What—?" Monica said.

"Get out of here."

Monica Cross didn't hesitate. She scrambled to her feet and crossed the cluttered room in less than a second. She flicked the deadbolt, turned the knob, and disappeared.

"She's gone," Kent assured him.

"Wise man, right to the end," Phythian acknowledged. "Now, put the gun to your head."

"I…what the fuck are you doing?"

"You know how this goes. Barrel to the temple."

Kent tried to conjure up an inner resistance, but he found himself doing what the most lethal man in the world was telling him to do—*ordering* him to do—gun in one hand, phone in the other.

"What kind is it?" Phythian asked.

"*What?*"

"Describe the gun to me."

The pain in his head was inexorable, agonizing to the point of wanting it to end, no matter how. This situation was going off the rails, certainly not the way Kent had envisioned it. He'd studied Phythian's dossier—Diana Petrie had insisted on it—and the third paragraph in the section titled "Personal Competency" noted that his mind-control skillset, while considered unique and extraordinary, was limited to a thousand yards, enough to make him a dangerous weapon of death and destruction, but finite in his reach. Right now, the motherfucker was on some Goddamned rock off the Scottish coast but, somehow, he'd managed to flip this phone call to his advantage.

If Kent had read the footnotes at the bottom of the page, he would have found the sentence: [3]*Asset has been known to apply these abilities to virtually unrestricted distances via wired and unwired communication devices, as observed both in documented training exercises and actual deployment in the field.*

"A Kimber Micro nine-millimeter with Crimson Trace Laser grips, white dot sights and sixteen-pound recoil spring, six bullet capacity," Kent found himself answering, as if he were reciting from the manufacturer's catalog.

"Decent weapon, unique cocking serrations on the slide and receiver front strap. And the trigger pull is solid, not too tight."

"Since when did you become a gun expert?"

"You'd be surprised," Phythian told him. "Now, go ahead and pull it."

"Do what?"

"You heard me, you son of a mongrel bitch. Give your finger a real good squeeze and let's put that trigger pull to a test."

Chapter 47

The Secret Service had spent most of the day sweeping the entire main floor of the Mayflower Hotel, as well as the one beneath it and the second level, one flight up. Security was tight at all street entrances, and metal detectors and explosive screening devices had been set up at the front elevators and the concierge desk. The elevators at the far end of the hall, near the Grand Ballroom, had been hijacked for the day, which snarled guest traffic and angered those who had unwittingly booked a room during one of the city's premiere power events.

The director of the Secret Service—a tall, sinewy man with thinning hair named Donald Poole—had sequestered himself and a small army of Treasury agents in a suite on the tenth floor, with windows overlooking traffic on Connecticut Avenue and DeSales Street. The four elevators that normally served guests entering from Seventeenth Avenue had been temporarily converted to their exclusive use, meaning the agency had unfettered access to every square inch of the hotel. No one came or went without their knowledge, and not without being recorded by at least a dozen of the forty-four security cameras that tracked their every movement.

Director Poole detested this annual burlesque show. Truth was, he detested every *ad hoc* event attended by the president and the vice president, because of the magnitude of what could go wrong compared to what had to go right—a solid family man who believed himself to be an optimist at heart, when it came to his job he turned into a worst-case-scenario fiend. His official punch list itemized a thousand things that had to be checked and double-checked, and if any of these seemingly minuscule items was overlooked—if one neglected detail allowed a gun or a bomb or even an unwanted protester to get inside—the results could be disastrous.

Not on Poole's watch. He'd never had a slip-up, not one scandal, and he was determined to take his spotless record with him when he retired just eight months from now. Still, the White House Media Dinner always gave him fits. Staged as a show of goodwill and camaraderie between the current Commander in Chief and the press corps that followed him and his covey of sycophants, it tended to be a poorly scripted free-for-all. Despite a tight agenda and precise timetable of events, the affair always went long and dragged well past the scheduled end time. Speakers spoke to hear themselves speak, and the eight hundred guests drank too much and then jockeyed their chairs so they could get a better view when the entertainment started.

Plus, they all expected unfettered access to President Mitchell—codename Keystone—and his understudy, Vice President Crittenden. This was the most dangerous part, because both men welcomed the handshaking and black-slapping that came with the event. At least they pretended to, although Poole wasn't sure the dodo from Mississippi liked much of anything about this town. Plus, he was a germophobe.

The first guests began arriving twenty minutes ago, even though the printed invitation said "Cocktail Reception Starts at 6:00 pm." These early-birds generally were those on tight budgets who wanted to be first in line at the open bar in order to take full advantage of free liquor before the main event began at seven. They pressed up against the velvet rope, jockeyed for position to see and be seen, and prepared to descend on the ballroom *en masse* like a spurt of sperm competing to reach the egg.

Carter Logan knocked on the door of the room on the eighth floor that Hilton Clark had rented for the evening. This way the deputy managing editor wouldn't get stuck in traffic following the event, and had ample space afterwards to write up the night's highlights for tomorrow's morning edition. It would be twenty-six column inches, not including captions for a half-dozen photographs depicting DC's power elite. A lengthier story would appear the following day, but the *Post* needed to own this event. In print, and online.

Logan's entire body was shaking as if he he'd been operating a jackhammer ever since the woman named Monica Cross had handed him the envelope and the shooting began. He'd scrambled down the stone steps and took off running, past the pedicab vendors and a line of taxis and rideshares, zig-zagging eastward along Madison Drive. He'd heard two or three more gunshots, but they'd ceased by the time he reached Seventh Avenue. From there he angled across the street toward the south entrance of the National Gallery of Art. Easy to get lost in there; he'd done it many times in the past without even trying.

Logan wondered what had become of her, this woman who'd put him in danger and then saved his life by pulling him down when the shooting began. After that she'd taken off at a sprint into the museum, and his brain told him to go a different way.

He'd thought about calling her, just to check in and see how she was. But his frontal cortex had screamed *bad idea*, since it was either his phone or hers—maybe both—that had tipped these bastards to their meeting in the first place. He'd just have to trust—and hope—that she'd gotten away, just as he had.

He'd run as fast and as far as he could, hadn't dared slow down long enough to look at the envelope Monica had given him. When he finally ran out of steam, he detoured into the east building of the National Art Gallery and found a corner in the museum's Tower Two, surrounded by the sculptures and paintings of Alexander Calder. It provided enough cover that he could keep an eye on anyone who looked suspicious; trouble was, with all he had just gone through, that meant just about anybody.

The standard number ten envelope contained a single sheet of paper and a USB flash drive. The drive had no markings on it other than the manufacturer's logo, but the paper was a note, handwritten in simple block letters. It read:

Mr. Logan:

Please accept my apologies, my much-delayed condolences, and my deepest sorrow for causing what I know must have been intolerable pain. I am referring, of course, to the disappearance and crash of the plane in which your fiancé was a passenger six years ago. It was an event I was hired to arrange and execute, although I made a few minor adjustments to the original plan. Particulars are not necessary, other than to say I guarantee your beloved Katya did not suffer, and endured no pain.

I accept all responsibility for her untimely death, and do so with all weight of guilt it bears on my being. However, I believe you should know that my mission to divert the plane and ultimately bring it down was assigned to me by a covert operation that, over the years, has engaged dozens of highly skilled operatives to carry out thousands of similar assignments around the world. That organization, which is called different things in different circles, is responsible for the deaths of princes and presidents, ministers and cabinet officials. Businessmen, academics, radicals, clergy, journalists, and even actors have died because of its actions and assignees.

The enclosed drive contains all the details of the operation that took the life of your future bride. These include the identities of the parties that arranged the hit, price paid, money transfers, dossiers, and surveillance photos. You also will find my name as the contractor of record.

Please do with this information what you will. I know it is in capable hands and, if you are half the journalist I believe you to be, expect there to be more where this came from.

Best regards, RP

PS: You are on the right track with Justice Wheeler. Do persevere.

Logan had been stunned, and it seemed as if the giant black Calder mobile overhead had uttered an audible groan. He dared not blink, found himself not even breathing as old thoughts and feelings and memories spun through his head with the force of a cyclone. *Katya.* Their first kiss. The first time they made love. Last time they saw each other, last time they spoke on the phone. Just a few words, knowing they'd be together again in mere hours. She'd been on a secret mission she couldn't tell him about, but insisted was huge. *Huger than huge.* A cache of information that would be a game-changer in the framework of global politics.

See you soon, my love.

Well, that never happened. She'd never come home, no hello kiss at the airport, no wedding gown or aisle to walk down. And no one had the slightest clue where she or the plane had gone. Couldn't explain how a leased King Air turboprop might just disappear like that. Not one scrap of wreckage was found where the plane should have hit the water, not even a black box to ping from the sea floor.

Yet now, six years later, he held the secrets of her last minutes in his hand, delivered to him by the woman who had discovered her body after all this time, dispatched by the murderer who had consigned Katya—and everyone on board—to a vile and brutal death.

All these thoughts kept crashing through Logan's mind as his old boss opened the door and ushered him inside. "So great to see you, my friend," Hilton Clark said, seemingly flustered by his repeated attempts to knot his bow tie. "Help yourself to a cocktail."

Logan desperately wanted a glass of wine. In fact, he'd already had one at a place a couple blocks up Connecticut, to help ease his nerves after the events at the Museum of Natural History a few hours earlier. He'd been shot at, for Chrissakes, right on the streets of the nation's capital—a scene straight out of a Hollywood movie. But any more alcohol might cloud his mind, and he wanted to be as sharp as possible for this meeting with his old boss.

"I think I'll pass," he replied instead. "Long evening ahead."

"Suit yourself," the *WaPo* deputy managing editor said. "If you change your mind..." He let his words trail off, a sweep of his hand indicating the array of bottles that had been set up in the suite.

"Much appreciated. And I want to thank you again for inviting me to this event tonight."

"Glad to have you here. Nice suit." While the dinner was "black tie suggested," many reporters showed up in their nicest business threads, since they didn't have pockets deep enough to spring for fancy rental duds.

Fact was, Logan had an old tux stuffed in his closet. He hadn't worn it in years and didn't know if it even fit him anymore. But after last night's encounter with the woman who called herself Giselle—obviously not her real name—and the shooting down on the Mall, no way was he going back to his apartment. He'd thought about calling Raleigh Durham, but he didn't want to disturb her at work. Besides, there was nothing she could do to help him. Nor did he want to place her in any more danger than she might already be in. She'd be at tonight's soiree, but she traveled in different circles than he did at these things, and he didn't want to crash her party.

Instead, he'd shelled out fifty dollars at the Goodwill store on South Dakota Avenue for a lightly worn black-ish suit, white shirt, tie, and a pair of passable shoes. It was not the dashing impression he'd hoped to make when he walked into the Grand Ballroom nor, for that matter, his former boss' suite. But the matter was out of his hands, and he felt fortunate just to be alive.

"I got caught up in some research and didn't have time to go home to change," he explained. "I hope I don't stand out too much."

"Forget it," Clark replied. "This town is way too stuck on convention, anyway. And since we're short on time, I'll get right to it. I want to hire you to investigate this Wheeler thing. My overlords seem to believe you may be on to something, and we hear the *Times* may be looking into it. Have you spoken with them, by any chance?"

"Not a word," he said. Not entirely true, but a reply email was not the same thing as a phone call.

"Keep it that way. Now, we're looking at a ten ninety-nine thing for starters. Independent contractor, no bennies, but we'll pay you at your old rate. Plus expenses. If it grows legs, or if you bring us something else solid, we can talk about making it a permanent arrangement."

It was a lot to soak in, but not too much not to foster an immediate reply. Especially since tonight's event had already set him back well over a hundred bucks, including clothing and a night's lodging at a Motel 6 in Silver Spring, where he'd changed into the second-hand suit and stashed the USB drive.

"That's definitely doable," he said. "And I think I may have just stumbled on something even bigger than Wheeler."

"Good to hear, Logan," Hilton Clark said, finally giving up on straightening his tie. "See you Monday. I'll be in by seven."

"I'll be there," Logan replied as his former—and possibly future—boss abruptly turned and wandered into the bathroom, sipping from the glass of amber liquid he'd picked up from the library table.

Logan considered filling him in on the shooting at the museum, the woman named Monica Cross, the flash drive, and the note that had come with it. But this was Washington journalism and competition for a good story was fierce, leading him to keep the details to himself. Instead, as he let himself out and he made his way down the hall to the working elevator bank, all he could think was *that's assuming I'm still alive by Monday.*

Chapter 48

Lior Eichorn rode in the middle car of a three-vehicle convoy from the Israeli Embassy on Reno Road. There were no flashing lights or DC Metro cops on motorcycles, just the occasional tourists gawking as the small procession passed by, wondering who might be inside. Local residents become inured to these sights in the nation's capital, but outsiders tend to be almost intoxicated by the overt display of power and influence.

Normally the Israeli Foreign Minister would have declined the invitation to attend such a drunk and disorderly affair as the White House Media Dinner. It was well beneath his dignity, but President Mitchell had extended the last-minute overture because Eichorn had announced a surprise visit to Washington, and it was a courteous thing to do. Besides, Mitchell needed an ally in Jerusalem, considering the hardline stance recently taken by the current prime minister and his loyal party sycophants. In return, Eichorn had said he had something he wanted to personally discuss with the president regarding West Bank settlements, and the annual event would be an ideal place for a brief and informal sit-down.

He rode in silence in the back of the Mercedes, digesting the news he'd received just that morning. His cousin had been found dead on the floor of a train bathroom, fresh gunshot residue on his fingers even though no weapon was found with him. Clearly this was a deliberate attack, and he believed he knew who was behind it. Just before leaving his office in Berlin, Hazan had shared with him the name of the person who, along with several ally nations, had arranged the plane crash that had killed his beloved Avigail. Eitan clearly had been killed for his betrayal.

That had made him even more pleased to have accepted the president's invitation to this evening's fete. Bittersweet as it was, tonight would avail him the opportunity to avenge the death of his beautiful daughter, and pay a debt of gratitude for his brave and heroic cousin, who had laid down his life in the pursuit of justice.

The small motorcade pulled up to the barricaded hotel entrance on 17th Street. A cluster of Secret Service agents descended on the black S 600 in the middle, in which they knew the Foreign Minister was riding. Eichorn and his embassy bodyguards climbed out and were whisked inside to a private room that had been reserved for special guests who preferred not to mingle with the great unwashed. That included dignitaries and government officials, television and movie celebs, athletes and recording artists, and Wall Street one-percenters. Several dozen members of this elite echelon had already arrived, and were either huddling in twos or threes, enjoying light conversation, or nursing cocktails on one of several couches arranged comfortably in quiet corners.

While the president had issued his invitation personally, Eichorn actually was here because of Mitchell's successor-in-waiting: the vice president. Three years ago, Crittenden's addition to the ticket had solidified enough states to help notch an Electoral College win, and it was no secret that the former Mississippi governor had his eyes on the top prize. Since Mitchell's job approval consistently hovered above fifty percent in the polls, however, the VP would have to be patient and maintain a humble profile through this and another full term if he intended one day to move into the Oval Office.

Eichorn had traveled a great distance to make sure that never came to pass.

Vice President Crittenden's motorcade left the official residence at the Naval Observatory at precisely twelve minutes after six. Unlike the Israeli foreign minister's, it consisted of six black vehicles, plus eight coordinated motorcycle officers on loan from the DC Metro Police. It was a trip of only a mile and half down Massachusetts Avenue, and took a total of five minutes. Crittenden and his wife, Raeanne, rode in the bulletproof Cadillac, third from the front of the caravan, flanked by two secret service agents.

The convoy pulled up to the 17th Street entrance precisely at seventeen minutes after six, and the couple was rushed from their limo into the hotel.

Three and a half seconds total, no shots fired. Even forty years after John Hinckley popped President Reagan with a ricochet in the left underarm outside the Washington Hilton, nerves were always on edge during the transfer of high-profile targets from vehicle to building, and vice versa.

Nine floors up, Donald Poole exhaled a sigh of relief: *one down, one to go*.

The Crittendens were escorted to yet another private room immediately adjacent to the VIP holding tank in which the other illuminati had been stashed. This room was almost empty, except for a small cadre of "image consultants" who were huddled around lighted mirrors and make-up tables loaded with matte foundation, stipple liner, face powder, lipsticks—the works. Their collective job was to make sure those who were seated on tonight's dais looked presentable, and at the moment they were hard at work on the well-known comedienne/talk show host who was emcee of tonight's affair. Crittenden had been forewarned that he and the missus would have to go under the brushes and powder-puffs, which made him even more convinced that, when he was president, he would do away with all this frivolity for good.

At one point a cocktail waiter approached with a mint julep for Raeanne Crittenden and a Johnnie Walker Black for the vice president— prearranged, of course. His Scotch of choice was the much pricier JW Blue, but the Secret Service insisted that the president and vice president could only be served from previously unopened bottles—the reasons were obvious—and neither the hotel nor the government was willing to crack a four-hundred-dollar seal just for this occasion. His taste buds would have to settle for the Black.

Crittenden was standing with his back to the door, eyeing the curves of one of the women who was straightening the comedienne's tux. He took a slow sip, enjoyed the mellow burn as it warmed his throat. His mind briefly flashed on Linda Fisher, but he pushed the thought away as quickly as it appeared.

"How classless to be wearing a man's tux rather than a gown," he said to his wife in a whisper intended to be overheard.

"She's a lesbian," Raeanne whispered back. "Very popular with both the straight and LGBTQ community."

"What about the FBI or CIA community?" the VP quipped, flaunting his political incorrectness with the one person in the room he knew would tolerate it. "Or the NSA or DIA, or even the ASPCA?"

"*Shush*, Jimmy," she said, politely swatting his arm. "Save that talk for your buddies at the club."

"I just want to know what the difference is between a G and a Q," he continued, with an innocent shrug. "Or a B and T. Sounds to me like some kind of sandwich."

"I'm sure she'd be happy to educate you," came an abrupt voice from behind him.

The vice president turned and found himself face to face with a man he had seen on the news a few times, but had never had occasion to meet. Tall, muscular, dark hair with lines of silver running through it—a professional dye job, considering he had to be in his sixties. He had a rugged face, solid chin, intelligent eyes that were boring into him—a leading-man type, if Central Casting had anything to do with it.

"Mr. Foreign Minister," Crittenden said, not in the least apologetic for his coarse remarks that the Israeli diplomat had overheard.

"Please…call me Lior," Eichorn corrected him. "And this must be your lovely wife I've heard so many wonderful things about."

"Indeed," Crittenden said. "Raeanne, please meet Lior Eichorn, the foreign minister from Israel. And please, Lior…call me Jim."

"Very pleased to make your acquaintances," Eichorn said to both of them. "I was next door in a stuffy room full of stuffy people, and someone let slip that you were in here. I hope you don't mind me crashing your make-up party, but I wanted a chance to get to know you."

"Why is that?" The vice president was known for being brusque and candid on occasion, and this was one of them.

"Because you never know how the scales of fate might tip one day. Ambition and politics write the dialogue of history."

Crittenden had grown up in the south, where regional vernacular was as thick as shit on a pig's ass and folks tended to say what was on their mind, although not always in an honest or straightforward way. He studied Eichorn's deep-set eyes, trying not to glance at the thin but noticeable scar that ran along the side of his face to his lower jaw, which he had no way of knowing was the result of a knife fight years ago during a military offensive on the Gaza Strip.

"I'm a simple man of simple origins," he told the foreign minister. "I'm not sure I follow your manner of speaking."

Eichorn grinned at that and said, "I believe you do, Mr. Vice President.

Jim. But I'll clarify my words to meet your regional sensitivities. Even though your country and mine may have some policy differences, you and I are really not all that different. For instance, we both know that, unless you're seated at the head of the table, you only see half of the room."

"He's talking about what comes next," Raeanne told her husband in a hushed voice as she lightly gripped his arm. "You know....*after*."

"Thank you, Rae," Crittenden told her. Then to the foreign minister he added, "I grasp the full import of your observation, and I'm very much pleased to make your acquaintance."

"Well, sir, I just wanted to say hello, and to thank you for the invitation to this wonderful soiree tonight," Eichorn said. Holding back on the urge to strangle the murderous sonofabitch right then and there, he gave the vice president a firm shake, using both hands to cement their new friendship.

"You are most welcome, Mr. Foreign Minister. Lior. Although you'll have to personally extend your gratitude to the president for that."

"Indeed, I will. *Shalom*, Jim. Ma'am."

With that he was gone, disappearing back into the stuffy, celebrity-packed room from which he'd come. Crittenden hardly thought about their brief encounter, having always been indifferent to Israeli affairs, except when it came to fundraising. But it was smart politics to have a colleague in Israel who seemed to understand his personal ambitions, a backchannel minister with whom he could consult on Middle East policy matters when the occasion arose, which would be much sooner than anyone could possibly suspect, if all went according to plan.

He pounded the rest of his Johnnie Walker Black, handed the empty glass to a waiter who passed by with an empty tray. It was then that he heard a commotion outside the room, down at the far end of the marble promenade, signaling that the president had just arrived. It was the man for whom he had harbored great disdain and contempt, even when he'd received the call that night almost four years ago, as he and Raeanne were sitting in the living room of Raven's Rest.

"Jim, I'll cut right to the chase," the governor of Pennsylvania had told him at the time. "I'd like you to join me in my run for the White House."

Those words had been like a wish fulfilled, even if it meant clinging to the coattails of a poser who shared virtually none of his core American values: baseball, babies, and the King James Bible. He'd said yes, of course, and the loathsome move had gotten him this far, just a heartbeat away from the main attraction of tonight's shindig—at least for an hour or two longer.

"I suppose we should go say 'hello' to the president," he said to his wife.

"It'll be good to see Kate," Raeanne said. "It's been since I don't know when."

They turned to go, and Crittenden straightened his black tie and made sure the flaps were out of the front pockets of his tux. That's when he felt a slight bulge in one of them, and when he reached inside, he found a small vial of brand-name hand sanitizer—the kind he almost always had with him, but did not recall picking up before leaving the official residence tonight. He figured his wife had probably slipped it into his pocket since she knew his phobia for germs at public events.

You never know where someone's hand has been, she'd told him on many occasions, and the notion struck him now as he guided her toward the door.

Angela Wilde had managed to cover her discolored skin with enough pancake makeup and mascara to have it pass for smoky eye. Plus, she wore a raspberry beret that she had, in fact, found in a secondhand store. Years ago, in New Orleans, and after she'd paid the six dollars, she'd sauntered out into the Bourbon Street steam humming the refrain to the Prince classic.

The simple yet fashionable headwear cast just enough of a shadow to deflect attention to her silver floor-length gown, strapless shoulders, sequined bodice, the sum of all parts guaranteed to distract from her injury. She carried a matching clutch purse that had passed through the security check point without much fuss, just a quick inspection by one of the Secret Service agents who seemed embarrassed when he found her feminine hygiene products.

Worked like a charm, every time.

Her cover tonight was as one of the image consultants, highly recommended to the production company contracted by the White House to manage all the optics for the evening's activities. That meant everything from staging to lighting to the make-up and accessories worn by the guests of honor. Her *curriculum vitae* had been impressive and the move to add her to the Media Dinner team had been strongly championed by a wealthy donor in Houston. No one bothered to press the donor for details; all that was known was she was a pro and had worked magic for a number of businessmen and politicians who came across in public as stiffer than bread sticks.

Homeland had vetted her through normal channels, and she was summarily added to the roster of associates working with the first couple in a secure, private room backstage, and later—on standby—out in the ballroom. She was dressed in style tonight partly because she had always enjoyed playing dress-up, partly because her research told her President Mitchell was a sucker for lovely goddesses in slinky gowns. It was critical that he feel comfortable around her, especially if he was going to obey her directions.

So far, that part had gone well. Running for president required a hefty ego, and she stroked his liberally, assuring him that he exuded a solid and confident presence, carried his body well, didn't let his shoulders droop to the right or left. Strong, sincere eyes that engaged with the lens or the audience, a voice for radio and a face for Hollywood. He was the complete package, one that expected to be out on the campaign trail next year, shaking hands and kissing babies.

The cocktail reception had already begun in the marble promenade outside the Grand Ballroom. Angela yearned for a Cosmo—no more of those tequila and bourbon concoctions that had almost knocked her on her ass last night—but tonight she was drinking sparkling water. The Dragon Lady on the phone had made it clear that this assignment could not go wrong, or she would pay the ultimate price.

Diana Petrie's threat was clear, and she had no intention of fucking this up.

"Good choice of necktie, Mr. President," she complimented him. "The red is just the right shade, and I love the gold threads woven through it."

"Why thank you, Miss...."

"Please, call me Vikki," she told him. "Do you mind if I make just a few adjustments to your jacket? The crease is bunched up, and the back needs straightening."

"Whatever you say, Vikki," he replied, turning her name over with his tongue as if it were entangled in a French kiss.

The Secret Service agent standing five feet away seemed not to mind that she was actually touching the president, straightening his lapels and gently tugging on the shoulders of his tuxedo. Thus, he paid no attention as she deftly slipped a pliable strip of C4 explosive manufactured at a factory in the Czech Republic under his collar in the back. Earlier in the evening she'd embedded the microscopic digitally-controlled detonator into the compound, which was formulated from cyclonite, plasticizer, and an inert binder composed of low molecular mass hydroxyl-terminated polybutadiene. Prior to leaving her rented apartment she'd inserted the entire device inside a cardboard tampon tube, then thoroughly wiped it—and her hands—to avoid detection from the Secret Service scanner, just in case security was tighter than she'd been forewarned.

"I think you're ready for your close-up, Mr. DeMille," she told him with a coquettish smile as she patted down his lapel one last time. "Go out there and break a leg."

Chapter 49

Carter Logan was on his second glass of Zinfandel when the doors to the Grand Ballroom opened and the lights blinked, like a Broadway theater signaling the audience it was time to be seated. He'd been invited to the event by Hilton Clark but, when he'd made it through the line at the attendees' check-in, he'd learned that he was not seated with any of his former *WaPo* colleagues. Instead, he'd been relegated to the hinterlands, aka the overflow space that had been set up in the adjacent Chinese Room.

The accordion wall had been folded open to create one large area that could hold a total of eight hundred guests sardined into eighty tables of ten. The stage, fitted with a lectern and a dais for the night's eight roasters, seemed light years away. But Logan didn't mind; two days ago, he'd planned on spending the night binge-watching *Bosch,* and now here he was, staking out a chair at a table in the back row at the top DC journo event of the year. He was a mere flea on the underbelly of the beast known as the Fourth Estate but, somehow, he'd managed to make it into *Downton Abbey.* Mixed metaphors, but that's what free wine was for.

His table included a professor of journalism at American University and five of his students, two cable interns, and a tech writer who had won a White House essay contest on the future of American media. Four of the ten were vegans, which was good news for them because all that was left by the time the servers got to their table was the quinoa bean salad and Mediterranean eggplant roll-ups. Logan didn't mind; Katya had been an animal rights activist and he'd learned to honor her dietary preferences, whenever he was with her.

It was a memory that momentarily reminded him of the flash drive and note Monica Cross had passed to him earlier that afternoon. Again, he wondered how she was doing, and if she'd made it out of Dodge.

Up on the dais the talk show host dressed in the blue tux and lace shirt was hurling one-liners at the president, who seemed to be taking her crude humor in stride.

"What's the difference between a politician and a banana slug?" *Pause.* "One is a slimy creature that leaves a slick trail everywhere he goes, and the other is a gastropod who eats animal shit." *Another pause.* "On second thought, maybe there's no difference at all."

The audience thought this was funny, the president guffawed, and she went on to her next ribald dig. Something about not caring for political jokes because she'd seen too many of them get elected to Congress.

Somewhere toward the tail-end of her monologue, something caught Logan's eye. Up there in the front of the vast ballroom, standing in a closed doorway that led out to the roped-off promenade where cocktails had been served less than an hour earlier, was the woman who last night had told him her name was Giselle—the one who had left Hobo's with him and then had come at him with a knife, just as he'd punched her in the eye with a hard, right hook.

The one whose face—before he'd clocked it—looked exactly like the woman in the surveillance video that his contact at the hotel had texted to him.

What the fuck was she doing here?

Standing that close to the president?

Up on the dais the comedienne told her final one-liner of the night, stating, "Presidential candidates are like a roll of toilet paper. Think about it: they're soft on the outside, hollow on the inside, and no matter which one you vote for, you end up getting an ass."

That drew lots of laughter, boos, hisses, and jeers, everything this dinner was all about. She gave a polite bow as the audience jumped to its feet to applaud, obscuring Logan's view of the front of the room. Even at this distance he remained convinced—*beyond any reasonable doubt*—it was the woman who had tried to kill him. And, if the surveillance video from the hotel was anywhere close to being accurate, she had killed Supreme Court Justice Colin Wheeler, then staged the autoerotic set-up in his suite as grand legerdemain.

As the audience collectively settled back into their seats, the comic hostess offered her heartfelt thanks to everyone in the room. Then she said, "Now, without any further ado, I present to you—joining us tonight from the most expensive public housing project in the entire city—the President of the United States, Frank Mitchell."

More applause and another standing ovation followed. Those who supported him clapped and cheered the most, and even those who opposed his economic and social policies put their differences aside for a moment. But Carter Logan, seeing his chance, did neither. Instead, he slipped away from the table of ten and edged toward the far wall, sizing up the situation as the eight hundred guests in attendance remained on their feet.

By the time he made it to the perimeter of the room most of them had taken their seats, and President Mitchell was standing at the lectern, adjusting the microphone.

"Good evening, ladies and gentlemen and all those millions of my fellow Americans who can't hear or see me, because this thing isn't on television," he began. "But rest assured, I'm sure everything that's said tonight will be live-streamed in a matter of minutes. Everything today is about going viral, like the summer cold I seemed to have picked up this morning that's spreading like lobbyists around this town."

While the audience had been on its feet, Logan had lost sight of the woman named Giselle. Even though folks now were seated, he couldn't spot her anywhere. She'd been standing a few yards from where Mitchell had been seated on the dais, but when he'd taken over the spotlight, she'd disappeared. Had she sat down at a nearby table, or maybe ducked out? She'd been wearing a silver dress that shimmered like the sea on a calm summer afternoon, but there was nothing like that to be found anywhere near the front of the ballroom.

"I've heard a lot of politicians give speeches throughout my career in government, and Lord knows I've made a lot of them myself," the president was saying at the front of the room. "I can tell you—and I quote from the great book of wisdom, otherwise known as *Mad* magazine—political speeches are like steer horns: a point here, a point there, and a ton of bull in between."

As Logan tried to find her in the crowd, he realized he could have been imagining things. He'd spoken with the woman no more than ninety minutes last night, and she'd had blonde hair that glimmered like a waterfall at high noon. Tonight, however, she was wearing a French beanie, reddish-purple in color, probably to shade the bruise that must have formed from the force of his blow. He tried to remember what she'd said she did for a living, realized she'd never told him. Which again begged the question: What was she doing here, hovering just ten feet from the president?

Up at the lectern President Mitchell was saying, "Another thing I learned here in Washington: Never, ever take friendship personally—"

Logan was now standing along the far wall of the expanded ballroom. Thus far, he had not drawn the attention of the Secret Service agents, twelve of whom he could count from his vantage point. He suspected more were lurking in the shadows, and some were probably planted at tables near the dais, pigtail devices stuck in their ears while they monitored every bit of motion anywhere even remotely near the president.

"Now, as I was saying—" Mitchell continued, but by this time Logan had tuned him out. He was one hundred percent sure that the woman named Giselle had left the room, which meant her role here tonight was done. He stood on his toes to give him a few inches of added height, surveyed the crowd at the front of the room. *Not there.*

Not anywhere.

The lady vanishes, Logan thought, although he doubted that even master director Alfred Hitchcock would characterize her as a lady.

Everything was set. The Secret Service agents had been oblivious to Angela Wilde's sleight of hand in the president's *ad hoc* green room, and Mitchell had been too busy admiring her assets to detect a thing.

His jacket collar was already stiff from the heavy dose of starch that the White House laundry had applied to the tux, and he had not felt the improvised explosive device she'd positioned two inches from his second cervical vertebrae—and, by extension, no more than three or four inches from his Medulla Oblongata, the section of the brain stem that controlled cardiac, respiratory, and vasomotor functions. The strip of explosive was the size and shape of a stick of Juicy Fruit and, with the detonator device attached, weighed about seven grams. Half of that was the C4 itself which, when triggered, would cause a blast radius of about six inches, which was seemingly small, but more than enough to take out a good chunk of the base of his skull.

The best part was, forensic analysis would trace it back to a Czech factory that was owned by a company controlled by a former KGB operative and longtime associate of the current Russian president.

Her job done, Angela had slipped out a side door of the ballroom just as the mistress of ceremonies finished her warm-up routine. She'd staked out her escape route two weeks ago, posing as a hotel guest and casually taking cell phone video of every angle of the marble promenade outside the ballroom and throughout the first floor. She'd counted fourteen surveillance cameras in all, and subtle scrutiny told her where the dead spots were, and where her face was most likely to be captured by a lens. She had sketched it all out in an elaborate floorplan, letting the live zones determine her path of egress once she had set the play in motion.

Her abrupt departure from the ballroom would have to appear genuine, since every frame of video captured by every camera in the hotel would be examined exhaustively over the coming weeks. Justice Department and Homeland Security analysts would fume and fuss over it, and countless Congressional task forces would run it through the equivalent of an electron microscope. The networks would run it backwards and forwards, and social media would tear it apart, hunting for every hint of conspiracy.

None of that really mattered. She had dressed in silver and raspberry in order to attract attention, to stand out in a crowd much the way Spielberg had dressed the girl in red in *Schindler's List*. When she slipped through the side door into the wide promenade, where the remnants of the cocktail reception were being cleared away, she made a beeline for the ladies' room. After a quick wardrobe change, she dumped her gown and handbag in a trash bin and casually sauntered back out of the lavatory. Instead of heading back to the Grand Ballroom, however, she turned to her right and confidently made her way toward the lobby. She had memorized the placement of all the cameras, confident she hadn't missed any during her stakeout, and made sure to casually pretend to look at something or glance down as she came into range of their respective lenses.

A few minutes from now she would be the most wanted assassin in the world; all she required was a few minutes' head start and she'd be home free.

And she would be ten million dollars richer.

• • •

Logan glanced to his right and left, saw that the only way to leave the annexed Chinese Room was through a set of double exit doors. Unguarded, which he found unbelievable. He inched his way along the wall and, when he got close enough, nudged one of them open just wide enough to slip through.

He'd been wrong about the unguarded part. A Secret Service suit with a pigtail in his ear was positioned just outside the door, alert and at attention. *Of course*, Logan thought. He's here to keep people out, not to keep them in.

"Where are you going?" the agent demanded, raising his hand as the door started to close behind him.

"Men's room," Logan explained. "Too much wine."

"No re-entry until after the president is off the stage."

Logan did a little jig while standing in place, indicating the urgency of the moment. "A man's gotta do what a man's gotta do," he said. "Besides, I didn't vote for him."

"Neither did I," the agent replied with a grin. "Have a good evening."

"Same to you."

The exchange took only fifteen seconds, but they were fifteen seconds he felt he did not have. He tipped a nod at the Secret Service man, then headed toward the rest room he'd used earlier, when he'd first come down from Hilton Clark's room. He was certain the agent's eyes were boring into the back of his head, which meant he had to at least enter the lavatory and remain there long enough to have relieved himself.

Considering the number of people seated right across the hall, it was remarkable that the men's room was empty. And for good reason: The White House Media Dinner was best-known for the president's scripted and acerbic comments, followed immediately by a bristling roast from a half dozen select politicians and celebrities. As the president had said a minute ago, it would all go viral within minutes, but no one in attendance would miss it for the world.

No one, that is except for whoever was in the ladies' room next door.

Logan was washing his hands when he heard a toilet flush through the tile walls. He figured someone was in there, checking her make-up, maybe applying a fresh layer of lipstick, even if she wasn't going to be let back inside the ballroom. He counted to five, then ten before he pushed his way back out into the promenade—empty, except for the agents standing guard outside every entry to the ballroom. He raised his hand in acknowledgment to the sentinel he'd spoken with a minute before, a brief motion that momentarily distracted him and almost caused him to miss her.

Giselle, or whatever the hell her real name might be, was casually sashaying through the promenade area toward the lobby. She'd lost the sequins and beret, replaced by tight jeans and a lightweight blouse, black New Balance shoes that made it easier to walk.

But it clearly was her; no question about it. Logan thought about calling out to her, but realized that would only draw her attention and cause her to run. And from the look of things, she definitely wanted to get away from there fast, while appearing to seem casual, almost blasé.

He started to follow her, trying not to let his pre-owned Oxfords make too much noise on the marble floor. She was about forty yards ahead of him by the time she reached the check-in desk in the main lobby. Then, without even the slightest of pauses, she pulled a cell phone out of a back pocket and took a quick glance at it. She tapped the screen, and Logan realized she had just speed-dialed a pre-set number.

What the fuck? he thought, at the very instant a defeaning blast reverberated from inside the Grand Ballroom behind him.

Chapter 50

Angela Wilde didn't flinch, didn't miss a step, didn't look back. She just kept walking as if nothing had happened, a seamless flow of movement that she knew the forensic analysts would note when they repeatedly viewed the time-stamped frames from the surveillance video.

But that was hours, if not days, in the future. Right now, she had about sixty seconds before the full force of the Metro Police, FBI, and Secret Service descended on the hotel and cordoned off every exit. As the extent and import of the carnage inside the ballroom became clear, they would extend that perimeter to a five-block radius; then ten. Within minutes the city would be shut down, flights and trains would be canceled, and every one of the bridges and highways would be hit with roadblocks.

The city would become paralyzed, the nation would be in mourning, and the entire world would be stunned by the loss of the American president. Not a very good one, she was more than certain, but very few of them were.

As she slipped through the polished brass doors that led outside to Connecticut Avenue, Angela allowed herself a quick breath of relief. That's when she heard someone behind her yell, "Stop, you bitch."

No way was she going to do that. In fact, she did just the opposite. Without even looking back she began to run.

"Stop," Logan yelled again. Louder this time, and a little closer. "Giselle—"

Screw you, she thought as she picked up speed. Whoever it was, he was using one of the many names she'd employed through the years—not since Dublin over a decade ago, in fact—not until last night.

No fucking way.

Angela kept moving, focused on reaching the car she'd parked earlier on St. Matthews Court, an alley that cut from Rhode Island Avenue to N Street, just four blocks away, no more than two minutes as she'd timed it on foot just yesterday. Although that time would be cut in half tonight, since whoever had yelled at her to stop had forced her to hoof it.

Even though she kept herself in prime shape—a requirement in her line of work if you planned to live long and prosper—she could hear him behind her. She didn't know how far away he was but now, as she racked her brain, she realized who it was.

The Goddamned sonofabitch who had punched her in the eye last night.

What the hell was he doing here?

Angela ran. Logan ran. There was no doubt in his mind she'd been there for some nefarious reason, and the resounding boom he'd just heard coming from the ballroom only reinforced his reasoning. He didn't care to think what had just happened in there, but the muted screams he'd heard suggested it couldn't be any good.

She still had a good twenty yards on him, and made good use of every one of them. She launched into a sprint up the sidewalk that was radiating heat from earlier in the day, then raced through the crosswalk at Desales Street. She was fast and well-toned, and seemed to have the stamina of a marathon runner. Whereas Logan had the initial push of a short-distance sprinter but eventually would run out of steam.

The twenty-yard gap had shortened to fifteen, then ten. By now she had reached the busy intersection at Rhode Island Avenue and M Street. The cross traffic had a green light and a bunch of pedestrians had clumped up at the crosswalk, waiting for the "don't walk" sign to change. Angela was forced to slow as she veered around them, then darted into the middle of the intersection. She dodged a cab and a delivery van as she made a sharp right and navigated the opposite curb effortlessly.

Anticipating her next move, Logan cut an even sharper right and darted behind the two lanes of cars that were beginning to slow as the green changed to yellow. She didn't see him coming at her on his dogleg route, but she could hear his shoes on the pavement. She dared not look back; even the slightest hesitation would throw her off her pace. It was going to be tight when she finally got to her car, since he would be on her long before she was even able to unlock the door.

She did what any respectable woman running from a man—self-preservation on her mind—would do. Without yielding even a fragment of her speed she yelled, "Help me. Please help me. My husband's trying to kill me!"

Logan was right on her heels now, and he followed her around the corner into the narrow alley he knew connected through to N Street. Almost right to the front door of the Tabard Inn, a boutique hotel and restaurant where he'd enjoyed a delicious four-course dinner with Katya just a few months before she'd died—and later, a lovely guest room on the third floor, tucked away from the street, with a bottle of *Billecart-Salmon* Brut Reserve on ice.

He was almost on top of her now, and he could see where she was going: the sea-green Jetta tucked into a space beside a dumpster. If he made a diving lunge, he might be able to tackle her. Then again, if he missed, he'd go face-first into the asphalt and she'd be gone.

Behind him he heard—much closer than he liked—the words "Leave her alone, motherfucker." A second later it seemed as if a Mack truck hit him in the back, and he was slammed forward with what felt like five hundred horses of pure diesel power.

The blow caused him to collide with the woman he knew as Giselle, who careened into the door of the Jetta. She struck it hard with a vicious crunch, just as Logan was driven down on top her. A flurry of punches connected with his spine and kidneys, exacting all the pain of a medieval torture chamber. Then he saw a galaxy of stars, as his entire world sank into an excruciating chasm of darkness.

Chapter 51

Monica Cross keyed both the lock and the deadbolt and pushed open the door to her apartment. Still hard to think of it as *hers*, rather than *theirs*, since she had spent more than five years sharing it with Phillip, after they had toured dozens of other places on the Upper West Side and down in the much pricier Village.

They'd settled on the twelfth floor of a postwar building between West End Avenue and the Henry Hudson Parkway. It had the three bedrooms they wanted, and it was just a short walk to the subway, which served the 1,2,3 lines that took them both within blocks of their respective offices. *Earth Illustrated* was located on Sixth Avenue near the Empire State Building, and Phillip worked as a white-collar defense attorney at a boutique law firm just a stone's throw from Thirty Rock. The apartment had a master bedroom with *en suite* and walk-in closet, a home office for him, and a third bedroom where Monica could practice yoga and which would be converted to a nursery whenever they decided to start a family. It also was a block from the parking garage where Phillip got a good monthly rate, which his employer paid for him as a perk.

She'd already told the landlord she would be moving out when the lease expired in November. The rent was way more than she could afford on a single salary, even with the payout from the law firm's insurance company. Phillip had been killed while driving back from taking a deposition up in Albany and, since he was officially on the clock—although not racking up billing hours—it had turned into a worker's comp claim. Strict money management had allowed her to stay put for now, but she'd already begun

317

sizing up neighborhoods where she could find an affordable one bedroom closer to her office.

After the shoot-out at the Museum of Natural History—and the unexpected gunshot she'd heard after fleeing the utility closet—she'd zig-zagged her way to Union Station. One block over, two blocks up, just as she'd done earlier. Her ankle seized up twice and she'd had to rest a moment and massage the pain away. When she finally entered the bustling terminal, she'd checked the timetable, saw there was a Northeast Regional leaving in ten minutes. Not bad, but it made about a dozen stops on its route up to New York, so she opted for the Acela that got her to Penn Station just a few minutes before seven.

She took a cab from there, and made it home around seven-thirty. The view of the river and the sunset over New Jersey helped to take the edge off, but she couldn't put the day's events out of her mind. It was hard to believe her morning had started in London, followed by a long flight and an attempt on her life—two of them, in fact—in the nation's capital. Then came the quick hand-off to Mr. Logan, which led to the gunfire and her close encounter with a mad man, before a phone call had intervened and allowed her to escape, an exceptionally close call, which was briefly explained to her halfway through her train ride north when a text landed in her phone:

Monica. You should be in the clear now. International alerts are called off, threat level is zero. Safe travels and enjoy life. P

She had wondered who "P" was, then figured it had to be the man named Phythian. He'd told her his last name but had never spelled it, and she'd assumed it started with an "F." *FITH-yun*. In any event, his words had helped her relax as the train raced through the Maryland countryside.

Even so, she was quick to triple lock the door as she slipped into her foyer. A tsunami of relief washed through her, and she sagged against the wall as she bolted it behind her. *Home at last, safe and sound.* She closed her eyes and just stood there, shivering even though she'd left the AC off when she'd left almost two weeks ago for Pakistan. She almost felt like crying from relief, but the tears wouldn't come. Not now, although she suspected they would eagerly find her later. They always did.

Monica wandered into the kitchen and headed straight for the wine fridge next to the dishwasher. Fifteen seconds and one corkscrew later she was sipping a glass of chardonnay, larger than it should have been, but she didn't give a damn. Not after everything she'd been through, and tomorrow was Sunday. She'd been tempted to call Arnie Kelso from the Acela, but the events of the day convinced her that her phone was compromised. His was, too, most likely, as were email and texts.

She took her wine into the bathroom, where she ran a full tub of hot water and Epsom salts, then soaked her bones until the water got cold. She was exhausted but too wired to climb into bed, so she wandered back out into the living room and sank into the sofa. She flipped on a cable news station, wondering if any of the talking heads might mention the shoot-out on the National Mall down in Washington earlier in the afternoon.

What she got was a scene of utter chaos. Block letters on the TV read "Assassination Plot Averted," accompanied by a split screen that showed the regular eight o'clock anchor and some kind of crazy commotion outside a hotel in downtown DC. Monica had trouble hearing what was going on, with the pandemonium of sirens and yelling in the background.

"What we're learning is that six people were injured in the blast, but there are no reported fatalities," the stern-faced anchor said. "The President, who at the start of his remarks had mentioned feeling ill, had just removed his jacket and handed it to a White House aide when an explosive device detonated. The aide and several other people standing nearby, including two Secret Service personnel, reportedly were wounded—"

Holy shit, Monica thought as she leaned forward in her seat. *Someone tried to kill the president? What is this world coming to?*

The image of the flashing lights was replaced with the face of a woman who appeared to be in shock, although she was doing her best to hold herself together. The anchor introduced her by saying, "Our local reporter, Raleigh Durham, was at the event tonight at the Mayflower Hotel, and she witnessed the explosion. Raleigh, what can you tell us?"

Raleigh Durham? Seriously?

"Thank you, Kurt," she replied. "As you said, the president was about halfway through his monologue when all of a sudden there was an explosion up on the dais, where he and other guests had just finished their dinners. I'm told—and this has not yet been verified—that a small explosive device detonated under the collar of President Mitchell's jacket, which he had just removed because he was not feeling well. The young aide who was holding the jacket—and again, this is unconfirmed—may have lost a hand in the explosion, and several Secret Service personnel also suffered burns and lacerations."

The anchor named Kurt nodded at her remarks, then inquired, "Is anyone saying how the explosive device came to be implanted in the president's jacket? Security at these events is tight…people must be wondering how this could have happened."

"Kurt, there's just too much chaos and confusion right now to get answers to that question," Raleigh Durham replied. She seemed to be thoroughly jolted by the events she was covering, or maybe it was just the three pear martinis she'd consumed earlier. "Certainly, this attempt on the president's life—and no one is disputing that's what it was—will be investigated thoroughly, but for now facts are few and far between. I can tell you, however—and this is from a reliable source inside the administration—the president is safe and resting comfortably after being rushed back to the White House."

There was more serious nodding from Kurt, who then put a hand to the side of his head and listened to what the earbud was telling him. Then he said, "We just received some breaking news on this ongoing story. Sources tell us—and again, this is unconfirmed—that a possible suspect, or suspects, have been detained by DC Metro Police. A man and a woman were seen running from the hotel just prior to the explosion in the ballroom, and they were both tackled by a good Samaritan who heard the woman scream. No confirmation on the identities of the two individuals, or if they were, indeed, connected to the assassination attempt at the Mayflower."

He appeared to listen to the earbud a few more seconds, then went on. "We've also just learned that Vice President James Crittenden, who was at the media dinner tonight, has been taken to a hospital. He was seated at the other end of the dais and, while he was not injured in the explosion, he apparently has become ill. As have several other guests whom he spoke with earlier, including Secretary of Commerce Arnold Everett and actress Jessica Howell. No word yet on what caused them to collapse, but it is not thought to be food poisoning or the flu."

Monica stared at the screen, her glass of wine frozen about a foot from her lips. She dared not move, as if any sudden motion might rejigger the universe in such a way that the planet would spin even further off its axis. And somewhere, way back in a deep crevasse in her brain, she couldn't help but think this somehow was connected to her, and the ordeal she thought she'd just put behind her.

Chapter 52

Logan spent thirteen days being bounced from one law enforcement agency to another, grilled by dozens of special agents, and some who weren't very special at all. FBI, Homeland, DC Metro Police, the State Department—any and every agency that had even a remote interest in the attempted, but unsuccessful, assassination of President Mitchell—made him swear on a Bible and reveal all he knew.

While all this was going on, Hilton Clark managed to convince his bosses and their bosses that, despite the allegations and the threat of potential federal charges, Logan could be a valuable asset to the paper. He had a unique perspective of an historic incident that no other reporter possessed and, once it finally was determined that he had taken down an assassin who had been paid handsomely to kill the Commander in Chief and disrupt the course of history, he quickly was lauded as a national hero.

Thirteen days after the events unfolded at the Mayflower Hotel, the *Post* printed two investigative pieces as part of a new contract that brought Logan back to fulltime status. He had to read them on his laptop because his limited finances didn't permit him to subscribe to the printed version of the *Washington Post*. Until his first paycheck cleared the bank he still counted every quarter, drank cut-rate cabs, and used the password Hilton Clark had given him to access the newspaper's online pay wall.

Justice Wheeler's Death Ruled Homicide After New Evidence Emerges
By Carter Logan, Washington Post Investigative Reporter

WASHINGTON, DC—July 9: The medical examiner for the District of Columbia yesterday revised the cause of death of Supreme Court Justice Colin Wheeler from accidental asphyxia to homicide, following additional toxicology tests that revealed traces of succinylcholine chloride in the victim's system.

The substance, also known as Quelicin, is a sterile, nonpyrogenic agent often used in emergency medical situations as a short-acting skeletal muscle relaxant. The district's chief pathologist, Regina Thorpe, MD, said it is likely Wheeler had been injected with the drug in order to temporarily subdue him prior to his death. The substance was not previously found because routine autopsy procedures do not require the thorough blood analysis that would identify it in a victim's system, she explained.

Additionally, one hundred twenty-six pornographic files found on a laptop computer belonging to Justice Wheeler were determined to have all been uploaded the night of his death. According to FBI digital forensic specialist Bruce Quinlan, the "create dates" for each of the images had been physically altered to make it appear that Justice Wheeler downloaded and installed them over an eighteen-month period.

The images were traced to several "Dark Web" chatrooms that cater to pedophiles and predators. Those websites have since been shut down, and fourteen individuals connected with them are in custody.

Federal authorities arrested Angela Wilde, previously charged in the attempted assassination of President Mitchell, for first-degree homicide in Justice Wheeler's death, as well as conspiracy to commit homicide. Surveillance video shot the night of the murder at the Franklin Pierce Hotel shows a woman bearing a strong resemblance to Wilde leaving the hotel around the time of his death. A subsequent examination of Wilde's apartment, leased on a month-to-month basis, turned up numerous items consistent with both assassination attempts.

Justice Department officials have refused to specify just what those objects might be.

Toxicology Tests Reveal Vice President Crittenden Died From Novichok Attack; Russians Suspected

By Carter Logan, Washington Post Investigative Reporter

WASHINGTON, DC—July 9: The medical examiner for the District of Columbia confirmed today that Vice President James Crittenden died from coming in contact with Novichok, a highly toxic nerve agent created by the U.S.S.R. at the height of the Cold War.

Crittenden fell ill during the White House Media Dinner June 26, the same event where authorities say Angela Wilde attempted to assassinate President Frank Mitchell with an improvised explosive device.

Homeland Security officials and an FBI task force are investigating whether the two events were connected.

"Novichok is an extremely dangerous and sophisticated nerve agent, much more powerful than sarin or VX," said Professor Howard Reese, a pharmacology expert at Georgetown University. "It is a highly toxic chemical that prevents the human nervous system from working properly. While known to be produced in different forms, they most often are made as a liquid, which can penetrate the skin easily."

In Russian, the name "Novichok" translates to "newcomer." The term applies to a series of highly advanced nerve compounds developed in the Soviet Union during the 1970s and '80s, under the code word Foliant. The production of these chemical weapons was revealed in the 1990s by Soviet scientist Vil Mirzayanov, who later defected to the U.S. and published the chemical formula in a report titled *State Secrets*.

Vice President Crittenden is believed to have come into contact with the nerve agent after repeatedly cleaning his hands with a well-known over-the-counter sanitizing product. A small bottle of the solution was found in the pocket of his tuxedo jacket, and subsequent forensic analysis found it contained a high concentration of the nerve agent. How the substance came to be in the bottle found in Crittenden's pocket is not known.

Because of Novichok's Soviet origins, and since it is not known to be produced anywhere except Russia, U.S. officials believe that country likely was involved with the attack on the vice president. President Mitchell is examining several options to redress the situation, including economic sanctions and other political and military measures.

Russian Minister of Foreign Affairs Mikhail Noskov said his country had absolutely no involvement in this heinous attack on the American government or its highly respected officials, and was "insulted that anyone would suspect our complicity in any way." In a strongly worded denial, he insisted that neither Russia, nor the Soviet Union before that, has ever been involved in the development of nerve agents that "in any way resemble the compound the west insists on calling Novichok."

He went on to say that the nerve agent used in the attack on the vice president could have been manufactured in the Ukraine, the Czech Republic, Israel, or even the United States.

Not to be outdone, Hilton Clark weighed in with his own report the same day:

Suspect In President's Assassination Attempt Found Dead In Jail Cell In Apparent Suicide
By Hilton Clark, Deputy Managing Editor

WASHINGTON, DC—July 12: Angela Wilde, the suspect in the alleged conspiracy to assassinate President Frank Mitchell seventeen days ago at the Mayflower Hotel in Washington, was found dead this morning in her jail cell at the Federal Correctional Facility in Southeast Washington.

According to a U.S. Department of Justice spokesperson, a corrections officer on a routine prisoner check discovered Wilde unresponsive just after six o'clock, and attempted to resuscitate her. The suspect subsequently was transported to George Washington University Hospital, where she was pronounced dead from cardiac arrest.

An initial investigation revealed the deceased tied a strip of her bedsheet around her neck and threw herself off the top bunk, which was empty at the time.

U.S. Attorney General Michael Grimshaw said he was "appalled" that such a high-profile suspect could possibly have taken her own life while in federal custody. "Not since the Jeffrey Epstein case has such an egregious oversight occurred, resulting in the death of a prisoner," he said. "The investigation into the suspect's involvement in a plan to assassinate the President of the United States, as well as the murder of Supreme Court Justice Colin Wheeler, will continue."

Wilde was observed fleeing the Mayflower Hotel just seconds after a small explosive device was detonated in the Grand Ballroom. The suspect is believed to have planted the IED under the president's collar earlier in the evening, while she was posing as a media image adviser. Several Secret Service agents have said they saw her in close physical contact with the president in an *ad hoc* green room prior to the White House Media Dinner, and traces of cyclonite, a component of the powerful explosive C4, were found in her apartment after she was arrested.

Secret Service Director Donald Poole has accepted full responsibility for failing to detect the murder plot, and tendered his resignation the following day. However, according to multiple unnamed White House sources, President Mitchell reportedly has refused to accept it.

Washington Post investigative reporter Carter Logan noticed the suspect fleeing the hotel at the time of the explosion, and followed her on foot. He chased her several blocks north to St. Matthews Court, where he and a pedestrian, Harold Jackson, of New Carrollton, tackled her to the ground.

Initially arrested as a co-conspirator in the assassination attempt, Logan explained to federal authorities that Wilde had tried to kill him the night before after he learned she might have been involved in the death of Justice Wheeler earlier in the week. Surveillance video from the lobby of the Franklin Pierce Hotel confirmed his suspicions, and Wilde was charged with murder, attempted murder, and conspiracy to commit murder in the Wheeler case.

Justice Department officials believe Wilde was hired by an unknown party to kill both men, but declined to say anything further, pending an ongoing investigation.

Logan was subsequently released from federal custody and allowed to return home. He has since returned to his fulltime job at the *Post*.

Chapter 53

A white disc of searing heat hung high in the sky, blazing down on a massive sea of scorched grass that was pocked with the skeletons of dried baobabs and acacias and vachellias. Phythian climbed down from the bed of the Toyota Hilux and brushed a layer of African dust from his trousers, instantly relishing the silence and solitude that was why he called this place home.

The village of Terrat had not changed in the two weeks since he'd left it. Why would it? The place was little different than it had been a hundred years ago, and was unlikely to shift much over the next hundred. Chickens and goats napped in the shade of the concrete huts that put this outpost on the map, just barely, seeking shade from a day that inarguably was going to be more blistering than yesterday. The faint odor of burned cow dung hung in the air, mixed with the smell of diesel fuel that powered the noisy generators along this dusty road that was Main Street.

He'd picked up the ride four hours ago in Namanga, a lonely checkpoint on the border between Kenya and Tanzania and the start of the main road that took tourists to Lake Manyara and Serengeti National Park. He was headed toward neither of those locales, but the town was the final destination of the bus he'd boarded at Jomo Kenyatta International Airport when his one-stop from London via Addis Ababa landed the night before. Fortunately, there had been a restaurant where he could find a meal of pilau and biriyani, and a half-decent glass of Syrah.

The paved highway that ran through town was the only north-south route within one hundred kilometers, and Phythian easily had found someone who eagerly agreed to take him as far as Terrat—for one hundred thousand Tanzanian schillings, paid in advance.

The driver dropped him off in front of the post office, where the usual half-dozen villagers sipped their tea while comparing notes on yesterday, today, and tomorrow. Phythian tugged his backpack out of the pick-up bed and hoisted it over his shoulder, then handed his driver a fifty Euro note. He had no use for it, but figured the gaunt African behind the wheel could find some way to exchange it. Once the rusty old Hilux rattled off in a swirl of sand and dust, he made his way inside the building, the same tired fan churning in the corner, same flyers flapping on the bulletin board.

Phythian wandered up to the laminated counter and said to Elimu, the young postal worker, the same words with which he always greeted him. "*Barua yoyote kwa ajili yangu?*"

"*Mshangao,*" Elimu replied. He was dressed in a short-sleeve cotton shirt that at one time had been white but had discolored from sweat, dust, and the ever-present sun. "*Ndio unayo kifurushi.*" You have a package.

"*Hiyo ni mshangao,*" Phythian said. "*Nashangaa inaweza kuwa nini.*" That's a surprise. I wonder what it could be.

In fact, it was not a surprise at all, and he knew precisely what the parcel contained. Phythian had mailed it to himself from Glasgow one week ago, the afternoon he'd left Gray Rock. This was several days after Adam Kent had been found lying in a pool of his own blood in the broom closet at a museum on the mall in Washington, DC.

Authorities had been baffled why a senior administration official would have committed suicide in such a place. Surveillance footage showed a woman hurrying through the rotunda and Ocean Hall, down the stairs, then back up and inside the small room just seconds before he had followed her inside. Some investigators speculated that she might have pulled the trigger, but further scrutiny of the security video showed Kent entering the lavatory with his gun drawn, and multiple witnesses reported that someone seemed to have been shooting at a man and a woman earlier, outside the museum.

The GSR on Kent's hands sealed the deal.

Phythian spent a total of five days on the tiny knob of granite in the Firth of Clyde. On his first morning there he transferred a sizeable sum from a G3 account in Grand Cayman to a bank in Glasgow as a reward for Gordy's many years of loyal service as caretaker, and to ensure his family would always enjoy the finer things Scotland had to offer. The generous gift also bought a promise of silence regarding the disposition of the island's previous tenant, and an occasional "check-in" to make sure all was in order when no one was in residence.

As soon as the old caretaker departed Gray Rock, Phythian dug a good-sized grave for The Chairman. The old man had followed his final sip of rum during the tempestuous storm with a shot of lead to the temple, about an hour after Adam Kent had met a similar fate. The 7.65×17mm SR cartridge had been fired at close range from a Mauser HSc, a commercial pistol adopted for military service by both the German Navy and Air Force. Unfortunately, the soil on the tiny island was, indeed, mostly rock, and it took a good part of the day to prepare a hole large enough to do the job.

Martin Beaudin arrived the evening of the second day. As he'd learned during Phythian's late-night visit in Andorra, it was difficult to say no to this enigma who had broken into his house and shared a bottle of expensive wine with him. Then, as now, he came to understand the changes Phythian had in mind, and agreed to execute them—not that he had much of a choice.

With over seven billion humans competing for space on the planet, there would always be greed and avarice, love and hate, retribution and revenge. The Greenwich Global Group had emerged from the ashes of World War II as a cadre of a few well-intentioned men intent on avenging Hitler's lethal regime and hunting down the Nazi scourge that remained. Over the years, however, it had evolved into a for-profit company that offered a permanent solution to personal or political conflicts that couldn't be fixed by any other means than death; a super-monopoly with which no one could compete, and few dared to cross. Sure, there were independent players who could step in to provide similar outcomes for a lower price, but a G3 contract carried a certain *cachet*. A mark of prestige, the ultimate seal of approval.

Nature abhors a vacuum, of course, and people would always want other people dead. If the G3 were to disappear, another player would quickly fill the vacated space. Plenty of outfits were ready to move in at the first sign of opportunity, which made it prudent to preserve a lucrative business model that yielded tens of millions of dollars in net profit every year.

Phythian decided it was time to shake things up a bit.

The data contained on the cloud server in Luxembourg was beyond priceless. The G3 had completed over six thousand discrete executions since the end of the war, with only two abject failures during that entire period. The most recent of these had been Vice President Crittenden's attempt to have President Mitchell assassinated less than two weeks ago, a plot that been foiled only by the hands of fate. Oddly enough, the VP himself had died that same night, a vial of hand sanitizer laced with a Russian nerve agent. Investigators were intent on tracking its origins back to the Kremlin, but Phythian suspected it would be wise to begin their inquiry in Jerusalem.

In any event, it all added up to a cache of invaluable intelligence for which countries, companies, organizations, and individuals would again pay handsomely—this time to prevent the details of their actions from being exposed to the public. Some with deep pockets would do so readily, albeit reluctantly, in order to protect their deadly secrets, while others would refuse to cough up one more dollar or Euro. Those who refused to reach a monetary settlement would pay with their lives, and eventually the other stragglers would get the message and fall in line.

Beaudin had willingly pledged his very soul to oversee the transition from one core strategy to the next. He hadn't really been given a choice, but he appreciated the sizable increase in personal compensation, as well as an equity stake in the new enterprise. So far, Phythian was proving to be a fair and reasonable employer, and had promised to be back in touch in a week or two when his plans were locked in place.

Elimu appeared anxious to see what might be in Phythian's package, which had been addressed to "Mr. Mzungu, Kambi ya Safari, Terrat, Tanzania," the Swahili part translating to Mr. White Man, Safari Camp, which was what he had come to be known in these parts.

But Phythian did not open the parcel, not now. Instead he made limited chit-chat with the postman, then turned to go. He had a long walk ahead of him, unless a truck happened to come along and offer him a lift, a likelihood that was possible but not guaranteed on any good day in the Tanzanian Serengeti.

He was almost out the door when Elimu called out, "*Karibu nikasahau. Wanaume wengine walikuwa wakiuliza juu yako.*"

Phythian stopped, took a moment to decipher what the young man was telling him. Then he said, "*Wakauliza juu yangu?*" There were people asking about me?

Elimu nodded, swatting a fly from his face.

"What did they want to know?" Phythian inquired in Swahili, knowing he was butchering both the question and the language.

"*Unaishi wapi.*" They asked where you live.

"And what did you tell them?"

Elimu shook his head and gave up a broad grin. "*Kwamba sijawahi kukuona,*" he said.

"Good answer," Phythian replied. "When was this?"

"*Jana usiku. Jua.*" Last night at sunset.

"*Asante,* Elimu," he thanked him.

He shuffled out to the dusty road and began walking south, his backpack slung over his shoulder and the small package the size of a shoebox tucked under his arm. All the while he was sensing, *the Russians are here,* knowing the powerful yet grieving oligarch had not personally come to Africa to seek revenge for the death of his son. Instead, he'd hired a surrogate, and Phythian had pulled the sniper's name out of the late Chairman's laptop on Gray Rock the night before he'd left the island.

He was smiling to himself and thinking, *it will be my greatest pleasure to see you to your grave.*

Less than an hour into his walk, Phythian heard a vehicle approaching from behind. He was acquainted with most of the subsistence farmers in the area, and had never found one who would pass by without stopping to pick him up. He turned and raised a hand to the air, a casual gesture indicating he'd like a ride, if the driver was willing.

The vehicle slowed, a fantail of dust churning up from its rear wheels. He recognized it as a Toyota Kluger, at least fifteen years old, a color that the factory probably had described as charcoal when it first rolled off the line. Despite its age it was in good condition, none of the customary dings and dents and caked-on mud embedded around the wheel wells, water being too precious this time of year to be used to wash away a little dirt. That meant it probably was a rental car, probably from Mombasa near the coast or, equally likely, Nairobi.

As the vehicle pulled up alongside him, there was no question in his mind who the occupants were, or where they were from: two white men, crisp safari shirts, stiff collars, aviator sunglasses that looked as if they'd been purchased just yesterday in an airport halfway around the world.

The driver cranked the window down and flashed Phythian a polite but cheerless smile. "Need a lift?" he asked in an accent that sounded Australian.

"Depends," Phythian replied. "Where are you going?"

"All the way through to Kibaya," the driver explained, seeming none too happy about it, even though it was a lie.

"What's in Kibaya?"

"Nothing, as far as I can tell. So how 'bout it, mate? You want a lift, or not?"

Definitely Australian. Same thing with his passenger, but not the elongated package in the back, which Phythian had already determined had been picked up in Kampala, and contained a SAKO TRG 42 bolt-action sniper rifle originally manufactured in Finland.

"I'm not going very far, only about twenty miles," Phythian told him.

"It'll be good to have company part of the way." The driver glanced over at the man in the passenger seat, added, "All Archie, here, does is snore and fart."

"Let's go," Phythian said. "As long as I don't have to sit behind him." The man named Archie looked offended, but Phythian said nothing as he opened the rear door and slipped in behind the driver with his backpack and shoebox-sized package. "There's an old baobab tree marking the road to my place," he said. "Can't miss it."

Phythian had expected retribution for the killing of the Russian poacher, and a quick mental grab of the two men in the front seat told him they were the recon party that had been dispatched to track him down. The third member of the team, the shooter who belonged to the crated gun in the back of the SUV, was in the vicinity and positioned to move in as soon as the target's identity and location were verified. While they didn't know Phythian's name, they suspected this hitchhiker was the man they were looking for, and both were almost giddy with excitement to have found him so easily. They'd been given strict orders not to harm him, just to confirm his whereabouts and try to get as much information out of him as possible.

Phythian found all this comforting, since it meant the person who had flown this pair of professional spotters halfway around the world from Melbourne didn't know the identity of their target, either—an interesting and convenient twist.

Because of their collective ignorance, they had no clue that he had already determined that the driver had a Glock G29 loaded with ten-millimeter cartridges tucked into his door pouch. Similarly, the gassy passenger up front—the driver had been spot-on about that—had stashed his SIG P226 in the glove compartment.

The driver's name was Russell, and he and Archie asked questions they believed were subtly designed to verify that their rider was the person they had traveled all this way to locate, but not touch—and certainly not kill. That was up to the boss lady, who was waiting for a signal that her mark was in-country, and back at his compound.

"How long have you lived here?" Russell asked as Archie passed gas beside him.

"About five years," Phythian explained. "It's a magnificent and unspoiled corner of the planet."

"Looks like a great place for trophy hunting," Archie said.

"If you're into that sort of thing," Phythian responded. "Personally, I don't see the fun in stopping a beating heart." He knew his words could be considered by many as the height of hypocrisy but, in fact, he'd never taken any pleasure in completing an assignment—other than checking his bank account later.

"Do you see many elephants out here?" Russell wanted to know.

"From time to time, but you'll find more of them in the national park. They're illegal to hunt there, but now and then we get some rich asshole who pays a fortune to take one down." Practically leading them by the hand to the confirmation they were looking for; the quicker they figured this out, the sooner it would all be over.

The two men in the front seat glanced at each other and regarded him warily. Phythian studied Russell's eyes in the rearview mirror, waiting for the dim bulb to go off in his head. Finally, he obliged, saying "We're looking for a man who is said to live around here."

"Shouldn't be difficult, since there's not many of us. What's he look like?"

"White man, about your age and height."

"What do you want with him?" Phythian inquired.

Both men in the front seat laughed. Then the one named Archie, the one Phythian could tell had a short temper, said, "He killed a man named Vasily Sokolov."

"You mean the Russian bastard who was in the wrong place, clearly at the wrong time."

The two men in the front seat didn't know what to do next. Their only job had been to hang around Terrat until the target showed up and they were able to confirm his identity. *Done.* This hitchhiker had all but confessed to shooting the young Russian hunter three weeks ago, and seemed indifferent to the presence of these two Australian men driving a rented Toyota SUV in the middle of fucking nowhere.

"Do you have any idea why we're here?" Russell asked him.

"Well, you're obviously not going to Kibaya; that much is certain. Which means you've probably come all this way from Australia, flew into Kampala to pick up the SAKO TRG 42 you have in the back there, for the purpose of settling a score. Then you drove here."

There was silence from the front seat, almost five seconds of it. Then Archie kicked open the glove box and pulled out his Sig, a black, double-action semi-automatic.

"Who the fuck are you?" he demanded, aiming the gun at Phythian. Even though he'd been forewarned that, under no circumstances whatsoever, was he to injure the target.

"You want to know rule number one in this line of work?" Phythian replied. "Never ask a question to which you don't already know the answer."

"How the bloody hell could you know what's in the back?"

Phythian let out a sigh of impatience, said, "There—you just did it again. Whoever said there are no stupid questions was wrong."

"Yeah?" Archie said. "How 'bout this one, then: Which one of us has the gun, fuckwit?"

"Archie—put that thing down," Russell told him. "You shoot the bloody wristy, we don't get paid."

"Listen to your friend, Archie," Phythian said. "You don't want to go back to Melbourne empty-handed. Or, more likely, shipped home in a box."

"You fuckin' kidding me? You're the one's gonna get himself killed."

"Put it down," Russell repeated. "Before you blow this whole thing."

Archie found himself in a conundrum from which he saw no escape. Russell, behind the wheel, was telling him to put the gun away and stand down. But if he did that, this crazy hitchhiker—whom he now was certain was the sniper who had killed the Russian kid, and somehow knew too much about their business—would do something crazy. He was sure of it. Plus, he was beginning to sense a headache coming on. Not exactly a headache; more like a large hose clamp tightening around his skull, the worm gear being turned one agonizing notch at a time.

Inexplicably, he found himself turning the gun away from this crazy scrote who was almost smirking at him from the back seat. He moved it in one slow but steady motion, pivoting it until the barrel was pressed up against his own temple. His hand trembled as he fought this growing impulse that had come over him with absolutely no warning.

In the seat beside him Russell screamed, "C'mon, mate…put it down—"

But he didn't—*couldn't*—put it down, as the clamp seemed to squeeze his head even tighter. At the same time it was filling his brain with a maelstrom of emotions, all of them very dark and disturbing. His eyes filled with fear as he felt his finger tighten on the trigger, the pull of which he had reduced by replacing the factory-original hammer spring.

The firing pin snapped forward, the explosive charge in the brass casing detonated, and the hollow-point roared down the four-point-four-inch barrel directly into Archie's brain.

"*Fucksakes*," Russell screamed from the front seat. "What the bloody hell—?"

His hands were shaking on the wheel, and the Toyota Kluger began to weave from one side of the dirt road to the other. Eventually he pulled it over to the edge and lurched to a stop, yanking the shifter into neutral. He whirled around in the front seat and yelled, "Who the bloody fuck are you—?"

But Phythian ignored his question, instead snatching the blood-covered SIG from Archie's limp hand. He pressed it against the driver's temple and said, "Give me your Glock, unless you want to end up like your friend there."

"My what?"

"The gun in the side pocket. Now."

"How the hell—?"

"I said *now*."

Russell reluctantly removed the gun from the door pouch and handed it over his left shoulder. Phythian accepted it, then stuffed both weapons into a pouch in his backpack.

"Listen up," he said. "Here's what you're going to do, but I'm only going to tell you once."

Russell was too nervous—*too bloody scared*—to do much listening, his dead friend Archie slumped against the passenger door, brains already simmering on the hot glass. But he nodded anyway and made like he was paying attention.

"Wherever your boss lady is, tell her she's down to just one spotter. She's going to have to improvise a bit, since it's too late to fly in someone new. Go ahead and give her the gun in the back. It's a fine weapon, and she'll think it'll give her an advantage. Which she's going to need. Tell her that. And make sure you also tell her that her old friend from The Farm says 'hello.' Got it?"

The driver nodded; yeah, he got it.

"And one more thing," Phythian said as he opened the rear door and climbed out, grabbing his backpack and the package. "Make sure she knows I'm waiting for her."

Chapter 54

Phythian slept well, knowing he was safe until sunrise. While some military snipers have been known to employ thermal imaging cameras and night scopes, he knew the illumination they provide was grossly insufficient for this particular task. Under optimum conditions it was possible to hunt a target in the dark, but the Serengeti was anything but optimum, especially at night. Lions, leopards, and wild dogs often were out in force long after the stars came out, and at the onset of the dry season competition among hungry carnivores could be fierce—and fatal to someone not familiar with the terrain.

After five years at *Utuliva*, he knew every hillock, tree, rock outcropping, stream bed, and dry lake within five miles of his camp. He'd studied the migratory patterns of the giraffes and zebras and wildebeests and bushbucks, and carefully analyzed the hunting customs of the predators. With all its beauty and elegance, the Serengeti was a brutal, lovely, vicious, and innocent nativity, teeming with the promise of life and threatened by the grim finality of death–every day on every level.

As the first thin sliver of sun emerged from the east, Phythian gazed out upon the vast blanket of grassland that spread out before him. In the weeks since the rains had ended it had turned from green to brown, and many of the animals had headed north to wherever water remained more plentiful. Sloppy mudholes existed at the lower elevations, often identified by the birds that might suddenly flush out of the grass without warning.

This morning, however, the land was calm and quiet. Near an acacia tree in the distance, maybe about a mile away, he saw giraffes reaching for a leafy morsel that hadn't dried yet, but mostly their world remained asleep. Except for Phythian, who had awakened from his hideout about an hour ago, when he'd smelled—very faintly, but definitely—a wisp of smoke. Not his would-be assailant, he was certain: she was far too good to make that sort of mistake.

But maybe it was her spotter.

Phythian had slinked out of camp shortly after sundown, stealthily working his way through the scrub to the rear of the fenced compound. Now that his stalker knew who he was, she would take great pains not to venture within a thousand yards of the place. Her G3 file listed her maximum shooting distance at one thousand, nine hundred twenty-one yards—a little more than a mile. Not enough to place her among the top elite of the special forces pack, but definitely a range of great value in the field, when surgical precision was key.

Not bad for a girl.

Diana Petrie had shrugged off the pervasive sexism within the military as the detritus of an archaic, male-dominated world order. She'd experienced gender intolerance her entire life, from when she tried out for boys' Little League or when she ran cross country with the men's team in college. She suffered through all the jingoism that her ignorant peers could hurl at her, all the slurs from dyke to butch to rug muncher, and endured the full spectrum of harassment and bullying and persecution that typified the adolescent female ethos.

When she'd enlisted in the Army after college—on an ROTC scholarship—no one asked, and she didn't tell. She took to guns swiftly and with great competence, and now here she was, in the far reaches of northern Tanzania. Stalking the most dangerous quarry she'd ever pursued and, all her personal affirmations and encouragement aside, she was terrified.

Terrified of who her target was, and what he'd managed to do to the rest of the G3 executive board.

Terrified that she was all that remained at the top of the once-great Greenwich Global Group.

The five million dollars promised by the Russian thug named Sokolov wasn't worth it, yet here she was.

She and her spotter named Russell had arrived a little after three in the morning, and had hiked to a spot just under two miles north of the camp. The night vision goggles had been almost useless, but the two had managed to find a good perch behind a scattering of rocks left over from an earlier epoch when this land had been a lake bed teeming with fish and birds and earlier versions of mammalia that long since had evolved out of existence.

What neither of them knew was that Phythian had followed them, silently inching his way and maintaining a smart distance as they assessed the fallen logs and mounds of earth. The roost they finally selected offered a good view of his camp, although at too great a distance for her to land a solid shot. No matter: what really counted was that she was well outside Phythian's mental range and, therefore, he could not possibly know where she was—unless, of course, he was already positioned four-hundred-ten yards to her right.

She considered the very real possibility he was not inside the main structure. He knew she was here, coming for him, so why would he remain in the compound? He wouldn't, but she knew how he functioned. She had recruited and trained him, instilled in him the confidence and patience of a bold and fearless killer. Thus, she was convinced that the Rōnin Phythian she knew would make her come to him.

The sudden and unmistakable spray of blood that washed over her where she now lay in the grass—rifle on a tripod extending out in front of her—changed her thinking in an instant.

A fraction of a second later, the crack of the McMillan Tac-50 long-range anti-materiel and anti-personnel rifle hit her ears, and she knew she'd grossly miscalculated the situation.

The force of the bullet, one of several that had arrived by post from Glasgow just a day earlier, struck the Australian spotter named Russell Gartner high in the back with enough force to sever his spine at the thoracic one and two. The slug also shattered his clavicle as it ripped through his flesh, the force of the blow thrusting his body sideways, causing his arm to hit the SAKO TRG 42 and knock it askew.

Then he toppled face-first into the dirt.

Petrie's first instinct was to scream, but she didn't. She didn't utter a sound, didn't flinch. She was paralyzed by the prospect of what might come next: a second bullet flying through the air at one thousand feet per second, fast enough that she would be dead before she even heard the retort of the rifle. She knew from the time gap between impact and gunshot that Phythian was about five hundred yards away and, because of the angle of the shot, she also had a general idea where. Russell was dead because he'd been propped a little too high up on his elbows, surveying their surroundings with his state-of-the-art scope—also gauging the wind (there wasn't any) and humidity (very low).

But Petrie was lying flat on the ground, out of sight, although she sensed Phythian knew where she was. The spotter would have been located close enough to her that any communication between them would be almost silent, or hand signals. That meant Phythian either couldn't see her where she was, or was positioned at such an angle that he couldn't hit her if he tried.

She also knew that, from five hundred yards away, he could read her thoughts, had tapped into all the hypotheticals that were racing through her mind. He held the advantage here, even though she had the superior gun and greater shooting acumen. Phythian knew the terrain, he had her pinned down, and he'd already killed her spotter, both of them, counting the one he'd shot yesterday. There was no way she could stand up without giving away her exact position, and trying to move to another location would be impossible without being detected.

I know you can hear what I'm thinking, Phythian, she thought. *Please confirm.*

She did not possess the same abilities he did, not on any perceptible level, but she had greatly strengthened his ability to push his own thoughts into anyone's mind, to within his cerebral range of a thousand yards, which he definitely was. So, he eventually replied, *You're in quite a quandary, Dee-Dee.* His name for her while he was studying at The Farm. *A real pickle, in fact.*

Help me out, here, she mentally pleaded.

You called this play, he responded.

What are you going to do, make me shoot myself?

An interesting thought, but impractical with a gun like a SAKO TRG 42.

I trained you, Rōnin. Now she was using his first name, going for collegial intimacy. She ought to know that wouldn't work. *I scanned your brain, up and down, inside and out. Identified the area in your cerebral cortex responsible for all this. Gave some form to the deformity, if you will. If it weren't for me, you'd be wandering around from guru to guru, mystic to mystic, trying to make sense of who you are.*

If it weren't for you, neither of us would be here.

I'm happy to walk away, she suggested.

Anastasia's checkmate, was his reply.

She flashed back to how the two of them had played chess in the early days of his training at The Farm, her instructing him to read her thoughts, thus training him to strategize several moves in advance and eventually take down her king, figuratively speaking, of course.

You learned well, she thought.

I had a fine instructor, was his pushed response.

So, the student becomes the teacher? she inquired mentally.

More like, the hunter becomes the hunted.

For eleven hours Petrie remained where she was—motionless, no food or drink. That was in her backpack two yards away, but she dared not reach for it.

At one point she had to urinate, but she knew Phythian wasn't about to agree to a ceasefire to permit such a trivial thing: same with the excruciating cramp that began biting into her left calf sometime around noon. He sensed her acute pain as her muscles tightened and twisted, driving her almost to the breaking point. Later she felt something wriggle up the leg of her trousers, but whatever it was backed around and slithered out. Flies and ants nibbled at her, and the scorching sun seared her neck and face. By early afternoon Russell's body began to smell, and vultures circled overhead. Eventually the stench attracted the attention of a young hyena trying to prove himself to his pack. He grabbed hold of the dead spotter's neck and dragged the carcass off, eyeing Petrie hungrily as he disappeared into the grass.

I'm going to stand up, she eventually communicated to him.

It will bring peace to both of us, was his mental reply.

You'll be quick?

If you wish.

Please. And Phythian?

Yes, Dee-Dee?

She hesitated a second at the use of her childhood nickname, then thought, *Don't let the animals take me. Promise me a decent burial.*

The least I can do, he agreed.

She waited another two hours sixteen minutes before she finally rose to her feet out of the tall grass, the only sound in the sizzling African air being that of a few flies buzzing around the dried pool of her dead spotter's blood. The sun was slipping near the horizon in the west, the sky ablaze with streaks of pink and violet and tangerine. She couldn't remember seeing such beauty in all her life, even when she was a little girl, and it almost felt as if the hand of God was reaching out to her.

Phythian kept his word.

Chapter 55

Monday, September 13
Long Island, New York
2:40 pm GMT, 10:40 am Local

It was a small beach, quiet this time of year. Quiet even in the summer, just a little stretch of sand on Long Island that few summer folks knew about. A pale sun was hanging in the morning sky over the Atlantic, barely visible through the veil of fog that swelled up over the stark dunes and danced across the sawgrass.

Through the rippling folds of mist the ocean took on the color of dull pewter, casting up white lines of foam where it nibbled at the shoreline. The ever-present gulls soared in lazy circles overhead, their incessant squawks breaking through the gray stillness as they searched for whatever might satisfy their hunger. Despite a bran muffin she'd eaten an hour ago, Monica felt hungry, but her appetite could wait until she had finished what she had come here to do.

She trudged along the sand with a canvas bag in one hand, a garden trowel in the other. Her eyes grew moist, but she forced the tears back, just for a few more minutes. She wasn't quite ready to let go, not yet. As she turned her tired eyes away from a gust of stinging sand, she recalled the last words she ever heard come from Phillip's lips as she kissed him good-bye.

"Indian food tonight?"

Simple, everyday words. Throwaway words. Nothing words. But she had hung onto them as a treasure, words that would linger in her mind forever. *Indian food tonight.* She had not known she never would speak to him again as he drove off that morning. He'd always been there, and then he wasn't. Nor would he ever be again.

The beach had been her sister's idea. Monica had avoided calling her for several days after returning to New York and, when she did, Kathleen readily conceded that some men in dark suits who claimed they were from the government had persuaded her to let them listen in on her conversations. That had put quite a damper on her late-night booty calls with Lance Hendrix, but she'd had no choice. Not really. *Did she?*

Monica settled for a secluded spot at the far end of the sand, back from the surf and out of view of the houses on the other side of the dunes. She laid out a beach towel and kneeled down, then began digging. When the hole started to fill with water, she knew this was as far as she could go.

She tipped her eyes to the heavens, followed a puffy cloud as it gently rolled in front of the sun. Then she said a silent prayer to her late husband, inhaling ragged gasps as she tried to hold back the flood of grief she knew might begin any moment. Finally, she loosened the ties on the bag and opened the plastic pouch inside.

"Goodbye, my love," she whispered as she sifted his ashes into the hole. Once the pouch was empty she carefully added some private sentiments from their wedding night on top: his boutonniere, the cork from the champagne they had drunk at their reception, the garter he had forgotten to remove from her leg at the wedding, and which he very much enjoyed working from her thigh later that night.

When she was finished, she sat on the towel for a good ten minutes, fully conscious that she was treading very close to an emotional abyss. But she'd felt a strong need to do this in order to purge the scars that were forming around the edges of her being. Just as the recovery of the phoenix began in the ashes of a smoldering fire, hers would begin on this cold, lonely beach at the end of her first summer without him.

A crisp chill coursed through every nerve in her body, and Monica knew it was time. She emptied a scoop of sand into the hole, then another and another. She was surprised at how quickly it filled up, and when she had nothing more to scoop, she stood up and stared out to sea.

She turned to go, and that's when she realized she wasn't alone. A man was standing at the crest of the dune behind her, silhouetted against the diminishing fog. Her entire body went rigid, until she heard his voice.

"Good morning," the man said.

"Mr. Logan," she said. They had spoken twice on the phone not long after the incident on the museum steps back in July, but neither had moved beyond formal salutations. He'd had plenty of questions for her, and she'd had even more for him. "You startled me."

"Please forgive my intrusion," he apologized. "I suppose I should have said something earlier, but I didn't want to interrupt."

Monica didn't respond right away. This was a personal moment, and she did not welcome the intrusion. But she was glad to see him anyway, even though she did not know why he was there, standing in a clump of beach grass looking down at her. Or how he possibly had found her on this empty stretch of beach.

"I should have phoned first," he continued. "I'll leave you for now, but there's something I need to tell you when you have a moment."

He turned to go, but Monica called after him: "No, please stay—"

Logan stopped in his tracks, then slowly turned back around to face her. "I've been told I have the decorum of a mastodon," he told her. "By the way, congratulations."

"For what?"

"Don't be modest," he replied. "That was an awesome photo spread in *Earth Illustrated*. I sense a Pulitzer on the horizon."

"Hardly," she said, although she liked hearing it. "Truth is, I thought those pics were lost forever, just like my phone. I totally forgot I'd set it to upload everything to the cloud as soon as it found a wi-fi signal, which I guess it did when I got to Islamabad. The phone never turned up, but when I found them…well, my editor jumped all over it. Brought me back on board full-time, too."

"He'd be a fool not to. A lot of people are falling all over themselves trying to explain how they overlooked those gunshot wounds." He hesitated a second, shifted his balance from one foot to the other. "And again, I'm sorry for just showing up like this."

"No worries, Mr. Logan. It's just that you're the last person I expected to see here."

"Thing is, I was in New York on a story and dropped by your office. After a little cajoling Mr. Kelso told me you'd taken the day off."

"Did he tell you why?" she inquired.

"No, and I should have asked." He started down the dune toward her, the wind blowing through his thinning hair. "All he said was you'd mentioned something about Mastic Beach, and I found it on Google. And before I make a total ass of myself, let me explain why I'm here."

"I'm listening." Still peeved, by curious.

Logan glanced out at the gray sea crashing on the sand, then said, "It's about your late husband."

His words startled her, and she did a noticeable double-take. "Phillip? What on earth are you talking about?"

"See? I should have called you on the phone—"

"Too late for that. What about him?"

He paused, not knowing the best way to go about this. He'd thought about it on the shuttle ride up from DC, and the entire drive out to Long Island from Manhattan. Even as a reporter—a profession that often required prying into other people's personal business—this sort of thing never came easy.

"It's about the night he died," he said at great length. Not looking at her, keeping his eyes averted to the horizon, out there somewhere past the gray.

"I don't see what that has to do with—"

"Please, Mrs. Cross," he said, raising a hand for her to save her breath. "I know this is all of a sudden, but I can explain."

"As you can see—" she swept her hand around the beach, and the hole she had just filled in "—I'm trying to move forward with my life."

"And what I have to tell you may help you do that."

She regarded him warily, wondering whether she should trust this man or not. Then she said, "Okay, tell me what you think you know about the accident."

"The thing is, Mrs. Cross—it *wasn't* an accident."

"Not a...what the hell are you trying to tell me?"

"Please...just hear me out," he said. "Remember that envelope you handed to me that day at the museum?"

"How could I forget?" she replied.

"Well, it contained some information that was very personal to me. It explained a lot of things that I don't want to bore you with now. But the thing is, every once in a while since then, I've received anonymous emails with details about old deaths that had been ruled accidents or suicides. Some even natural causes. I suspect these emails are coming from the same person who gave you that envelope. And as I've looked into them— and written about them—I've found the information they contain to be incredibly accurate. Names, dates, suspects, motive—everything."

"I know," Monica said. "I've been reading your articles."

"My advertisers and I appreciate it," he quipped. "Thing is, several weeks ago, I got a message that recommended I look into the accident that killed Phillip Cross. Your husband."

"I'm sure there are a lot of men who have that name," she said.

"Several hundred of them, in the U.S. alone. But only one who was killed in a supposed accident on the Thruway last winter, right after Christmas. Correct?"

She said nothing, just nodded.

"At the suggestion of my anonymous benefactor, I looked into it." He let his words hang there as he formulated his next thoughts. "Your husband was driving his new Tesla, right?"

"He'd picked it up new just a few weeks before," Monica confirmed. "He loved that car. If there was a way to get it up the elevator into our living room, he would have."

Logan grinned at her words, then went on. "The police investigated the accident and ruled it just that: an accident. His car skidded on the slick pavement, slid off the highway, and crashed into a tree. The impact shattered the panoramic glass roof, and your husband...well, he was killed."

"That's what I was told."

"But there's one thing the state cops overlooked, something they didn't know about at the time."

She just looked at him, waiting for him to go on.

After a second he did. "Your husband's Tesla was fitted with a system called Sentry Mode," he said. "It's a feature that turns on the car's cameras when it senses something is wrong. If someone keys the vehicle, or even leans on it, the cameras begin recording."

Monica was staring at him with eyes almost too large for their sockets. "Are you telling me his car recorded the accident?"

"Like I told you, it was no accident. Not according to what the cameras picked up. I know this is hard for you to hear, Mrs. Cross—"

"Please, I think it's time we started using first names. Mine is Monica."

"Monica, then. And you can call me Carter. The truth is, your husband's car was forced off the road during the storm that night. And after he collided with that tree, someone came down the shoulder from the road and made sure he was dead."

"Oh my God...you're sure of this?"

"I have the video, if you want to see it."

"You mean here on the beach?" she asked, incredulity in her voice, and a lingering annoyance from having her intimate time with Phillip disrupted. "Now?"

"I'm sorry...I get a little impulsive about work. We can do this another time—"

Monica suddenly felt a hollow ache in her gut that told her no, she most certainly did not want to see whatever Carter was talking about. But she shook it off and said, "You came all the way out here to show it to me, so go for it."

"You're sure?"

"No, but let's do it anyway," she told him. "Before I change my mind."

Logan didn't reply at first, just edged closer and turned his cell phone to give her a clear view of the screen. Then he said, "This is just a short segment of the whole thing, but it's enough to convince you that what I'm saying is true."

"Go ahead."

He touched a finger to an icon that launched the video clip. It began with several seconds of blurred chaos as the car skidded, flipped, and crashed top-first into the tree, followed by about twenty seconds of nothing. Then a shadow appeared from the darkness and the outline of a man in a dark coat moved into the frame.

"The car's headlights remained on after the impact, and Sentry Mode turned up the console display to maximum brightness," Carter Logan told her. "That's important to know during the next few seconds."

Again, she said nothing, just watched as the man moved further into the range of the car's side camera. He was dressed in a black parka, wool cap, black gloves. Squarish face, a day or two of stubble on his chin. Dark eyes, but that could have been caused by the time of day or the hat he was wearing. His breath was steaming from the cold as he peered through the driver's shattered side window.

"I don't know if you want to watch this next part," Logan warned her. Just as before she didn't, but she couldn't pull her eyes away.

"This is where it really gets cruel," he said.

Cruel was hardly the word for it. The man in the wool cap peeled away the remaining crystals of shattered glass, then reached inside with both hands. He appeared to wrap them around something, then gave a rapid twist.

"Holy *shit*," Monica said. A ripple of glacier water rushed up her spine and she felt herself grow light-headed.

"I did some research," Logan told her then. "It's really not that easy to break a person's neck, not unless the victim is already in restraints. Which your husband was, because of the seatbelt. I think that maneuver was just for insurance."

"Do you have any idea who that sonofabitch is?"

"I do, and so do the New York State Police. His name is Buddy Weber, former Army MP with a "big chicken dinner" on his record."

"Excuse me?"

"It's military slang for bad conduct discharge. Anyway, he's a mob iceman who freelances on the side, and he was sent by the company hired by the plaintiff in the case your husband was working."

"It was some sort of whistleblower thing," Monica said, her mind awash with confusion. "He said he couldn't talk about it."

"And he went up to Albany that day to take a deposition," Logan said.

She nodded, remembering again how he said he'd be home in time to go out for Indian food. The snow had made him late, but the restaurant didn't close until ten. "Where is this Buddy Weber now?" she asked, her voice barely a whisper.

"In federal custody, as of ten o'clock this morning. Murder, attempted murder, assault, conspiracy. The police didn't want to tell you about it until he was behind bars."

"And you took the initiative," she replied.

"My idea, not theirs."

This was all too much for Monica to absorb. She'd come out here to the beach to say a final farewell to Phillip, in some feeble attempt to conquer the grief she continued to feel for the husband she would never see again. Just her, the waves, the sky, and the memories she literally had chosen to bury in the sand.

Now this.

She said nothing for a long time as she let Logan's story sink in. Everything he said made a strange, horrible sort of sense. And there was an additional layer of—*what, relief?*—that Phillip had not died accidentally, but in fact had been killed doing something he believed in.

"Why?" she finally asked. "Why did they have to kill him?"

"He was the man who knew too much."

"But he'd gone up to Albany to take that deposition," she said, shaking her head. "Anything he thought he knew would have been part of the legal record."

"Carmen Zaffino—he was the scheduled deponent that day—never showed. Your husband took care of some other business, then headed home early because of the storm."

"And this Buddy Weber...he ran Phillip off the road." A statement, not a question.

"The video makes a strong case for it," Logan said.

Yes, it did, but there was something that was bothering her.

"You said you got this tip from the person who's been feeding you other stories?" Monica asked. She had a good idea who that person was, but didn't want to go into it. Not with Carter Logan, not with anyone. She'd been left alone, unharmed since the day she thought the man in the museum closet was going to blow her head off, and she didn't want to mess with fate.

"I did," Logan told her. Leaving out the deeply conflicting apprehension he had about accepting intel from the person who was responsible for his Katya's death. Something he would deal with in due time, in a manner he had yet to conceive or comprehend. Patience truly was one of his virtues. "Once again, he had names, dates, photos, even the dollar amount that changed hands."

"You're sure this was a paid hit?"

"No question," he replied. "Every tip I've received from this source somehow involves a contract killing, arranged by the same bloody dark web outfit that brought down that plane you found. And killed my fiancé. I'm sorry...I've already said too much—"

Monica shook her head, said, "No...please, go on."

"It's a long story," he warned her.

"If you talked to my boss, you know I have the day off."

"In that case, maybe we can talk over a cup of coffee. If I remember correctly, I saw a place about mile up the road."

Monica's mind was spinning from the story she'd just heard, the video she'd seen, and a growing sense of trust for the man who had told it to her. "I'd like that," she said.

She gathered up the beach towel and garden shovel, took one last glance at the hole she had just dug and filled. Then Carter crooked his elbow and she gripped it with her cupped hand, the motion so natural that she no longer noticed the sharp wind biting her face.

A change of season was in the air, and Monica Cross was struck by a reassuring sense that the long, dark tunnel of winter might just have a glimmer of light at the end of it.

Author's Notes

Project MINDGAZE is a fictitious government program loosely based on the Stargate Project, the official code name for a very real clandestine U.S. Army unit begun in 1978, under the auspices of the Defense Intelligence Agency and SRI International. While no known useful research came from the hundreds of millions of taxpayer dollars spent to investigate "remote viewing" and other "extrasensory phenomena," it was the basis for the book and film titled *The Men Who Stare At Goats.*

Rōnin Phythian is a fictional character developed to illustrate the potential magnitude and deadliness of Project Stargate, had it ever produced actionable results. As noted in the book, the name comes from the Japanese term for drifter or wanderer—essentially, a samurai without a master—as similarly referenced in the John Frankenheimer film of the same name. A classic, which I highly recommend.

Assassination conspiracies abound throughout history and literature. The Greenwich Global Group is a combination of several of these, both proven and alleged, including:

- The Hashishin, a cult of Isma'ili Muslims led by Hassan-is-Sabbah in the 11th and 12th centuries. The word "assassin" derives from the name of the group of killers that formed an *ad hoc* guild of killers, which was responsible for the deaths of numerous political and military leaders for a century and a half, until they were wiped out by Mongols in 1256.
- Murder, Inc., an organized crime ring and a branch of the so-called National Crime Syndicate, allegedly responsible for up to one thousand assassinations in the 1930s and 1940s. The loosely based gang was mostly composed of Italian-American and Jewish mobsters that reportedly operated out of headquarters in the Midnight Rose Candy Store, located under the elevated portion of the 3 subway train in Brooklyn.

- The Nokmim (Hebrew for "avengers"), a cadre of Jewish assassins who hunted down unpunished Nazi war criminals in Europe after World War II.
- The Werewolves, a band of thousands of German volunteers selected largely from the ranks of the Hitler Youth and the Waffen SS. Trained in sabotage and silent killing techniques, they engaged in only a few, sporadic assassinations toward the end of the war, before the German military machine ground to a halt.

J.H. Black Headwear LLC is a fictitious pseudonym for the Greenwich Global Group (aka the G3), and was named for an innocuous office for a global apparel company I'd once seen on an upper floor of the Graybar Building in New York. Made me wonder what actually went on behind those closed doors.

Beechcraft does make a long-haul aircraft known as the King Air 350 ER, which stands for extended range. I took the liberty of modifying it for a longer flight by adding the letter "X" and the word "extra" to its description, in Chapters 1 and 2. Also, much appreciation to Steve Saslow, who advised me on the mechanics and flying of this particular aircraft. Anything I got right is because of him; any mistakes are on me alone.

Several characters in this book are prone to quoting authors, playwrights, politicians, and philosophers. In some cases I worked the source of said quote into the manuscript, but sometimes that was impractical without making the prose sound clunky. To give credit where it is certainly due, here are the origins of quotes or aphorisms I incorporated into the pages of this book but did not cite therein:

- *Anxiety is a thin stream of fear trickling through the mind.* –Arthur Roche, English archbishop of the Catholic Church.
- *The search for a scapegoat is the easiest of all hunting expeditions.* – President Dwight D. Eisenhower
- *The devices of the wicked lead only to treachery and perfidy.* –Cobbled together from numerous Bible quotes, especially those found in Job and Exodus
- *Conscience is the window of our spirit, evil is the curtain.* –Douglas Horton, American Protestant clergyman
- *Golden lads and girls all must, as chimney-sweepers, come to dust.* – William Shakespeare, in Cymbeline

- *When the debate is lost, slander becomes the tool of the loser.* –Widely attributed to Socrates, who actually wrote nothing. Thus, the origin of this phrase remains unknown.
- *What's past is prologue.* –William Shakespeare, in The Tempest
- *Hate the sin, love the sinner.* –A twist on St. Augustine's Letter 211
- *The best-laid plans of mice and men often go awry.* –Robert Burns, from his poem "To A Mouse"
- *As she has planted, so does she harvest. Such is the furrowed field of karma.* –Sri Guru Granth Sahib
- *A man who lives a full life is prepared to die, but the coward trembles as time grows near.* –Paraphrased from a quote by Mark Twain

Fans of the marvelous Scottish film *Local Hero* will find several "Easter eggs" hidden toward the end of the book, including the names *Ceilidh*, *Urquhart*, and *Gordon*. If you've never seen the film, please find time to watch it.

As always, I would like to thank my magnificent editor and friend, Kimberley Cameron, for her continued encouragement and diligent efforts in getting my books in print. Also, continued appreciation to my parents for instilling in me the love of the printed word. Additionally, I would particularly like to offer a shout-out to all the folks at Epicenter Press/Coffeetown Press in Seattle, particularly Phil Garrett and Jennifer McCord for all their support along the way.

Last, but by no means least, I offer hugs and kisses to my wonderful wife Diana, whose unyielding confidence and optimism have kept me plugging away all these years. It's your fault. Love actually, and always.

About the Author

Reed Bunzel is the author of a half dozen crime novels and thrillers, as well as several nonfiction books. He also is the author of BunzelGram, a weekly newsletter that focuses on mysteries and thrillers both in print and on the screen.

A former media industry executive, Bunzel was editor-in-chief for United News and Media's San Francisco publishing operations, overseeing the weekly publication of The Game Report and Chairman.

Earlier in his career he was editor-in-chief of Streamline Publishing's Radio Ink and Streaming magazines, as well as an editor at Radio & Records and Broadcasting magazine. Additionally, he served in an executive capacity at both the National Association of Broadcasters and the Radio Advertising Bureau.

A graduate of Bowdoin College in Brunswick, Maine, Bunzel holds a Bachelor of Science degree in Anthropology cum laude. A native of the San Francisco Bay Area, he resides with his wife Diana in Charleston, South Carolina.

About the Author

Reed Bunzel is the author of a half dozen crime novels and thrillers, as well as several nonfiction books. He also is the author of *BunzelGram*, a weekly newsletter that focuses on mysteries and thrillers both in print and on the screen.

A former media industry executive, Bunzel was editor-in-chief for United News and Media's San Francisco publishing operations, overseeing the weekly publication of *The Gavin Report* and *Gavin.com*.

Earlier in his career he was editor-in-chief of Streamline Publishing's *Radio Ink* and *Streaming* magazines, as well as an editor at *Radio & Records* and *Broadcasting* magazine. Additionally, he served in an executive capacity at both the National Association of Broadcasters and the Radio Advertising Bureau.

A graduate of Bowdoin College in Brunswick, Maine, Bunzel holds a Bachelor of Science degree in Anthropology, *cum laude*. A native of the San Francisco Bay Area, he resides with his wife Diana in Charleston, South Carolina.

CPSIA information can be obtained
at www.ICGtesting.com
Printed in the USA
BVHW071917221022
649854BV00004B/33